Noble
BENEATH *the* SHIELD

R.C. MARTIN

Noble
BENEATH *the* SHIELD

R.C. MARTIN

CONTENTS

prologue

T HE NIGHT BEFORE WAS THE LAST STRAW. Mitzi Bates couldn't wait anymore. She needed to get out of Bedford County and far, far away from Shelbyville, Tennessee. This, of course, had always been her plan—when she was ready. When opportunity came knocking. Or when she could sucker her opportunity into inviting her along for the ride. The longer she waited, the stronger her resolve.

She'd been rejected from her dream school twice. She had the grades and the talent, but the private school didn't accept very many applicants. Not to mention, without one hell of a scholarship, paying New York tuition was going to be a bear, even with her parents help. Mitzi didn't love sticking around her hometown, working full-time at her daddy's dealership while the rest of her friends journeyed into their sophomore year of college, but her mind was made up. There was only one future she would accept.

Fashion school had been her dream since she was twelve years old and her mother insisted on the most ridiculous pageant outfits imaginable. No matter how hard she tried to convince Dolly Bates she could do a better job of designing her own pageant attire, her mother wouldn't budge. She was a purist. It drove Mitzi nuts. She never wanted to be *Little Miss Shelbyville* anyway. That was her older sister's title, until she went on to be crowned *Miss Teen Bedford County* three years in a row. Scarlett was also cheer-captain her junior and senior year of high school, and prom queen to Trace Whitfield's prom king.

In many ways, Mitzi and Scarlett weren't actually all that different. They had the same dark brunette hair, so long as neither of them hit the salon feeling experimental; the same hazel-green eyes, a gift from their daddy; and the same sweetheart shaped lips their mother never let them forget was a trait for which she deserved all the credit. Scarlett got all the height, standing five inches taller than Mitiz's five-foot-two frame, but that just meant Mitzi always got to fly the highest when she was suited up in her cheerleading uniform.

Around town, they were known fondly as the Bates sisters or Dolly's girls. They were pretty and sweet, like the southern belles they were raised to be. Their mother had seen to that, grooming them the only way she saw fit—as close to perfect as possible. And yet, what the Bates sisters wanted out of life had them on very different paths with very different mindsets. This was obvious, even at a glance.

It seemed like Trace was all Scarlett wanted since she was fifteen years old. She'd gone on a few dates with a couple guys before she could finally catch Trace's attention. Though, the way she pranced around school in her cheerleading skirt, it was all but inevitable she'd catch the quarterback's eye. Once she had it, Scarlett was fitted with a pair of blinders, preventing her from seeing any other guy on the planet.

Mitzi, on the other hand, never let a guy get too attached to her. The last thing she wanted was to fall in love too early. She'd seen what falling in love did to people. Her mother, her sister, her best friend—the decisions they made always factored in the guys who stole their hearts. Happy as they seemed, Mitzi wanted to *live* a little before settling down. She told all the guys the same thing: she wasn't easy, but she was fun. They could take it or leave it. Didn't matter to her either way.

Dolly seemed to dislike Mitzi's wild-hearted ways most of all. The longer she stuck around Shelby after graduation, and the closer Trace and Scarlett's wedding got, the more irritated Dolly was. She believed her youngest daughter was wasting the beauty she swore had an expiration date. Not that her mother had a foot to stand on. At forty-two, Dolly was still pretty as the prom queen to Sterling Bates' prom king, circa 1968. If anyone in town forgot, they were certainly reminded at the wedding of the freaking century.

Mitzi sighed as she scrolled through Facebook, looking at the images people had been posting all morning. It was like all anyone cared about was sharing proof they'd been in attendance at the Whitfield-Bates union. While the Bates family were certainly well off, given how hard Sterling always worked to provide for all his girls, Mitzi's new in-laws were definitely at the top of Bedford County's list of elite. Papa Whitfield made a name for himself in commercial real estate. He passed his fortune and his business down to his son. Everyone knew after Trace graduated college, he'd follow in his daddy's footsteps. Trace and Scarlett's future was as predictable as they came.

Shaking her head, Mitzi stopped on a photo of Trace kissing his bride at the altar. Mitzi stood close by as one of Scarlett's bridesmaids. Studying the image, she was relieved her forced happiness seemed genuine in the captured moment.

All Scarlett wanted was the picture-perfect wedding, in her ten-thousand-dollar dress at a venue Mitzi knew Sterling would be paying off until Scarlett bore her first child. It didn't matter to Scarlett if the groom waiting for her at the end of the long aisle was an asshole. No one seemed to care about that except for Mitzi.

Regardless of the fact that she'd been trying to warn her sister off the guy for years, she was completely blind to his douche-bag ways. Mitzi swore up and down he was destined to be nothing more than one of the spoiled Whitfields who lived in some alternate reality where he reigned in his glory days of old as the high school's star quarterback. He was attractive and rich, a lethal combination which led him to take whatever liberties he wanted while he kept her sister around for arm candy. Somehow, in the eyes of their town, he could do no wrong. So, of course, when he made a pass at her during the reception, it was *Mitzi* who bore the brunt of Scarlett and their mother's wrath. She, in her aimless and selfish ways, tried to steal the spotlight and ruin the event of the year.

Not wishing to relive the heated argument mumbled through clenched teeth and fake smiles the evening before, Mitzi closed out of Facebook and powered down her computer. As she stood from her desk, turning to stow the laptop in her luggage, she felt her stomach drop. Much as she knew it was time, she could hardly believe what she was about to do.

Mitzi never thought she'd be running away from Shelbyville, but she hadn't really been left with much of a choice. After the wedding from hell, where she had to paste on a smile for the four hundred guests Scarlett *had* to invite to her big day, Mitzi knew it was time to let go of her excuses. Whatever setbacks or shortcomings had stood in her way weren't greater than her need to flee. She'd figure it out. She'd have to.

After lugging her second heavy bag down the stairs, the doorbell rang. It was a sound she'd heard a million times, but it still made her jump. She clutched the fabric of her t-shirt over her belly, drew in a deep breath, and went to answer. Nora-Jean was the only person she'd told about her escape, and her best friend was to be her ride to the bus station. Still, it came as no surprise when Mitzi opened the door to find Lawson standing on the front porch, his arm casually slung over her best friend's shoulders.

"I know you said to keep my mouth shut, but—"

"You're crazy as hell, Mitz," Lawson started, a lazy smirk curling the side of his mouth. "Always liked that about you."

"He just showed up, you know? I couldn't lie," insisted Nora, leaning into her lover's side.

Mitzi rolled her eyes playfully and then hitched her thumb over her shoulder. "Well, make yourself useful, muscles."

Lawson only replied with a wink before he snuck by her and into the foyer. As if her bags weighed nothing, he picked them up, both girls moving out of the way as he headed for the truck Mitzi was sure he'd parked in the driveway.

"You're sure about this?" asked Nora as Mitzi took one last look at her home.

What she was about to do, she'd never be able to take back.

"Your mama's gonna have a cow. Leavin' while she and your daddy are out of town?"

Mitzi shrugged. She knew Nora was right. Dolly and Sterling were away for the weekend—a post-wedding trip they'd both earned. They'd be back the next evening, but Mitzi couldn't wait that long. Every time she thought about her mother, she saw the look in her eyes as she reprimanded her daughter for being a spoiled, jealous brat at her own sister's wedding.

"Maybe," she finally murmured. "Or maybe she'll be relieved."

"You didn't do anything wrong," Nora replied, reaching for Mitzi's hand. "Trace is a dog. Hell, I guarantee he'd have hit on me if Lawson didn't have his eyes on me all night."

Mitzi couldn't help but chuckle as she gave Nora's hand a squeeze. "He had more than his *eyes* on you."

Nora grinned but demanded, "Don't change the subject."

"It's time, Nora-Jean. I have to go. Now. I'll call them when I get there."

"Yeah, well, I'm gonna hold you to that."

"We hittin' the road or what?" hollered Lawson.

Mitzi looked down the walkway and saw him standing with his hands on his hips, waiting impatiently.

"Bus doesn't leave the station for another hour, Lawson Steele. Chill, would you?"

"I don't know what bus you're talkin' 'bout. This truck is city bound, and it's leavin' this station in two minutes."

"Wait—what?" she called out as he began to walk away.

Nora laughed, and Mitzi's brow furrowed in confusion.

"What's he talkin' about, Nora?"

"He loves me somethin' fierce, you know," was her only reply.

"Uh, yeah. Wouldn't be surprised if everyone in Shelby knew that boy only has eyes for you. What does that have to do with anything?"

"My best friend is movin' to New York City. That's nine hundred miles away. And I thought it was hard leavin' you here for Knoxville."

"Nora..."

Lawson started up his truck, and the sound of the idling engine wafted up to join the girls on the porch.

"It's like he said. We're your ride."

Mitzi's jaw fell open for a second. "Serious?"

"It'll soften the blow, your daddy knowin' you weren't all alone. And how else am I gonna make sure you call your parents when you get there unless I'm standin' right next to you when you do it?"

Mitzi squealed in excitement, throwing her arms around Nora, who giggled and squeezed her right back. Lawson honked the horn and Nora reached down to smack Mitzi's backside.

"Come on, Mitzi Belle, before he changes his mind."

chapter one

Eleven and a half years later...

M ITZI STARED AT HER REFLECTION in the circle mirror hung in the entryway of her flat. She'd spent way too long on her hair and makeup, but it helped calm her nerves. Her hazel-green eyes were big, round, and striking all on their own, but that never stopped her from playing with a bit of eyeshadow to make them stand out even more. With her expert application of eyeliner and a generous amount of mascara, she looked like the pretty-little-thing her mother raised her to be. Her eyebrows were shaded-in to perfection, and she wore a neutral, pale-rose shade of lipstick that gave her just the right amount of color in an effortless sort of way.

Her hair had known various hues over the years. Jet-black or caramel-blonde were among her favorites, but these days she felt good as a natural, dark brunette. It'd been nearly a year since she'd turned thirty, chopped off six inches of her beautiful mane, and started sporting the long bob she loved. She wore it down most days, and styled it with big waves, which gave her a desired amount of body. Today, it was half up, a messy knot on top of her head, and the rest hovering a couple inches above her shoulders.

It was the middle of October, her favorite time of year in the city. The weather was perfect. The colors were downright inspirational. And, best of all, there was a football game on television five days a week. Autumn in the northeast meant dressing in layers. Mitzi loved throwing together pieces that would keep her warm and fashionable at the same time. The raincoat she wore over her outfit was from Sterling Thread's fall collection the previous season, but she loved it so much it would never go out of style.

The woman staring at her in the mirror was beautiful, smart, ambitious, and proud of the life she'd built in the city that never slept—and yet, the thought of leaving her flat in order to head to her boutique terrified her. It was why she needed to get away. She'd been so anxious the last couple weeks. Her stomach churned constantly. A trip home would do her good; but getting there was going to be the hardest part.

Titan barked, and Mitzi drew in a breath as she looked down at her beloved companion. Her adorable, three year old, pale brown maltipoo stared up at her in excitement. The poor thing was probably dying to get outside. She hadn't taken him on a long walk since the incident.

"I know, sweet boy. We're going."

He barked again, his whole behind wagging as he turned to face the door, and Mitzi decided to follow his lead. She strapped her purse and Titan's travel duffle over one shoulder, extended the handle of her small, roller bag, grabbed her keys, and forced herself on her way.

She lived just eight blocks from the boutique. She and Titan moved into her dream apartment a little more than two years ago, soon after she finished paying her investor back for the generous loan she needed to open her shop in the first place. Business was good and growing steadily year over year. Mitzi worked hard to keep her brand relevant, her fashion line fresh, and her storefront someplace people wanted to visit.

Online sales had been what helped catapult her onto the fashion scene in the first place. She still remembered what it was like sewing orders at all hours of the night, trying to keep up with the supply and demand that humbled her and inspired her in equal measure. She was twenty-three, working two part-time jobs, barely making ends meet, and yet as determined as ever to give Sterling Thread every ounce of dedication she could muster.

She'd come a long way in seven years. Mitzi wasn't sewing online orders from the corner of her postage-stamp sized bedroom in the flat she shared with four other women in Sunnyside, Queens. In fact, she wasn't sewing any of the clothes sold online or displayed on the floor of her boutique at all. She had a team of amazing seamstresses who could piece together her designs in record time. Mitzi found herself sitting at her sewing machine only after she was happy with her sketches and ready to see them come to life.

As she walked briskly through the streets of Carroll Gardens, Brooklyn, she tried to think of things she loved. Her work. Her store. Her friends. Her life. It was the middle of the day, the sun was peeking through the clouds, and she was surrounded by strangers who were more like the accessories she needed to blend in, but it didn't make her breathe any easier.

She heard the jingle of Titan's tags and glanced down at her pup. He didn't seem to mind their quick pace, too busy enjoying the cool breeze through his hair. She was comforted by the reality that she was giving him something he needed—a chance to really exert some energy. Unfortunately, it wasn't long before she was reminded *why* she'd neglected his exercise, and her own, keeping both of them cooped up in her flat unless he needed a chance to relieve himself.

Her anxiety made her usual fifteen-minute trek only twelve, and Mitzi was sweating under her arms by the time she reached the store. She barely took a moment to appreciate the new glass, which had been installed to replace the door someone shattered when he smashed it open with a crowbar a couple weeks prior.

Someone, she muttered in her mind. *You know who was to blame for the attack, even if the cops can't prove it. Even if the perp in custody won't cough up his name.*

Mitzi locked the door behind her before she blew out a lung-full of air. The familiar scent of Sterling Mist filled her nose. She tried to hold onto the truth that she *loved* her line's fragrance collection. She didn't want to recall the way *that* scent was the last she remembered before it happened; before she passed out after being conked on the side of the head, landing hard on the floor in the center of the shop thirteen days ago.

"Hey, boss—you okay?" asked Adalynn, startling Mitzi.

She spun around quickly and came face to face with her assistant. Adalynn hugged a stack of items to her chest, an apologetic grimace pinching at the features of her round face. Her honey-blonde hair was braided across the front and pulled back into a high pony in the back, the way she liked to style it best. As if it were business as usual, the twenty-six-year-old looked as put-together as always. She'd dressed up a pair of jeans with a rust-yellow blouse, a leather-suede combo jacket, and a pair of brown leather booties which put her head and shoulders above Mitzi.

"I'm fine," she answered, forcing a smile.

"Right. Stupid question. You're not fine. But you will be. That's what this trip is for, right?"

Mitzi relaxed a little, a small, genuine smile replacing her forced one as she looked into Adalynn's kind, blue eyes. She knew better than to lie to her assistant. They'd been together going on three years. Sometimes it felt like Adalynn was taking up residence inside of Mitzi's head—making sense of things she couldn't.

"I know your flight leaves in a few hours."

She took a careful step toward her boss. Easing Mitzi's bags off her shoulder, Adalynn set the doggy duffle on the floor and then opened the oversized purse in order to tuck away Mitzi's laptop and sketch books, which had been in the back office since she'd been holed up at home.

"I really don't want you to worry about things here, okay? Gianna is all set to re-open the shop tomorrow morning. The staff is certainly looking forward to being in-house again. All the destroyed inventory has been replaced. You see the door was fixed. The sign guy will be here this afternoon with the decal—seriously. We've got this."

"Yeah. Energizer Bunny, over here, hasn't missed a step," teased Gianna, Sterling Thread's CFO and the shop's co-manager. As she strode toward them, she went on to say, "She's right, by the way. We're all good here. Take all the time you need. Especially if that southern air will inspire you to get going on your spring line."

Adalynn eased Mitzi's purse back onto her shoulder. She hardly noticed the extra weight it carried as she kept her focus on Gianna. If it was her assistant who helped her decipher and order her jumbled thoughts and responsibilities, it was Gianna who took Mitzi's vision and made sure it was moving forward, full speed ahead, at all times. Sterling Thread was Mitzi's baby, but Gianna loved the brand as much as if she had dreamed it up herself.

They'd been in business together for almost six years. Drew, Mitzi's ex, had been the one to introduce them. In spite of being six years Mitzi's senior, which came with a load of professional experience Mitzi would have to learn along the way, it wasn't long before their friendship blossomed into the single most important business relationship either of them had ever known. Gianna had proven her loyalty many times over, including taking Mitzi's side when she and Drew finally split.

In her nude, stiletto heels—which she never left home without —Gianna stood as tall as Adalynn. In another life, she could have been a runway model. Her oval face and high cheek bones, her incredibly lithe frame, her perfect olive tone skin, and her gorgeous black hair, grown halfway down her back, all contributed to her stunning appearance. She was wearing a pair of fitted, black trousers and a matching blazer over a t-shirt Mitzi designed. It was part of her summer collection, and it was obvious Gianna was trying to get as much wear out of it as she could before it got too cold in the city.

"Honey," she spoke gently, rubbing a comforting hand up and down Mitzi's arm. "Why didn't you let us bring you your things? You didn't need to come in. You're obviously still a little shaken."

Mitzi pulled in a breath, closed her eyes, and shook her head. She wasn't sure how long she'd gone without responding. When she opened her eyes once more, she was met with two shades of worry —one in blue, the other in brown. She appreciated their concern, but she didn't want their pity.

"You guys have been great, and I don't know what I'd do without you, but I can't avoid this place forever. I can't be afraid of this city. I refuse to be that pathetic."

"Mitzi," Adalynn breathed, sounding aghast. "You're not pathetic. You were attacked. The store was robbed. That would shake anyone."

"It could have been either one of us," said Gianna. "And if it was, you'd be doing what we're doing right now—telling us to get out of here until we felt up to coming back."

"It'll just be a few days, I swear," insisted Mitzi, hoping it was true.

"Like I said, take all the time you need." She picked up Titan's duffle and continued, "A few days, a few weeks—you're brilliant, honey, but we can run things without you. What we *can't* do is design the clothes that define the brand. Clear that head of yours and get to sketching, all right? That's an order."

"Yeah," said Mitzi on a quiet laugh. She took the duffle and glanced around the store. She hadn't noticed upon her entrance, but Adalynn was right. The space looked as good as new, no thanks to her. Unfortunately, the view of her beautiful store didn't calm her anxious belly or erase the memory of that dreadful night.

"Okay, out you go," mumbled Adalynn.

She took hold of Mitzi's shoulders and spun her boss toward the door, gently escorting her out into the cool, late morning.

"Text me when you land. And if you need anything, you know I've got you covered. Day or night."

Gianna followed them out, Mitzi's roller bag in tow, hailing a cab as Adalynn spoke. The next thing Mitzi knew, they were all exchanging farewell hugs before she was sliding into the backseat of a taxi, headed for home on a one-way ticket.

MITZI DIDN'T FIND HERSELF in the Nashville airport often, but it didn't make Tennessee feel any less like home. After she moved to New York, where she was determined to make a life for herself—come hell or high water—it was two years before she made her first trip back.

Nora had been right about how Dolly and Sterling would take the news of her departure. There were more than a few heated phone calls followed by a stretch of no communication at all, which hurt more than Mitzi thought possible. Blame was launched across state lines, landing with bitter and resentful destruction. Misdirected anger was left unresolved, creating festering sores that grew infected in the silence. Even in a city comprised of millions, there was a loneliness Mitzi was forced to grow out of all on her own.

It was Scarlett who broke the silence when, a year and a half after her wedding, she called to announce she was pregnant with her first child. The news was a band-aid which failed to fix what had been broken, but it was something. Predictable as her sister's life was turning out to be, Mitzi was happy to hear such news. It was when Charlotte was born that she scraped up every penny she had to make the trip down to meet her niece.

Since then, she'd been home a handful of times. Whatever tension existed between the Bates and Whitfield clan didn't erase the fact that they were family. Soon after the launch of Sterling Thread, Mitzi's days weren't long enough, and her dollar didn't stretch far enough for her to make it home for the holidays. While this did nothing to heal old wounds, it became the norm. Mitzi did make it back to meet Brooks, Scarlett's second child, born three years after his sister. However, it wasn't until Nora-Jean got pregnant with Evelyn that Mitzi started to realize exactly how far away from Shelby she really was.

Things in Tennessee were complicated. There was no other way to describe it. Even so, much as Mitzi had in the city, a decade hadn't made it home. What happened at the store served as her reminder that whatever success she'd found didn't make New York any smaller or compassionate. Until recently, she'd been happy and content in Brooklyn, but she'd be lying if she said something wasn't missing. That something being the part of her that was most at ease in a smaller town traveling at a slower pace with the people who understood her best.

Except, more than a decade hadn't healed all the wounds the Bates family had inflicted and endured under friendly fire. There was a reason why, soon as Mitzi got off the plane, it was her best friend she was looking for outside the terminal. There was a reason why she hadn't called her folks after the robbery, and why she hadn't yet told them she was planning on a visit. Eleven and a half years was a long time, but it didn't change the way she left or why. Nothing could change that, and not one in the bunch could dispute it.

Titan whined from the inside of his travel duffle, and Mitzi hugged the bag a little closer. "I'll let you out in just a minute, baby. Let mama get her suitcase, okay?"

Her calming tone seemed to soothe him, and he quieted down as she continued toward baggage claim. Mitzi's phone sounded from within the pocket of her raincoat as she arrived at her first stop, and she was quick to extract the device. She'd texted both Adalynn and Nora as soon as she touched ground. It was no surprise Adalynn had been first to send a reply.

> **Adalynn:** Glad you made it safely! The sign guy just showed up. I'll send along pics as soon as the job's done.
>
> **Adalynn:** The insurance company called. You should see an email come through. It's been handled but thought you should have a heads up.
>
> **Adalynn:** I promise, we're all good here. Unplug a bit, boss. You deserve it.

Mitzi read the messages twice, grateful for the subtext Adalynn seemed intent on driving home. After the break-in, Mitzi didn't want *anyone* at the shop for the first week. Until the detectives assigned to her case had the person responsible for her concussion and the missing eight hundred in cash from the till, she swore it wasn't safe. Turned out, even after they caught the perp who'd done the deed, Mitzi wasn't convinced it was a good idea to open up shop right away. Gianna and Adalynn disagreed. They even got the NYPD to back their argument that even if Mitzi suspected someone else was at fault for the robbery, they'd caught the guy who actually saw it through. The only thing to do now was move forward.

Every time Adalynn or Gianna assured her all was under control, it wasn't the business to which they were referring. It was their belief the shop would be fine and anyone in it would be safe. Both women swore they'd never be at the boutique alone, but Mitzi still couldn't shake her unease. There was a rational part of her that knew they were right. Crime in Brooklyn was nothing new. The incident had been dealt with, and there was nothing left to do but keep on keeping on. It was her rationale that calmed her conscious enough to get her on the plane, but it was her own personal anxiety she needed to wrestle into submission.

It had been months since she'd seen her ex; but whatever peace of mind time had granted her was eradicated after the break-in. Now, it didn't matter how at ease her team felt. It didn't matter what the cops said. She didn't trust Nolan. He was too unpredictable. And in a city as big as Brooklyn, she'd never see him coming—just like she didn't see the hooded man with a crowbar until it was too late.

The baggage carousel powered on, and Mitzi blacked out her screen, pocking her phone as she searched for her luggage. Soon as she spotted it, she wiggled her way through the crowd of travelers and snatched it up. Before she headed for the exit, she freed Titan from the confines of his duffle. He gave himself a shake, happy to be free, and then Mitzi clipped on his leash. They were on their way outside when Mitzi's phone began to ring.

The sight of Nora-Jean's name lighting up her screen brought a smile to her face. Suddenly, it settled in. She was *home*.

"Hello?" she answered.

"You're here," Nora breathed, sounding as relieved as Mitzi felt.

"I am. Are you? Titan and I were just getting ready to head outside."

"Oh, my god—I see you! Damn, you look good."

Mitzi couldn't fight her grin as she turned her head left and right, searching for her friend. "You see me? Where are you?"

"I knew that haircut was hot, but this is the first time I'm seeing it in person. I was *this close* to forgivin' you for lettin' someone else put their scissors to your hair. Now, I'm jealous all over again."

"Nora-Jean, *where are you?*" Mitzi demanded on a laugh.

"Right where you left me, Mitzi Belle."

This time, when Nora spoke, Mitzi heard her voice from behind. She whipped around and saw her best friend smirking at her, her phone still pressed to her ear as she closed the remaining distance between them.

The two women had been close for more than twenty years. Mitzi knew just about everything there was to know about Nora-Jean Barton. And yet, after nearly two years of nothing but video chats, text messages, and phone calls, Mitzi somehow forgot just how gorgeous her friend was. It wasn't merely her thick, chestnut-brown hair, her pretty green eyes, or the body Mitzi swore was bikini ready all year long. It wasn't her easy smile, or the raspy tone of her voice, which made her sound sexy even when she wasn't trying. It was deeper than that.

When Mitzi looked at Nora, she saw the strength of a single mother, the resilience of a dreamer, and a love so unique and precious, no amount of distance or time could make Mitzi let go. One look at her best friend, and her churning belly relaxed.

"Hi," Nora whispered, her phone still pressed to her ear.

"God, it's so good to see you," Mitzi whispered back.

Neither one of them bothered to hang up as they reached for each other. They both held on tight, breathing each other in.

"You smell good."

Laughing, Mitzi mumbled into Nora's ear, "You're wearing Sterling Mist for Her."

"Every day," she replied, holding her friend tighter. "Tell me you're okay, Mitzi. You were vague over the phone. The fact that you're here and not there after your shop was robbed—you're not tellin' me somethin'."

Titan barked, as if to voice his dismay at being left out of the affection.

"I should get him out," said Mitzi, pulling away from her friend's embrace.

"MB…" Nora's tone was drenched in warning.

"Trust me, the whole story requires booze."

"Well, then—good thing Evie-B is with Aunt Darlene for the rest of the afternoon. By my watch, we've got an hour and a half to grab a drink and then hit the road before rush hour."

Nora took hold of Mitzi's roller bag and started for the exit.

Mitzi followed without a word of protest.

chapter two

NORA-JEAN AND EVELYN LIVED in a two-bedroom apartment five minutes from downtown Shelby. The building was as old as their friendship, and it showed. While the fixtures and appliances had been updated since the building's construction, Mitzi knew they'd been around as long as she'd been in New York. It was a far cry from her upscale flat in Brooklyn, but it was also undeniably cozy and inviting.

Having always been a fan of prints, Nora sprinkled them throughout the apartment. From the botanical theme in her bedroom, to the pink peonies aesthetic in Evie's room, Nora brought a special touch to every square foot. The navy and white Aztec rug juxtaposed with her gray and dusty-yellow striped throw pillows in the main room burst with color and contrast in a tasteful and mature design. There were knickknacks and keepsakes on hanging shelves and end tables, but there wasn't any clutter. Nora made the place her own, and Mitzi loved it. The rest she got while sleeping on the overstuffed, gray sofa underneath the fluffy, cream throw blanket had been the best she'd had in weeks.

She sat up and stretched, looking around the living room as she allowed herself a moment to become fully awake. Glancing toward her feet, she noticed Titan wasn't curled up there, and she wondered where he'd wandered. She checked the wicker basket swivel chair, but the cushion was empty, save the pillow Titan napped with upon arrival the previous evening. Before she could put too much thought into where else her pup might be, Evie came running into the room. Mitzi giggled when the little girl, dressed in lavender, floral-print, long john pajamas, stopped only when she was nestled into her side.

"Hi, Auntie Belle," she greeted, smiling up at Mitzi.

Evie always called her that, as Mitzi was still a bit tough for her to pronounce. Mitzi preferred it, anyway. The name was something they had it common, and it was a reminder of how much each of them were loved by one particularly special woman.

Evie had sleep in her light brown eyes, and her long, golden brown hair was a tangled mess, as if she'd been wrestling with her dreams all night. Still, she was the most adorable four year old in the world. She'd doubled in size since Mitzi's last visit, and she still couldn't get over how big the little woman was.

"Hi, Evie Belle," said Mitzi, brushing a bit of hair out of her stunning eyes.

"Are you gonna hang out with me today?"

"You bet I am," she promised, genuinely looking forward to it.

Regardless of the fact that Mitzi knew she was going to have to bite the bullet and go see her parents eventually, there was only so much truth sharing she could handle at one time. She wanted to ease into it. Spilling the whole of her situation to Nora had been one thing. Confiding in her parents wasn't going to be as easy. They were never in love with the fact that she chose New York over them. While that wasn't exactly how she viewed it, she had yet to change their perception of her life choices. Learning of their daughter's attack was not going to go over well.

"Yay!" cried Evie, kicking her legs in excitement and effectively nudging Mitzi's negative thoughts away. Leaning into her auntie, Evie's eyes grew wide as she asked, "Can Titan come, too?"

Another giggle danced its way out of Mitzi as she recalled the previous evening, when they'd arrived at Nora's aunt and uncle's house to pick up Evie. She'd been so excited to see Mitzi, in part because Titan came trotting alongside her. Evie was barely three the first time she met the maltipoo, but it had been love at first sight. There wasn't a single video chat between Nora and Mitzi that didn't involve Evie saying hi to Titan.

"Titan can *definitely* come," insisted Mitzi.

Evie gasped, clasping her hands together against her chest as she declared, "I don't want you to ever leave!"

Mitzi's smile fell a bit. Less than twenty-four hours in Shelby, and she was feeling the same way. Before she could think of a reply, the sliding glass door opened, and they both looked toward the apartment's balcony patio. Titan walked in first, jumping up into Mitzi's lap right away. As Evie reached to pet him, he rolled onto his back, signaling his desire to have his belly rubbed.

"She didn't wake you, did she?" asked Nora, closing the door behind her.

The small notebook in her hand was Mitzi's clue she'd been out there writing. She wondered how long her friend had been awake, and what was on her mind, begging her to get it on paper.

"I didn't, mommy," Evie insisted.

"She didn't," echoed Mitzi.

"Good. I was gonna hop in the shower before I get Evie-B ready. Sorry I couldn't clear my calendar today. Reese's schedule is pretty fixed these days, and I didn't want to make her wait until her next weekend off before I fit her in."

"Are you kidding? I don't mind. Really. I invited myself down.

You don't have to go out of your way for me."

Nora rolled her eyes. "My best friend is in town. My best friend who I haven't seen in person in almost two years. After Reese's appointment, expect nothin' but girl time."

"But Titan is a boy," interjected Evie. "Auntie Belle said Titan can come, too."

"Okay, girl time plus Titan. How 'bout that?"

Evie jumped off the couch, expertly skirting the coffee table as she ran toward her mother. She crashed into Nora's legs before wrapping her arms around her hips and craning back her neck. "Mommy, will you braid my hair for girl time?"

"If you want me to."

"I do."

"Then I will. Soon as I get out of the shower, 'kay, mini-me?"

Evie nodded, but didn't let go of Nora before she said, "Kiss."

Mitzi's heart melted as she watched Nora bend to meet Evie's puckered lips with her own. Satisfied, Evie then raced for her room. Titan, intrigued by such energy, jumped from Mitzi's lap and followed after her.

"Every time I visit, she reminds me just how far away I am. She's getting so big."

"I keep tellin' her to stop growin', but she won't listen." Quirking an eyebrow, Nora went on to say, "I'd tell you to move home if I thought you would."

"You're kidding, but..." Mitzi hesitated, wondering if she was crazy for voicing her flippant thoughts. It only took her a second to come to the conclusion that if she could share her half-baked ideas with anyone, it was her oldest and closest friend. "It's stupid, but if it didn't make me a total coward, I'd consider it."

Nora scowled, folding her arms across her chest as she muttered, "That's not stupid, and I'm *not* kidding. I would never kid about you movin' back. And it *would not* make you a coward. Real talk—you'd move home?"

"I don't know." Mitzi shook her head and ran her fingers through her hair, pulling it away from her face.

Tossing her notebook on the coffee table, Nora made her way to the couch. She studied Mitzi closely as she sat sideways, propping her bent knee against the back of the sofa. "Don't play with me, Mitzi Belle. You know if you put this idea in my head, I'm gonna have a hard time lettin' it go."

"Real talk?"

"With me, always."

Mitzi shifted until her position mirrored Nora's. "I've been homesick since you got pregnant."

"MB, when is it goin' to sink in that you bein' here and not there probably wouldn't have changed anything? Lawson and I—I screwed it up. And Creed was a huge mistake. Possibly the biggest mistake of my life. Except, without him, there'd be no Evie. And I wouldn't trade my mini-me for the world."

"I know. Doesn't change the fact that for the last five years, only one thing has kept me in New York. But that one thing is my dream come true, and I can't just leave it behind."

"Or maybe you've got it backwards. Maybe you're usin' your dream come true as your excuse for not comin' home."

Mitzi didn't respond but wondered what truth might have been embedded in Nora's statement. She never imagined one night in Shelby would lead to such a conversation. She needed time away from the city, but she hadn't stopped to consider how long that desire had been buried, or how deep its roots had been spreading.

"Listen to me—I'll support you no matter what, you know I will. But how many times have you told me Sterling Thread is what it is because of online sales? You've managed to build a brand that can follow you wherever you go. Not to mention, you pay people to help manage your business. Now, there's a reason you're sleepin' on my couch and not in that fancy apartment you've got."

"Yeah. Because I got spooked. So, what, I'm supposed to run

away when things get hard?"

"No, of course not. But is that really what you think this is? You've struggled before without comin' home. Maybe this is fate."

"Fate? My bad dating decisions led to a break-in and anxiety that had me running home with my tail between my legs?"

"Maybe. Kind of like your sister's scummy husband was the catalyst to the argument that drove you away from here in the first place. And look at you now. People don't admit it like they should, but you're like our hometown hero."

"Oh, shut up," Mitzi scoffed.

"Don't tell me to shut up," argued Nora, playfully smacking Mitzi's knee. "It's true. You didn't just leave town; you made a name for yourself. Half the people 'round here have somethin' from Sterling Thread in their closet."

"Twenty-thousand people live in Shelby—no way half of them even know me."

Nora scrunched her face with a scoff. "Half the people in Shelbyville are drivin' around with a *Sterling Bates Dealership* decal on the back of their cars. And if you don't think your daddy framed that article about you in *Marie Claire* for all to see in his office, you're wrong. I'm just sayin'..."

"What? What are you saying?" Mitzi demanded to hear, feeling desperate for a reason that made sense.

"I hate what happened to you. I hate how scared it made you —but maybe a knock on the head is what you needed to get your stubborn behind home. I'm sayin'...think about it."

"Mommy?" Evie called before she raced into the room, Titan right on her heels.

"Yes, Evie-B?"

Gone were her floral print pajamas. She was now clothed in a white, long-sleeve dress covered in pink and purple butterflies. In one hand she held a hairbrush, and in the other was an all too familiar, giant white bow.

"Is that what I think it is?" Mitzi chuckled, pointing at the old, cheerleading headpiece.

Speaking through a grin, Nora nodded. "I was digging through some old boxes not long ago and she found it."

"Mommy, I changed my mind. I want to wear this."

"Tell you what," Nora started to say, running her fingers through her daughter's long, wavy mane. "We'll do two half braids, a high pony, *and* the bow."

"Yes, please!" she replied, holding out the brush and the bow.

"Can I shower first?" Nora teased.

"Oh. Yeah."

"While I'm at it, put something on those legs. It's chilly out. Leggings or tights."

"Okay," she said before racing away.

This time, Titan watched her go, then jumped up into his mama's lap.

"I'll be quick," Nora promised. "Think you can be ready to go in forty minutes? Thought we'd stop by Rock-N-Joe before we hit the salon."

"Are you kidding? I can be ready in thirty if it means I'll get a cup of Billie's coffee."

Laughing, Nora rose and said, "If you're ready in thirty minutes, coffee's on me."

"You're on."

AN HOUR LATER, IT was Mitzi who offered her card to pay for their lattes, but she wasn't sorry. It went against her own personal code to leave the house wrinkly, even if it meant losing a bet. Her cropped, lightweight, tan sweater fared well in her suitcase, but her high-waisted, knee-length, printed skirt needed her attention. Fortunately, Nora knew Mitzi was incapable of getting ready in just a half hour and had a few extra minutes to spare before meeting Reese across the Town Square.

The smell of coffee filled the shop, and Mitzi's mouth watered in anticipation of her drink order. It wasn't an exaggeration to say Billie had the best coffee in all of Tennessee. To anyone living outside of Bedford County, Rock-N-Joe was Shelbyville's best kept secret. For anyone within its borders, it was where you went if you wanted the best cup of Joe east of the Mississippi. It was also one of the coolest places to hang out before dark.

The shop used to be Billie's uncle's record store. A few years back, when sales were lower than low and he was on the verge of going out of business, his niece stepped in with an idea that turned the place around. Half the store was still dedicated to music. No matter where you were in the place, rock-n-roll jams were always streaming. As Mitzi and Nora waited on their order, Led Zepplin played through the overhead stereo system.

"Auntie Belle, can I hold Titan's leash?" asked Evie as she twirled the end of her ponytail.

"When we get back outside, okay? You can walk him to the salon."

"Mitzi Bates, is that you?"

Evie, Nora, and Mitzi all turned their necks at the sound of his voice, and Mitzi couldn't keep the grin off her face even if she tried —which she didn't. Two uniformed cops stood at the register, both of them formidably handsome in a way no woman could deny. As she took them in, she remembered them dressed in uniforms of a different sort. Her memory brought forth who they were more than twelve years ago, and she was struck with a sense of familiarity which brought with it comfort and security that went beyond what their police shields signified.

Jedidiah Donahue was two classes ahead of Mitzi. After Trace graduated, Jed took his spot on the field as Shelby High's starting quarterback. Good looking and talented as he was—standing a foot taller than Mitzi, with his dirty blond hair and baby blue eyes—he was nothing like Trace, which only made Mitzi like him more. As memory served, he was also a great kisser. They'd made out a few times, usually after a couple beers down by the river on a Friday night following a game. He took her to his senior prom, too, even though what they had was nothing serious.

Bishop Sharpe graduated a year after Mitzi, but he started as the Dragon's running back his freshman year. At five-ten, he was far from the tallest on the team, but he was definitely the quickest. He also had what was arguably one of the best smiles in all of Shelbyville; his smooth, brown skin a perfect contrast to his straight, white teeth. Not to mention the way his grin made his almond shaped eyes brighten as they narrowed.

"It's me, in the flesh," answered Mitzi, speaking through her lingering smile.

As he pocketed his wallet, the men came closer and Jed asked, "What are you doin' down here?"

"Nice to see you too, Donahue."

"You know I didn't mean it like that." He extended an arm, and Mitzi didn't hesitate to greet him properly with a hug. "It's been a while."

"Yeah. I was overdue for a visit."

Jed let her go just as Bishop reached for her. Their embraces felt like more than hello. They felt like an invitation—a reminder that she was always welcome.

Or maybe you're just reading too much into it, she told herself, stepping away from Bishop.

"How've you guys been? How's Lex?"

Bishop's whole face lit up at the mention of his wife, Lexy. He folded his arms across his chest, and Mitzi swore she saw him puff up a little before he replied, "Pregnant with number three."

"Oh, my gosh, congratulations!"

Bishop and Lexy had a history of creating the most adorable offspring—with pale brown skin, Bishop's dark eyes and curly mane, but Lexy's blonde hue.

"Rumor has it, Bish is finally giving Lex a girl," teased Nora.

Mitzi raised her eyebrows as she laughed. "Good thing her daddy's a cop and his daddy's the chief. She comes out lookin' like your boys, you're in trouble."

A sly smile tugged at the corner of his mouth as he reached down and patted his weapon. "I'm always carryin'." Nodding toward Jed, he added, "And I've always got backup."

"Got that right." Jed held up his fist and he and Bishop knocked knuckles.

"Nora!" called out another familiar voice. "Mit—Mitzi?"

This time, their whole group looked behind the commercial espresso machine to find Billie peeking around at them. Her jaw dropped as her gray eyes, decked out in her usual black eyeliner and a generous amount of mascara, grew wide. Her light blonde hair was pulled into a stumpy ponytail on top of her head, a few loose strands framing her round face.

She glanced toward the register, no doubt checking the Saturday morning rush-hour line still stretched through the store. She hesitated only a moment, then threw her hands up as if to say— *to hell with it.* Mitzi laughed as Billie came out from behind the counter. She was in a pair of holey, black jeans, a faded AC/DC t-shirt, and a worn, denim button-up she wore open with the sleeves rolled up her elbows. She looked as rock-n-roll as she always was— except when she was in a cheerleading uniform.

"Oh, my god!" she cried, crashing into Mitzi. "You think you can just walk in here and order a drink like you do it every day?"

Billie smelled like coffee and flowers, and she held her friend for a long hug, all of which made Mitzi feel calm and welcome.

"What are you doin' here?" she asked when she finally pulled away.

Before Mitzi could answer, Billie looked down and spotted Titan. She gasped and then immediately dropped to her knees. "I finally get to meet this Instagram star? You are *adorable.* I mean, I'm sure havin' you in here breaks at least a dozen food/safety codes, but it's worth it."

"Sorry about that," murmured Mitzi guiltily. "He kind of comes with me everywhere."

"Oh, it's fine," she said, scratching behind Titan's ears. "Nobody's goin' to report me." She peeked up at Bishop and Jed, tossing them a wink before she smiled at Mitzi.

"I've got to run," said Nora, lifting her coffee. "I don't want to be late. Can I leave Evie with you?"

"Of course," Mitzi replied. "We'll be just behind you."

"'Kay. Bye, y'all," she said to the others before making her way toward the exit.

"How long are you in town?" asked Billie as she stood.

"Uhm…" Mitzi hesitated, thoughts of her conversation earlier that morning flittering across her mind. Thinking about going back to New York twisted her stomach, but she tried to ignore it as she vaguely replied, "A few days."

"Okay, well—how do you feel about girl's night? Tonight? My place? Jay's gonna flip when she finds out you're here."

"Sounds fun. Your place pet-friendly?"

"For that little guy? Yeah."

"Then we'll be there."

"Donahue. Sharpe," called out another barista.

Billie glanced back behind the counter and then grimaced apologetically. "I've got to get back to it. I'll text you and Nora-Jean the details later today."

Before getting back to work, Billie tapped the tip of Evie's nose, making her giggle. As she headed to the sink to wash her hands, Mitzi, Bishop, and Jed grabbed their coffees and made their way to the door.

"I'm sure you've got a lot of people to see, but if you've got time before you head back to the Big Apple, swing by the house. Bring that dog of yours. The boys would love it."

"Yeah, okay," Mitzi agreed, handing Titan's leash to Evie.

"It was good seein' you, Mitz," said Jed. He waved as he and Bishop headed for their radio car, parked right up front.

"You, too, Donahue."

As the two men folded into their seats, Mitzi paused a moment and watched them depart. There was something about being on a first name basis with guys who wore a shield. She knew it was unfair to compare her situation in Brooklyn to the life she knew in Shelby, but she couldn't help it. It put her at ease knowing, if anything were to happen to her, the police officers in town would take it personally.

"Auntie Belle?"

Mitzi shook away her wandering thoughts and looked down at Evie, who peered up at her curiously. "Sorry, babe. Got distracted for a second. Ready?"

Evie nodded and then they were on their way, walking through a downtown area she'd taken for granted growing up. The Town Square was full of mom-and-pop shops which colored her childhood and adolescent years. It was quiet in comparison to what she'd gotten used to up north, but the storefront windows they passed were a statement that businesses got the foot traffic they needed to keep their doors open.

Mitzi listened as Evie chatted about what she was learning in preschool. She knew from Nora that Evie was in a program that met weekday mornings, and she'd started a little over a month ago. It was obvious Evie loved it so far. She'd even made a friend whose name was Olivia. Olivia *always* had a pretty bow in her hair, which was a trait Evie seemed to admire.

Just as they were nearing the end of the block, Mitzi caught sight of an empty storefront. The windows were covered, save for the glass front door, but she found herself stopping to get a better look. With most of the natural light blocked out, Mitzi couldn't see all the details of the vacant space, but she saw enough to know it was a decent size floorplan. Whatever was in there before had been cleared out entirely. All Mitzi could see was a stretch of counter near the back wall, which might have been the check-out area.

"Auntie Belle!" called Evie.

"One second, Evie-B. Wait for me, okay?" Mitzi mumbled, barely tearing her eyes away from the empty shop.

She took a step back and looked on either side of her. There was one store to the right, taking up the corner. The sign that hung above the door read: Dahlia & Co, and Mitzi noted it was a floral shop. To the left was a cake shop that had been there forever. Frosted by Faye was where Scarlett had ordered her six-tiered wedding cake. The skill Faye had would keep her busy until she decided to hang up her apron, too tired to bake another thing.

Mitzi wondered what the two shops used to sandwich and why it was no longer there. It was a prime location, especially considering how much business Faye saw on a regular basis. The longer Mitzi stood staring, the harder her heart beat. Again, she recalled the conversation she'd had with Nora-Jean that morning. Nora had called her situation fate. The longer Mitzi thought about it, the more valid Nora's statement felt.

She took a slow sip from her latte. As she swallowed the heavenly beverage, her eyes focused in on the leasing agent's contact info on the door. Her stomach dropped as she read his name over and over again. Trace Whitfield. It wasn't a surprise his family's agency was the one renting out the space. They represented most of the commercial real estate in all of Bedford County and the surrounding region. What startled her was how it seemed like the stars were aligning, and life itself was telling her what she needed was far greater and more complicated than a weekend home.

"Auntie Belle—it's *Dedective* Steele!"

Mitzi looked away from the shop just in time to see Evie take off toward the corner. Titan, spurred on by her excitement, took off right along with her. Only, his four legs moved quicker than hers. Unprepared for his speed, Evie lost her loose grip on his leash.

"Oh, no!" she gasped, her feet not missing a step. "Titan, come back!"

The sight of her maltipoo and her best friend's preschooler heading for the street was enough to clear Mitzi's thoughts completely. Moving as fast as her heeled ankle boots and skirt would allow, she started after the both of them. Before she could get Titan's name out, one of the two men crossing the street hurried up onto the sidewalk and scooped Titan into his arms.

"I'm sorry. I'm sorry. I'm sorry," Evie murmured over and over, coming to a stop in front of Titan's rescuer.

"Evie, babe—you can't leave my side like that," chided Mitzi gently.

"I'm sorry. I didn't mean to. I just wanted to say hi to Dedective Steele."

"It's my fault," said the detective.

Mitzi lifted her eyes to meet his handsome brown ones, and her words got caught in her throat. It had been ages since she'd seen Atticus Steele. He'd always been easy on the eyes, with his perfectly sculpted jaw line, his full lips, and his intense stare. In high school, Steele was tall and lean, which made him the kind of tight end who could really move out on the field. Everyone called him Steele not just because it was his name—but because he was as tough as steel, and stronger than he looked.

Mitzi got to see him play a few games when he suited up in orange at the University of Tennessee, too. As soon as he graduated college, he went on to join the police academy up in Nashville. Right around the same time, Mitzi was leaving for New York. After Nora and Lawson's split, it didn't really come as a surprise that Mitzi never ran into the oldest Steele boy during her infrequent visits.

At the sound of his sure, deep voice, and the look of his tall, lean body wrapped in jeans, a button-up, and a really great sportscoat,

Mitzi was sorry she couldn't remember the last time she saw the man. He wore the last decade extremely well—his frame a little fuller and his face a whole lot sexier with the dark stubble that dusted his chin.

"I take it this little guy belongs to you," said Steele, setting Titan back on his feet. He then took the leash and held it out for Mitzi.

"Uh—yes. Yes, he's mine. Thank you."

"Hey, Evie," greeted Steele's companion. "Who's your friend?"

"This is my Auntie Belle," she replied chipperly.

"Otherwise known as Mitzi Bates," added Steele.

The stranger smirked, the expression making him look intriguingly distracting.

"As in *Sterling* Bates?"

Steele smiled, effectively capturing Mitzi's full attention as he clarified, "As in Sterling Thread."

"You—you know my fashion line?" she asked, suddenly breathless.

High school was a long time ago, but Atticus Steele was still that illustrious and enticing older brother of a friend that was off limits. He was in Scarlett's graduating class, hung out in the same crowd, and caught more than enough female attention to keep him occupied, if he so chose. Given their age difference, he was gone before she was old enough for him to take notice of her, but she had certainly noticed him. Now, all these years later, to learn she wasn't completely invisible to him—to learn he'd kept some sort of tab on her—she didn't know what to make of it.

"I don't live under a rock, Mitzi," he laughed quietly. "It's been a long time. You look good."

Mitzi felt herself blush, and she was suddenly sixteen all over again. She shook her head, in an attempt to ward off her girlishness, knowing good and well he was just being polite.

"It *has* been a long time. I hear you're doing well, *detective*."

The stranger cleared his throat loudly, and Steele's smile grew before he said, "Mitzi, this is my partner, Detective Abernathy. Abernathy, Mitzi."

His distracting smirk still pulling at his lips, he dipped his chin in a nod. "Reed, for anyone with a smile like you've got. I take it you don't make it home often. What brings you to town?"

Mitzi's eyes flicked back and forth between the men. She exhaled her amusement as she inquired, "I'm sorry, detective, am I a suspect of some kind?"

Both men laughed, which was doubly disarming. "I apologize," Reed drawled. "I didn't mean for it to sound like that. Just curious."

"Well, it's like you said," she murmured with a shrug. "I don't make it home often. It was time."

Her stomach fluttered at the sound of her answer. The meaning behind her words was starting to shift as the day wore on, and it made her feel unsettled.

"Dedective Steele?" Evie pipped in softly, graciously rescuing Mitzi from her thoughts, yet again. "Do you have one?"

"Does he have what, Evie Belle?"

Mitzi's gaze moved from Evie to Steele, stopping when she caught sight of the grin he offered the little girl.

"Always, Evie," he said, reaching into his pocket. He pulled out a Dum Dum sucker and offered it to her.

She was quick to snatch it up and hug it to her chest. "Thank you."

"Don't eat it until your mom says you can, copy?"

"Copy."

"Wait, you always have Dum Dums in your pocket?" asked Mitzi.

"You should see the stash at his desk," muttered Reed.

Steele shook his head at his partner and then answered, "It's like I said, it's my fault she took off earlier. Evie knows I've always got a sucker in my pocket. I'd offer you the same, but—the little lady took my last one."

"It's all right," she said, speaking through the smile he'd

inspired.

"Auntie Belle, can I hold the leash again? I promise not to let go this time," Evie whispered pleadingly.

"How about after we cross the street?"

"Steele, I think our work here is done," said Reed.

"Yeah," he agreed. "Don't mean to keep you. Maybe we'll see you around."

As the two men walked away, Mitzi couldn't stop herself from catching another glimpse. When Steele did the same, both of them locking eyes over their shoulders, Mitzi's belly fluttered in excitement. She drew in a deep breath as she focused her gaze in front of her, then took another slow sip from her latte.

"Come on, Evie. Let's go before your mom wonders where we are."

With every step she took, Mitzi tried to convince herself her most recent chance meeting wasn't fate. It couldn't be. Shelby was a small town, and that was all.

chapter three

"YOU BE GOOD, YOU HEAR?" instructed Nora.

Evie, whose arms were wrapped around Nora's hips, looked up at her mother and nodded.

"I'll pick you up after breakfast in the morning."

"Auntie Belle will still be here?"

"I'll still be here, babe. Promise," chimed in Mitzi.

"Uncle Wayde's powering up the Wii, munchkin," said Darlene, in an attempt to get Evie to let Nora go.

Instantly, she pushed up on her tiptoes and demanded, "Kiss!"

No sooner did Nora's lips meet Evie's than the little girl was racing into the house.

"Bye, mommy. Bye, auntie. Uncle Wayde, wait for me!"

"Thanks for this, Aunt Darlene," said Nora.

"You know thanks isn't necessary," she replied, shooing the women off her porch.

It was true. Darlene and Wayde filled the role of Evie's

grandparents more than Nora-Jean's parents ever would. It had been that way since the second Evelyn was welcomed into the world. Yet, routine as it was for Nora to drop Evie with her aunt and uncle for any stretch of time, Mitzi knew she'd never stop saying thank you. She appreciated the way Darlene and Wayde loved Evie as if she were their own.

"Y'all have fun tonight. Don't do anything I wouldn't do," she added with a wink. "See you in the mornin'."

With a wave farewell, Nora and Mitzi headed back for Nora's car, where Titan waited patiently in the front passenger seat.

"Is there a Kroger on the way to Billie's?"

"Close enough. Why?"

"I thought I'd pick up a few things for tonight."

Nora laughed as they both closed themselves inside her old Honda. "You remember our host, right? You don't need to bring anything."

"I swear, it'll only take a minute. She put this whole night together so quickly, I'll feel bad if I don't bring something."

"She's gonna give you hell," Nora teased, easing out of the driveway.

Mitzi rolled her eyes. "I'll survive."

An easy moment of silence settled between them, and Mitzi thought ahead to the company she would be keeping that night. Billie and Jay were a lot like Mitzi and Nora—thick as thieves for as long as any of them could remember. It wasn't just the nature of their small town that forced the girls into a circle of friends, either. While Billie had been on the cheer squad with Nora and Mitzi, Jay wasn't the type to rustle a pom-pom. She was, however, one of Lawson's biggest fans. She never missed a game. Seeing as Lawson had nothing against his kid sister hanging about, she and Billie were part of the crew all through high school.

Thoughts of Jay reminded Mitzi of the run-in she'd had with Steele that morning. It was impossible to replay their encounter without remembering how he'd looked back at her the same moment she'd looked back at him. His self-confidence was a trait he'd always had; but seeing it directed her way was a new experience.

"So, I meant to ask…" she murmured, feigning a casual air.

"Ask what?"

"Steele and his partner—what was his name, Reed?"

"Yeah. What about 'em?"

"Evie seemed to be quite familiar with them."

Nora lifted a single shoulder in a shrug, glancing at Mitzi before focusing her attention back onto the road. "The station's not too far from the Town Square. Between runnin' into them at Rock-N-Joe or seein' them around town, we're not strangers. Anyway, Steele's always been real sweet with Evie. In the beginning, I thought it was out of spite, on account of me breakin' his brother's heart but—he's not like that. Deep down, I knew it then and it's unquestionable now."

"And what about Lawson? He moved back, right? Do you run into him?"

"I have a couple times. The security company he works for? It's in Tullahoma. Jay says his work has him anywhere between there and Nashville, mostly. Even if he's not far, he's not *around*, you know?"

"Ever wish he was?"

Nora coughed out a soft, humorless laugh. "The masochist in me, sure. Why?"

"No reason. I just—I haven't seen Steele in a long time. He looked…"

"*Hot?*" Nora finished presumptuously.

Mitzi tried not to grin, but her efforts were fruitless. "Yeah," she fessed. "Was he always that good looking?"

"Yes," replied Nora, as if Mitzi's question was ridiculous. "The Steele men come by it honest, you can't have forgotten that. You know with our history he's like a brother to me, but soon as he made detective and ditched the patrol uniform, he's turned more than a few heads around here. Smart, attractive civil servant dedicated to his work? He's got half the town wonderin' why he's still single."

"Well, if you had to guess?"

Nora took her eyes off the road a second time, smirking at her friend. "Why, you interested?"

"Just curious," murmured Mitzi, lifting her hands in surrender.

"Uh-huh," teased Nora. "Steele always struck me as the kind of guy who would hold out for someone special. I don't know him as well now as I did back in high school, but I don't think much has changed. The way Jay tells it, the last woman in his life did a number on him. That was a couple years ago. He's been all about the job since."

"I can relate," Mitzi replied as she absentmindedly rubbed behind Titan's ears.

She thought of Nolan, which reminded her of the break-in at the shop, and the flashback brought on a wave of fear she hated. Mitzi knew she wasn't to blame for the lifestyle of her ex. She'd tried to *help* him, but she couldn't help a man who didn't want to be helped. The fact that she was still paying the price for his downfall, and in ways she never saw coming, made her resent him almost as much as she felt sorry for him.

"Okay, this is your last chance to change your mind," warned Nora as she turned into the Kroger parking lot.

Mitzi shoved aside the negativity threatening to sour her mood and glanced out the window at the grocery store. Unbuckling her seatbelt, she said, "Tell you what, you stay here with Titan, and I'll be ten minutes. That way, you won't even be considered an accomplice."

"Deal," Nora laughed.

As promised, Mitzi was in and out of the store in a matter

of minutes. While she wasn't able to find exactly what she was looking for, she made do. By the time Nora parked in the visitor's lot near Billie's townhouse, it was a little after six-thirty. The sun was setting behind rooftops, and the temperature was starting to cool. The smell in the air was clean, the quiet neighborhood was quaint, and Mitzi found herself relishing all the finer details of an evening in Tennessee.

When Nora and Mitzi made it to the sidewalk leading to Billie's front porch, they could hear music and laughter coming from inside. This was all the evidence Mitzi needed to know that Jay had arrived. With Titan in one arm and her bag of groceries occupying her other hand, she let Nora ring the doorbell. Not five seconds later, Justice Steele stood grinning in the doorway.

Earlier, Nora mentioned how the Steele men had inherited their good looks—and they certainly weren't the only ones. Justice, who everyone knew fondly as *Jay*, was—put simply—a knock-out. But it wasn't just her looks; it was a combination of what you saw and what you got. There was an irony about her that made her undeniably likeable.

The tallest in their bunch, she stood just shy of five-nine. She was thin from top to toe, her feminine curves as slight and delicate as the features of her face. Her eyes were a greenish brown, and it was the only color her face ever saw. She'd never been one for makeup, outside of mascara and a little lip-gloss. But she didn't need it. Her skin was flawless. Yet, as dainty as she appeared, she was far from it.

She wore her straight, brunette hair in a layered pixie cut, the front thick and long enough to drape across her face. That night, she wore it coiffed and pinned back out of her eyes. The plaid, flannel button-up she wore hugged her every curve, and the rolled-up cuffs revealed a hint of the artwork that covered her right arm in a full tattooed sleeve.

Justice Steele was a sweetheart and a badass all wrapped into one.

"Oh, my god, hi!" she gushed before stepping onto the porch in her bare feet. She wrapped Mitzi in a hug, careful not to smush Titan. "It's so good to see you."

"It's even better to see you," Mitzi insisted.

As Jay pulled away, she nudged Nora and greeted, "Hey, girl."

Just like Steele, Jay never let what happened between Lawson and Nora sully their friendship. While her loyalty was always going to leave her siding with her brother, the truth was: life happened, people changed, but friendships were precious.

"Hey. You gonna leave us out on the porch or what?" Nora jibbed.

"That depends," said Jay, folding her arms across her chest. She lifted an accusatory eyebrow at Mitzi and inquired, "What's in the bag?"

Nora laughed and Mitzi shook her head.

"Hey," chimed in Billie as she came to stand in the doorway. "Get your booties in here."

"I spot contraband," Jay said, looking over her shoulder.

"You guys, it's just a little cheese and crackers. Maybe some sausage, too."

Billie narrowed her eyes at Mitzi. "What kind of cheese?"

"Brie..."

There was a pause. Jay and Nora exchanged a look, and Mitzi didn't miss the way Jay tried to suppress a smile.

"Hand it over, city girl," Billie finally demanded, reaching for the bag. "And get inside. Reese will be here any minute."

While Billie Holt, co-owner of Rock-N-Joe, was all rock-n-roll, *Willamenah Holt* was nothing more than a southern woman who kept fresh flowers in the house year-round, decorated in a soft palette of white, gray, and blue with a splash of navy in a style that could be described as nothing other than farmhouse chic, and she was—hands down—the most gracious hostess of their generation. Alternative rock was playing on the living room sound system. As they all followed Billie to the kitchen, Jay stole Titan from Mitzi's grasp for a dance.

"I've got sweet tea, for anyone who wants to start slow. Otherwise, there's beer in the fridge, couple bottles of red on the counter, and as soon as I add Mitzi's contraband to the appetizer platter, we can get this party started."

"Your house is gorgeous, Billie," said Mitzi, her gaze soaking up the room.

"I forgot you've never been here before. Soon as I check on dinner, I'll give you the full tour."

A couple minutes later, just as Billie set out her homemade charcuterie board, complete with the brie, sliced sausage, and crackers from Kroger, the doorbell rang. It was Nora who went to answer, and she returned to the kitchen with Reese in tow.

Reese, like Jay, was a bit of a badass in her own right, but you wouldn't know it just looking at her—with her silky blonde hair, her light brown eyes, and her five-foot-three frame. She was the youngest in the girl posse, a couple years behind Mitzi and Nora, but she was also the smartest. She became a cheerleader in high school to combat the stereotype that all mathletes were nerds. Now, she wasn't only the prettiest cop in all of Shelbyville, she was also the *only* female cop they had. These days, she walked around town in short skirts or tight jeans to combat the stereotype that female cops were butch.

There were hugs all around before Billie gave Mitzi the grand tour, Titan following them in and out of every room. Soon after, they all sat down at Billie's kitchen table with their drink of choice. For hours they ate, drank, and laughed. It felt like old times. When Billie brought out dessert and served everyone coffee, it wasn't just Mitzi's belly that was full. Her heart was overflowing. Whatever fear she left behind in Brooklyn was temporarily forgotten, and her anxious thoughts were drowned out by the music and gossip she'd only ever had at home.

"So, Nora-Jean, when's the next time we get to see you and the Pick-a-ninnies on stage?" asked Jay before shoveling a bite of brownie in her mouth.

Nora smiled down at her coffee mug and admitted, "Actually, we're playing next weekend in Tullahoma."

"Whiskey-N-Boots?" asked Billie.

"Yeah."

"Dang. I'm on duty next weekend," said Reese, frowning in disappointment.

"You didn't tell me you had a show coming up," murmured Mitzi.

"It's not a huge deal. Just a local gig."

"Shut up." Mitzi smacked Nora's arm and then pointed at her as she insisted, "Every show's a big deal. Big stage or little. Especially after what happened with he-who-shall-not-be-named."

"Here, here," agreed Jay, raising her coffee mug.

"You still gonna be here?" asked Nora.

Mitzi's heart swelled at the subtle invitation. In it was a plea she knew no one else could hear, and it made her feel good to have a valid reason to stick around for another week.

"I'll be there. Front row center."

"Me, too," promised Billie.

"Me, three," added Jay.

The women finished their dessert before taking their coffee to the living room. They got comfortable on Billie's sectional, talking until well after midnight. Jay was the first to start cleaning up; and, against their hostess' protests, everyone joined in. Finally, around two, they said goodnight and went their separate ways.

They were halfway to Nora's place, riding in a comfortable silence, when she reached over and blindly grabbed hold of Mitzi's hand. She gave her fingers a squeeze and murmured, "I'm glad you came home."

Mitzi leaned her head back against the headrest and peered

through the darkness at her friend. She squeezed Nora's fingers in return as she whispered, "Me, too."

MITZI WOKE WITH A GASP, startling Titan, who slept at her feet. He leapt to his paws, and the sound of his jingling tags helped ground her in the present moment. As she worked to catch her breath, she looked around the room. Dawn cast a faint glow of light across Nora's space, and Mitzi buried her fingers in her hair, sweeping it out of her face and holding tight to the strands. She tried to breathe evenly, so as to calm her racing heart. She closed her eyes for just a second, and the nightmare she'd recently escaped was still there, so she sat up and shook it off.

Nightmares weren't exactly the norm for Mitzi. She knew everyone dreamed, but she rarely remembered hers. She couldn't recall the last time a dream frightened her enough to rip her from the clutches of sleep. Then again, much as she wanted it to be, her nightmare wasn't merely a figment of her imagination. She'd lived it. Unfortunately, her mind saw fit for her to *relive* it in slumber.

Titan padded atop the blanket over Mitzi's legs, climbing over her knees before sitting his bum on her thighs and resting his body against her stomach. Appreciative of his presence, Mitzi hugged him close, lowering her face until her nose felt the warmth of the top of his head.

After a minute of snuggling her pup, her pulse had slowed, her breathing had grown even, and when she closed her eyes, it wasn't her boutique in Brooklyn she saw. She saw Donahue and Sharpe folding themselves into their radio car. She saw Reese, Nora, Jay, and Billie sitting around a table, half-eaten dinner plates in front of them, and two empty bottles of wine as their center piece. She saw Evie holding onto Titan's leash as she chatted about every thought that came to mind. She saw Steele glancing back at her from over his shoulder—and she saw the empty storefront he passed as he did so.

"What do you think, baby?" she whispered into Titan's hair. "Would you like it down here? Should we move? Hmm? Think mama could open up shop at home?"

Titan tilted his head back, his wet nose grazing the underside of Mitzi's chin before he licked her. She giggled, accepting his kisses before freeing a heavy sigh. She felt a little crazy entertaining the thought of packing up her life and moving back to Shelby on what felt like little more than a whim—but the anxious feeling she got in her belly at the thought wasn't the same anxious feeling she had two days prior, walking the short trek from her apartment to her boutique. Instead, it seemed more like the anxious anticipation she felt when she hopped into the cab of Lawson's truck eleven and a half years ago. She'd followed her gut then. Shouldn't she do the same now?

"Come on, baby. Let's go for a walk."

Understanding her perfectly, Titan jumped out of her lap and searched for the door. Mitzi rummaged through her roller bag until she found the oversized sweater she was after, throwing it over the tank she'd worn to sleep. Keeping on her plain, black leggings, she pulled on her walking shoes, grabbed Titan's leash, and met him at the door. They walked for an hour, wandering up and down the quiet streets as the sun came up. Under-rested as she was, Mitzi felt refreshed as she and her maltipoo climbed the steps leading back to Nora's unit. She'd also made up her mind.

It was another half hour before Nora emerged from her room. She stopped at the end of the hallway, squinting sleepily at Mitzi, who sat with one of her legs folded against her chest, her foot propped on the edge of her seat as she held a steaming mug of coffee to her lips.

"Hey," Nora clipped pathetically. "How long you been up?"

"A while." She raised her mug and pointed out the obvious. "Made coffee."

"Music to my ears."

Mitzi took a slow sip, watching as Nora went about doctoring herself a cup. She waited until her friend was sitting before she asked, "How would you feel about me staying with you for a couple weeks?"

"MB, you know you're welcome as long as you need," she murmured, lifting her coffee for her first sip.

Mitzi smiled. "Great. Hopefully it doesn't take too long for me to find my own place."

"Wait—what?" Nora whispered, her eyes suddenly more alert.

"So, yesterday, when Evie and I were walking to the salon, I noticed there's a vacancy in the Town Square."

"Shut up," she gasped as her spine straightened.

"Okay," taunted Mitzi.

"I mean—don't shut up!" Nora set aside her coffee, now fully awake and on the edge of her seat. "Are you serious?"

"Doesn't count as running away if I open another Sterling Thread boutique, right?"

"Oh, my god! Put your coffee down so I can hug you!"

Mitzi did as she was told before Nora launched across the distance between them. Her joy was contagious, and soon they were both laughing.

"My best friend is movin' *home?*"

"Don't tell anyone. There's a lot I have to figure out. I haven't even seen my family yet, but—"

"I won't say a word, I swear." Nora pulled away and settled back in her seat. "This is the best news. I can't believe we'll have our own Sterling Thread in town."

Sucking in a deep breath, Mitzi arched an eyebrow and said, "One guess as to who's the agent in charge of leasing the space."

Nora's excitement was instantly damped, and she pinched her lips together in a frown. "Okay, that does suck. But..."

"But what?" prompted Mitzi, already certain what her friend

was thinking. "But maybe it's time to bury the hatchet?"

Lifting a single shoulder in a shrug, she replied, "You can't really deny how it kind of brings things full circle."

"I know. I wish I could."

"So, when *are* you goin' to go see your folks?"

"Today." She traced the tip of her middle finger around the rim of her mug and sighed. "If I'm really going to do this, I've got to make a move before someone else gets that space, which means I'll talk to my parents today, I'll go see Scarlett tomorrow and then—then I guess I'll stop by Trace's office."

Nora nodded, relaxing a little as her temperament began to sober. "I know a part of you thinks the timing of all this is like you runnin' away. But nobody runs from trouble into more trouble. You comin' home is brave, Mitzi Belle."

"You really think so?"

"I do." She took a breath, held it in for a second, then grinned as she said, "I also think you need to tell your folks pronto, because I can't promise to keep this secret for more than forty-eight hours."

Mitzi shook her head, but she couldn't stop from laughing as she declared, "Holy hell, I'm movin' home."

chapter four

I T WAS MID-AFTERNOON BY the time Nora was able to hand over her keys so Mitzi could borrow her car to get around town. Mitzi knew kick-off for the Titans vs Texans game had just passed. She hated to miss the beginning of the game, which is why she hoped her dad would be where she assumed he was. Otherwise, she'd likely miss most of the first quarter making two stops.

When she pulled into the lot at Gypsy's, there was a small thrill that raced through her at the sight of so many cars parked out front. It wasn't that Mitzi couldn't find a sports bar with football fanatics up in New York—she just never found one where she wasn't the only one in the place rooting for her boys in blue. At Gypsy's, it was Tennessee or bust.

She found a vacant stall at the back of the lot and was quick to grab her purse and her game-day gear from the passenger seat before getting out of the car. The jean jacket had been one of the last things she stuffed into her little suitcase. It was a tight squeeze, but Mitzi had been wearing her custom denim going on seven seasons. She had no intention of missing a Sunday, regardless of her circumstances or location.

The front was fairly simple, a single Titan's logo patch sewn onto the left breast pocket. On the right breast pocket were two, monogram patches—a red M and a navy B. Down the right sleeve, she'd sewn Titan-blue patch letters that spelled out *Tennessee* in cursive font. On the left sleeve she had an NFL patch at her shoulder, an American flag just beneath it, and a navy football with white detail just above her elbow. Across the top back panel of the jacket, in big, capital, block, navy letters with a white outline, it read: *Bates*. Below her name were two large zeros, like on a jersey. Scattered in the remaining blank space were little stars in red, white, grey, and Titan blue.

Win or lose, she always wore it with pride.

As she made her way inside, she fidgeted with the cuffs, rolling them up over her wrists nervously. Part of her thought it was silly, the way her insides twisted whenever she came face to face with her parents—especially her dad. No matter what happened between them, they were always going to be family. That had been proven over the span of years comprised of mediocre attempts at salvaging what had been broken with words and actions that couldn't be taken back. Except, her heart knew what her mind was too afraid to admit.

She wanted the family they'd been when she was little. When it was just the four of them. When Scarlett and Mitzi swore their daddy hung the moon, and their mama was the prettiest and wisest woman in town. When Mitzi wanted to be just like her older sister, and boys weren't on either of their radars. The four of them had been close once. She missed it. But there was a part of her that hoped, somewhere down the line, they might be able to get some of that closeness back. Hard as it was to admit, she knew if that was ever going to happen, she'd have to play her part. *That's* what made her nervous. *That's* what twisted her insides.

If she was going to stick around town, *somewhere down the line* had arrived.

Once inside the bar, she allowed herself a second to appreciate the crowd. There were jerseys, t-shirts, and ball caps showcasing Tennessee pride all over the room. It smelled like beer and fried bar food, and there was a loud hum of conversation battling with the sound of the game—plastered on every TV in the place.

Yeah. She was home.

Lifting up onto her tiptoes, she tried to search the crowd for his face. She'd only just started looking when a curvy, young redhead came her way. She stopped at the hostess stand and offered Mitzi a smile as she asked, "You look like you're lookin' for someone. Maybe I can help?"

"Uh, maybe," replied Mitzi, settling back down on her heels. She didn't recognize the woman, but that didn't mean the woman didn't know her dad. "Any chance you've seen Sterling Bates drop by in the last hour?"

"Oh, yeah," she said, as if they were old pals. She pointed toward the bar. "Mr. Bates is where he always is when the Titans are playin'. Sittin' with Redd."

Mitzi nodded and waved her thanks as she made her way to the center of the room, where the bar was situated. Redd, Gypsy's son, was standing in the corner, a dish towel thrown over his shoulder, his neck craned back as he looked up at one of the screens behind the bar. Just like the redhead said, Sterling was sitting at the counter, a cold glass of beer perched in front of him.

Sterling used to sport a head full of hair. Now, it was down to a buzz cut to help soften the blow of his receding hairline. Nevertheless, age hadn't bested his good looks. What hair he lacked on his head, he made up for on his face, with his full, salt-n-pepper goatee. While he still had a couple years ahead of him before he reached sixty, he took care of his body as if he was still forty. He looked good, in a blue button-down and jeans.

He always did say Dolly wouldn't let him leave the house in a t-shirt.

Glancing up at the TV, Mitzi noticed the teams were in between plays. The opening was obvious, so she walked right up to the man and said, "Hi, daddy."

Sterling jolted as he turned to look at his daughter. At first, he didn't say anything, his eyes too busy taking her in. She smiled, sure she looked different than she did the last time they saw each other—almost two years prior. Her hair was shorter; and while she was a little older, she liked to think any evidence of her age was found only in the wisdom held in her eyes.

"Look at my girl. Pretty as the day is long."

Mitzi's smile grew as Sterling slid off his stool and wrapped his youngest in his arms. She held on tight, the familiarity of his embrace one she missed even more than she knew.

"It's good to see you, daddy."

"What are you doin' here?" he asked, letting her go.

It wasn't lost on Mitzi how nearly *everyone* she ran into asked her the same thing. It stung acknowledging the blame she owned in that regard.

"Well, for starters, I was hoping to catch the game with you."

"I'd say that's a good place to start. Fred, move down a seat, would you? Make room for my baby girl."

Fred complied just as Redd folded his arms and propped himself against the bar. "Well, I'll be damned," he began with a half-cocked smile. "If it isn't Mitzi Bates." He jerked his chin and added, "Nice jacket."

"Thanks, Redd."

While Shelby was filled with many natives, Redd was a towny through and through. All he ever wanted was the simple life. He'd been working behind his mama's bar since it was legal for him to pour liquor. Twenty years later, and he still showed up to work with a smile that was contagious and a wink that made all the girls feel noticed. He knew one day he'd take over ownership of Gypsy's. The bar would be his family's legacy, and he wouldn't have it any other way.

"What'll it be?" he asked, knocking his knuckles against the counter.

"I'll take a Stella, if you've got it," Mitzi answered as she hung her purse and climbed onto her barstool.

"Comin' right up."

When Mitzi glanced up at the television closest to her, she saw both teams lined up, the Texan's quarterback calling out the play. She watched as the ball was hiked, her eyes glued to the men who made up the defensive line. The quarterback danced, looking for an opening, and Mitzi shook her head. She always hated it when the opposing QB had more than enough time to throw the ball. When he gave up his hunt and started to run the ball himself, Mitzi could keep quiet no longer.

"Take him down, for cryin' out loud!"

A second later, in hopes of dodging a hit, the man slid onto his side for a gain of three yards. Sterling chuckled just as Redd served Mitzi her beer.

"With that attitude, this one's on the house," he said with a wink.

Mitzi grinned, raised her glass in thanks, then took her first swig.

"When did you get in?" asked Sterling.

Mitzi shrank a little in her seat, setting aside her beer as she met her dad's eyes. "Friday afternoon. I've been staying with Nora-Jean."

It was impossible to ignore the wounded look in his gaze. It only lasted a second, but it hurt to see. Mitzi felt his disappointment even as he pasted on a smile and said, "It's good of you to make time for your old man."

"Daddy…"

"How long are you in town?" he asked before she could figure out what else to say. He shifted his focus back onto the game, but she kept her gaze trained on him as she prepared to come clean.

"Actually, that's why it's taken me so long to come see you. I needed a couple days to figure that out, myself."

This caught his attention, and he met her eyes as he waited for her to go on.

"Something happened at my boutique. Everything's fine, or it will be. I just—I needed to come home. Until this morning, I didn't know for how long."

"What do you mean, *somethin' happened?* What happened?"

Mitzi straightened her spine, turning in her seat until she was facing the man directly. "Don't freak out, but...the shop was robbed. It was late. We were closed. I was there alone. There was only eight hundred dollars in the till, as my assistant had made a bank run after closing. Damage to the shop was minimal. I ended up with a mild concussion, but—"

"*What?*" he all but growled.

Mitzi could tell by his posture he was not heeding her request to not freak out. When he started to get red in the face, she sealed her lips closed and braced.

"He put his hands on you? When did this happen? Why am I just now hearin' about this?"

"It was a couple weeks ago. But daddy—"

"Couple *weeks* ago? You get robbed and knocked over the head a *couple weeks* ago, and you don't think to call your mother and me?"

"Dad—"

"At least tell me they caught the sonofabitch," he demanded, cutting her off.

Mitzi blew out a sigh then reached up to run her fingers through her hair. She could feel the attention of the patrons at the bar, and she cursed the commercial break that made them the center of attention.

"Sort of," she admitted.

"*Sort* of? What the hell does that mean?"

"It means they arrested the guy who did it but not the one behind it. And because I don't know where he is and the man in custody won't sell him out, he's still out there. But, dad, listen—"

"Oh, I hear you loud and clear, sweetheart, and I don't like what I'm hearin'."

"Daddy! I'm moving home," she blurted.

This shut him up a minute. He stared at her blankly before he finally managed, "I beg your pardon?"

"I got freaked. I was barely leaving my apartment to take my dog out. I came home to clear my head and then I got here and, I don't know. I don't want to go back. It's not that I don't love the city and everything it taught me. For the most part, it's been good to me. But I was walking around downtown yesterday, I saw there's an empty storefront, and I'm thinking about leasing it. Honestly, I can run my business from anywhere. I've got a great team behind me. But I like having a store to go to every day. Having one in Tennessee—it just feels right. I figure, if I can open a second boutique here, maybe a move might also be good for business."

Again, Sterling took a long pause. His eyes flicked up at the game, then dropped back down to stare at Mitzi. He moved his beer glass, as if he was going to pick it up, but it never made it to his lips as he continued to process all she'd said.

"You're really movin' back?".

"Pretty sure, yeah," she murmured with a nod.

"I know the spot you're talkin' 'bout." He studied her carefully, as if she might change her mind any second. "Trace has had a few bites on it. I'll give him a call, tell him to hold off if you're serious."

Ignoring how much she wasn't looking forward to seeing her brother-in-law, she forced a smile. "Thanks, daddy. I thought I'd stop by his office tomorrow."

He nodded, glanced up at the game, and then back at Mitzi. "This guy—the guy behind the robbery—he was targetin' you?"

"I don't know if *targeting* is the right word, but it wasn't a coincidence."

"And he's still runnin' free?"

"Yeah." It was Mitzi's turn to break eye contact in order to peek at the game. Texans had the ball, which meant she'd missed the last Titan possession, but it looked like they hadn't scored. "Listen, I told you, I don't want you to freak out about it."

"Right. It's got you freaked enough to move home, but you expect me not to worry about it?"

"Daddy, he's not a threat to me here."

He paused contemplatively, then mumbled, "You don't know that." Before Mitzi could say another word, he twisted in his seat and hollered, "Steele? Steele, son, get over here, would you?"

Mitzi's spine straightened as her mouth fell open. She hadn't clocked him when she walked in the door but, sure enough, there he was—at a high-top table with a couple unfamiliar people, one new acquaintance, and a face she hadn't seen in a long time. She watched as Lawson looked her way before recognition struck. A slow, half smile curled his lips, and he dipped his chin in a quiet *hello* just as Sterling yelled, "Abernathy, why don't you come on over, too."

Mitzi managed a small wave at Lawson before Steele and Abernathy stood. It wasn't until the two men were headed toward her that Mitzi realized what her dad might have been up to. The closer Steele got, the more discombobulated she felt. What she wanted was to wrap up the discussion she was obligated to have with her dad and get back to the game. What she didn't want was to invite more people into the conversation. Least of all Atticus Steele, who looked good in a sports coat and jeans on a Saturday morning, but was also just as enticing on a Sunday afternoon in a long-sleeved t-shirt, just tight enough to hint at his toned body, a well-worn and faded, trucker-style, Tennessee Titan ball cap, covering his head full of hair, and a bottle of craft beer in his hand.

Mitzi forced herself to breathe.

"Mr. Bates," greeted Steele as he and his partner came to stand beside them. "Mitzi."

Like his brother, he acknowledged her with a nod and a subtle smile. Unlike his brother, his gaze lingered on her face until Sterling gave him a reason to look away. Mitzi knew better than to read into what he chose to do with his eyes, but she felt *seen* by the man who hadn't seen her a decade ago. It would be a lie to say it didn't feel good.

Man like that stares at you a second longer than he should, creeped out isn't how any woman would feel. Quite the opposite, she admitted to herself before her dad brought her back to the moment at hand.

"Mitz, pull out your phone. Y'all exchange numbers."

Mitzi's eyes grew wide as she stared daggers at Sterling. "Excuse me?"

"You heard me. You plan on openin' a store down here, people will be in and out of that place all day. Might even get some out-of-towners. Somethin' happens, I don't want to be the last to hear about it. You call the cops, you call Steele, you call me—in that order. You understand?"

She blinked a couple times as she processed his command. Somewhere in there was a vote of confidence she didn't want to let get away. He thought she'd draw business from out of town. Being a businessman himself, she believed he wasn't just saying that to be nice. What he said meant a lot—but his worry that something might happen seemed unfounded.

"Daddy," Mitzi began softly, "This is Shelby we're talking about, not Brooklyn. I don't need to have a detective on speed dial."

"Wait, you're openin' a store in Shelby?" asked Steele, sounding genuinely interested.

Again, Mitzi tried not to read into it as she looked up at him and answered, "That's the tentative plan. I have to meet with Trace about the option to lease the space and talk with my CFO, but—yeah."

"So, you're movin' back?"

"Yes. But I don't imagine I'll need to contact you for an emergency." Furrowing her brow, she went on to admit, "I don't really know the crime scene around here, but something tells me you have better things to do than worry about hypothetical calls better suited for dispatch to dole out to the patrol officers."

The bar erupted with shouts of excitement, and Mitzi, Sterling, Steele, and Reed were all quick to turn their heads in search of the nearest television screen. They caught the tail end of the Titan's carry, earning them a first down with thirty extra gained yards. Now, even more than before, Mitzi wanted to ditch any personal conversation in favor of watching the game while she finished her beer. Fortunately, no one was interested in talking so long as the Titan's had the ball. When the drive down the field led to the first score of the game, there were cheers all around.

Unfortunately, Sterling was happy to pick up where they'd left off as soon as the game was interrupted by a commercial break.

"Come on, now. Get out your phone and let these men get back to the game."

"Dad—"

"We don't mind, do we, Steele?" piped in Reed.

Steele glanced at his partner. Mitzi saw their quick and silent exchange before he held out his hand and replied, "No. I don't mind, at all. Always happy to help where needed."

"Okay. Fine," she conceded, throwing her hands up in defeat. She then twisted in her seat and dug inside her purse for her phone before she unlocked it and handed it to Steele. It was when she saw a smirk tug at the corner of his mouth that she remembered the background image on her phone. It was a selfie. A close up of her and Titan cheek to cheek taken in Central Park over the summer.

This time, she had a hard time pretending his smirk meant

nothing. He liked the picture—and she liked that he liked the picture.

After he put in his contact info, he moved to hand the device to Reed, but he declined. "I'm always with you, partner. She needs both of us, I'll be there. Kick ass jacket, by the way." He clapped Steele on the shoulder, winked at Mitzi, and then started back for his table. "Go Titans," he muttered as he walked by Sterling with a pat on the back.

Steele then handed the phone to Mitzi and said, "Guess I really will be seein' you around. You two enjoy the game."

Mitzi held her phone in her hand as she watched Steele make his way back to his table. The only reason she didn't get caught staring was because before he took his seat her dad spoke.

"While your phone's out, call your mother. She's makin' pork chops for dinner. There won't be enough if she doesn't know you're comin'." Eyeing her carefully he verified, "I expect you *are* comin'?"

Mitzi offered him a small smile and a nod. "Yeah, daddy. I'll come for dinner."

chapter five

"**I**'LL TELL YOU THE GOD'S honest truth, it's a wonder you lasted as long as you did without somethin' like that happenin' to you," said Dolly as she and Mitzi drove through town the next morning.

They were on their way to the dealership, as previously discussed over dinner the night before. Her daddy wouldn't have her driving all over town in a borrowed vehicle. If she was sticking around, she needed her own set of wheels. This Mitzi couldn't argue. When Dolly offered to pick her up the next morning, she accepted graciously. Now, even though Mitzi knew her mother didn't have much more on her agenda than maybe a trip to the grocery store, she was sitting next to a woman who was dressed and ready for anything. Big blonde hair. Made-up eyes. A flattering shade of pink lipstick. A short-sleeved, belted, navy blue dress. Like always, dressed to impress.

While Sterling had made his fuss about the incident at Gypsy's, he dealt with it the way he saw fit and it was over before the Titans and the Texans started the second quarter. He got flustered, laid down his law, recruited one of the finest detectives of the Shelbyville Police Department to be on standby, and that was that. He could let it go. Dolly, on the other hand, heard the news and had brought it up every fifteen minutes while Mitzi was at the house; now, not five minutes in the car together, and she was still speaking her piece.

"You got that pretty face of yours from your daddy and me, but you inherited your great grandmother's height, on your daddy's side, God rest her soul. What I'm sayin' is, you're a target in a city like that. Hate to admit it, but you were probably long overdue. Thank heavens it wasn't worse."

"Mom, please," Mitzi begged as she stared out the passenger window.

"I still don't know how you can stand it. All those people all the time. No one's safe."

"Mom," Mitzi tried again, her tone a little gentler. She turned to look at Dolly, took a breath, then said, "There's nothing wrong with New York. Crime exists everywhere. What happened to me wasn't as bad as it sounds."

"Brought you home. Could barely get you here for a Christmas, and yet here you are."

With a sigh, Mitzi let her head fall back against the headrest of her mother's fully loaded, Q7 Audi SUV. She'd earned that comment. Much as she wanted to argue how Sterling or Dolly never suggested a trip up north, she knew the spacious vehicle wasn't large enough to hold the can of worms that comment would unleash.

"Never mind the reason. I'm just glad you came to your senses. Maybe now that you're home, you'll settle down. It'd be nice of you to give me some grandbabies before I'm too old to enjoy them while they're young."

Mitzi couldn't help but laugh. First of all, she knew just because Dolly said *never mind the reason*, "the reason" would come up again. Likely in another fifteen minutes. Furthermore, she'd barely made up her mind about her relocation, and it was just like her mother to start dropping hints about what other major life decisions it would be nice of her to make.

"I don't know what on earth you think is funny. I'll be sixty soon, you know."

Grinning at her mother, Mitzi said, "You just turned fifty-six. You're far from ancient, mom."

"Well, I'm not gettin' any younger," she mumbled as she flicked on her blinker, signaling her intention to turn into the lot of their destination.

They parked right out front and the two of them walked into the dealership together. Mitzi didn't mind having an escort. It might have been a while since any of her dad's salespeople had laid eyes on her, but Mrs. Bates was familiar enough for them to know not to approach. Much as she loved her daddy, Mitzi had never been particularly fond of a car salesman.

Sterling was on the phone when she and Dolly invited themselves into his office, but he was quick to wrap up the call on account of his company. Claiming a laundry list of errands she had to run, Dolly only stayed long enough for a kiss.

On her way out, she pointed at Mitzi and said, "Soon as you start lookin' for your own place, you keep your mama in the loop. We'll find you someplace nice. Guarantee it'll be a sight bigger than what your money can buy in the big city."

Mitzi forced a smile and tamped down the temptation to be overwhelmed by the speed at which her mother's mind operated. She hadn't even called Gianna or Adalynn with her news, and her mom was ready to have her settled in a neighborhood with her stamp of approval.

"Okay, mom," she managed.

Dolly gave Mitzi's shoulder an affectionate squeeze on her way out, and Mitzi took a deep breath, letting it out slowly as she focused her attention on Sterling. He only grinned before he asked, "Ready to pick you a set of wheels?"

An hour later, Mitzi was driving off the lot in a silver, Ford Fusion Hybrid while her dad headed back to his office to get the necessary paperwork started. She was to return to the dealership after she met with Trace. If she still loved the vehicle, she and Sterling would make it official. She felt odd, driving around town in what would likely be her new car. Aside from the little Chevy her parents let her drive everywhere during high school, Mitzi had never had her own car. She'd never needed one in the city. Behind the wheel, her future started to feel that much more *real*.

Deciding noon was still too early in the day for her to endure the company of her brother-in-law, she drove the opposite direction of his office, following the GPS instructions to his residence. Mitzi wasn't sure whether or not Scarlett would be home, but it was a detour and a procrastination tactic she thought would be well worth her time. They were blood relatives, after all. It was only fitting she tell her sister the news before her husband found out.

Trace and Scarlett owned a five-bedroom, three bathroom, four-thousand square-foot home with a three-car garage on a plot of land just shy of the next town over. On both the inside and the outside, it looked like something out of a *Southern Living* magazine. Mitzi was sure the Whitfield home ranked third on Scarlett's list of pride and joy—coming in just after Charlotte and Brooks. Like their mother, she was a homemaker through and through.

When Mitzi pulled into the wrap around driveway, the first thing she noticed was the front porch decked out in fall décor. White and orange pumpkins. Dried, decorative corn stalks. Black lanterns with white candles inside, all of it arranged around their welcome mat. It was classic Scarlett, which made Mitzi smile to herself.

Upon exiting her vehicle, Mitzi ran her fingers through her hair, sweeping a bit behind her ears. She took a deep breath before she rang the doorbell, holding the air in her lungs until she heard her sister's approaching footsteps.

Scarlett opened the door and, much like their dad had done the day before, she didn't speak right away. It was obvious Scarlett wasn't surprised to see her sister on her porch, her gaze one of curious assessment. Mimicking her sister, Mitzi gave the woman a once over, too.

She'd always been slim, but Scarlett was the thinnest mother of two Mitzi knew. She wore an over-sized, dark green knit cardigan over a thin, heather gray t-shirt tucked into and a pair of skinny jeans that accentuated her narrow hips and long legs. Her hair was grown out well past her shoulders, the silky brunette strands accented with caramel highlights. She'd pulled it half up, in a perfect messy bun, with the rest styled in big, loose, curls. Her makeup was flawless and subtle, which made her look both classy and casual at once. Not for the first time, Mitzi acknowledged how beautiful her sister was.

"Hi," Scarlett finally spoke.

"Hi. I'm guessing mom called and told you I was in town."

"We *do* talk every day," was her only reply.

Mitzi nodded, forcing her smile not to slip. "Can I come in?"

Scarlett stepped aside, holding open the door to grant her sister entrance. "Can I offer you a drink?" she asked as she closed them both inside. "I've got some iced tea. I can make you a coffee, if you want."

"Tea sounds nice."

With a nod, Scarlett started for the kitchen.

"I like your hair short like that. It's cute."

"Oh. Thanks," replied Mitzi, genuinely flattered.

"I think about choppin' mine off all the time, but Trace likes it long."

Like it always did, hearing Trace's name made Mitzi want to scrunch her nose in dislike. Knowing he was the reason Scarlett hadn't changed her hair in nearly twenty years just made her flat out irritated.

"He can't know he wouldn't like it any different if you never give it a shot."

"He's got eyes, Mitz," she retorted, opening up her fridge. "He doesn't need to see it on me to know what he does or does not like."

"I'm just saying, you should cut your hair if you want to."

Scarlett set the pitcher full of tea on the counter before reaching up into her glass-faced cupboard for two glasses. "He's not my warden. He's my husband." She paused and looked back over her shoulder as she went on to say, "What I *want* is for him to like my hair. You don't have a husband. I don't expect you to understand."

Before Mitzi could think of a response, Scarlett began filling their glasses with ice. The clattering noise the ice machine made was enough to silence Mitzi long enough to accept it was time to change the subject. She set her purse on the floor and then settled in one of the chairs tucked beneath the lip of the kitchen's long, white granite countertop island. After Scarlett served Mitzi her tea, she occupied the seat next to her.

"Mom says you're movin' back."

"Yeah. I'm still working out the details, but that's the plan. Actually, my next stop is Trace's office. The vacancy, next to Faye's place? I want to open a shop there."

Scarlett nodded, took a sip of her tea, carefully set her glass back on the counter, and then shook her head contemplatively. "Must have been real bad, whatever happened to you."

"What do you mean?"

"I mean—no one leaves Shelby for someplace bigger and better only to come back. What's the story? The *real* one."

"Sounds like you got the full story. The *real* one. Seriously, the robbery wasn't any worse than I described it. Did it put me on edge?

Yeah. I'd be lying if I said otherwise. But my decision to move home is bigger than this one incident."

"Sure," replied Scarlett, clearly not convinced.

"My family's here, Letty. My family and my oldest friends. New York was just a chapter in my life. A pivotal one. If I hadn't gone—"

"You mean, if you hadn't run away?"

Mitzi paused a moment, neither looking away from her sister's stare nor cowering to her challenge. "If I hadn't gone," she began again, "I wouldn't have Sterling Thread. But no place has felt like home the way Shelby does."

"Well...I know daddy called Trace this morning so, I imagine the place is all but yours if you really want it."

Recognizing this was as close to a *welcome home* as she was going to get, Mitzi smiled, relaxed, and decided to move the conversation along.

"So, what's new with you? How are the kids?"

The two women talked for the next thirty minutes. When Scarlett got up to put their empty glasses in the dishwasher, she mentioned she had a few things she needed to get done before it was time to pick up Charlotte and Brooks from school. Mitzi knew it was time to get her meeting with Trace over with anyway, so she gathered her things and followed Scarlett to the door without protest.

"Brooks has got a little league game on Saturday," Scarlett mentioned as Mitzi stepped out on the porch. "It'd be good of you to come."

Mitzi smiled. "I'd love to come. Text me the details?"

"I will."

Each of them waved goodbye before they went their separate ways. Twenty minutes later, Mitzi was walking into the Whitfield commercial real estate agency. She was greeted by a receptionist she guessed was no older than twenty-five. Somewhere deep inside she knew, if she were walking into any other business anywhere in the world, she'd feel inclined to compliment the blonde on her dress or her perfect choice of accessories—but it wasn't *any* office. It was Trace's office. Rather than appreciate the woman's fine tastes, she disliked the woman for being so gorgeous. It wasn't fair, but it was the truth.

Any woman that *pretty shouldn't be allowed anywhere* near *Trace Whitfield.*

"Hi, welcome in. How can I help you?" she greeted kindly.

Willing herself to be pleasant in return, Mitzi replied, "Is Trace available?"

"I'll have to check. Is he expecting you?"

"I don't have an appointment, if that's what you mean."

"All right, well, let me just pop back and see—"

"No need, Cordelia."

Both women looked toward the short passageway leading toward the building's private offices. Trace filled the hallway almost as well as he filled his navy suit. Even though it had been years since he'd graced the field in pads and a jersey, he still looked like an athlete—tall, toned and sculpted. He didn't wear a tie, the collar of his pale blue button-up undone, but that only seemed to add to his charm. Mitzi wished his eyes weren't so blue or that his head full of light brown hair was thinning, but facts were facts. He was aging well.

Trace smirked at Mitzi and she bit her tongue as she watched his eyes take her in from top to bottom and back again. When his gaze settled on her hazel-green irises, his smirk transformed into a grin. It took everything in her not to turn on her heel and march right out the front door.

"Mitzi, you're lookin' good. It's been a while."

"Yeah. I'm sure you've heard I'm moving back. I suppose we'll be seeing more of each other."

"No complaints here."

God, I don't like you, thought Mitzi as she plastered on a smile.

"I was just with Scarlett. She mentioned daddy called you this morning. I assume you know why I'm here."

"I do. And I have good news for you. Come on back."

Much as Mitzi didn't like her brother-in-law, she couldn't deny he was good at his job. Not only that, but he was also prepared for her visit. As soon as she sat down on the opposite side of his desk, he pulled out a folder of documents in relation to the retail space in which she was interested. He went over everything. By the time he was finished, Mitzi was feeling even more confident about her decision.

"What do you say? Ready to close this deal?" he asked, leaning back in his chair.

"Just about. Can I have twenty-four hours? I would like my CFO to look over this, and of course my lawyer should glance at the lease before I sign."

"I understand. Let me know where to send it, and I'll shoot over the electronic version of everything we discussed. And I'll tell you what—you're family. I'll give you forty-eight hours. In the meantime, I'll grab the keys to the space. You can spend a little time there and get a feel for the place."

"Thanks, Trace. That's very generous of you," she murmured, meaning every word. "You mentioned there's a renovation allowance. I obviously haven't had a chance to explore the shop yet, but I'm sure I'll be doing some remodeling. It'd be great to get some video footage to send to my team."

"You remember Palmer Reynolds?" asked Trace as he stood to his feet.

"The name rings a bell."

"He's my top contractor recommendation. If you plan on being on site tomorrow, I'll give him a call and tell him to stop by." Before Mitzi could thank him, he came out from behind his desk and instructed, "Sit tight. I'll go grab you those keys."

Much as she hated to admit it, when Mitzi left five minutes later, she felt glad to have sat down with her brother-in-law. He was all business, something she wasn't used to from him. While this didn't exactly change her opinion of him, she chalked it up as yet another sign she was exactly where she was supposed to be doing precisely the right thing. Now all she had to do was figure out how she was going to tell her business partner and just how she intended to relocate her entire life.

Folding herself behind the wheel of her Ford Fusion, she knew that could be decided the following day. Right then, she had a date at the dealership. Soon as she claimed the car as hers, she was off to pick up her first passenger. She was sure Titan would love it.

chapter six

"**M**INI-ME, YOU'RE KILLIN' MOMMY," mumbled Nora as she stood at the front door. Her purse was slung over her shoulder, Evie's backpack dangled from the hand at her side, and she stared up at the ceiling in an obvious show of depleted patience.

Mitzi fought a smile from where she sat, her legs folded beneath her in the chair she occupied at the kitchen table. She'd learned the day before it was best for her to stay out of the way when Nora was trying to get the two of them out the door in order to make it to preschool on time. This is why she sat silently, still in her sleep attire, Titan curled up in her lap, and a steaming mug of coffee in front of her.

"Evelyn Belle!"

"But mommy, these aren't the socks I want," whined Evie. "Where are the ones with stripes?"

"Baby, I don't know. They're probably dirty. You'll have to settle with what you've got. *Now*. I mean it. This train is leavin' the station in *one minute*."

"But mommy—"

"Fifty-nine seconds!" Nora interjected.

Mitzi chuckled into her mug at the sound of Evie's small feet scurrying from whence she came. Nora rolled her eyes and shook her head at her best friend, then changed her tune completely.

"Want to meet up for lunch today? I want to hear how it goes with Gianna."

"Definitely." Grinning, Mitzi added, "I can't believe we're going to be work neighbors."

Nora waggled her eyebrows. "Barton and Bates reunited at last. This town's not ready." They both laughed before Nora turned her head and called out, "Forty-five seconds, Evie. I'm not kidding."

"No, you can't leave without me." No sooner had she said the words than Evie came hurrying down the hallway. Nora held out her backpack when her child was in reaching distance, and Evie was quick to grab it.

"See you later." Nora opened the door and began to guide her daughter through it.

"Bye, Auntie Belle."

"Have fun at school, Evie," said Mitzi before she and Titan were left in the apartment alone.

After another swig of caffeine, she reached for her laptop and propped it open. She'd been up late the night before, working on the logistics of her move. Even though it wasn't her job to crunch numbers, she never liked to be left in the dark as far as Sterling Thread finances were concerned. She trusted Gianna to work out the finer points of the pending lease deal, but she wanted to make sure she had a strong case when she presented to her CFO later that morning.

Mitzi had also gone over the terms of her apartment lease. Fortunately, it was New York and there was always someone looking for someplace to live. The cost to break her contract wasn't overwhelming, and she had enough in savings to pay the fine as well as the movers she would need to help relocate her life. She felt incredibly fortunate to be in such a stable place professionally to realistically pull off a move that was just as impromptu as her decision to leave Shelby.

Eleven and a half years ago, she had little more than a couple suitcases and a prayer. Now, it was so much more than that—and yet, things were falling into place.

"We just have to convince Gianna and Adalynn I'm not crazy, huh, baby?" Mitzi murmured, scratching behind Titan's ears.

Anxious to get her day started and to step foot into what would soon be her new store, she helped her pup out of her lap, abandoned the last of her coffee, and gathered what she needed for a shower. Having only packed for a few days, her outfit choices were just about gone, but she managed to look presentable nearly an hour later. Dressed in a burgundy, corduroy, overall shift dress over a long-sleeved, off-white, mock turtleneck, she hoped the mild weather would continue to make her bare legs acceptable. She styled her hair parted down the middle, curled just enough to give her a desired amount of volume. She used warm, neutral shades in her eyeshadow to compliment her dress, and a dark, maroon lipstick for that added bit of flair. After donning her heeled booties, she tossed Titan's leash into her purse, along with her sketchbook and her laptop.

Keys in hand, she strapped on her purse, scooped up Titan, and finally took her leave. It was a few minutes after nine when she unlocked the front door of the vacant retail space. As soon as she crossed over the threshold, she set Titan at her feet and then locked them both inside. Taking in a deep breath, Mitzi looked around. She wasn't sure where the light switch was, but there was enough sunshine pouring in through the door that she didn't feel in any rush to find it. Instead, she immediately started to imagine what the blank canvas before her could be.

It was perfect.

Making her way toward the built-in counter space she'd seen a couple days earlier, she set her bag down and pulled out her phone. She'd waited long enough. It was time she shared the news, and the space, with her team. Without hesitation, she pulled up Gianna's contact info and initiated a video call.

"Hey, gorgeous," greeted Gianna upon answering. Mitzi could hear the boutique's music playing in the background. Gianna was making her way through the store to a more private space.

"Hey," said Mitzi, her smile a reflection of how good it was to see her partner. "Do you have a minute?"

"For you, always. You look good! Refreshed. How's Tennessee?"

"It's great, actually. How are things for you?"

"All good. Sales were through the roof this weekend," she reported as she slipped into the back merchandise space. "Word got around about what happened, and people wanted to show their support."

"Oh," Mitzi hummed as her heart swelled. For a second, and for the first time in days, she missed Brooklyn. "That's really nice."

"Yeah. It was. Anyway, what's up? Do you know when you're coming back? No rush, of course. Just wondering."

"Actually—is Adalynn around?"

"Yes. I think she's been holed up in the office all morning, catching up on emails. One second."

Mitzi waited, watching as Gianna looked for her assistant.

"We've got a call," she announced with a sly smile as she entered the small, back office.

She held the phone so both of their faces were in the screen, and Adalynn grinned broadly at the sight of Mitzi. "Hey, boss. You look great. How are you feeling? Everything's under control here, by the way. We're holding down the fort."

"I had no doubt you would," chuckled Mitzi. "Listen—I've been doing a lot of thinking. And you might think I'm crazy, but I have something to show you."

Mitzi hesitated a moment, eyeing both women as they peered at her in curiosity. She then flipped the camera on her phone and panned her way around the empty shop.

"What are we looking at? Where are you?" asked Adalynn.

"Well, as soon as I clear it with my CFO..." Mitzi paused and flipped the camera once more. "This is going to be our second Sterling Thread boutique."

"Oh, my god," Adalynn gasped.

Gianna covered her lips with her fingertips, saying nothing at first. Mitzi waited, staring at the woman who was obviously instantly deep in thought.

"This is—this is brilliant," said Gianna.

"You think so?" Mitzi asked, feeling instantly relieved.

"Yes. Oh, my gosh—yes. Why didn't we think about this before?" Her gaze grew unfocused as she began to process aloud, "This has always been our flagship store, but maybe that could all change. You're talking about opening an upscale clothing boutique in a small town, what, an hour outside of Nashville? It would be a destination, for sure. We could sell it as *your* home store. I need to get our marketing team on the phone."

Mitzi laughed. "Wait, I'm so glad to hear you're in support of this, but let's get the papers signed. I'm going to send you everything I've got as soon as we hang up. Can you make sure our lawyer sees the lease agreement? If we need to do any negotiations, I'd like to have it all squared away as soon as possible. Tomorrow, if that's not unthinkable."

"Done," said Gianna resolutely. "I will make it happen."

"Wait, so, you're moving?" asked Adalynn, sounding apprehensive.

"Yes. And I was hoping you could help me with that. I don't think I'm coming back. I'll need my apartment packed so all my things can be brought here. I can arrange for—"

"I can do it. Of course, I can help however you need," she interjected. "But—um, what about me? Should I be thinking about moving, too?"

Mitzi wished she could reach through the phone and take hold of Adalynn's hand as she insisted, "I know how much you love the city. I couldn't ask you to leave it. In a few months, when I hope to have this place ready to open, I would love for you to come visit and help me get things going—but you're also needed there."

"I'd do it, you know. For you."

Bringing a hand to rest over her heart, Mitzi replied, "That's unbelievably sweet, and I love your for saying that. In a couple months, I might take you up on the offer. For now, I'll just get my bearings and we'll go from there."

"Okay, boss."

The three of them continued to talk for another forty minutes, each second boosting Mitzi's confidence in her plan of action. After they finally wrapped up the call, she was quick to open up her email app in order to forward all the documents previously discussed to Gianna. With that done, she set aside her phone and pulled out her sketchbook.

Mitzi was no architect, but she'd been the one with the vision for the layout of the Brooklyn boutique. She always knew, if people were going to make the trip to come into the store, she wanted them to feel like they were entering into her creative space. She wanted it to be personal, because Sterling Thread *was* personal. From where she stood, near the back of the vacant shop, she looked around and knew she had an opportunity she wouldn't dare take for granted. Her future boutique, in Shelbyville's Town Square, was going to be the epidemy of personal. Her brand in her hometown. Just as Gianna said, this was going to be her home store, and Mitzi wanted it to be gorgeous.

She'd just flipped her sketchbook open to a blank page when she heard the rattling sound of someone trying to open the locked door. He pulled at the door again and Mitzi saw it as the man lifted his hand to wrap his knuckles against the glass, but she couldn't see who it was. Panic blinded her, and all she could remember was the sound of a crowbar shattering a door three states over. She grabbed her phone and ducked behind the counter, her breaths coming faster as her heart beat rapidly.

"Titan, baby, come 'ere," she insisted in a frazzled whisper. He obeyed and she gathered him into her arms, holding him close as another knock sounded against the glass.

Mitzi sealed her eyes closed tight, trying desperately to remember where and when she was—but she was afraid. Her gut told her to call the police. Then she remembered. She gasped, opened her eyes, unlocked her phone, and dialed the number she thought for certain she'd never need.

STEELE LOOKED AWAY FROM his computer as he reached into his pocket for his ringing device. His brow furrowed at the sight of a New York number displayed on his screen. For a second, he thought about ignoring it. He didn't know anyone in New York, which meant it was likely a solicitor. But before he silenced the call, the memory of Mitzi sitting at the bar in her decked-out denim jacket came rushing to the forefront of his mind. The smirk which pulled at the corner of his mouth couldn't be helped. She was beautiful all on her own—but her Titan pride made her sexy as hell.

If it was her on the other end of the line, it was worth the risk of answering the unknown number. He slid his thumb across the screen and lifted the phone to his ear as he answered, "This is Steele."

"Steele," Mitzi whimpered. "Someone's outside. I don't know who it is. Will you please come?"

Not at all expecting her frightened tone, Steele was instantly on high alert. "Slow down. Where are you?"

"I'm in The Square—in the empty store next to Faye's cake shop.

Nobody knows I'm here. Except—except Nora. I don't know who could be trying to get in, but I'm by myself and—"

"Take a breath, Mitzi," he said calmly as he stood from his chair. "I'm on my way. Three minutes. Just breathe. I'm gonna hang up now, okay?"

"Okay. Please hurry."

Reed, whose desk was across from Steele's, looked at his partner in confusion. "What was that?"

"I don't know. Let's find out."

As he grabbed his keys and snagged his jacket from over the back of his chair, Reed followed suit. When Steele jogged from the front door of the station to his department issued SUV, Reed didn't need to be told to keep up. Steele didn't bother switching on his sirens in order to make it the couple blocks to his destination in two minutes, but he did light up when he pulled alongside the curb and parked illegally in front of the empty shop.

"Isn't that Palmer?" asked Reed before he and Steele hopped out of the vehicle.

This time, it was Steele who frowned in confusion. "Yeah."

"Trace, let me call you back," said Palmer into his phone as the detectives approached. He looked at the men suspiciously and asked, "Detectives, how can I help you?"

Reed looked to Steele, folding his arms across his chest as if he was wondering the same thing.

"Shop's empty. Can I ask what you're doing here?"

Palmer coughed out a laugh, as if he found Steele's question ridiculous. "Look, I don't know what's going on, but Trace Whitfield told me to drop by the space today. Apparently, his sister-in-law is plannin' on leasin' it and she's got a mind to do some renovating. I was told she'd be here."

"Oh," muttered Steele. He hesitated, glancing toward the door before he reached inside his pocket to retrieve his phone. "Did she know you were coming?" Steele inquired, this time sounding more curious than authoritative.

"Trace said he mentioned it, but I haven't spoken to her, no. I was just droppin' by."

Steele nodded, pulled up his most recent call list and said, "Give me a second."

He turned his back to the guys and took a step away as he initiated the call. It rang once before he heard Mitzi whisper, "Hello?"

"Hey, I'm outside with Abernathy. Palmer Reynolds is with us— the contractor. He says he thought you knew he might be stoppin' by."

"Oh, my god," Mitzi breathed. She then groaned and repeated, "Oh, my god. I'm so sorry."

"It's okay," said Steele, speaking through a smile. "Want to come to the door?"

"Yeah. Yeah—give me just a second."

They disconnected and Steele was quick to add Mitzi as a contact to his phone as he turned to face the door. With his gaze trained down at his screen, he missed the inquisitive stare he got from Palmer before everyone's attention was drawn through the glass as Mitzi freed the lock. With her dog clutched against her chest, she pushed open the door, her cheeks flushed as she breathed a pathetic laugh.

"This is *so* embarrassing. I really am sorry." Looking to Palmer she explained, "I forgot you might stop by. When I heard you at the door, I panicked. Steele, Reed, I don't even know what to say. Thank you for coming. I'm *so sorry* to have pulled you away from whatever far more important things you were doing."

"It's not a problem. We're just around the corner," said Reed.

It was obvious, from the expression on Mitzi's face this didn't make her feel any better.

"You goin' to be okay?" asked Steele, looking from Mitzi to Palmer and back again. He couldn't exactly explain why, given

Palmer wasn't a threat, but he felt apprehensive about leaving the two of them alone.

"Yes. Everything's good here."

Steele nodded, but he didn't turn to take his leave until after Mitzi waved and headed back inside with Palmer following after her. As he made his way back behind the wheel of his SUV, he thought about how odd it seemed that Mitzi would have such an intense reaction in response to a simple miscommunication. There was an explanation, and he wanted to know what it was.

"Not gonna lie," said Reed, shutting himself into the passenger seat. "Was hopin' she'd call so maybe your ass would have a reason to finally put yourself out there again—but that wasn't some contrived way of gettin' your attention. That was weird, right?"

"Yeah," mumbled Steele as he shifted into drive. "That was weird."

MITZI SMILED TO HERSELF as she sat at the kitchen table, listening to Nora-Jean as she sang Evie to sleep. Her eyes lost focus, and the information on the computer screen in front of her grew blurry as she got lost in the beautiful, raspy tone of her best friend's voice. She missed moments like this. Not merely hearing Nora's signature tone but hearing it in a way that was thoughtless and natural; hearing it as if the performer didn't realize she was performing at all. She thought about her weekend plans and how she was going to get to see Nora on stage with her band again. She couldn't wait. And for the millionth time, Mitzi was relieved to be home.

Nora's singing put Mitzi into a trance, and her thoughts wandered, stopping dead on the incident she'd caused earlier that day. She scrunched her brow in embarrassment even now, mortified by her own actions. The look on the detectives faces when she came to the door made her wish the ground had swallowed her whole.

She'd told Nora about what happened over lunch, and Mitzi couldn't blame her friend for laughing. It really was ridiculous, given the setting. Nora assured her she'd laugh about it one day, too —but Mitzi wasn't sure that was true. Not merely because the fright she felt before Steele showed up was very, very real, but because she'd made a complete fool of herself in front of the man who was, quite possibly, Shelby's most eligible bachelor.

Not that she was trying to throw her hat in the ring or anything.

"That wasn't at all exhausting," said Nora on a sigh, plopping into the seat across from Mitzi.

She shook away her thoughts and tried to play back what she'd just heard, but she was too distracted. "What?"

"Nothing," Nora replied. She reached up to sweep her hair away from her face as she said, "If she wasn't four, I'd swear she had PMS. Ten years from now, I am in for a world of trouble."

Mitzi flashed a guilty grin. "I wish I could argue otherwise, but you don't call her mini-me for nothing."

Narrowing her eyes into slits, Nora muttered, "I'm gonna let that slide."

Before Mitzi could think of a response, there was a knock at the door, which had both women looking in its direction. They then looked at each other as Mitzi queried, "Are you expecting someone?"

"No," murmured Nora as she got to her feet. Titan followed after her dutifully as her backup.

From where she was sitting, Mitzi couldn't see who was standing outside when Nora unlocked and opened the door. Neither could she see her friend's surprised face as she greeted, "Oh. Hi."

"Hi."

Immediately, Mitzi's eyes grew wide, and her mouth fell open at the sound of his voice. As if it had been minutes rather than *hours* since she'd last seen the man, her face grew warm with a blush as her heart beat wildly in her chest.

"Is Mitzi here?"

It was in that moment when Nora leaned her head back and smiled in Mitzi's direction. In spite of Mitzi's gut reaction, which was to shake her head *no*, Nora smiled and replied, "Yeah. MB? It's for you."

Capturing her bottom lip between her teeth, Mitzi tried to get a hold of herself. Her plan had been to avoid detectives Steele and Abernathy when at all possible for the foreseeable future. She wasn't prepared for whatever exchange was about to commence.

It seemed *fate* had other plans.

She drew in a deep, calming breath and then forced herself onto her feet. Slowly, she shuffled her way to the door. Steele was no longer in the slacks and sports coat he'd had on earlier in the day. Instead, he wore a pair of faded jeans—the kind of faded that couldn't be manufactured but came from years of wear—and a plain white t-shirt underneath a great black, leather jacket. He looked less official, but no less handsome. Somehow, this made Mitzi less embarrassed.

"Hi," she breathed.

"Hey," he greeted with a small, crooked smile. "Wanted to check on you. Can we talk for a minute?" he asked, nodding out rather than in.

"Uh, sure. Yeah. Okay."

As Mitzi stepped out into the hallway, Nora scooped up Titan. Before she shut the two of them on her doorstep, Nora made a face that silently said—*oh, my gosh, wow!* Mitzi suppressed the urge to respond in kind.

"I hope you don't mind my stoppin' by," Steele began, tucking the tips of his fingers into the pockets of his jeans.

"I don't, but you really didn't have to. Earlier—it was a mistake to call you."

"Not at all. I'm glad you did."

Mitzi dropped her gaze down to their feet; his covered in a pair of cowboy boots, and hers completely bare. She shook her head and insisted, "You're just saying that. Much as I appreciate your kindness, something tells me you don't usually make house calls, which means this is the second time you've gone out of your way for me today." Lifting her gaze once more, she added softly, "I'm sure I've exceeded my quota."

"Mitzi, you called me for a reason. You felt threatened. As a cop in this town, I take everyone's safety personally. I'm glad you called. But I'm hopin' you might shed some light on *why* you called."

"Oh. Well, it's like I said—I forgot Reynolds was coming. He scared me, that's all," she replied, unconsciously folding her arms across her chest.

Steele nodded slowly, as if he could see through her half-truth, but she didn't offer him more. She'd convinced herself the whole truth would add insult to injury. She'd overreacted earlier. If he knew the real reason why, it would make her reaction even more unfounded in his eyes.

"I'm a detective, Mitz." A smirk curled the side of his mouth. "Damn good one, if you ask the right person. I know there's more to the story."

"I'm fine," she assured him, holding herself tighter. "I promise. What happened today won't happen again."

"Okay." He freed his fingers from his jeans. "Fair warning, I intend to get to the bottom of this anyway. Maybe over dinner. Friday."

Momentarily speechless at his sudden shift in tactics, Mitzi's mouth opened a couple seconds before she had any words to fill it. "Uh, like—like a date?"

His smirk grew into a smile. "Just lookin' for the truth. The whole truth." He turned to take his leave, glancing back at her from over his shoulder as he added, "I'll pick you up at seven."

Mitzi stared after him, mouth agape, until he disappeared into the stairwell. When she was alone, she laughed, more shocked than amused at what had transpired. As she finally walked back inside, she did so while shaking her head in disbelief.

"What's that face mean? I can't tell. What happened?" asked Nora before Mitzi even had the door shut. She was back at the table, Titan perched in her lap as he studied his mama carefully. While Mitzi made her way back to her chair, Titan leapt off of Nora's legs and followed. She sat, and he curled up at her feet.

"He wanted to check on me," Mitzi mumbled, still processing the conversation in the hallway.

"Got that much," Nora replied, speaking through a grin. "And, honestly, it's not all that surprising. He always was the noble type. What'd he say?"

Mitzi hesitated, staring apprehensively into Nora's green eyes before she admitted, "I think he just asked me on a date."

Nora's eyebrows shot up. "You think or you know?"

"He didn't use the word *date*. In fact, he didn't even really *ask*, but he wants to go to dinner. Friday. He—he said he'd pick me up at seven."

"Wow, look at you. Not back even a week, and you've got men fallin' at your feet" she teased.

"It's not weird, right?" asked Mitzi, too taken aback by the whole of the situation to dwell on such a joke. "If I go out with a Steele guy, you're okay with that?"

Nora's amusement slowly morphed into an expression that could be read as nothing short of disappointment. "Mitzi Belle, are you interested?"

Mitzi paused to genuinely consider the question. There was no doubt in her mind she found the man attractive. Disarmingly so, in fact. Every time she saw him, she wondered how she could forget how good looking he was—but did that mean she wanted to *date* him? She'd been single for a few months. Certainly long enough she wasn't pining over the demise of her last relationship. Even if that had been the case, the break-in would have been enough to eradicate the residue of any residual feelings for the man. Still, Nora had said it. Mitzi hadn't even been back a week. Moreover, her being *back* was still in the works.

Then again—she was, indeed, sticking around. Any reservations or second thoughts had been driven away that morning. First, after her chat with Gianna. Then, after her panic attack, which had her calling Steele in the first place. He was right when he insisted there was a reason she freaked. Of course there was a reason; embarrassing as it was to admit, it brought her to Shelbyville, and she wasn't leaving. If Atticus Steele wanted to see more of her, what good reason did she have to say no?

"I don't know. Maybe," she finally answered.

"Okay, then go out with him and figure out which it is," demanded Nora. "It's Steele we're talkin' about, not Lawson. And even if it was Lawson..." Her voice trailed off and she shrugged, as if Mitzi was supposed to fill in the blank.

"Come on. You can't fool me. Any woman in this town goes after him and she's not you—I hate her."

A sad smile played across Nora's lips as she whispered, "Yeah. Me, too."

A moment of silence passed between them, heavy with regret for both women.

"Anyway, the point is, Steele's a good guy. Everyone knows it. If you're interested, I want you to go for it. You've had your share of duds. It's about time that changed."

"Thanks. Though, it's possible, after what happened this morning, he probably just feels sorry for me."

"About that, I've been thinkin', and I'm sorry I laughed when you told me over lunch."

"Nora, don't be silly. I overreacted, plain and simple."

"Except, it really isn't. Plain and simple, I mean. It's actually the opposite. Truth be told, Palmer's not your average guy. I wouldn't call him creepy, but there is somethin' different about him. It's not just him, though—it's the whole situation. I didn't intend to belittle how you felt, given what happened in Brooklyn."

Mitzi nodded, but she wasn't sure if she deserved the *out* her friend was giving her. Part of her knew her fear wasn't born from nothing; but it didn't change the fact that there was practically nothing in Shelby that should scare her after more than a decade in *the* biggest city in the country.

"That's what makes this whole thing so stupid. This *isn't* Brooklyn. It was Shelby, in the middle of a sunny day."

"Okay, stop. No excuses. It happened, and we can't brush it off. In fact, I have a solution."

"All right. Shoot."

"First, next time you're expecting Palmer, I'm there with you."

Mitzi furrowed her brow in disapproval. "Nora—"

"Don't give me lip. I'm right across The Square. And what is it you told me about your boutique in New York? No one is allowed to be there alone? I think the same rules should apply here, at least until you get a security system installed. And it so happens, that hot guy who just left? He knows someone who works at a security company. Rumor has it, they offer top of the line stuff. And if you don't feel like asking him for details, we'll talk to Jay."

Mitzi fought a smile as she stared at her friend. "You're not going to let this go, are you?"

"Nope. I just got you back. I'm not letting anything scare you away."

"Fine. We should have the lease finalized in the next couple days. I don't expect I'll be ready to meet with Palmer again until after I talk to an architect, so you're on standby until further notice."

"I can live with that. Now…" Nora paused, folding one leg over the other as she smirked at Mitzi. "What are you gonna wear Friday?"

This time, Mitzi didn't try to suppress her grin. She shook her head in reply and said, "I definitely didn't pack for a date. I think I'll need to do some shopping."

"Fantastic. I'm in!"

chapter seven

M ITZI PUT ON AN EXTRA COAT of mascara before assessing her handy work in the mirror. Satisfied with the way her dark lashes stood out against the gray, smoky eye she'd created, complete with a pop of rose-hued eyeshadow, she twisted the lid back on and then tossed her mascara into her makeup bag. She dug for the matte blush lipstick she'd planned on wearing. When she found it, she smoothed the color over her lips effortlessly.

"Wow," whispered Evie, admiring Mitzi from where she sat on top of the closed toilet seat. "You look so pretty."

Mitzi had to admit, she *felt* pretty. It had been a bit of a chore finding something worthy of a night spent at dinner with Steele. She longed for her own wardrobe, carefully curated over the years; or the stash of merchandise in the back room of her boutique; or even her sewing machine and a few yards of fabulous fabric—but she settled for the black, half-sleeve, mini wrap dress she'd found, which belted in a knot at her side, accentuating her narrow waist.

It was simple, but it fit her well. With her hair styled just the way she liked—parted down the middle and curled in big, soft waves—along with her full face of makeup, and the strappy, nude, high heeled sandals she'd bought, she thought the whole look came together quite well.

Mitzi patted her lips together as she winked at the mesmerized four-year-old. "Thanks, babe." She was just getting ready to recap her tube of lipstick when she thought better of it. Turning toward Evie, she instructed, "I think you should have some, too. Tilt your head back for me."

Evie obeyed immediately, sitting extremely still as Mitzi painted her lips.

"Okay, now, you must always remember to blot," she said, setting the lipstick aside. She then grabbed a tissue and kissed it before holding it out for Evie to do the same. This, of course, was so adorable, Mitzi couldn't keep from grinning. "Beautiful, darling."

Evie giggled, squirming in her seat before she asked, "Can I come on your date with Dedective Steele?"

"You're not allowed to go on *any* dates for *at least* another fifteen years," hollered Nora from the kitchen.

Mitzi raised her eyebrows playfully, surprised Nora could hear them, and Evie laughed again. "I think we should listen to your mom."

She didn't bother to clarify that, in fact, she wasn't entirely certain if her evening plans could be officially labeled a date. It walked like a date and talked like a date, but Steele neglected to call it as such; even when he texted to confirm he'd be by to pick her up at seven the previous afternoon. In the days following his visit, they hadn't run into each other, there'd been no phone calls or flirty text exchanges, it was all so straight forward. Part of her wondered if he really was simply after the truth and nothing more.

But she bought the dress, just in case.

"Evie-B, dinner's on the table."

"Coming!" called the little one as she catapulted from her seat.

Mitzi watched her go and then checked the time. Her stomach twisted nervously when she saw it was less than ten minutes before the top of the hour. She gave herself another once over in the mirror, fussed with her hair a little, then zipped up her makeup bag, snagged her lipstick, and headed for the living room.

"What if he shows up in a baseball cap and track pants?" she muttered as she searched for her purse. Finding it, she chucked her phone and lipstick inside before setting it on the coffee table.

"He's not gonna show up in a baseball cap."

Mitzi could hear Nora's eyeroll in her tone as she made her way to the kitchen.

"Also, Steele doesn't strike me as a guy who owns track pants. Who wears track pants any...?" Her voice trailed off as she turned and got a look at her friend. Her face lit up in obvious approval before she rested her hands on her hips and declared, "You look *hot*."

"Are you sure I didn't overdo it?" Mitzi asked, glancing down at herself. "What if this really *isn't* a date?"

"What you're *doin'* is overthinkin' it. If all that man is after are some answers, he could have called you to the station. This is a date. Where's he takin' you?"

Mitzi frowned. "I didn't ask."

"Well, as long as it's not Gypsy's or Chili's I think you've got nothin' to worry about," she said as she went back to platting her own dinner.

Mitzi's frown only deepened at Nora-Jean's comment. The thought of walking into Gypsy's in her wrap dress and heels was slightly mortifying; not because it wasn't done, but because when it *was* done, the woman wearing the dress was sending a message— a message Mitzi had no intention of broadcasting to the bar crowd on a Friday night.

But it was more than that. Nora might have been teasing about

Chili's, but the truth was—Chili's was on the higher end of the spectrum when it came to Shelby's dinner options. She was no longer in foodie heaven. Outside of Smithy's, which was the nicest restaurant between home and Nashville, the pickings were there, but they were slim.

Mitzi didn't notice Nora was standing right next to her until she felt the pop of her finger as she flicked the side of Mitzi's head.

"Ow," she whined as she flinched.

"Stop it," Nora demanded with a scowl. She then continued to the table, taking the seat next to her daughter as she went on to say, "The way you're worryin', I think it's safe to assume you're *definitely* interested."

Before Mitzi could open her mouth to respond, there was a knock on the door. Titan barked, jumping out of the wicker basket chair in excitement. Mitzi drew in a breath at the same time Evie gasped and pleaded, "Mommy, can I get it?"

"It's for Auntie Belle, not you. Eat your dinner."

"But it's Dedective Steele. What if he has a sucker? Mommy, please?" she begged.

"I don't mind," said Mitzi as she went to get her jacket and her purse. Titan circled around her feet, as if silently declaring he intended to go, too. "Sorry, baby, you can't come this time," she told him.

Soon as she slipped into her favorite raincoat, she hooked the straps of her bag over her elbow and then looked expectantly toward the table. Evie glanced between Mitzi and Nora, and Nora shook her head, obviously fighting a smirk as she stared at her friend, seeing right through her play.

"Okay, Evie. Make sure it's him before you open it," she acquiesced.

Without hesitation, Evie hopped off her chair, headed for the door. Titan hurried to join her as she called out, "Who is it?"

"Detective Steele," he replied.

Evie looked to her mother, who offered her a nod, and then she twisted the locks and opened the door. Mitzi's breath caught in the back of her throat at the sight of him. He wasn't wearing a baseball cap, and he certainly didn't look like a man who owned a pair of track pants. He wore a denim button up underneath a tan sports coat. His shirt was tucked into his dark washed jeans, and he'd tied the whole outfit together with a pair of red-brown boots. He looked really good. He looked dressed for a date. But it was the smile he had aimed at Evie that did Mitzi in.

"Hi, Evie. How are you?"

"I'm good. I'm eatin' dinner."

"Oh? Probably shouldn't give you a sucker then, huh?"

She clasped her hands together against her chest and stared up at him hopefully as she replied, "I promise I'll eat all my food!"

"Even the green stuff?" he asked, reaching into the breast pocket of his jacket.

"Yes. Promise," she declared, holding out both her hands.

"Okay. Remember, if mom says no, you have to save it for later. Deal?"

She nodded and he handed her a Dum Dum. Bouncing in excitement, she thanked him and then returned to her seat at the table, leaving Steele in the doorway. Soon as she was gone, he lifted his gaze and found Mitzi.

He raised his eyebrows, taking her in from top to toe before he murmured, "Wow."

He'd said one word, and Mitzi's body temperature went up a notch.

"You ready?"

Mitzi nodded, not trusting her voice, and finally started for the door. She smiled and waved goodbye to Nora then knelt to say goodbye to Titan before stepping out into the hallway, shutting the door behind her.

Steele started for the stairs and said, "You look beautiful."

"Thanks," Mitzi whispered as she felt her cheeks warm.

Part of her thought she was being silly. Men had been telling her she was beautiful for years; but there was something about hearing the words uttered by Atticus Steele that made her insides tingle.

Yeah, she was interested. And this was definitely a date.

"I was plannin' on takin' us to Gypsy's," he muttered, reaching up to rub the back of his neck. "You're probably a little over dressed for that, so I'll have to opt for plan B."

"Oh, my god," Mitzi gasped, her feet coming to an abrupt halt. "Are you serious?"

He grinned, chuckled, and shook his head. "Not at all."

Capturing her bottom lip between her teeth, Mitzi tried not to laugh and failed. "Funny. Very funny," she grumbled as she continued toward the building's exit. Or, at least, she'd meant to sound disgruntled. Instead, her tone was wrapped in the amusement that all but chased away her nerves.

"Allow me," Steele insisted. He extended his elbow for support as they approached the stairs.

She smiled up at him, accepting his offer as she informed him, "I'd say thank you, but I'm not sure you deserve it after that stunt."

"That's all right. Your laugh'll do."

Damn, he's good.

"So, where *are* we going?" Mitzi inquired, hoping to steer their conversation along.

"Mexican sound good to you?"

"Bottomless chips and salsa always sound good to me."

"Noted."

Mitzi made it down the stairs just fine, letting go of Steele's arm as he stepped in front of her to open the door that led outside. When he started making his way toward the cerulean blue, Chevy classic she couldn't properly name, her brain had trouble communicating with her feet. Her pace slowed to almost a stop a few feet away from the vehicle. Steele noticed only after he reached to open the passenger side door.

"What's wrong?"

She pointed at the beauty, her eyes wide as she stared at the man who just got a whole lot hotter—a feat she didn't know was possible. "*This* is your car?" she asked lamely.

He gave her a crooked smile, and she swore she was sixteen years old. It was like being home made her a kid again, a date with Steele was too good to be true, and he was totally out of her league.

"Were you expecting the squad car? Sorry to disappoint. I prefer the Chevelle when I'm off duty."

"Right," she mumbled with a nod, trying to get a hold of herself. "Right, that makes sense."

Forcing one foot in front of the other, she made her way around him, folding herself into the passenger seat before he shut her inside. The interior looked almost as good as new, and she was impressed.

"This car is in such great condition," she said as he opened the driver's side door. "What year is it?"

"Thanks. She's a '72. She's kind of a pet project of mine. Has been for the last eight years."

Mitzi had every intention of asking him more about the Chevelle until he closed himself in and moved to buckle his seatbelt. As she breathed in his scent, she froze. She couldn't believe it was possible. It didn't make any sense. It was one thing for him to have heard she'd started a fashion line—it was another thing entirely for him to know she had a fragrance collection, too.

No. Not just know, but to *own*. Unless she was imagining it, and she swore she must have been, he was wearing Sterling Mist for Him. The scent of the cologne mingled with his natural musk in such a way it only served to enhance what she'd had bottled for her customers.

It couldn't be. It just *couldn't* be.

"Mitzi?"

The sound of her name on his lips made her gasp, and she jerked in the act of turning to meet his dark brown eyes, warmed by his obvious amusement.

"I'm sorry, what?"

"Might be off the clock, but I've always got my badge. Seatbelt."

"Of course," she sighed as she buckled herself in. All the while, she tried to breathe deep and clear her mind—which didn't work out as well as she hoped, as it only served as a reminder how *great* Steele smelled. Moreover, she could tell he hadn't doused himself in the mist. The reason she could smell it so well was because it wasn't just *on him*. It was in the car, like he wore the fragrance all the time.

"How are things goin' in The Square? Is the spot officially yours?" he asked, mercifully rescuing her from her thoughts as he drove out of the parking lot.

"Um, actually, yes."

She tucked a bit of hair behind her ear as she contemplated her answer. It was wild to think that only a week ago, she was getting on a plane for a short trip home. In just seven days, she hadn't merely decided to make a major life change. She'd put things in motion and all but eliminated the option for her to change her mind.

"All the paperwork was signed yesterday. I was there this morning, taking pictures to go along with the blueprints I had sent up to the same architect I used in New York. My boutique in Brooklyn, it turned out exactly as I envisioned. I want something similar down here, but with an added bit of charm. I want it to feel more personal. Anyway, I imagine it'll be a few months before I'm ready to open. I'm willing to be patient in order to get it right."

"And what about you? Are you in for a lot of back and forth for the next couple months?"

"Me? No. I'll be here."

Steele glanced her way. Mitzi, noticing his movement, turned to meet his quick gaze. She only had his eyes for a second, but it was long enough to note the confusion he showcased there before he queried, "Just like that? You're here to stay, without saying goodbye to anyone? Without packin' your things?"

Shifting her focus down at her lap, she took to heart his question. When it came to her things, that had seemed as easy a task as Adalynn made it out to be. A crew had already been hired to pack her belongings starting Monday, and a truck would deliver her life in a pod the following weekend. Hard as she worked for the apartment she loved, the peace she'd found at home was worth so much more.

As for the people in her life, she wasn't quite sure what it said about her or her social circle when she admitted the thought hadn't really crossed her mind to say goodbye to anyone. The people she spent the most time with would still hear from her on a regular basis, as they were integral to her business. Outside of her CFO and her assistant, there were a handful of people she owed a text or, at most, a call—but she had never made friends in Brooklyn the way she did in Shelby. Everyone was always so busy, including her. She had dinner companions and acquaintances she was more than happy to meet for drinks. Being a part of the fashion industry, she knew a lot of people, just not people who would be all that concerned about her change of address.

Then, of course, there was her love life. Or, recently, the lack thereof. For some reason, the surprise in Steele's voice made her feel self-conscious about what it meant that for the second time in her life, she was making a split-second decision that would change everything, and she did so in a manner some might consider reckless or perhaps even extraordinarily selfish.

"Mitzi? You okay?"

She closed her eyes and shook her head, a self-deprecating laugh forcing its way past her lips. "Yeah, I...I guess I just realized how ridiculous it sounds that in the last decade, I haven't made connections with people in the city the way I have here. Aside from my team at Sterling Thread, there's not anyone to make a big deal about my relocation."

"Ridiculous seems a bit harsh."

"Does it?" she asked, looking his way. Dusk casted him in a mysterious light. As she stared at him, she felt suddenly desperate to know what he thought of her circumstances.

"It does." He flashed a knowing expression her way. "You grew up here. Any of us who did would be lying if we said the friendships we made outside of this town are comparable to the ones that make this place home; the relationships that keep us here or, in your case, draw us back. Add to that the fact that you left here to make a name for yourself in a city literally four hundred times bigger than Shelby—I imagine it's four hundred times harder to make meaningful connections up there."

"You're not wrong," she murmured. "Half the time, I had my head down just trying to make it. It's not easy finding friends in a crowd you're constantly competing with."

"They say it's lonely at the top."

"I do all right, but I wouldn't consider myself at the top," she said modestly.

"Around here, you sure as hell are," Steele replied matter-of-factly.

Flattered, Mitzi directed her proud smile out the passenger side window. All at once, she found herself not caught in some warped version of the past, where a date with *Atticus Steele* was too good to be true and he was totally out of her league; rather, she was planting roots in the present, where a date with Steele might still have been too good to be true, but he wasn't out of her league. There were no leagues, just a hot guy in his sweet ride, and a woman who was growing more than a little interested as she saw herself through his eyes.

"Have you started lookin' for a place of your own, or will you be with Nora-Jean for a while?"

"I've started looking. I'm having my apartment in Brooklyn packed up next week, and I'll need someplace to settle when my things arrive. As my best friend, Nora's obligated to love me, but I don't want to overstay my welcome. She and Evie have a routine, and Titan and I need to create a new one of our own."

"Ah, yes, Titan. Can't forget him."

Smiling his direction, Mitzi insisted, "Never."

They arrived at *El Mexico* a couple minutes later, and the parking lot was nearly full. On a Friday night, this wasn't surprising. The family-owned restaurant served some of the best authentic Mexican food in town. As she climbed out of the Chevelle, Mitzi wondered who they might know inside.

A week at home was more than enough time for her to remember, it was rare to go anywhere without running into someone she knew. While there were quite a few new faces around town, that would change, especially after she opened up shop. But Steele had been around almost as long as she'd been gone. Not to mention, he was the eldest son of one of the most prominent judges in the county; and as an officer of the law himself, he took every local citizen's safety personally, which meant he wasn't just known, he was *known*. No doubt, as soon as they were seated, word would start to spread about their date like wildfire.

As Steele reached for the front door, pulling it open for her, Mitzi swallowed a laugh and fought the urge to reach for her phone in order to shoot Nora a text. First chance she got, she had every intention of casting her bet on how long it would be before Dolly Bates got word her youngest was seen out with Gale Steele's boy.

Her amusement and appreciation for the predictability of Shelby's small-town charm lingered as Steele informed the hostess they desired a table for two. It then vanished when—after the woman grabbed a couple menus and started for the dining room —she felt Steele place a hand in the middle of her back as they followed after her. Rather than amusement, she felt another, warmer sensation. One she hadn't felt in a long time. It wasn't familiarity or possessiveness so much as it was gentlemanly care. When they arrived at the table and he pulled out her chair for her, she looked up at him feeling suddenly speechless. The last man to pull out a chair for her was her daddy.

"Thanks," she murmured.

Mitzi had to will her body to keep moving rather than to stare at the man who dipped his chin in acknowledgement. She slipped out of her jacket, draping it over the back of the seat along with her purse before she sat, Steele easing the chair closer to the table when she was ready. A menu was placed in front of her, but she didn't look at it, wishing to watch Steele as he settled in the seat across from her. They hadn't even been served their chips and salsa yet, and already he seemed to be sweeping her off her feet with little effort.

"I've never been to New York City, but somethin' tells me they've got great food." He picked up his menu then glanced over at her. "Will you miss it?"

"The restaurants? Sure." Picking up her own menu, she nodded and continued, "Or, at least, the accessibility of a great variety. Nashville's just up the road, I know, but it won't be quite the same."

"What's your favorite thing about livin' in the city?"

This time, she paused as she contemplated his question. It wasn't just for the sake of conversation she wanted to give him an honest answer. As someone who had never been to Brooklyn, she felt as though she owed it to him, and the borough, too.

"There are a few things I love," she said just as their server arrived at the table.

They were given a basket of chips and warm salsa before their drink orders were taken. Steele opted for a beer, Mitzi wanted a strawberry margarita on the rocks, and as they were left to consider their dinner options, Mitzi spoke freely of the things she enjoyed most about New York. The energy, the hustle, the diversity, and the culture.

"I don't really consider myself an artist, per say, but I am a creative. As such, I'm drawn to art and the way it makes me feel. In the city, there's always something new to see and experience. In a lot of ways, it's inspiring. I learned *so much* up there. Not just about fashion or business, but about myself and people."

Mitzi grew silent when she noticed the expression on Steele's face. There was a knowing glimmer in his dark brown eyes, a ghost of a smile playing at his lips.

"What? Why are you looking at me like that?"

He didn't respond right away, and then their server returned with their drinks. While neither of them had spent much time looking at the menu, they managed to make their selections on the spot before they were left alone once more.

Rather than answer her previously posed question, Steele picked up his bottle, met her gaze and suggested, "How about a toast?"

"A toast?" she queried as she raised her glass. "For what?"

"You. Congrats on your new store."

"Oh," she murmured graciously. "Thank you."

They drank to her success, and before Mitzi could return her glass to the table, Steele said, "You never say no to bottomless chips and salsa, but in the last ten minutes, you've been so busy tellin' me about why you love Brooklyn, you haven't eaten a single chip. What happened up there? What changed?"

Mitzi sat back in her chair, exhaling slowly as she dropped her gaze onto the chips he'd mentioned. He was right, of course. He'd totally set her up, and she fell for it. She shook her head, her lips curling upward in spite of the annoyance she felt toward herself for the way she totally played into his hands. He wanted the truth. He'd said as much the night he asked her out.

He also said he was a damn good detective, she remembered. *He wasn't lying.*

"New York was never meant to be forever," she said, peeking over at him from beneath her lashes.

"Fair enough. But why come home now?"

"Why *not* now?" she deflected a second time.

Steele rested his arms on the table, clasping his hands together as he leaned toward her. His furrowed brow made his eyes seem even darker, but his gaze was still somehow soft and patient.

"Pretty girl like you makes it out of Shelby, she doesn't come back," he reasoned, his voice low and mild. "Pretty girl like you launches a business of her own, a brand that sells all over the world, she comes home at Thanksgiving and Christmas, spreads her love, then goes back to the city that inspires her. Pretty girl— what happened?"

A sad smile spread across her mouth as she stared at him, feeling suddenly desperate. The truth was, she liked the way he looked at her. It made her feel good, the way he talked about her; the way he talked about her brand. A couple days ago, she didn't want to tell him what happened at her boutique because it would make the incident in The Square that much more ridiculous. Now, it was more than that.

"If you knew, I would no longer be the pretty girl who was brave and bold enough to get out of here and rewrite my story."

"Mitz, you'll always be that pretty girl. Comin' back doesn't change that. Comin' back and claiming a part of Shelby as your own, bringin' your brand home—you're still bold. But something brought you here. Somethin' that scared you. I'd like to know what it is. Can't have a pretty girl like you walkin' around scared in my town."

Damn, she thought as she reached for her margarita.

How could she deny him after that?

She took a big swig of her drink, set the glass back on the table, and let the words fall from her mouth as fast as she could get them out.

"I fell in love with a model. His name is Nolan. We were together for a couple years. Only, the last six months of our relationship, we were pretty off and on. His career was taking a turn, not in a good way, and he started getting into drugs. It got bad. It got dangerous. I wanted to help him, but as much as I tried, I couldn't.

"At the beginning of the year, I ended things. I just couldn't do it anymore. I didn't love the version of him he'd become, and he didn't love me. It was unhealthy. I felt horrible for a while, like I'd given up on him. He'd come around, asking for money. I never gave him any, of course." She shook her head and forged on, all the while trying to ignore the way her story made her belly ache.

"The last time I saw him was a couple months ago. I told him I didn't want to see him again, that he needed help, and he couldn't keep coming to me. When I didn't hear from him after that, I thought we were finally finished." She paused long enough to suck in a deep breath and huff out a sigh before she continued.

"A couple weeks ago, I was at the boutique with Titan. It was after close, and I was alone when someone broke in. He had a crowbar. He used it to shatter the front door and knock me over the head. While I was unconscious, he robbed the till. There wasn't much there, but he took every dime. It wasn't Nolan, and the cops ended up catching the perp—but just because it wasn't Nolan doesn't mean he wasn't behind the robbery. I can't prove it, but I just know it was him. He owed someone something, and they came to me to collect."

"Shit," Steele murmured, his brow still furrowed, and his stare aimed intently at her. "The cops pick up Nolan for questioning?"

"No. They said they didn't have probable cause."

"Any other stores on your block get hit?"

"No," Mitzi whispered.

"And the guy with the crowbar, he explain why he picked your place?"

"Not really. But this wasn't his first offense, so they chalked it up as another bad decision."

Steele's brow dipped even further, and she watched the muscles around his jaw flex as he clenched his teeth together. "They closed the case and told you unless you got attacked again, Nolan wasn't their concern."

"In a manner of speaking."

"You came home because you didn't want to be a waiting target."

Hearing him wrap his own words around her reason put her at ease. She didn't know how many open cases the detectives assigned to her had on their plate, but she could guess in a city of millions they were busy. She didn't blame them for the anxiety she felt every time she stepped outside of her apartment; but Detective Steele offered her more in two sentences than the gold shields gave her in Brooklyn.

She felt heard and understood. She felt justified, which is why she went on to admit, "I barely left my apartment after it happened. He's still out there, doing only God knows what, and throwing my name around. For two weeks, I was too afraid to go back to the scene of the crime. And that's what sucked the most. My store had become a *crime* scene. Even after it was cleaned up and ready for business again, I couldn't shake it.

"I came home because I needed the space to breathe. I'm staying because—impulsive as it is, it feels like the right decision."

Blowing out a slow breath, Steele sat up straight and reached for his beer. The bottle was halfway to his lips before he hesitated and spoke. "Sorry that happened to you, Mitzi. I'm sorry it scared you out of the city. But I'm not sorry you're here," he offered before taking a pull from his beer.

Feeling relaxed again, Mitzi grabbed hold of the sense of comfort found in Steele's validation and finally reached for a chip.

chapter eight

H E LIKED HER BIG EYES. He liked how, whether she was talking or listening, she was always communicating something with those hazel-green irises. He saw her smile in her gaze. When it was coupled with her laugh, that shit was contagious.

He'd known *of* Mitzi Bates fifteen years ago. It was hard not to. She and Nora-Jean were practically attached at the hip, and Nora-Jean was still the only woman his brother ever loved. Back then, wherever Nora was, Mitzi and Lawson were likely close by. To Steele, Mitzi was first introduced as Scarlett's younger sister. Both Bates women were gorgeous, not unlike their mother—but Mitzi had been his kid brother's girlfriend's best friend. She wasn't on Steele's radar.

After two strawberry margaritas, half a plate of fajitas, and enough chips to justify her unfinished dinner—Mitzi Bates was definitely on his radar. This was why, the first time he felt his phone vibrating in his pocket, he ignored it. Ten minutes later, when it started ringing a second time, he hated to look away from Mitzi as he reached for the device to check the caller ID. When he saw who was trying to reach him, his eyebrows knit together in a frown.

"I'm really sorry. I wouldn't normally do this, but I've got to take this call," he muttered regretfully, sliding his thumb across the screen even as he stared into the hazel eyes across from him.

"Oh, okay. Sure," she replied with a nonchalant shrug.

He was bothered by her body language. In her shrug, he didn't read forgiveness for his rudeness. Instead, he saw acceptance; like men taking calls in the middle of dinner didn't faze her because it had happened enough for her not to be bothered by it. He took note of this, then blinked and focused on the interruption itself.

"Lieutenant?" Steele answered.

"Need you at the station, Sarge. Hate to disrupt your evenin', but I'm callin' everyone in."

"Everyone?"

"All my guys in the CID. 2130 hours."

Steele flipped his wrist, checking his watch for the time. It was just after nine, which meant his date had come to an unexpected end. He sighed through his nose, jerking his chin in a nod his Lieutenant couldn't see. Disappointed as he was, he was equally as curious about what could be so important the whole Criminal Investigation Department was getting called down to the station on a Friday night.

"Copy that."

"See you in a bit."

Lieutenant Carlson hung up without further ado, and Steele offered Mitzi an apologetic smile as he pocketed his phone.

"Did you get enough? We've got to go."

"Um, yeah." She spoke in affirmation, but as she looked down at her plate and then back at him, she shook her head, signaling a negative. Unlike a moment ago, she didn't accept his news nonchalantly. Her gaze was as uncertain as it was curious. She gave voice to his observation when she inquired, "Is everything okay?"

"It was work. I've got to go in," he said before waving down their server.

"So...*no*, then."

Smirking, he replied, "I don't like to jump to conclusions."

He knew she was right. Nothing good called him into work when he was off duty—but after hearing about the truth behind why she'd called him away from his desk a few days before, he thought it best to keep it vague. He didn't want to give her any reason to be on her guard. That was his job. Besides, what he told her was true. He wasn't one to jump to conclusions, and he had no idea what was waiting for him at the station.

Steele settled their bill, and they were on their way to the parking lot less than ten minutes later. He thought about Mitzi's lips almost the whole drive back to Nora-Jean's apartment. If he had it his way, soon as they reached their destination, he'd get out of the car, meet her on the passenger side as she did the same, then lean down for a taste. Her sweetheart lips were plump. Every time she laughed, when her mouth spread into a smile, it was like she was begging to be kissed. He was more than happy to oblige.

Unfortunately for him, he didn't have time to have it his way. Soon after he pulled into the parking lot of the apartment complex, he stepped out of his Chevelle, made his way to the passenger side of the vehicle, and reached for Mitzi's hand, instead. He felt her fingers squeeze his in surprise, and he smirked down at her, pleased when those big eyes smiled up at him.

"Hate to drop and run, but duty calls," he said as they walked toward the building.

"I'd make a joke about whether or not I believed there was really an emergency; how maybe this is *actually* your desperate attempt at cutting the night short—but I think it'd fall flat."

Steele paused at the building's entrance, holding the door open while at the same time gently tightening his grip around Mitzi's hand, signaling her to stop. When he had her attention, he assured her, "If it was anyone else, I wouldn't have even bothered to answer the call. Sorry I had to."

He watched as the amusement on her face softened into something else; something that made him want to kiss her even more. "I understand," she murmured.

She continued through the open door, taking Steele with her. The trip up three flights of stairs was mostly a silent one, but Mitzi held onto him until they were approaching Nora's door. He watched as she reached inside her purse for her key, palming it before she smiled up at him.

"Thank you for dinner. And for...listening to the truth you were after without judgement. I had a nice time."

"Me, too. We'll talk soon."

"Okay."

He reached for her, grazing the soft skin under her chin with a bent finger. "Goodnight, Mitzi."

"Goodnight, Atticus."

The only people who called him by his first name were the people who shared his last. Sometimes, not even them. Hearing his name pass her lips was like confirmation they understood what that night meant, and they wanted the same thing. *More.* He winked at her as he lowered his hand down to his side, and the way her eyes lit up caused a slow smile to tug at the corner of his mouth. As he gave her his back, his smile grew. He was grinning to himself by the time he hit the stairwell.

Mitzi Bates was home grown and pretty as could be. He wondered if she was just who he was waiting for.

On his way to the station, he felt his phone buzz with a text alert. He didn't bother to check it as he focused on the road. Instinct told him it was his partner, inquiring about his ETA. He hadn't told Reed his evening plans.

Eight minutes later, and almost ten minutes late, Steele unlocked his glove compartment, extracted his firearm, then got out and jogged toward the familiar building. By the looks of the parking lot, he was the last of the nine-man crew to arrive. When he spotted the guys and Lieutenant Carlson gathered in the outdated conference room, he headed that way. He could tell, by the hum of conversation around the table, they were waiting on him to start.

Soon as he crossed the threshold, the Lieutenant saw him and immediately called the room to order. Spotting Reed standing on the opposite side of the room, his arms folded across his chest, and his shoulder propped up against the wall, Steele made his way toward him. The guys got quiet as the Lieutenant started speaking, but it was obvious Reed wasn't paying attention as he gave his partner a once over, a sly smirk announcing his thoughts.

"And where are *you* comin' from?" he mumbled as Steele planted himself at his partner's side.

Steele fought a smile and won—just barely—as he replied, "Don't worry about it."

"...but we all know crime doesn't give a damn about our schedules," Carlson began. "Y'all might remember, a few months back, murder of a woman up in Nashville. Twenty-eight year old, resident at a hospital up there. The case got cold real fast. Report came in a little while ago, there's been another murder. Same M.O. Victim in her late twenties, surgical resident—only it wasn't in Nashville. It was in Franklin. Right now, we can't say for sure if it's the same perp, but we might be lookin' at a serial killer. Not a whole lot of information at this time, but the word is bein' spread. We're to be on the lookout. Didn't want to sit on this through the weekend."

The meeting lasted a few minutes longer, some of the guys asking follow-up questions. It was after ten by the time they were free to go. Still, as the members of Shelbyville's CID began to file out of the room, Steele remained. His thoughts drifted toward Mitzi. He still remembered her scared whisper in his ear Tuesday morning. That coupled with her confession—how afraid she was to leave her apartment for two weeks after she was attacked—he wondered how she'd respond when news spread there was an unidentified killer on the loose. From the sound of it, Mitzi didn't fit this guy's M.O., but logic was rarely a formidable opponent when it came to fear.

"Where's your head at?" Reed asked, pulling Steele from his thoughts.

Steele shook his head then ran his hand over his mouth and down his chin. "Nowhere."

Reed chuckled, the expression on his face arrogantly knowing as he replied, "Bullshit."

This time, Steele didn't try to conceal his amusement. "Maybe."

"Sports coat, collared shirt, clean jeans and a fresh face on a Friday night? You, my friend, were on a date. How was it?"

It didn't go unnoticed how Reed was curious about the *how* and not so much the *who*. Not that Steele was surprised. His partner had been there the first time he laid eyes on Mitzi a week prior. Then again at Gypsy's, and again when she called them to The Square. Reed was right on the nose, but Steele wasn't going to let him do a victory lap just yet.

He shrugged, started for the door, and answered, "Interrupted."

chapter nine

"**A**RE YOU SURE YOU'RE GOOD HERE?" Nora asked for the fifth time.

She was standing in the mouth of the hallway, dressed in a flannel button-up and a pair of holey skinny jeans. She managed to make her top look trendy as opposed to frumpy, and her bottoms were a reminder of her truly great legs. Her hair was half up and half down, the knot at the crown of her head thick and neat, and the sight of her took Mitzi back.

There was something about Nora-Jean—a quality she possessed which Mitzi sometimes envied. She was *so good* at making the best of things. When they were growing up, Dolly instilled in Mitzi the mindset that every time a woman left the house, she had to look like she was doing it on purpose. To this day, Mrs. Bates wouldn't be caught dead at the grocery store without a full-face of makeup. Much as she hated to admit it, Mitzi internalized many of Dolly's beliefs.

But Nora-Jean didn't have Dolly as a mother. Earlene could hardly be called a mother at all, in Mitzi's opinion. It was a wonder Nora grew up with any sense of modesty, but she did. Moreover, she'd always been able to make hand-me-downs look like a million bucks. Even without a lick of mascara, there was something about the way Nora carried herself that made her look like she was leaving the house on purpose in a way Mitzi always admired.

"Earth to Mitzi. Is that coffee even workin'?" Nora frowned a little, pointing at the piping mug of the freshly brewed nectar she held in her hands.

It was barely eight o'clock on Saturday morning, and Mitzi was curled up on the couch still wearing her sleep clothes. Titan was pressed against one hip, and Evie was anchored to her opposite side, her attention entirely engrossed on the cartoon she'd picked not thirty minutes prior. She, like Mitzi, was still in her pajamas— though, upon her mother's request, she'd washed her face, brushed her teeth, and sat still long enough for Nora to braid a couple pigtails before she began to indulge in a story Mitzi was still trying to figure out. Something about a lady bug and a cat with superpowers.

While it had been an early night and she'd gotten plenty of sleep, Mitzi was wading through the haze of morning lazily. It'd been exactly a week since she'd first woken on Nora's couch, and her whole life had changed. That afternoon, she had plans to go check out a possible rental property. From what she saw online, the place looked promising. She was cautiously optimistic about finding a house to call her own so quickly. Given the cost of living and the size of the town, she wasn't all too worried about her next address. What clouded her thoughts more than anything was *Atticus*.

Mitzi took a slow sip of her coffee, staring at Nora as she shoved thoughts of Steele aside for a moment. She swallowed and finally replied, "Your lack of confidence in me is offensive."

Nora grinned, folding her arms across her chest as she insisted,

"It's not about trust. I don't want you to think I'm takin' advantage of you bein' here."

"Go to work," Mitzi demanded. "Evie and I will be fine. We're gonna watch cartoons, we're gonna go to a football game, we'll grab some lunch, and we'll meet you at the house around two."

Nora dipped her chin in a decisive nod, as if Mitzi's latest reassurance she didn't feel *used* had finally sunk in. She then shifted her focus onto her daughter and said, "Mini-me, look at mommy."

It took her a second, but Evie dragged her attention away from the television obediently.

"When Auntie Belle tells you it's time to turn off *Miraculous* and get dressed, you need to listen. Be good at the game, eat all your lunch, and I'll see you this afternoon."

"'Kay, mommy," she mumbled before returning her attention to her show.

A smile played at Nora's lips even as she rolled her eyes.

"Evie-B?"

"Hmm?"

"Kiss."

This time, Evie hurried off the couch and across the room, stopping when she was toe-to-toe with her mother. Tilting her head back, she puckered her lips, and Nora was quick to dole out the affection for which she'd asked.

"Love you."

Her back already turned as she raced toward the couch, Evie called, "Love you, too, mommy."

With a shake of her head, Nora went to grab her purse and keys before heading for the door. After reminding Mitzi Evie could have cereal or yogurt should she get hungry, she then called out a farewell to which only Mitzi responded. She locked up behind herself, and then it was just coffee and cartoons until a text alert diverted Mitzi's attention.

She set aside the last few sips of her caffeine as she reached to unplug her phone and check her latest notification. When she saw she had a message from *Steele*, her face mimicked the excitement she felt in her belly. Then she read the text, and her bottom lip was suddenly captured between her teeth so as to contain her grin.

Steele: Morning, pretty girl.

Staring down at her screen, Mitzi marveled at the way he was able to get away with calling her that without making her feel patronized or objectified. She knew, if it were anyone else, she'd roll her eyes. But it wasn't anyone else. It was Atticus. And while whatever they were doing was just starting, it was impossible to deny how much she liked the reflection she cast in his eyes.

Pretty girl like you launches a business of her own, a brand that sells all over the world, she comes home at Thanksgiving and Christmas, spreads her love, then goes back to the city that inspires her.

Mitzi wasn't exactly famous, but she was known in the fashion industry. Her success wasn't something that went unnoticed in the city; and even though there were a handful of people who made a big deal of her brand at home, she never considered someone like Atticus would have taken notice from so far away. It made her feel good that to him she was so much more than a pretty face.

Me: Good morning. How are you?

In an attempt to be cool, after Mitzi sent the text, she put her phone face down in her lap. She looked up in time to see another episode of *Miraculous* had come to an end. Nora didn't usually plant her daughter in front of the television for hours on end, often encouraging other forms of entertainment which didn't require electricity. One glance at Evie was all the evidence she needed to know the four-year-old was in lady bug heaven.

"Evie Belle?"

"Hmm?" she hummed, looking up at Mitzi.

"Let's make a deal. One more episode, then you take a little break to get dressed and get some breakfast. After you eat, I'm thinkin' you could get in three solid episodes while I get ready to go."

She took Mitzi's proposal under advisement before she presented a counter. "How 'bout I get dressed and then eat breakfast *while* I watch *Miraculous*?"

Narrowing her eyes playfully, Mitzi pretended to think over Evie's offer. When her phone sounded with another text alert, she relented. "Okay," she agreed. "But you still have to eat at the kitchen table."

"'Kay," she chirped happily.

As Evie re-emersed herself in the happy land of lady bug heaven, Mitzi flipped over her phone and got lost in another sort of mystical realm—one where a knight's shining armor was a police shield, and he had the power to make her stomach flutter with just a single text.

Steele: *Preoccupied. Got a pretty girl on my mind. What are you up to today?*
Me: Cartoons. Little league football. House tour. I've also got front row tickets to the one and only Nora Jean and the Pick a ninnies tonight. You?
Steele: *Some renovations with Judge. Gypsy's and college ball after.*
Steele: *Which neighborhood you lookin at?*
Me: McKeesport. The house is adorable.
Steele: *Rent? Buy?*
Me: You and your questions…
Steele: *Occupational hazard. Which is it?*

Mitzi bit her lip, denying her face the satisfaction of a grin at their exchange.

Me: Rent. Of course Mrs. Bates knew someone who owned a few houses in the county. No doubt, if I love

it, mom'll try to sweet talk the owner into selling
it to me.

Steele: *New subdivision. Safe place. Hope you like*
it.

While Shelbyville wasn't known for its crime, the members of
the SPD didn't spend all day twiddling their thumbs. Mitzi was
drawn to her simple town because it brought her peace of mind;
that said, it meant a great deal to have *Detective Steele* assure her
the neighborhood in which she was interested was a decent part of
town. Moreover, it warmed her insides to know Atticus wasn't all
talk.

He'd heard her the night before, and he wanted her in a good
neighborhood. Atticus Steele took the safety of Shelby's citizens
personally—including hers.

Especially hers.

Me: I'll let you know…
Me: What are you and your dad renovating?

Atticus didn't respond right away and still hadn't by the time
Evie's current episode came to an end. Mitzi set her phone aside
and reached for the remote, pausing the continuous streaming
progression. She didn't even have to remind Evie of their deal
before the little girl was racing from the couch in order to go get
dressed.

"What do you want for breakfast, babe?" cried Mitzi as she
stroked the hair down Titan's back.

"Yogurt!" Evie yelled.

"Yogurt it is," she mumbled before planting a kiss on top of
Titan's head.

When she stood from the couch, she grabbed her coffee mug on
her way to the kitchen. Her pup stretched, gave himself a shake,
then hopped down and followed close behind. By the time Evie was
dressed, Mitzi had her bowl of blueberry topped yogurt on the table.

Not surprisingly, she'd opted for a pair of black leggings covered in daisies and a long-sleeve white t-shirt. The girl was so much like her mother and all about the prints.

"I'm going to get ready," said Mitzi as she started the next episode. "When I'm done, we'll go, okay?"

"Mmmhmm," hummed Evie distractedly.

As per usual, it took Mitzi an hour to make herself presentable. She'd officially stayed longer than she'd planned, which meant she'd already worn everything in her suitcase at least once. While she was certainly longing for the items in her own closet, she wasn't shy about raiding Nora's. They weren't the same height, but the two women had been swapping tops for ages. That morning, Mitzi donned a pair of holey black jeans and matched it with one of Nora's simple, cream, cable knit sweaters. It draped over her frame, giving her exactly the look she was going for—casual, cute, and cozy for an autumn day spent outdoors.

"Evie Belle?" she murmured from the bathroom as she zipped up her makeup bag. "Put your shoes on, babe."

"Auntie Belle, it's almost over. Please?"

Mitzi smiled at her reflection. She didn't have it in her to say no. She was such a sucker.

Sticking her head out into the hallway, she replied, "Five more minutes."

It was another ten minutes before they were all out the door, and fifteen minutes more before they were at the park where Brooks was to play. They made it with a couple minutes to spare before the start of the game. Mitzi carried Titan in one arm, holding Evie's hand with her free one as they walked across the field, looking for familiar faces. When Mitzi spotted Trace, her stomach turned; then she pulled in a deep breath, straightened her shoulders, and willed herself to suck it up.

As they drew near the front of the small crowd, stretched from one endzone to the other, Mitzi saw Scarlett sitting in a collapsible chair, Charlotte laid out on her belly across a blanket in the grass.

"Hey," Mitzi greeted, the word aimed at her sister.

Scarlett looked over her shoulder, her eyes covered by her sunglasses, but she didn't have a chance to respond before Charlotte.

"Aunt Mitzi!" she gasped as she jumped to her feet.

It still startled her how excited her niece got every time she came around. Brooks was usually polite and kind, like his mother raised him to be, but Charlotte saw Mitzi in a different light. Given the rocky relationship between sisters, and the distaste she harbored for the girl's father, it was almost miraculous how much she was adored.

"Goodness, who are you and what have you done with my niece? You're practically a grown up; you can't possibly be her," teased Mitzi.

Charlotte grinned, her smile all the proof anyone needed she belonged to Trace. Even though she was almost as tall as Mitzi, she still had a girlish charm about her; her face round and her body slight and void of the feminine curves which were likely right around the corner.

"It's me, I swear," she insisted with a hair flip.

This made Mitzi chuckle before she let go of Evie's hand to invite Charlotte into a Titan sandwich.

"Your dog is so soft," she murmured, reaching up to pet his curly mane. "Mom says we're never gettin' a dog."

"That's right," sang Scarlett lightheartedly. "So don't even waste your breath tryin' to guilt me into it."

When Charlotte rolled her eyes, Mitzi was forced to tamp down her amusement. She might have gotten her daddy's looks, but she was full of her mama's spirit.

"Can I play with him?"

"Absolutely, so long as you make it a party of three. You remember Evie?"

At the mention of her name, Evie clung to Mitzi's leg. But when Mitzi looked down at the little girl, the wide-eyed gaze she had pinned on Charlotte spoke of her silent admiration.

"Hi, Evie," Charlotte greeted kindly, one of her hands still diligently stroking Titan. "I like your leggings."

At this, Evie let go of Mitzi, took a step forward and fidgeted with the hem of her denim jacket as she murmured, "Thanks. You're really pretty."

Mitzi's heart melted at the compliment. She could tell Evie meant it just as much as Charlotte appreciated hearing it. Right then and there she knew Evelyn Belle was going to make one hell of a best friend to a lucky someone someday.

"Come on. You can sit with me and play with Aunt Mitzi's puppy while we watch the game."

"His name is Titan," said Evie, the hint of excitement in her tone evidence of her burgeoning confidence.

"How long's it been since you've stood on the sidelines, Mitz?" Trace asked as the girls got settled on the blanket.

Mitzi straightened and looked up to find Trace smirking down at her. She wasn't entirely sure what he could be getting at, but she forced a small smile anyway. "It's been a while."

"It was good of you to come," said Scarlett, giving reason for Mitzi to shift her focus.

"We're going out for pizza after the game. Hope you'll join us."

Mitzi wished she could take Trace's invitation at face value. His desire for her to join the rest of the family for a meal should have been innocent; but she didn't trust him. Even more, she didn't like the way his eyes grazed over her every time she looked in his direction. That said, she couldn't pass up the opportunity to spend time with her niece and nephew. Regardless of how Trace made her feel, she wouldn't be fixing anything with her parents or her sister if she didn't accept the invitation.

"I'm sure Evie would love some pizza."

The referee on the field blew his whistle and the boys came running out onto the field. This captured Trace's attention, and he clapped his hands, stepping away from their group as he called out, "Al'right boys! Let's go Cyclones."

"Where are mom and daddy?" asked Mitzi.

Scarlett signaled across the playing field with her chin. "Daddy likes to pretend he's the assistant coach. Between him and Trace, Brooks has always got someone hollerin' at him up and down either sideline. Mom's around here somewhere. You know how she is. She's got friends everywhere she goes."

"Remind me of Brooks' number?"

"Fifteen, like his daddy. They've got him playin' wide receiver."

Mitzi looked out on the field and saw right away the Cyclones were currently playing defense. When she thought she heard her phone sound with an alert inside her purse, she took advantage of her opening and reached for the device. Upon seeing Atticus had sent her two messages, she smiled to herself and was quick to open them.

Steele: *Currently, my kitchen. Last room in the house that needed my attention.*

The second text he sent was a picture, the image that of his gutted kitchen. Before she could respond, a third text and a second picture came through—this one taken in what she assumed was his yard. Keaton Steele was hard at work, bent over a table saw, and Mitzi was officially impressed.

Me: Looks like maybe I should hire me a couple Steeles to remodel my new store.

"Is that my youngest, on her phone, in the middle of a game? My, my, that city's done a number on you," said Dolly as she approached, capturing Mitzi's attention.

As if she were a teenager, caught doing something she shouldn't be, she pressed the screen of her phone against her chest as she greeted, "Hi, mom."

"Who is he?" asked Scarlett, peering up at her sister.

"Who?"

"Mom's right. Not much could pull your attention away from a game, but I saw how quick you reached for your phone a minute ago."

"You know, I did hear a rumor," said Dolly, occupying the empty seat beside Scarlett.

Of course she did, thought Mitzi, amused. *What's it been, sixteen hours?*

"Patricia told me she saw Gale's oldest out last night with a woman who looked an awful lot like my baby girl."

At this news, Scarlett twisted her whole body to better fix her gaze on Mitzi. Her lifted eyebrows could be seen peeping over her sunglasses as she muttered, "Steele? You went out with Steele last night?"

"What if I did?" retorted Mitzi, tucking her phone into the back pocket of her jeans.

Scarlett coughed out a quiet laugh as she righted herself in her seat. "Tread lightly with that one."

"What's that supposed to mean?"

"Now, Scarlett, be careful how you speak about our law enforcement. It's families like the Steele's who keep this town safe."

"I'm not sayin' he's bad at his job. I just mean, there's got to be a reason a guy who looks like him is my age and still single. Whatever he's got going worked for him in high school, but we're adults now."

Bristled by the comment, Mitzi didn't think twice before she replied, "Marital status isn't everything, you know. Some of us spent our twenties focusing on our careers."

Scarlett had no come back, and her immediate silence made the taste of regret dance across Mitzi's tongue. She hadn't meant it as a jab at her sister's lack of professional life, but intentions didn't mean much when the truth struck a nerve.

"Girls," Dolly interjected, her warning clear in just one word. "Keep it sweet."

Thankfully, the Cyclone offense took the field, and Brooks' first few minutes in the game captured everyone's attention. Knowing it was for the best, Mitzi didn't reach for her phone for the duration of the game.

In the first half, Brooks had three carries—Trace and Sterling cheering him on the loudest. The spark of excitement Mitzi always got when she was watching a good game made her antsy at halftime, and she understood why the men followed the boy up and down the field every time his team had the ball. Confident Evie was in good hands with Charlotte, Mitzi stole Titan at the start of the third quarter and journeyed to the opposite side of the field to pace the sideline with Sterling. She was glad she did. And not merely to put a little breathing room between her and Scarlett.

When Brooks scored his first touchdown of the game, he headed straight to his Pops for a fist bump. High from his moment of victory, he lit up at the sight of Mitzi, who extended her hand in a congratulatory high five he didn't refuse. In the end, Cyclones took the win by a single touchdown, and Mitzi couldn't deny she was looking forward to a celebratory lunch with the star of the hour.

MITZI GLANCED DOWN THE table at Evie, sandwiched between Charlotte and Brooks, pleased at what she saw. Brooks, still amped from his team's victory, had been goofing off and making Evie laugh for the last hour. Noon brought with it just enough heat to make the patio seating at the Pizza Joint comfortable; and aside from Scarlett's snide attitude and the obvious way she doted on her husband throughout the meal, Mitzi didn't have anything to complain about.

"So, Mitz, your mother tells me she found a couple available houses in the area. You takin' a look at any of 'em?" asked Sterling. He leaned back in his chair, settling his gaze on his youngest as he rested his arm across the back of Dolly's seat.

"I'm actually scheduled to meet Mr. Birch about his place in McKeesport this afternoon."

"That's a perfect place to start," said Dolly approvingly. "Mr. Birch is a good man, and his wife is a sweetheart. I know for a fact that house is in tip-top shape. They bought it for their daughter and son-in-law just last year. Then Will went and got himself a job up in Nashville. They moved out only a couple weeks ago. I tell you, the timin' is so perfect, it's uncanny."

"Well, if you like it and you end up stickin' around for a while, might be worth negotiating rent with an option to buy," Sterling suggested.

It came as no surprise that her daddy would recommend such an arrangement. Earlier in the day, she'd told Atticus she surmised her mom would try to negotiate such a deal. What surprised her was how his comment implied he didn't think she was moving home for good. Even after she bought a car from him and leased a vacancy in the Town Square, he was still hanging onto his doubts; almost like he didn't want to get his hopes up. She knew she was responsible for his doubt, and she hated it.

"Daddy, I'm not going anywhere," she murmured. Mitzi then paused a second, staring into his eyes all the while, hoping the truth would sink in. She went on to say, "I'm also not anxious to buy right now. I know, ultimately, it's a smart financial move, but a lot has happened in a week. I want to give myself a chance to catch my breath."

"No matter how you slice it, gettin' out of that city is smart. You can't tell me New York isn't a financial risk for anyone. And don't even get me started on their politics."

"New York isn't all bad, mom. I wouldn't have stayed a decade if it was. Not to mention, my fashion line wouldn't even exist if I'd never gone."

"Wasn't all *good* either, or else you wouldn't be sittin' here," chimed in Scarlett.

Mitzi opened her mouth to respond, but then thought better of it. There was no use in defending Brooklyn, especially not to two women who'd never even stepped foot into the city. They saw the world differently than she did. They always had. Rather than justifying herself, in an attempt to prove she was as good as they were, Mitzi needed to accept herself and learn to accept them, too. It was a hard lesson to learn, and Mitzi's actions rarely reflected any evidence it was taking root, but at that table, she forced herself to concede her point and take the high road.

After all, Scarlett wasn't exactly *wrong*. The city she loved wasn't *all* good. No place was.

chapter ten

"I WAS IN NORA'S CHAIR A couple days ago, and she mentioned there was a house you were goin' to check out this weekend. Did you?" asked Billie as she lifted her mint julep to her lips.

She wore her hair down and curly that night, likely to show off her freshly trimmed chin-length bob and killer highlights. Even with her hair giving her a pretty sun-kissed glow, her dark eyeliner and smokey eye made her look as fierce as she was hot. She had a different ring on six of her ten fingers, a feat Mitzi knew not everyone could pull off; and her burgundy, long-sleeved, snap-front, bodycon mini dress only amplified the amount of attention they were getting at their table, just to the right of the main stage.

To be fair, Billie wasn't the only one dressed for a proper night out with the girls.

Jay had on a black and white printed, long-sleeve romper, complete with a Sterling Thread tag. The short cut begged anyone with eyes to check out her legs—at the bottom of which were a pair of fantastic strappy, black heels with fringe wrapped around her ankles. As always, her makeup was all but non-existent, and she topped her outfit off with velvet, tri-black Benson.

Mitzi made do, pairing one of her skirts with another one of Nora's tops. It wasn't exactly up to her fashion standards, but she was running low on options. What she lacked in wardrobe she made up for with lipstick. That night, her dark red lips gave her all the confidence she needed walking into the restaurant with her crew.

Whiskey-N-Boots was the best place to hear local artists outside of Nashville and within twenty miles of Shelby. The venue had a great vibe, with a little something for everyone. There were pool tables and dart boards to the left of the dining room, and a full bar to the right. During the summer, there were a set of garage doors at the bar that opened up onto a patio, where there was another stage and plenty of sitting room. As it was the tail end of October, and the sun went down earlier and earlier every night, Nora and the Pick-a-ninnies were set up inside. The tables grouped around the little dance floor were full, as was expected on a Saturday night, and there was nowhere else Mitzi wanted to be.

"I did. I went and saw it this afternoon."

"And?" Billie goaded.

Mitzi grinned, thinking back on the walk-through she'd taken with Nora and Evie trailing behind her and Seeley Birch. The three bedroom, two bathroom ranch was better in person than in the photographs she'd seen. Dolly had been right about the condition of the home. It was practically brand new, with white appliances, granite countertops, and white cabinetry. It wasn't quite as upscale or modern as her apartment in Brooklyn, but there was a certain charm about the place she couldn't deny. It also had plenty of room for the pod full of things she expected to be delivered the following week.

"I sign on the dotted line Monday, and I move in Saturday."

"You're really not wastin' any time, are you?" Jay took a sip of her beer, eyeing Mitzi all the while.

"You know me once I make my mind up about something," she replied with a shrug.

"I guess I still can't believe it. Don't get me wrong, I love it here. Shelby's home—but you were our city girl."

"True. But Dolly Bates raised me to be a southern belle. You can take the small-town girl out of Tennessee, but you can't take Tennessee out of the girl, even if she does get lucky in the city."

"Oh, stop. Luck's got nothin' to do with it. You're a talented designer. Always have been."

"Thanks," Mitzi murmured graciously. She was still thrilled as she always was to see one of her designs out in the world. Especially on someone who wore it as well as Jay. "Anyway, Shelby's home for me, too. Now that I'm back, I need to get settled in and get this store up and going."

"Speakin' of which," Billie interjected, "if you need any help with that, I'm on the other end of the block. You've got my number, and I expect you to use it."

"God, how incredible is this? Back in the day, did you ever think we'd all be kicking ass and makin' a name for ourselves, drawin' business to The Square?" Jay leaned back in her chair, shaking her head in awe.

"I always dreamed we'd go places," said Billie, a half-smile exposing one of her shallow dimples. "I never imagined we'd stick around and people would come to us."

"The way I hear it, your skills draw people across state lines." Mitzi nudged Jay's knee with her own under the table. "Much as I hate needles, I might need to get some ink from our local tattoo legend."

A coy smile tugged at the corner of Jay's mouth as she teased, "Get in line, babe."

"I think there's just one of us not livin' out our dream. That girl was made for brighter lights than these."

Mitzi looked at Billie and saw her gaze directed at the stage. Turning to look over her shoulder, she watched as Nora-Jean made her way to the front, her acoustic guitar strapped to her back. They'd been at the restaurant for nearly an hour, waiting for their friend to take the mic. Nora-Jean and the Pick-a-ninnies had a two hour time slot, the first half-hour all instrumental followed by Nora taking centerstage for two forty-five minute sets.

"Hi, y'all," said Nora, speaking over the melody the banjo, fiddle, and double bass players were plucking. "I'm Nora-Jean. Hope you don't mind if I sing a while."

All three women at the table erupted in loud support, a number of the other patrons welcoming Nora with a round of applause. Nora grinned, chuckling under her breath as she shook her head and adjusted her guitar across her front. She then looked down at Mitzi, winked, and began the first verse of her opening number.

A few minutes later, she was on the last chorus of her rendition of "Jolene" when Mitzi's phone vibrated with a text on the table. Mitzi turned her device face up and smiled at the sight of Steele's name lit up across the screen.

Steele: *So?*

It took only a second for Mitzi to remember she told Atticus she'd let him know if she liked the house in McKeesport. After the game, she'd been so preoccupied with other things, she forgot to send any updates. Part of her was glad she forgot. It felt good having Atticus follow-up.

Me: This time next week, if you want to drop by, guess you'll have to use your detective skills to find me.

"Okay—I'm only a couple beers in, but I see my last name on

your phone. I'm not textin' you, seein' as I'm sittin' right next to you, which means you're textin' the only guy in my family who barely responds to the name my mama gave him."

"Oh. Um, yeah," mumbled Mitzi, placing her phone face down on the table.

"*Um, yeah?* That's all I get?"

Mitzi knit her eyebrows together, turning her body in Jay's direction. "I'm sorry, it didn't cross my mind to ask—which is ridiculous, because you're my friend and his sister and I should have—but, it's not too weird, right?"

Jay's jaw fell open as she coughed out a laugh. "Shit, are you serious? You and Steele are—"

"One date. We've been on one date."

"What? When? This is breaking news. I've got to tell Lawson," she insisted, reaching for her phone.

"Wait, no, I—wait, please," Mitzi begged as she grabbed hold of Jay's wrists. "I don't want to make this a big deal if he doesn't want to make it a big deal. It really was just one date."

With lifted eyebrows, Jay glanced at Billie and then back again. "Babe, you've been gone a while, so I get it that you don't understand. But if Atticus Steele took you on a date, it's a big deal."

"He didn't waste any time, did he? Good for him," said Billie swirling around the contents of her cocktail.

Mitzi looked between the two women and then sighed as she settled her gaze on Jay. "You're going to text Lawson as soon as I let you go, aren't you?"

Grinning, Jay replied, "You bet your ass."

"Right," Mitzi conceded.

"And for the record, it's not weird. We're all adults. If you're interested, I say go for it. If it doesn't work out, well…" She paused, glanced up at Nora, and then shrugged. "Been there. Done that."

"All right, so—*details*," insisted Billie.

Mitzi scrunched her face and shook her head, not sure she was ready to gab about Atticus with his baby sister. Besides, what she said was true. They'd been on one date. Mitzi wasn't particularly superstitious, but whatever was happening between them, she didn't want to jinx it.

"I'll say this much: I've never been on a date with a cop before. We ended the night early when he got called in. I don't know what for, but my guess is it wasn't for a lost kitten."

"If it was Steele and his team called in, I'd guess it had somethin' to do with that murder in Franklin," Jay speculated as she finished constructing her text. She set her phone aside, looking up as she continued, "It was all over the news this morning. The killer's still on the loose."

"Oh, my god. I was watching cartoons with Evie all morning. I had no idea."

"Don't freak out." She insisted, this time nudging Mitzi with her knee. "It's part of the job. They just need to be in the know. There's no evidence that says he's headed in our direction—but he is out there, hidin' somewhere. Anyway, it's just my guess."

"Also, clearly he's not too worried if he's chattin' you up on a Saturday night," said Billie.

Mitzi fought a smile and was quick to divert attention in another direction. "How about we talk about you. When's the last time you let someone take you out?"

"Let me?" Billie guffawed. "Honey, I'm *this* close to puttin' on a short skirt and some stilettos and strollin' my way into Gypsy's."

Mitzi laughed. Her amusement was so contagious, even Billie couldn't pretend her statement wasn't on the verge of ridiculous. "Come on, the dating scene isn't that bad around here. Right?" Turning her attention onto Jay, she asked, "Who was it you were being cryptic about the other night? Liam?"

"Please," grumbled Billie. "Liam is *exactly* what's wrong with the dating scene in this town."

"Hey!"

Billie raised her eyebrows, propping her forearms on the table as she leaned toward Jay. "You know I love you, Jay Bird. You also know I've been your best friend for long enough that I'm obligated to tell you the truth, even when the truth sucks—and *Liam* has been playin' with you for months."

Jay hesitated to respond, taking a long pull from her beer. "I'm just...I'm just waitin' for him to realize what we have is worth holdin' on to."

"And if he doesn't?"

"I'll cut him loose."

The look on Billie's face was an outward expression of what Mitzi felt hearing Jay's answer. She understood relationships were complicated. In a lot of ways, she knew what it felt like to hold onto someone longer than it made sense. Much as she hated to learn how haphazardly this Liam guy was holding on to Jay's heart, Mitzi was certain only Jay could put an end to it, regardless of what her friends wanted.

Sensing it might be time to change the subject, Mitzi finished off the last of her Manhattan and was about to suggest another round when she caught sight of a group of guys walking from the entrance into the dining area. One glance, and she was certain she'd been right before. No way the dating scene was *that bad* so long as there were fine men like *them* out on a Saturday night.

"I don't know what Liam looks like, but I spot four guys who might solve all the problems at this table."

Billie grinned. "Where?" She turned to look back over her shoulder and then laughed as the men approached a table crowded with women. "Think again. It looks like they're spoken for." Righting herself, she went on to say, "Blondie, for sure. That's my neighbor. I met his girlfriend not too long ago."

"How did I not know the blond one was your neighbor?" asked Jay.

"He's not the most social guy. The day I met his girlfriend was the first time he'd stepped foot into Rock-N-Joe, and we've shared a wall for a year."

"That's the guy who just put in the security system at Skin Deep. Him and the tall, lean one. Dax and Finn, I think."

"You know what, I think I did know he works for a security company," Billie said, squinting contemplatively. "I didn't put the two together."

"Wait, those guys work with Lawson?" asked Mitzi, pointing at the table across the dance floor.

"Yeah. That's how Zeke found out about them. Building security isn't exactly my issue, but from the sounds of it, Zeke and Harlan are cool with them. Lawson says they run a pretty tight ship at Vollucci Security, and that's just the way he likes it."

Mitzi got a flashback of the moment she heard a crowbar shatter the front door at her boutique, and a wave of fear came with it. She pulled in a breath, shook her head, all the while reminding herself she wasn't in New York anymore. She was home. She was safe. She was in a town small enough where it was more than likely she'd run into a couple cops on patrol picking up her morning coffee, and one of the most trusted detectives was only a phone call away. Nevertheless, she remembered what Nora had said about getting a security system set up at her new place.

"Do you think you could introduce me?"

"I never really met the guy. Billie?"

"Now?"

Mitzi grimaced apologetically. She knew Whiskey-N-Boots with her girls after a couple drinks wasn't the most professional combination of circumstances by which to make such a connection, but it was another coincidence she couldn't ignore.

"Yeah. Just really quick. Maybe he has a card or something."

"Sure. Jay—order us another round?" asked Billie as she stood.

"You got it."

chapter eleven

MITZI TIGHTENED THE LITTLE PONYTAIL she'd thrown her hair into as she looked around Nora's living room, making sure she hadn't left anything behind. Not that she had much to worry about in the first place. While it had only been two weeks since she'd known the comforts of her own home, she'd be lying if she said she didn't miss her closet full of clothes. There was no doubt in her mind she'd be unpacking the wardrobe that made her feel most like herself before anything else.

"You ready?" asked Nora as she came into the room.

"I am. Also, in case I forget to tell you later, thanks for taking the day to do this."

Nora waved her off. "You know you don't have to thank me. I wanted you home and you're here, so I'm basically obligated to help you move in. That's not to say you won't owe me a drink."

"Deal," Mitzi laughed.

"I'm just hopin' when we open that pod all the heavy stuff is in the back."

"You and me both," she muttered, sweeping her fingers across her forehead.

Adalynn had sent pictures of her apartment when it was all boxed up and ready to go. It was so strange to see her belongings hidden in boxes, having last seen them out and precisely where she intended. She knew she had a lot of unpacking ahead of her, just as she knew how heavy some of her furniture was.

"My dad won't be there until after noon. Can your uncle Wayde still make it?"

"Yeah, he said he'd swing by."

"Good," she breathed, somewhat relieved.

While Mitzi knew it wasn't ideal to recruit a couple of the oldest men in her life to do the heavy lifting, she also knew family would help without complaining. She was acquainted with plenty of able-bodied men in their prime, but asking friends to move wasn't as easy as it had been when she was nineteen, with little more than two bags to her name. She would never claim to be a particularly strong woman physically—but mentally, Mitzi had enough fight in her to get the job done with what little help she could find.

Thinking of the men she could have asked, Atticus crossed her mind. She'd only seen him in passing over the last week, and hardly even then. According to the news Tuesday morning, she didn't need to hear it from him that work had him busy. Nora and Mitzi stopped in at Rock-N-Joe after dropping Evie at school, wanting to hear about what happened from the woman who had been right next door.

Shootings in Shelby weren't exactly the norm, but neither were the circumstances surrounding Billie's neighbor, Dax—or, more accurately, his girlfriend, Kyra—both of whom Mitzi had met at Whiskey-N-Boots the previous Saturday.

According to Billie, the situation had been handled and the case closed. It was a crazy story of desperation and misconstrued love.

Knowing what little she knew, Mitzi tried not to be disappointed that Atticus wasn't exactly free to jump at the chance to take her out again. Still hoping for another date, she decided using him for his muscles wasn't going to earn her any points.

She sighed, shoving aside thoughts of the man who'd been wandering around her mind all week and then bent to scoop Titan in her arms. "Let's do this."

"Evie-B! Let's go, baby," called Nora.

Soon as the little ball of energy came rushing into the room, they took their leave, piling into Mitzi's car before heading for her new home. They pulled into the neighborhood a few minutes after nine. When Mitzi turned down her street, she slowed to barely faster than a crawl, her mind distracted by what she saw in front of the house.

"MB?" Nora questioned, her tone echoing the surprise Mitzi felt.

"Oh, my gosh. Is he for real?"

Nora chuckled. "I think I'm gonna call Uncle Wayde. Looks like we won't need his help after all."

Mitzi parked her car on the street, behind a big, gray Chevy truck. As Nora pulled out her phone to call Wayde, Mitzi opened her door and began to step out of her car. Titan hopped out of Nora's lap, and Mitzi picked him up, unable to combat the giddy feeling blossoming in her belly. As she made her way around the truck, the five men she'd spotted as soon as she turned onto the street were all looking her way. Bishop and Jed were sitting on the curb next to her driveway, Lawson, Reed, and Atticus leaning against the side of the pod which had arrived the day before.

Atticus smiled around his sucker in her direction, a mischievous and cunning gleam in his dark eyes. Like it had been more than a few days since she'd last seem him, her heart jumped at the sight. In a way that made no sense, he was hotter than she remembered; and she hadn't forgotten him in the least.

As Mitzi drew near, he pushed himself away from the pod and

helped close the distance between them. He was wearing the jeans she kind of loved—well-worn, faded, and fitted just right—and an Army-green t-shirt. He rolled his sucker across his tongue, until it was held captive in his cheek, and Mitzi's belly tingled.

Tucking his fingertips into the front pockets of his jeans, he skipped over hello as he said, "Told 'em there was pizza and beer in it for 'em. Think you can manage that?"

Mitzi shook her head; not in response to his question, but in the confusion she still felt even as she stood toe-to-toe with the gorgeous man in front of her.

"How did you—?"

"As for me, I want more than pizza. I'll settle for a steak at Smithy's, though. Tonight. I'm buyin', you just be ready to go, lookin' pretty when I pick you up at eight."

"Atticus!" she laughed, the sound breathy even to her own ears.

"Shouldn't be too hard for you," he replied with a grin and a wink that would make any woman swoon. He then glanced over his shoulder at the four men now standing in wait. "We're ready when you are."

You didn't have to do this...

The words were on the tip of her tongue, but she didn't have to say them. He already knew. It was why he didn't tell her he was going to gather enough men to have her moved in before lunch. It's why he used his detective skills to find her house, the address of which she'd never shared. He claimed she owed him a date, but after a week of little more than a few text messages and missed opportunities for them to see each other, she would have said yes even without his kind gesture.

As it stood, she owed him more than her presence over steak. A lot more. It was a Jimmy Choo kind of night. Fortunately for her, her favorite shoes had finally made it down to Shelby.

"Okay," she said with a nod. "I just have to grab the keys. I'll be right back."

Mitzi hesitated a moment, staring up at Atticus. When she suddenly felt jealous of the sucker in his mouth, she bit her bottom lip in an attempt to tamp down her giggle and turned her back to him. She shook her head all the way to her car. As she approached the driver's side, Nora was letting Evie out of the backseat.

"Evelyn Belle, you are *not* to consume any candy this early in the mornin'," she called as her daughter took off toward Steele.

At this, Mitzi freed her giggle, earning her a smirk from her best friend.

"Looks like someone's day has been made."

In spite of the lighthearted way she'd said it, Mitzi's amusement began to wane as she thought about the *other* Steele who had volunteered his morning. She glanced back toward Lawson and then sighed as she met Nora's green eyes.

"I really wasn't expecting him to arrange this. Are you going to be okay?"

This time, it was Nora who looked Lawson's way before she redirected her attention over the top of Mitzi's Fusion. "If there was such thing as a good kind of torture, this would definitely be it." She shrugged then tilted her head toward the house. "Come on, MB. Let's get you settled."

BY NOON, NOT ONLY was the pod completely empty of all her belongings, but the guys had also taken it upon themselves to mount Mitzi's television and hang all her wall décor. Even with most of her things still in boxes, it was already starting to look like she belonged there. In her bedroom, the oak canopy bed was positioned perfectly between the two windows on the back wall. She knew, the white bedding she'd later unpack would brighten up the space, making it look even bigger than it really was. Of course, the room really *would* have a lot more space after she unboxed her wardrobe.

The spare bedroom was where she had her workspace set up.

Mitzi never invested in a desk, as she had grown accustomed to sketching wherever she was the most comfortable. She did, however, have enough necessities to fill the room. Her cutting table, which doubled as a storage cabinet, was on one side of the room, her sewing table on the other. Both pieces of furniture had belonged to her for a few years, but any time she walked by her at-home studio, she couldn't help but to pause and be grateful. After her first couple years in New York, she knew better than to take space for granted.

Kitchen boxes were scattered around the living room and stacked on top of her coffee table, but the table and her navy sofa were both in their final resting place, on top of her faded-print area rug. Nora had found her box of throw pillows and arranged them on the couch and on Mitzi's taupe, media lounge chair. This was obviously Evie's favorite piece of furniture, as she'd been stretched out on the thing, Titan by her side as she played alphabet games on Nora's phone.

A few minutes before noon, Mitzi ordered enough pizza to feed an army, and then handed her debit card over to Nora, who made a quick trip to the nearest grocery store to grab a couple six-packs of beer. The Steele men were putting away their tools when lunch arrived. Their hard work behind them, the guys were sitting around Mitzi's dining room table in the nut hued leather slope chairs she still loved as much as she did when she first bought them. None of them wasted any time diving into the pies, not the least bit concerned that Mitzi's plates were still wrapped in a box somewhere.

"You know, for a little lady like yourself, you sure do have a lot of shit, Mitz," Jed jeered, taking a huge bite of his slice.

"Hell, half of it is clothes," said Bishop, food still in his mouth.

"Boys—little ears, here," Nora chided as she lifted Evie up to sit on the kitchen's bar counter. Evie giggled as her mother handed her a slice of cheese pizza.

Bishop chuckled, swallowed, then smirked at Mitzi before he added, "Just remind me not to let Lex step foot into your closet."

"Mmmhmm." Mitzi folded her arms across her chest. With one raised eyebrow, she propped her side against the bar on the other side of Evie, tossing her playful attitude toward all the men at her table. "I notice guys like to give women a hard time about the amount of clothes they have, but they never seem to complain when she walks into the bar in a new dress that makes everyone stop and stare."

"Let the record state, you didn't hear me complainin'," Atticus said, lifting his beer to his lips.

Mitzi followed the sound of his voice with her eyes, but he didn't see her smile from where he sat at the other end of the table. This made his casual comment a hint she promised herself she'd remember.

"Heard Dax is puttin' in security at your new shop," said Lawson, changing the subject.

"Oh?" This time, when he spoke, Atticus sought out Mitzi's gaze.

"Yeah. I met him the other night and gave him a call a couple days ago. He's going to drop by Monday, take a look around and draw up a proposal."

"MB and I made a deal. Until she's got a security system installed, she's not allowed to be at the shop alone."

Remembering her company, Mitzi was quick to add, "Not that I don't think you gentleman do a fine job of keeping this town safe. Lately, I'm a little jumpy." Her eyes bounced between Steele and Reed, and a small smile played at her lips at the sight of his knowing smirk. "I thought it best to be cautious."

"It's a good call, Mitz. We do our best, but Shelbyville isn't perfect," said Bishop.

"Not to mention, we can't be everywhere at once."

"When do you think you'll be openin' your doors?" asked Reed.

"I'm not sure. I don't want to rush it. I also have a spring line I've got to design. So…couple months? Maybe longer?"

"Knock, knock."

Sterling didn't actually knock, but everyone turned to see him walk through the door. In jeans and a t-shirt, it was obvious he'd come ready to work.

"Hey, Mr. Bates." Jed started the chorus of hellos, and Mitzi smiled at her dad as she greeted, "Hi, daddy."

"Hi," said Sterling, his neck twisting right and left as he surveyed the space. "Looks like I'm late to the party."

"Still some pizza left. Mitzi ordered enough for a whole defensive line," Reed joked.

Mitzi rolled her eyes, but her facial expression broadcasted *annoyed* wasn't how she really felt. "I meant to call you, but I got caught up. Sorry you made the trip and you didn't have to."

"It's a father's business to know where his daughter lives."

Her smile fell a bit at his comment. The beat of silence that followed was pregnant with all she didn't dare say. Part of her wanted to believe he was just trying to put her at ease for not calling; but it couldn't be ignored how he had no idea where she'd been living for the past eleven years. Not really, anyway. Where she lived and how hadn't been his business for a long time. Now that she was almost thirty-one years old, it felt too late to change that.

Nora, as if she knew exactly where her friend's thoughts were headed, nudged Mitzi with her elbow and suggested, "Why not give him the grand tour, MB?"

"Yeah." She nodded and pushed away from the bar, slipping her fingertips into the back pockets of her jeans. "Yeah, of course."

After walking around the cluttered house, Sterling stayed for a couple slices of pizza and a beer. It was early afternoon when the guys decided they had better things to do than sit around Mitzi's dining room table. Hard as she tried to send them on their way with pizza, she was still left with half a box she tucked into her empty fridge.

Atticus was the last out the door, Mitzi following him to the porch.

"Thank you, again, for all this help. I kind of forgot how it is around here. Every small town is full of neighbors."

"You're not wrong, pretty girl—but I'd be lyin' if I said I didn't have an ulterior motive."

Grinning, Mitzi tilted her head and stared up at him as she replied, "You know, if you wanted a second date, all you had to do was ask."

"Yeah," he smirked. "I know." Backing his way off the porch, he added, "See you in a few hours."

She waved goodbye, lingering just outside the door until he closed himself into his Chevelle. When he peered through his passenger-side window for one last look, she pulled her bottom lip between her teeth and turned on her heel, headed back inside.

"Al'right, my mini-me's out," said Nora just as Mitzi closed the door. "I say we've got an hour, maybe an hour and half before she wakes up. After that, I've got to get her out of here; take her to a park or something. Think we can unpack your closet by then?"

Mitzi waggled her eyebrows, linking her arm through Nora's as they started for her bedroom. "We sure can try."

STEELE HAD HIS KEYS in hand, his feet leading him toward his garage, when his phone rang from inside his pocket. He halted and closed his eyes as he blew out a slow breath. His gut told him if he answered, he'd regret it—and his gut was rarely wrong. There was only one person he wanted to hear from, and something told him it wasn't a pretty girl on the other end of the line.

His integrity took control of his mind, forcing his hand into his pocket. When he pulled out the device and saw who was calling, Steele knew he'd be betraying the oath he'd sworn to protect and serve if he didn't answer.

"Last person I want to hear from right now, partner," he said instead of hello.

"Hate to do this to you, man. I really do; but we're up to catch, and you're gonna want in on this."

Steele dropped his chin to his chest and stared down at his boots as he grumbled, "What is it?"

"Armed robbery. Hit the convenience store on Union Street. Perp had a knife."

His head popped up as his brow furrowed with his frown. "You've got to be shittin' me."

"Told you, you were goin' to want in on this."

"He's in the wind?"

"Until we catch him."

"Officers still on the scene?"

"Yup."

"Damnit," Steele breathed. "I need thirty minutes."

"Copy that. I'll meet you there."

They disconnected and Steele paused a beat before he pocketed his phone and turned back toward his bedroom. He grabbed his gun from the safe in his closet and then resumed his trip to his vehicle, stowing the sidearm in the glove compartment before he started the engine. Behind the wheel of his Chevelle, he was as pissed as he was regretful. After the week he'd had, all he wanted was to sit across the table from Mitzi Bates, listening to her laugh while he enjoyed a medium-rare steak. His stomach turned as he remembered the way she smiled at him when she rolled up to the house that morning, and again when they said goodbye. He was certain that wasn't the look he'd get when he showed up on her doorstep, asking for a raincheck.

What pissed him off wasn't Reed calling to ruin his night. What pissed him off was Kevin Casey. Steele knew, even with what little details he'd been given, the perp with a knife was an old collar of his who'd done three years for the first time he was caught. Steele knew then what he knew two weeks ago, when Casey was released —he should have been locked up for a hell of a lot longer than three years. He was a loose cannon. He was also a sneaky sonofabitch who had a knack for hiding.

Fact of the matter was, Steele had Casey to thank for his promotion to Sargent and his pick of departments. He was the last collar Steele made still in uniform. Catching him had taken weeks, and he had a scar on his left bicep from the wound Casey inflicted the night Steele took him down. He'd never forget the black of the man's eyes. He was fearless. He was empty—and now he was back out on the streets.

Steele cursed under his breath, pressing down on the gas a little harder.

He pulled into Mitzi's neighborhood in less than ten minutes, parking on the street. He killed the engine, locked his gun in the car, pocked his keys, then hurried up the driveway. Hesitating a moment, he opened the front of his sports jacket, rested his hands on his hips, tilted his neck back, and stared up at the night sky. He huffed out a sigh and then reached out to knock on the door.

When she swung open the barrier thirty seconds later, he took one look at her, and the weight of his disappointment sank straight down into his boots. She looked perfect. Hair pulled back. Face done up. The dress she wore was cut wide at her shoulders, the neckline plunging just low enough to fill his mind with inappropriate thoughts. The sleeves were sheer, probably worthless against the cool breeze on an early November night, and the hem of the skin tight dress stopped mid-thigh. Mitzi Bates wasn't tall, but in that green dress with those heels—her legs seemed to go on for days.

"Damnit," he breathed.

"That's not happiness to see me," she replied, the smile on her lips belying the worry in her eyes. "What's wrong?"

Steele reached up and grabbed the back of his neck, forcing his gaze to stay locked with hers. If he looked anywhere else, he wouldn't have the strength to leave.

"I swear this doesn't happen all that often—but I caught a case. I've got to go in."

"Oh..." He watched closely as she processed this news. She switched her weight from one foot to the other as she asked, "It has to be you?"

He bit back another curse. If the dress and those shoes hadn't said it all, her question sure as hell did. It'd been a long time since he wanted a woman more than he wanted to chase a case, and walking away from her was not going to be easy.

"I'm afraid so."

She laughed, almost as if to herself, and then said, "I'd make a joke about how you're bad at coming up with excuses for getting out of spending time with me—but in this case, I think it'd fall flat."

Steele forced half a smile. "Raincheck?"

"Of course."

Before he changed his mind about leaving, he took a step toward her, pressed his lips against her forehead and mumbled, "You outdid yourself, babe."

When he felt her fingertips graze the front of his shirt, he straightened and turned for his vehicle.

"Be safe," she called as he stepped off her porch.

He paused, glanced over his shoulder, and nodded as he assured her, "Always am."

FOR THE SECOND TIME that day, Mitzi watched Atticus fold himself into his car. This time, she stood in the doorway and watched him drive off before she turned and shut herself inside. Her gaze fell down to her feet, and she sighed at the sight of her toes tucked into her best shoes. The Jimmy Choo, four-inch heels were backless, with a black, suede, pointed toe. Attached at the heel of the sole, slinking up the back of her foot, and wrapped around her ankle was the crystal embellishment which made the shoe remarkable.

"Sorry, guys. Looks like we're not going anywhere tonight."

It was only a second date. Mitzi wanted to convince herself her canceled plans weren't a big deal—but the disappointment which churned in her belly said otherwise. She'd spent half the afternoon unpacking her wardrobe and the other half picking which dress to wear before she was forced to go on a hunt for her steamer. She'd taken her time getting ready, using only her favorite moisturizers and perfumes. It took her an hour to get her hair and makeup the way she wanted, but she knew it would all be worth it in the end.

The look on Steele's face when she opened the door proved her right. She still felt the warmth of his kiss on her forehead, and her eyes fell closed. She liked the way he looked at her; but more than that, she liked that he didn't call or text to ask for a raincheck. He came to her door, like a gentleman, and looked her in the eyes as he broke the news. Nora-Jean had called him noble, and Mitzi was beginning to realize how badly she wanted to be on the receiving end of all the attention and affection of such a fine man.

Her stomach growled, and she began to pout without shame. Having skipped a trip to the grocery store in favor of necessary date-prep, all the food she had in the house was leftover pizza from earlier in the day. In no mood to change her circumstances, she twisted the deadbolt home, dropped her clutch on the entryway table, and started for her bedroom. It was practically sacrilegious to don her Jimmy Choo's for less than fifteen minutes, but she considered it worse to wear them while eating reheated pizza.

Titan, who'd been keeping watch from the arm of her living room couch, jumped down onto the floor and trotted after her. Mitzi slipped out of her shoes, setting them on the tuft bench seat at the foot of the bed before unzipping her dark green dress. The garment pooled at her feet and she stepped out of it, leaving it abandoned as she went to change into something more comfortable.

Once dressed in a pair of gray leggings and an old, light-weight, pink pullover fleece, Mitzi gathered Titan in her arms and snuggled him all the way to the kitchen. She preheated the oven then leaned her hip against the counter and rubbed her pup's belly.

"I like him, baby. Much as I love you, I was really looking forward to that date. But I guess it's just you and me tonight, huh? Detective Steele is out chasing bad guys."

Soon as the words were out of her mouth, the reality of what that meant started to take shape in her mind. It was easy to see him as a good looking man with a big heart and a protective streak that made him the kind of cop everyone wanted in town. His job and the sacrifices which came with it made him, and all the guys she knew like him, admirable. Except, lately, what she knew about the crime in Shelby planted a seed of worry in her belly.

As a kid, she wasn't exactly one to follow the news. Far as she knew, the worst crime to happen in Shelbyville, Tennessee was someone driving drunk after a night out at the lake. When she left, everyone in her closest circle was in the midst of figuring out what they wanted to do with their lives. How half the men she knew ended up on the police force, she wasn't sure. Nevertheless, it made her trust them all the more. Problem was, she was all grown up, too, and no stranger to the news. Shelbyville was a safe place to live— but it wasn't merely because everyone who lived there was a saint.

The oven sounded, notifying her it was ready for use, and Mitzi shook thoughts of what Atticus might be up to out of her mind. She reminded herself he'd been wearing a badge long enough for her to trust he knew what he was doing and he'd be all right. She'd cash in her raincheck soon.

While she warmed her pizza, she went to find her box of dishes. Before she knew it, she was eating her leftovers and emptying boxes in an effort to clear out her living room. At eleven, she knew she should be tired, but she wasn't. Glancing at her television, she wished she'd arranged for the cable guy to come that day; not because she wanted to watch TV, but because she was curious if whatever Atticus was up to had made the evening news. Unable to shake her curiosity, she found her phone and started to do a little investigating of her own.

It didn't take her long to find reports of a local armed robbery at a gas station convenience store on the edge of town. Anxiety settled in the pit of her stomach as she watched the clip of that night's breaking news. Memories of the robbery at Sterling Thread came racing to the forefront of her mind, and she felt the sudden urge to pace the floor. After a couple trips around her kitchen, she forced herself to stop and take a few deep breaths. If she was ever going to get to sleep that night, she needed to clear her mind.

She set aside her phone and went to the bathroom to wash her face and undo her hair. When all the pins were out, she pulled half of it up into a top knot, slathered her face in moisturizer, and went in search of her sketchbook. When she was distracted, she never drew anything great—but the sound of her pencil scratching the paper helped refocus her mind. After an hour on her couch, and a couple pages of scrapped concepts, she got an idea. She was so lost in her design, she didn't know what time it was when a knock sounded at her door.

Titan, who was curled up next to her, growled as he lifted his head. Mitzi frowned and didn't move, sure it was too late for anyone she knew to be out on her porch. When another knock came, her heart started to race, and she looked toward the kitchen, where she'd left her phone. She was getting ready to jump up to grab it when she heard his voice through the door.

"Mitzi? You up?"

Suddenly, her heart was racing for a different reason. She set aside her sketchbook and hurried for the door, Titan right on her heels. She raised up on her tiptoes to check the peephole—just in case—and bit her lip in excitement when she saw Atticus standing there, his gaze trained down at his feet. Without wasting another second, she twisted her locks free and swung open the door.

He looked tired, and it wasn't something she only saw in his eyes. The jacket he had on earlier was gone, the sleeves of his collared shirt cuffed and pushed up his forearms. His hair was mused, as if he'd been running his fingers through it; and his shoulders weren't so straight, like his night had been a rough one.

"Hi," Mitzi murmured.

"Hey." He took a step toward her and propped his shoulder against the doorjamb. "Was drivin' by, saw the light through your front window, thought I'd stop."

"Couldn't sleep. I saw the news. It kind of brought back memories."

"Yeah. Thought it might."

"Oh," she breathed as her chest filled with the warmth of realization. "Did you catch him?"

Atticus shook his head slightly. "Not yet, but we will."

Mitzi nodded, trusting his every word. "Do you...do you want to come in?"

"It's late. I just wanted to check on you."

Not ready to see him go yet, she replied, "You look like you could use a hug."

"You offerin'?" he asked, a hint of a smirk tugging gently at the corner of his mouth.

"Yeah."

He straightened when she took a step toward him. Given the difference in height between them, Mitzi's easiest option was to aim for his waist. But it was after one in the morning. He'd driven by to check on her. He stopped when he saw the light on, and that deserved better than *easy*. So she reached for his shoulder with one hand, took another step closer, then pressed up on her tiptoes as she wrapped her other arm around his neck. He came without resistance, both arms snaking around her back as he pulled her even closer, lowering his forehead until it was propped against hers.

They stood this way for the slowest, most enjoyable thirty seconds Mitzi could remember, all of her weight held by the man she was supposed to be holding. His face, lit by her porch lamp, yet covered by the shadow of their proximity, was stoic—like he was there with her but somewhere else at the same time. His breath smelled like butterscotch, and it reminded her of the sucker he had in his mouth that morning; it reminded her of how jealous she'd been of the candy. She wondered if the taste of his last sucker still lingered on his tongue. She bet it did. Then, her brain too tired to think twice about it, she titled her head and leaned in to find out.

The instant their lips met, whatever part of him was somewhere else came to take ownership of their kiss. His grip around her tightened as he straightened, taking her with him until her feet were no longer touching the floor. Her breath caught, her belly fluttered, and an excited giggle got lost in her throat when he sealed his lips around hers.

He started slow, as if he were savoring it. Or maybe her. Either way, Mitzi liked it. When she thought she might go crazy if he didn't give her more, she had a mind to open up and beg for it—but he beat her to the punch. One flick of his tongue, and she was putty in his hands.

And she was right. He still tasted like butterscotch.

"Comin' in," he mumbled against her lips, carrying her inside.

With one arm still holding tight to his neck, her other hand buried in his soft, wavy hair, all she could manage was a moan of affirmation, her mouth otherwise occupied. She heard the door close behind them, but he never let her go. They stood by the door in a clench—or, rather, *Atticus* stood and Mitzi held on until he lowered her down to her feet and slowed their kiss.

His lips still grazing hers, both of them short of breath, he paused and muttered, "Been on my feet a while, pretty girl. Mind if we sit?"

She shook her head in response, her words lost somewhere in the haze of a great kiss, but she didn't let him go. It wasn't until she heard his low chuckle that she realized she was sending mixed messages. Before she could start to pull away, his grip around her waist tightened, and he leaned in for a hard, closed mouth kiss. The hand she had buried in his hair slid down to the side of his slightly-stubbled cheek, and he lifted one of his own to take hold of the back of her neck as he tilted his head and parted his lips.

This went on for a while, until he pulled away a second time. Rather than wait for her foggy head to clear, he bent to scoop her into his arms and carried her out of the small entryway and into the living room. He sat her on one side of her lounge chair and then she watched as he sat next to her before reaching down to rid his feet of his boots. It took him a second, his slow, intentional movements cooling the moment. When he was finished, he leaned back against the pillows and sighed, running his fingers through his hair. Then he looked her way, their eyes met, and Mitzi saw his exhaustion—as if a break from their kiss had brought him back to reality, putting him in two places at once again.

Part of her wanted to bring him back. She wanted all of him. She'd already been robbed of his presence earlier. But she knew better. History had taught her when a man was battling something, she couldn't save him from it. All she could do was be there and hope it was enough for him; hope that he would fight his way back to her. Nolan didn't. As she stared at Atticus, her heart ached with a longing that *he* would. If it were anyone else, she'd think herself reckless for even entertaining such a thought. They didn't know each other very well. Not really. Except, they knew where each other was *from*—and *that* mattered just as much.

Rather than reach for another kiss, Mitzi got up and twisted the switch of the lamp on the end table beside them. She then turned off the overhead light, locked the door, and took up the blanket she'd been sketching under on the couch, Atticus silently watching her all the while. Then she sat in the spot next to him, spread the blanket over their laps, and curled up into his side. He didn't say a word, but what he did made her belly flutter and she fell for him a little harder.

He wrapped his arm around her, he pressed a kiss against her forehead, and then he switched off the lamp. Without a word, he made a promise to which she clung. He wasn't going anywhere.

chapter twelve

MITZI WOKE IN ALMOST THE exact position in which she'd fallen asleep, tucked into Atticus' side, her cheek resting against his chest. One of his arms was draped lazily down her back, his opposite hand gently holding the side of her neck, keeping her close. His fingers were tangled in her hair, and the feel of his touch reminded her of the way he tickled her nape until sleep found them both.

She never wanted to move.

It'd been a while since she'd woken in the arms of a man. Even longer since she'd slumbered with someone who didn't seem to want to let her go. She couldn't remember the last time she felt so safe. When she breathed in deep, the scent of detergent, faded Sterling Mist cologne, and *Atticus* filled her nose. He smelled so good, she wished she could bottle up *redolence of Steele* and keep it.

At the sound of Titan's pathetic whine, Mitzi came fully awake. She glanced down at her lap and saw him standing there, obviously anxious to be let out. Realizing it was him who must have pulled her from slumber, she scratched behind his ears, letting him know she understood. Then she shifted slightly to look up at Atticus.

Maybe it was the soft morning light. Maybe it was sleep deprivation. Or maybe it was just fact—but he was more beautiful in that moment than her memory could recall. Much as it pained her to extract herself from his hold, her baby needed her. Fortunately, Atticus was still so deep in slumber, he didn't wake when she got up and tiptoed toward her bedroom. She quickly rummaged through her dresser, cooing at Titan as his whine turned into an impatient growl. With her feet in a pair of socks, she started for the back patio door, Titan beating her to it.

The morning was a cool one, and the breeze cut through her old fleece. The sun looked to have been up for an hour or so, but it didn't warm her as she stood on her shadow-covered porch, watching her pup become acquainted with their new yard. He'd never had his own before, and it made Mitzi happy how her decisions enabled her to change that. Accustomed as he was to being indoors—accompanying her anywhere and everywhere she could take him around the city—he loved being outside. Now, being outside *and* off leash, he was busy marking his territory.

Mitzi jumped, startled at the feel of Atticus' hands as he took hold of her waist. When she felt his lips against her left temple, her eyes fell closed as her surprise melted into glee. She leaned back into his warmth, and he wrapped his arms around her, making her belly flutter.

"Hi," she murmured.

"Mornin'," he muttered in return, his voice deep, gravely, and far too sexy first thing in the morning.

Knowing she'd be doomed to couple that voice with the sight of his face, she rested her arms over his, pressed her cheek to his chest, and stared down at his sock-covered feet as she queried, "Did we wake you? I was trying to be quiet."

"Felt you get up. Got impatient waitin' for you to come back."

His response brought a smile to her face, and she couldn't deny herself the sight of his any longer. Soon as she tilted her head back to see him, he descended for a kiss. He pressed his lips to hers once, pulled away for a second, and then went in for one more, causing the fluttering sensation in her belly to travel all the way up to her heart.

He hadn't woken up in two places. That morning, she had all of him.

"Careful, Atticus Steele. A girl could get used to this," she teased.

He smirked. "Countin' on it."

She allowed herself a second to bask in his response before her inner hostess started to wake. "Are you hungry? I could make us breakfast. It is my specialty."

His smirk grew into a smile as he chuckled down at her. "Is it?"

"Yes." She nodded as she turned around in his hold, slipping her arms around his hips as she beamed up at him. "Don't let my designer brand fool you. I can make a mean biscuits and gravy."

"Biscuits and gravy? Really?"

"What kind of self-respecting southern woman would I be if I couldn't whip up some biscuits and gravy?"

"Got me there."

"Of course, I don't have any of the ingredients to make you breakfast. But a quick trip to the store would change that."

He stared at her for a second, his dark brown eyes dancing around her face, openly expressing he liked what he saw. Then he lifted one of his hands, grazed his thumb along the side of her jaw, and curled a finger beneath her chin as he sighed. "Much as I'd like to take you up on that, I can't stay."

"Oh. Okay," she murmured, trying not to sound as disappointed as she felt. In truth, she had plenty she needed to get done before her weekend came to a close. Much as she wanted to bask in Atticus' undivided attention for a while longer, she wasn't going anywhere, and she had a house full of her things to prove it. They had time.

"Raincheck?"

"I'm racking those up, aren't I?" She regretted the words almost as soon as she said them, the look on his face all the evidence she needed to know it wasn't the right thing to say. "Sorry—I didn't mean anything by that. Raincheck. Definitely."

"I know I'm not buildin' a great track record, but I'm not a flake."

"Atticus, I know," she insisted, tightening her grip around him. "I shouldn't have said that."

"It's Sunday. I've got church with the family, then Sunday dinner I can't miss, and after I leave there, I've got to get to the station to put in some work on this open case. I want to promise you dinner tonight, but if things go the way I need them to go, I'll be on a stake out with Reed all night."

"Atticus—"

"Mitzi, I need you to hear me. I don't have to go because I don't want to be here. I have to go because I've got responsibilities I can't push off to another day."

This time, Mitzi took a moment before responding. In the beat of silence that passed between them, she let her eyes roam over his face. His thick eyebrows were knit together, causing a crease to form above his nose. It bothered him for her to misunderstand his intentions.

"It was me who caught him three years ago," he mumbled, filling the silence. "The judge took it easy on him. Three years behind bars, another two on probation. I don't know what the hell he was thinking. Didn't make sense then, makes even less sense now. I've got to get this guy."

"I hear you," she assured him. She then reached up and gently smoothed a couple fingers between his eyebrows, silently insisting he relax. "We'll have other mornings."

His brow lifting, he mumbled, "Just mornings?"

"And afternoons," she said with a playful shrug.

"Yeah?"

Mitzi couldn't silence her laughter as he took her hips in his hands and teased her by tracing the tip of his nose along the length of hers, bringing his lips close—but not nearly close enough.

"Nights are good, too."

"Nights into mornings are my preference."

With no better words to voice her agreement, Mitzi pressed up onto the balls of her feet and stole the kiss for which she was too impatient to wait. Atticus surrendered what she took and then some. He no longer tasted like butterscotch—but it didn't matter. He still managed to kiss her into a fog of his own making.

"HEY, BOSS. HI, TITAN!" greeted Adalynn via video chat.

Mitzi, who stood in front of her laptop on the only counter in her shop, didn't take offense that Adalynn seemed more excited to see the maltipoo tucked against her side.

"Morning," Mitzi giggled. "How are things going up there? It's only been a couple days, but I feel like I haven't checked-in in forever."

"Business as usual. I'll have last week's repots over to you this morning. A few items sold out over the weekend with online sales. I've made a note to add inventory to our next team meeting agenda. I know Gianna is really anxious to hear about how your spring line is coming. She won't be so worried about restocking winter items if our seamstresses are going to be busy producing new material."

"I've started sketching, but I've barely considered fabric. Send me our inventory list, okay? I want to make sure we've got our hottest items as people start Christmas shopping."

"You got it, boss."

Before Mitzi could say anything more, a knock sounded at the door. She smiled when she looked across the shop and saw Nora out on the sidewalk, her hands full with two Rock-N-Joe coffee cups.

"Could you hold on just a sec, Adalynn?"

"No problem."

Mitzi sat Titan on the floor and the two of them went to let Nora inside.

"It's been a long time since I was so excited on a Monday morning," she said instead of hello.

"And what's so special about today?" asked Mitzi, accepting the cup with her name scribbled on the side.

Nora's eyes gleamed as she took a sip of her hot beverage, and Mitzi took the opportunity to taste her own. It wasn't surprising how the Americano with a splash of vanilla and creamer was prepared precisely the way she liked it.

"Well, the last two nights I went to bed and my best friend was no longer sleeping on my couch. Usually that means you've left Shelby in your rearview. But here we are—Monday morning, enjoying the best coffee in town in your new store."

"Cheers to that," she replied, raising her cup. "I've got Adalynn on the phone. I want to make sure I have everything lined up for later today. Give me a minute?"

"Of course. Do your thing."

With a careful grip around her Americano, Mitzi hurried back behind the counter. Soon as she was on screen, Adalynn started in as if Mitzi had never left.

"Everything is all set for your planning meeting. Gianna's going to take the call from the architect's office, and Reynolds will be onsite with you, correct?"

"Yes, that's the plan. And did you loop in—"

"Yup. I spoke with Dax at Vollucci Security right before this call. He had some availability on his calendar, and he said he'd be happy to join the meeting. He won't draw up a formal proposal until after he walks the space this afternoon, but he was more than happy to jump in this early in the process so he can work around the contractor's schedule."

Mitzi shook her head. "I don't pay you enough."

"Not nearly," she replied, speaking through a grin. "Anyway, how'd your move go? Have you started unpacking? Was it nice to sleep in your bed again?"

The memory of her first night in the house rushed to the forefront of her mind. She laughed to herself as it dawned on her how the first chance she had to sleep in her own bed had been foiled by a man she never saw coming. Then, as thoughts of the previous night followed, her amusement began to wane.

Sterling invited her to the house for dinner and Sunday night football. After a day of unpacking, she welcomed the excuse to get out for a while. When she got home later that night, she acknowledged the fact that she hadn't heard from Atticus since he left that morning. She assumed his silence meant he was hard at work, likely on the stake-out he'd mentioned. Like the previous night, thinking about Atticus versus an armed robber made her anxious. It didn't matter how he was far more equipped to take him down than she'd been the night of her own incident. The whole thing made it difficult to find sleep.

"What's that face? Did the movers do a shit job? Did they break something?"

"No, no. Nothing like that. It's just—it's funny. I've been in my own place for a couple nights now, and I haven't slept in my bed yet. I've woken up on the couch twice."

"Well, it might be home, but it's still new. You'll be settled in no time. And before you know it, the new store will be up and running."

"Yeah, you're right. Listen, thank you for this morning's sync. Let's do this again tomorrow, okay?"

"You got it. If you need anything before then, just let me know."

"I will, thanks."

They said their goodbyes, and Mitzi sighed as she closed her laptop and reached for her phone. It was after eight, which meant it was still pretty early; but it was also late enough she guessed Atticus was likely back at work. She wondered how he was doing and if he was any closer to closing his case.

"You've spent the last two nights on your couch? What's up with that?" asked Nora.

She set her phone aside as her best friend propped her hip against the opposite side of the counter, lifting her cup to her lips.

"Remember how I told you my date didn't happen Saturday?"

"Is this about the robbery? You know, from what I hear, this guy likes to stick to the outskirts of town. Not to mention, this place isn't even open yet. I know, given what you've been through—"

"It's not that. Not exactly. Atticus...he came over later that night. He was driving by, he saw my light on, and we fell asleep on my couch."

Nora giggled and shook her head as she muttered, "When that man knows what he wants, he sure does go after it. I'm gonna have to get used to you callin' him *Atticus*, though."

"Nothing happened. We kissed, we slept—that's all. I could tell he was exhausted and preoccupied with this case. Anyway, I haven't heard from him since he left my place Sunday morning."

"I'm sure he's just busy. After all he did this weekend, I really don't think you need to worry about what he wants. He's made that pretty clear."

"I know. That's not..." Mitzi blew out a sigh and grazed her fingers across her forehead. "I left a city of millions where crime is inevitable. I'm not naïve enough to believe there's no crime in Shelby but—I move back and there's a murderer on the loose and a felon who likes to rob people at knife point? And the two nights Atticus and I are supposed to be on a date, we get interrupted both times because of these criminals? I don't know." She reached for her coffee as she concluded, "If fate got me back here, allowing everything to fall into place so perfectly, what's it saying now?"

"MB, that's not fate sabotaging you. It's real life. And you're not some sort of crime magnet. For you to even think that is ridiculous."

"I guess I just—I don't want us to miss our chance. I *really* like him, Nora-Jean."

"My advice? Don't go makin' up excuses for why you won't. He's a cop. You hitch your wheel to his wagon, and your exposure to his job is gonna make you see Shelby in a way you didn't when you were nineteen. But, busy or not, that man wants you. Give him time. Give *yourself* time. You're not in the big city anymore. Your life doesn't have to move so fast."

Mitzi narrowed her eyes as she stared at her friend, pondering her wisdom. "When did you get to be so smart?"

"I don't know what you're talkin' about. I've always been this way." She pretended to be offended, turning up her nose as she took another swig of her coffee. Then, dropping the act, she bellied up to the counter, leaning on her forearms as she murmured, "You know you'll never get out of this conversation without giving me more than *we kissed, we slept, that's all.*"

Mitzi tried to hide her burgeoning smile behind her cup, but it was no use.

"You made out with *the* Atticus Steele. Former Shelby High *and* University of Tennessee star tight-end with the tight end, *current* unofficial but most eligible bachelor in this town, and the finest detective walkin' our streets."

Her laughter belied her furrowed brow as she replied, "How many times have you told me he's like a brother to you?"

"Yeah, so? I'm not the one he's kissin'. That'd be my best friend. Let's have it."

"Let's just say, he could kiss a girl stupid."

Chuckling, Nora righted herself as she raised her drink. "Cheers to that."

STEELE TOSSED HIS KEYS onto his desk and pulled his fingers through his hair in frustration. The case at the top of his priority list was getting colder by the hour, and he hated how out of control he felt. He and Reed had spent half the night parked in the shadows watching and waiting for Casey to slip up. He hadn't, which was why the detectives had been chasing their tails all day.

"You boys still comin' up short?"

Steele rested his hands on his hips as he shifted his attention onto his Lieutenant. Carlson looked the way he usually did at the end of the day—his shirt sleeves rolled up his arms, his tie loose, and his collar undone. Seemed like everyone's workload was getting heavier as of late, which made the boss's burden heavier. The last thing Steele wanted was to deliver no news. As if Reed was in his head, he spoke up before Steele could.

"Few leads we had took us nowhere. He's a sneaky bastard, wherever he is, and he's playin' us. That's for sure."

"Casey was a tough catch the first time. Three years behind bars, nothin' to do but stare at the walls night after night, he's not gonna be any easier to find this time. Don't beat yourself up about it. There's still an active APB out for his arrest. Night units know to keep an eye out. You two have been pretty hard at it the last forty-eight hours. Y'all go home tonight. Watch the game, get some rest, come back and put fresh eyes on it in the mornin'."

"Copy that," said Reed.

The lieutenant raised his eyebrows at Steele who offered a nod of acknowledgement. Satisfied with the silent response, Carlson continued on his way. Steele watched him go before he finally calmed down enough to sit.

"He's right, you know. This guy is smart. We've got to be smarter. A night off might help. What do you say we hit Gypsy's? Kick-off's in about an hour."

Steele looked at his partner across from him as he remembered the last time he'd watched the Titans play at Gypsy's. There'd been a pretty girl there, distracting him from the game every time she yelled up at the TV. The memory was soon casted aside by another, until all he could think about was the way she tasted. He thought about what it felt like to hold her and how much he liked her holding onto him. He knew there was only one person he wanted to watch the game with that night—and he sure as hell didn't want to do it in a bar full of people.

"Raincheck," he finally said, extracting his phone from his pocket.

Reed flashed an all-knowing grin his way, chuckling as he stood. "Sure, buddy. Raincheck." He then rapped his knuckles against his desk, grabbed his keys from his top drawer, and headed out for the night.

Steele didn't watch him go, his attention already focused elsewhere.

"Well, hi there," answered Mitzi on the second ring.

Dropping his chin, he marveled at the way just her voice made him smile. "Hey there, pretty girl. Game starts in an hour. I'll text you my address."

"That's quite presumptuous of you, Detective Steele. How do you know I don't have plans to watch the game elsewhere?"

His smile stretching into a grin, he ignored her question and postured one of his own. "Wings or burgers?"

She hesitated to respond, and he imagined her warm, hazel eyes lit up in quiet laughter, just the way he liked. "Burgers—but only if you let me contribute something."

"You just bring that Titan spirit. I've got the rest. See you in an hour."

chapter thirteen

MITZI APPLIED A LAYER OF pale-pink lip gloss, smeared her lips together, and then gave herself a final once-over in the mirror. She'd used a neutral palette of colors on her face earlier in the day and was satisfied with just a touch-up of powder and gloss to freshen her appearance. Her curling iron was still cooling from her efforts to rejuvenate the wavy texture she liked to add to her hair, and she approved of her casual but made-up state.

She'd changed into her favorite pair of distressed, dark wash, mom-jeans, into which she'd tucked the hem of her simple, over-sized white t-shirt. With her gloss still clutched in her palm, she pinched at the shoulder seam of her shirt, until the wide, V-neck collar draped over one of her bare shoulders. Studying herself a second longer, she decided subtly sexy was exactly the look she was going for. She hoped Atticus fell for it, hook, line, and sinker.

Glancing at the items scattered around her bathroom sink, she thought about how she'd teased the man of being presumptuous when he all but *told* her how she'd be spending her evening and where. She wondered whether or not it would be presumptuous to pack a toothbrush.

Would it be presumptuous or practical?

She stood, stared, and let the question circle around her brain long enough to make her feel ridiculous, and then she grabbed her toothbrush. And her make-up remover. And her facewash. Just in case. Returning to her bedroom, she dropped her belongings into her purse, then ventured to the kitchen to pack a measure of dog food for Titan, in the event he got hungry before they came back home. All this she did without second guessing herself.

It's practical to come prepared, she insisted, ignoring the urge to find Titan's travel bowls.

It was when she went to tuck her feet into her printed, pointed-toe, slip-on flats that she realized an extra pair of panties might be a good idea, too. After tossing the lacey garment into her purse, she admitted she wasn't being presumptuous *or* practical. With every item she added to her purse, she was getting her hopes up. Given their short history, it wasn't exactly smart to assume they could have a whole night together, completely uninterrupted—but matters of the heart were rarely smart.

"Titan, baby, where are you?" she called, anxious to get out the door. If she didn't leave soon, she'd never be able to get out of her head about it. "Time to go, baby!" she cooed, donning her Titans jacket as her dog came toward the sound of her voice.

Shelbyville hadn't changed much, but it had grown enough and Mitzi had been away long enough she needed the GPS to navigate the ten minute drive to Atticus' house. He lived in an older neighborhood with bungalow style homes, many of which were well past the point of starting to show their age. Except, even in the moonlight, as Mitzi came to a stop in his gravel driveway, she could tell he'd given his home a facelift.

His porchlight let her know his house was painted taupe with white trim. The dark copper iron railing leading up his steps and around his front porch was an obvious upgrade. At a glance, the only thing that could make his place more inviting would be a couple of rocking chairs on which to sit and watch the sunset.

"Come 'ere, little guy. Let's go see what the inside looks like," she murmured as she took Titan into her arms.

After knocking on the front door, she reached up and scratched behind her pup's ears in an attempt to keep from fidgeting in anticipation. Her whole body relaxed even as her belly fluttered when Atticus filled the doorway. He was in jeans and a faded SPD t-shirt, which had obviously seen its fair share of washes, his feet bare as if proclaiming he was home for the night. His head full of hair was covered by the same trucker-style Titans ball cap she'd seen him in at Gypsy's, and he had a bottle of beer clutched between his fingers and thumb at his side.

"She hardly goes anywhere without you, does she?" he said instead of hello.

Mitzi grinned, kissed the top of Titan's head, and then met Atticus' eyes as she replied, "You said bring my Titan spirit. Is it okay that he's here?"

He took a step toward her, causing her to crane her neck to keep eye contact with him. He then leaned down until she could feel the heat of his breath against her lips. "So long as he doesn't steal all my kisses, he's welcome."

"There's plenty to go around," said Mitzi, laughing softly.

She was soon silenced by his kiss, a kiss she'd been craving since they'd said goodbye Sunday morning. He didn't linger long, and she willed herself not to be disappointed when he straightened to full height. Then he jerked his head, inviting her inside, and her disappointment disappeared.

The front door opened into his living room. To Mitzi's right was his brown leather, L-shaped sectional, which looked masculine and comfortable in equal measure. It was situated atop a printed, grayish blue area rug. The two-tiered coffee table in the center had iron legs and a glass top, the bottom shelf adorned with a few books and auto-magazines. At the end of the couch closest to her was a wicker basket full of folded blankets. At the other end was a modern standing lamp with an antique design. On the wall behind the couch were five framed photographs of old, classic cars.

The polished, dark, hardwood floors were beautiful and a stark contrast to the beige hued walls. Mounted on the opposite side of the room was his big screen television. It was already turned on, the pre-game show turned down low. The wooden credenza below the screen had glass doors, showcasing Atticus' sound system and another collection of books. She'd barely stepped foot inside, and she was already speechlessly impressed.

"You want a quick tour? We've got a few minutes before the game starts."

"Yes, please," she replied, setting Titan at their feet.

As soon as her hands were free, Atticus took one of hers in his and escorted her through his living room and further into his home. He guided her to the guest bathroom first, where she learned that's where his renovations started, a couple of years ago. There wasn't much to see in his guest bedroom. The floors and the walls were finished the way he wanted them, but the space was still being used as a staging area—paint cans, wall tiles, and tools scattered everywhere. At the opposite end of the hallway was *his* bedroom. When Mitzi stepped inside, she finally found her words.

The master suite was perfect. He'd installed a beautiful farmhouse door along the wall that opened into his bathroom. The wood of the door matched the wood of his headboard and the bench placed at the foot of the tall bed. His linens were dark gray, with white sheets; and on either side of the bed were two, simple, iron nightstands with glass base lamps and cream shades. In the space next to his closet was a black, leather chair beside a wooden table that clearly served as his drop zone. On the chair was what

Mitzi guessed was the shirt he had on earlier, and the slacks he must have changed out of before she arrived. On the table was his wallet and his keys. It was the only clutter in the whole room.

"You did all this?"

"Most of it. Judge helped when I let him. Can't take credit for the design, though. Mama's got a knack for that, so I let her have at it when the time came."

"What about the kitchen? Is it finished?"

"Almost. Not quite," he said, leading her in its direction.

Mitzi could barely contain her gasp upon entering the kitchen. Even though it wasn't finished, it wasn't a long way off from being gorgeous. He had fantastic butcherblock countertops throughout, with white cabinetry below. The backsplash lining the room was clean, white subway tiles. On either side of his kitchen sink, he had floating wooden shelves which held most of his dishware. On the opposite wall, on either side of his stove, was what was left unfinished. Remembering the photos he'd sent her a couple weeks ago, she tried to imagine the empty space filled with the last of his cabinetry. Finally, just beyond the boundaries of his kitchen was his dining room table—large enough for six.

"That picture you sent me—"

"I took that about a month ago, when I first gutted it. The last bit of cabinetry still needs a coat of paint, but they'll go up as soon as I can make it happen."

"I can't believe you put so much work into this house. It's beautiful, Atticus."

"Thanks. It's something to do. Workin' with my hands helps clear my head."

She stared up at him then, thinking how clear his head must get with all of his efforts. Then she remembered the look in his eyes just a couple days before—how his attention was divided, the weight of his job clouding his thoughts. She understood how his home wasn't just a place for him to lay his head. It was a project through which he could ease his burdens.

"Want a beer? Burgers are keepin' warm in the oven."

"I'll take a beer, sure."

"'Kay," he mumbled as he leaned down for a kiss. This time, after he pulled away, he came right back for another before he let her go in order to fetch her that beer. After he popped the cap and handed it to her, Mitzi thanked him and watched as he filled the countertops with burger toppings and condiments. She'd had a glimpse of Detective Steele in his element. Seeing him move about his home, a place where he'd invested so much of his energy, she was seeing *Atticus* in a new light.

Mitzi understood what it meant to pour her heart into a creation of her own making. She knew the value of her ability to design and make something to share with someone. She might not have known the thousands of people who purchased her creations, but that didn't take away from their unspoken bond. The longer she stood in the middle of one of Atticus' creations, the harder it was for her to comprehend why there wasn't already a woman sharing his home and staking her claim on such a man.

As soon as the thought crossed her mind, Scarlett's voice was in her head, warning her the only explanation was there was something wrong with the man. Mitzi shook away the thought as she took a sip of her beer. If there was one thing she knew for certain, it was that life was complicated and relationships messy. Scarlett didn't know Atticus. Not really. Not anymore. High school was a long time ago.

"Can I help with anything?" she asked, needing the sound of her voice to drown out her sister's.

"You could grab a couple plates." He stopped what he was doing to smirk in her direction. "That is, if you can reach 'em."

Chuckling, Mitzi replied, "He's got jokes."

A few minutes later, their dinner plated and their beers in hand, they made themselves comfortable in front of the game. The

Titan's won the coin toss, opting to receive at the half, and kick-off started the game clock. Mitzi was only a quarter of the way through her burger when Atticus got a phone call. She was mid-chew when she heard it, and she wondered what it would mean if their plans were interrupted again. Surely, it was a sign. Suddenly, her dinner wasn't sitting right.

"Mitz?" Atticus called softly, ignoring his phone as he reached for her chin.

She glanced at his vibrating pocket before shifting her gaze to align with his. "Hmm?"

"Not goin' anywhere. Not tonight."

He meant it, and she could see it in his eyes. Still, she wanted more. She needed it. It was when he got the call that she realized how high her hopes had gotten. "Promise?"

"Yup."

"Okay."

He still had hold of her chin at the sound of the whistle. She cut her eyes toward the screen, and he snickered as he let her go. When she felt his lips pressed against her temple, her stomach began to settle and she reached for the remainder of her burger. Not five minutes later, there were footsteps outside his front door. Titan, who was curled up at Mitzi's feet, lifted his head when Atticus' guest tried and failed to twist open the doorknob.

Atticus grabbed his beer and took a long pull as a loud knock brought Titan to his feet. Mitzi spoke not a word as she looked to Atticus, who took his time before getting up to answer the door. After twisting his locks free, he barely opened the barrier, blocking Mitzi's view. Or, perhaps, his unexpected guest's view in.

"Why aren't you answerin' your phone? And why is your door locked?"

Mitzi recognized her voice immediately, and the irritated way Jay spoke to her brother brought a smile to her lips.

"Bullet—you notice a car in the driveway when you pulled up?"

"Yeah, so? That doesn't explain why you locked me out."

"I didn't lock you out. You don't live here."

"What does that have to do with anything?" she asked, still irritated.

The game cut to a commercial, and Mitzi thought about getting up, but she stayed put and continued to listen instead. It wasn't all that surprising, her and Atticus being interrupted again. Only this time, rather than feeling disappointed, she was kind of amused. There was also something about their exchange which made Mitzi jealous. The fact that Jay showed up, expecting she'd be able to walk right into her brother's house uninvited, it spoke of a bond between siblings. She imagined Jay had been barging into her older brother's room since she was old enough to twist a doorknob; except now, his room was a house across town.

"What are you doin' here?"

"Liam and I got into it. I needed a cool down. I didn't want to be home alone."

"Why didn't you go to Billie's?"

"Not in the mood to hear *I told you so*."

"And Lawson?"

"He hates Liam's guts, you know that."

"Yeah. I'm not his biggest fan, either—especially tonight."

"Atticus Montgomery, I don't want to hear it. Let me in."

"I'm busy, *Justice*. And, as we've already established, I'm not alone."

"It's Monday night and the Titans are playin'. You're not busy, you're watchin' football. And I'm no detective, but that looks like Mitzi's car in your drive. If it's her cute little ass on your couch, there's not a move you can make that'll get you laid before the end of the fourth quarter—so let me in."

Mitzi's laughter was unstoppable. Jay always did shoot straight.

Atticus looked back at her from over his shoulder and Mitzi laughed even harder. Their fate was sealed, and their date-night-in had just acquired a third wheel.

Her eyes still locked with his, Mitzi spoke through her smile as she asked, "Jay, you want a beer?"

"I'd love one," she called out in return. Then, addressing her brother, she mumbled, "Glad *someone* around here has some manners."

Atticus shook his head, but the smirk he wore let Mitzi know he wasn't really all that irritated. She winked as she started to get up, and that's when he finally made room for Jay to come inside. "Sit, pretty girl. I'll get it," he demanded.

She did as she was told, reaching for her own beer as Jay threw herself across the opposite side of the couch.

"Want to talk about it?" asked Mitzi.

Jay inhaled deeply and exhaled slowly, mulling over her answer. "No, thanks."

Mitzi nodded, respecting her friend's need for a little space. Recognizing whatever happened made her upset enough she didn't want to be alone, Mitzi wished she could do more. At the sound of Titan's jingling dog tags rattling as he scratched himself, she knew just what could cure her ailing friend.

She set aside her beer and reached for her pup, kissing the top of his head before she got up and laid him across Jay's stomach. "He's a great snuggle buddy. Give his belly a rub, and you'll feel better. I promise."

"Thanks, Mitz."

After Atticus returned with a beer, all three of them settled in an indiscernible silence. Easy as it had been for Jay to talk her way through the door, none of them was prepared to spend the evening together. Laid back as Mitzi wanted to pretend she was, she and Atticus were still exploring what existed between them. Having his little sister around—not to mention one of her oldest friends— Mitzi wasn't exactly sure *how* to fill the silence.

Then the game came back on, the Bill's quarterback fumbled the ball, and Mitzi had something to get excited about.

"I swear, you came out of the womb wavin' pom-poms," said Jay.

Mitzi only grinned in reply, not the least bit offended. After she was finished with her dinner, she was surprised when Atticus tugged on the back of her jacket. She looked at him in question even as he draped an arm around her shoulders, signaling precisely where he wanted her.

With her rigid back pressed against his side, he lowered his lips until they grazed her ear as he mumbled, "Planned on watchin' the game with a pretty girl under my arm. That okay with you?"

Mitzi hesitated for only a moment. Her gaze drifted toward Jay before she made up her mind. Rather than relax against him, she leaned forward and reached for her beer as she kicked off her shoes. Propping her bare feet against the edge of the couch, she then leaned back against Atticus, exactly where she wanted to be.

Jay didn't say much throughout the duration of the game. Every time Mitzi glanced toward the opposite side of the couch, her friend was either staring absentmindedly at the television or down at Titan, sprawled on his back and in and out of a doze. He jerked awake every time he heard his mama's voice, raised at the players as if they might hear her. And every time she got riled up, she felt rather than heard Atticus' quiet laughter. This, inevitably, brought a smile to her face. It'd been a long time since Mitzi dated someone who cared about football. Having a man at her back who understood her passion to the point of amusement made her want him all the more.

In the end, Titans took the win. During the final seconds of the game, Jay freed a heavy sigh and pushed herself upright. She gave Titan one final rub, then put him on the floor, where he immediately gave himself a full body shake.

"I should go," she announced, raking her fingers through her hair.

As she stood to her feet, Atticus moved to get up, too. "I'll walk you out." Before he rose, he pressed his lips against the side of Mitzi's head and mumbled into her hair, "Stay put."

"Night, Mitzi," said Jay with a lame wave. "Thanks for lending me your dog."

"Anytime."

She watched the siblings as they stepped out onto the porch and disappeared behind the closed door. In spite of the command Atticus left her with, Mitzi lingered on the couch only a few seconds before she decided to take advantage of her moment alone with Titan. She slipped on her shoes and scooped her pup into her arms, wandering through the house and toward the back door. She wasn't the least bit surprised when she stepped outside onto a finished deck, complete with a grill and five deck chairs circled around a table she bet money doubled as a fire pit.

"Go potty, baby," she cooed, setting Titan down at the top of a short set of stairs. He looked up at her, as if in question, and she encouraged him with a wave. "Go on."

He finally obeyed, wandering into the darkness beyond the reach of the patio light, and Mitzi wrapped her arms around herself in an effort to ward off the night's chill. She took a second look around the deck, mentally walking through the inside of the house and seeing all the amazing work Atticus had done. Between his house, his Chevelle, and his job—it was no wonder he was still single.

Or maybe it's not just the job he's been trying to forget.

She thought back a couple weeks and the first time she'd laid eyes on Atticus since her return. Later that same day, Nora-Jean had mentioned how, rumor had it, the last woman he'd been with had done a number on him. Mitzi had no idea how long it'd been since his heart had been broken; but from what she could tell, any woman who thought it was a good idea to give up Atticus Steele was crazy.

Soon as Titan had done his business, he hurried back up onto the deck, and Mitzi lead the two of them back inside. When she walked into the living room and saw no sign of Atticus, she slipped out of her jacket, draped it over the arm of the couch, and started to clean up their dinner mess. She'd finished rinsing their dishes by the time she heard Atticus come back inside. She cut off the faucet and dried her hands as he shut off the television. Mitzi turned and leaned back against the sink just as he entered the kitchen.

"You didn't have to clean up," he murmured, reaching up to rub the back of his neck as he looked at his cleared counters.

"It's okay. I wanted to." He dropped his arm as he continued to make his way toward her, and Mitzi frowned at the stain she saw on his shoulder. When he was in reaching distance, she lifted her hand and grazed the wet spot with her fingers. "Is Jay okay?"

"She will be."

Mitzi nodded. "You're a good brother."

"She seems to think so." He paused, propping his hands on either side of the counter behind her, caging her in. "Sorry tonight didn't go like I thought it would."

Mitzi slid her arms around his waist, smiling up at him as she replied, "The Titans won, and you kept your promise. We made it through the game and we're both still standing here so—I think that's a win."

A lazy smirk curled the corner of his mouth as his eyes danced around her face. She watched him stare at her for a long moment before he asked, "Where've you been all my life, pretty girl?"

Her face lit up as her grip around him tightened, her whole body responding before she spoke a word. "I had to go away for a little while, but I'm back now. I'm home, where I belong. I'm right underneath your nose, Atticus *Montgomery*, and I'm not going anywhere."

Chuckling, he tilted his head and brought his lips a hair's breadth away from hers. "Promise?"

"Yeah."

Mitzi barely got the word out before he was kissing her. Unlike his sweet kisses earlier in the night, this one spoke of the same desire she felt in the pit of her stomach. This kiss wasn't one that could stand to be interrupted. It was deep and delicious, and Mitzi hummed of her approval as she readjusted her grip. One arm went around his shoulders, while she used her free hand to blindly reach for the bill of his cap. Soon as it was off, his hands were holding her hips and she was airborne.

She gasped, sucking in a mouthful of his exhale as he lifted her up until she was sitting on the edge of the sink. He made room for himself between her legs, and she hitched her knees on either side of his hips, dropping his hat on the counter beside them before taking hold of the side of his face. When he buried his fingers in her hair, cradling her head as he kissed her deeper, she couldn't silence her whimper. If their first kiss was amazing, this one was sensational. She felt him everywhere they were connected—and every part of her he wasn't touching yearned for him.

After Atticus had kissed them both breathless, he kept a gentle hold of the back of her neck with one hand, while using his other to tug at the wide collar of her shirt. He dragged his lips away from her mouth, across her cheek, kissing his way down her neck before he tasted her bare shoulder. Mitzi shuddered, and he lifted his head until his forehead was pressed against hers.

"I'll stop when you tell me to," he breathed.

She shook her head, tilting her neck back in an attempt to reach his lips as she brazenly replied, "I'm not gonna tell you to stop."

Atticus, taking her at her word, dropped his arm around her waist and hugged her to him. With his other hand wrapped around the side of her thigh, he lifted her off the counter and took her directly to his bedroom. He sat her on the edge of his bed, pressed a hard kiss against her lips, and then let her go. Mitzi watched him in heightened anticipation as he switched on one of his bedside lamps before disappearing into the bathroom. He was gone long enough to find a condom, and Mitzi felt her lady parts flutter in excitement when she saw him carry it out. Then he reached over his head, grabbed the back of his shirt, and rid his body of the garment. Mitzi didn't have time to catch her breath at the sight of him before he slipped his tongue into her mouth and eased her onto her back.

Atticus didn't take his time, but neither did Mitzi feel rushed. As he rid her of her clothing, it didn't feel like she could be anyone or that he was only taking what he wanted. Every touch and each kiss belonged to her, and she knew it without him having to say it or slow down. When both of them were in nothing but their underwear, his hands exploring every dip and curve she could boast of, Mitzi burned with an awareness she didn't want to take for granted.

She planted one foot on the bed, bucked her hips against his, then rolled them both until she was straddling his lap. The bulge of his erection was an unmistakable and unavoidable reality between her legs, and she bit her lip as she felt her own arousal continue to soak her panties even as she denied herself the friction she craved. With her palms flattened against Atticus' chest, she felt her way down his hard, lean abdomen and up again. As his hands slipped up her thighs and around her backside, she moved to cup her own around his face and stared down at him, knowing two things to be absolutely certain.

What they were about to do, they'd never be able to take back. But more than any man she'd ever given herself to, *this one* felt right. *This one* came with consequences unique to life in a tight-knit community; consequences that, if things turned sour, might make her wish she never came back. And yet, she knew she'd regret it for the rest of her life if she didn't take the risk. Fast as things were moving between them, she was on fire with a reckless desire she hadn't felt in so long.

They'd known each other since they were kids. While that was a long time ago, and their history didn't weigh much, the moment he was inside of her, everything would change. Her insides burned with a longing to have him—all of him. Staring into his deep brown eyes, she felt like she was coming back home. Not just to Shelbyville, but that place wrapped in a feeling she only ever got on a Friday night, sitting around a fire down by the river after a game.

The man in her grip wore the scent of his respect; he knew where she came from, where she'd been, and he had confidence in where she was going. There was still so much to learn about each other, and yet their small town made them far from strangers. It was beautiful and familiar—it was wild and daring, in that way coming home would always be for Mitzi.

Atticus slid his hand up her side and around one of her breasts, reminding her the only things left separating them were easily removable. She rolled her hips, eliciting a moan from them both, and then lowered herself until her lips were grazing his.

"Take me, Atticus," she pleaded.

And so he did.

chapter fourteen

MITZI KNEW SHE NEEDED TO get up and wash her makeup off her face, but she didn't want to move. She was exactly where she wanted to be—propped up against a pillow, covered in the shirt Atticus had on earlier, her legs tucked beneath his rumpled blanket. She was cozy, sated, and deliriously happy. The scent of Atticus was all over her, and it was almost as intoxicating as his touch.

At the sound of his returning footsteps, she shifted her gaze toward his bedroom door. The boxer briefs he'd slipped into hugged him low around his hips, and she unknowingly slid her bottom lip between her teeth as she allowed herself to appreciate the view from top to toe.

"You keep lookin' at me like that, we'll never get to sleep," he teased as he came to a stop beside the bed. He drank from the glass in his hand and then handed the remainder of the water to Mitzi.

She smiled at him, her mind suddenly crowded with memories

of round two, and silently accepted the glass. Parched from exertion, Mitzi drank until the water was gone, and then handed it back to Atticus.

"You good? Need more?"

"I'm good, thank you."

Satisfied with her response, he set the empty glass on his nightstand and climbed back into bed. As if he'd done it a million times before, he lifted one arm around her shoulders, positioning them so she was leaning back against the side of his chest. She closed her eyes and freed a sigh when she felt the pressure of his kiss in her hair. Now, the thought of getting up to wash her face seemed utterly ridiculous.

They sat a moment in a comfortable silence before Atticus inquired, "Were you that flexible in high school?"

Mitzi opened her eyes as she laughed. "You don't get to be the top of the pyramid just for being short."

She felt rather than heard his chuckle, and she liked that. She liked laughing with him in bed. She liked the weight of his arm resting across her chest. She liked getting to experience this side of him—the man beneath the shield. Still, she couldn't help but wonder why there wasn't already another woman claiming the opposite side of his bed, half the bathroom sink, and three-quarters of his closet.

Glancing down at his arm, holding her possessively, she already hated the idea of not having him. Much as she wished it wasn't so, Scarlett's warning crept into her head, casting a shadow over her bliss. She reached up with both of her hands in order to fidget with his fingers, hoping to chase away reality with the memory of all he could do with them.

"What's on your mind, pretty girl?"

"How do you know something's on my mind?"

"Had a hunch. Your question proved it."

She hummed her acknowledgement, resting her head against

his shoulder. He paid attention to her. How she was feeling. What she was thinking. It wasn't the first time. Given his profession, she knew it wouldn't be the last. She'd never had that before. Not with a man. Sometimes she swore Adalynn had a key to her mind and could read her thoughts with nothing more than one hard look. With Atticus it was different. It was investigative. While it was true a girl liked to have her secrets, his awareness of her made her feel wanted. His awareness made her want to be honest.

"In high school, if you and I ever messed around—I would have wasted you. You wouldn't have been more than a good time. Back then, I was so adamant about finding my own way. I didn't want to be tied down. I didn't want to fall in love and get stuck here before I had a chance to go anywhere."

"And now?"

She hesitated as she thought over the last few weeks. If he'd asked her that question a month ago, her answer would have been different. Yet, in the moment in which she found herself, she harbored no doubt about what she believed would make her happy. "Now, everything is different," she admitted. "Shelby. Me and what I want."

"And what do you want?"

"I want this place to be home again. I want to feel like I'm part of my family. And—this…" She laced her fingers through his, holding onto him as she shifted under his arm. Pressed into his side, she slid one of her bare legs between his and sought out his gaze with her own. "*Us.* I want whatever this is."

"Good."

Mitzi wished she could be satisfied with his response. It was simple, she didn't need more to know he wanted her. Nora had been right on the nose earlier that day. There was no misinterpreting his actions. Nora had also reminded her the two of them had time to figure one another out; only, her sex-muddled brain put her in a vulnerable position, and she felt incapable of keeping her mouth shut.

"Atticus...you're a really good guy. You're hot, you're great in bed, you come from a good family, you wear a police shield, and you walk around this town like it means something to you."

"It does."

"What I'm saying is, you're a catch. Everyone knows it, and it's certainly not lost on me. But you haven't been caught, which begs the question—"

"What's wrong with me?"

"No. No, I don't mean that," she insisted, a frown pulling at her brow. She let go of his hand in order to cup the side of his face. Grazing her thumb against his cheek, she murmured, "I guess what I mean is, if you wanted a woman, you'd have one."

"Yeah," he muttered, closing the short distance between his mouth and hers. He kissed her then stayed close as he said, "Workin' on it."

Mitzi couldn't help her smile at the feel of his tongue, and she didn't deny him a short, wet kiss. Still, she wanted more. She knew Atticus could sense her real desire when he pulled away, studied her face a moment, and then started talking.

"Back in the day, you and I weren't so different. The only thing I was serious about was football. My grades were as good as they were because Judge wouldn't let me play otherwise. Girls were part of the deal. You know how it was.

"Things changed in college. I got off the bench, but I knew my time on the field was runnin' out. I was smart enough to plan ahead and think about life after ball. There were a couple girls in Knoxville I thought might be worth my while, but neither of them made it back here. That was the thing. Big as the world is, I never wanted to plant roots anywhere other than Shelby.

"After the police academy, found my way back home. Suddenly I was wearing a new uniform." He smirked and shook his head at the thought. "Got me as much attention as it did when I was wearing a jersey. I soaked it up for a while, until I met Faith." He looked away from Mitzi then, his amusement erased from his face as he continued. "Lost four years on her. Half the town was sure I'd be her ticket down the aisle."

"What happened?" Mitzi whispered.

"She didn't want a man. She wanted a puppet. She even mapped out my whole career. Wanted me ridin' a desk. Took me a while to realize it. Too long. Then I ended it, and shit went from bad to worse. Took nearly a year to shake her off. And I'll own some of that. Mistakes were made. But when it was finally over?" Atticus sighed as he reached up and combed his fingers through his hair. Mitzi tickled the side of his jaw with her fingertips, and he aligned his gaze with hers once more. "Took me a while to clear my head. I focused on work. Made Sargent. Became detective. Bought this house...

"Truth is, you're not the only one wonderin', Mitz. What folks don't get is I know what I'm lookin' for. I've just been waitin' on her to find her way home."

This time, it was her turn to initiate a kiss. Slipping her hand around the back of his neck, she drew him to her and relished in the feel of his plump lower lip closing around hers. He indulged her for only a minute before he lifted his head, his smirk returning as he demanded, "I showed you mine. Pay up, pretty girl. Smart, talented, gorgeous woman like you—would rather join a man then give him hell for watchin' football all weekend—and you haven't been caught?"

"Okay. You're right. It's only fair." She pulled in a breath and tried to think where to begin. "I told you about Nolan."

"The model turned junkie."

"Yes...well, before him was Drew. He's a stock broker. I met him when I was out one night in Manhattan. This was when I was still living in Queens, sewing clothes all hours of the night to keep up with my online sales. He, um...he's actually the reason I was able to open my first store. He took a chance on me and backed Sterling Thread. He's also how I met Gianna, my CFO.

"Anyway, we were together for almost three years. I think I only loved him for half of that. He was a successful guy who was constantly chasing status. He wanted to be among the elite and I couldn't relate to that. Sure, I wanted my brand to take off; and since I started dreaming of having my own fashion line, I've wanted to make a name for myself—but it's never really been about the money. I love designing. I love sharing it with people. I love getting to do both for a living; but buying a vacation home in the Hamptons has never been on my bucket list.

"In the beginning, I was convinced he believed in me. Somewhere along the line, it wasn't *me* he was pursuing. It was my potential as a designer and what it meant for him to have the owner of Sterling Thread on his arm. I stayed with him longer than I should have. I felt guilty breaking up with him before I could pay him back. Then Evie was born. I came home to meet her, and seeing my best friend making it as a mama on her own—I remembered why I left. I didn't need Drew. I needed to stay true to myself."

She dropped her hand down to his chest, her eyes following suit as she got lost in her own reverie. "My truth?" she murmured. "I've always been a small town kind of girl with big dreams. I left Shelbyville to chase those dreams. How I left, when I left, it wasn't great. But at the time, fighting with my mom and Scarlett is what got me fired up enough to leave, and I'm not sorry I did. I could blame my career on why I haven't found *the one*, but I don't think it's that simple. I just couldn't find someone who understood me or where I came from. And I think I've been in denial about where I really wanted to be.

"Maybe one day, I'll look back on the break-in at the boutique and I won't feel scared but grateful that it brought me home. I got everything I wanted out of New York, and it was time for me to come back, even if it was easier to stay away."

Atticus curled a finger underneath her chin, lifting her head until he had her eyes again. "Can't say I'm ever gonna be grateful some sonofabitch broke into your store, hit you, then robbed you for a score. Pisses me off just thinkin' about it. But you—under these sheets, in nothin' but my t-shirt—pretty damn glad about it."

"Yeah?" she managed to whisper before he captured her lips in a kiss.

"Mmmhmm," he hummed in reply.

He pulled her closer and she held on tight, no longer craving words.

Mitzi never did get around to washing off her makeup.

SHE FELT HIS FINGERS, submerged in her hair, massaging the nape of her neck as she slowly made her way out of sleep. His voice could be heard in the distance, like he was on the opposite end of a tunnel, and Mitzi wanted to get to him. She breathed in deeply, and the scent of him woke her instantly. He smelled like body soap, aftershave, Sterling Mist, and *him*. Peeling her eyes open, she pulled in another lung full of air, in love with his unique aroma.

"Mornin'," he mumbled affectionately.

This time, when he spoke, she smelled something else. Toothpaste and...something fruity. Mitzi squinted in confusion and focused on the man in front of her. It took her a second to realize he wasn't still in bed. He'd bathed—his dark, wavy locks damp from his shower—and he was fully dressed. They were at eye level with one another because he was squatting beside the bed, coaxing her out of sleep. And the handsome, crooked smile he wore was wrapped around the Dum Dum which was captured in the corner of his mouth.

"Morning. What time is it?" she whispered, her voice airy and scratchy from lack of use.

"Seven-thirty."

"Oh." Mitzi frowned, disappointed morning had come so soon. "You're already dressed?"

"Yup. I've got to get goin'."

"Of course. Work. I should get up, too. I can be quick."

"Nope." Before she could move to sit up, he pulled the sucker from his mouth and leaned in for a kiss. "You get up now, I won't get to walk out the door with the image of this pretty girl still in my bed. I was lookin' forward to that. Besides, I'm not stupid, babe. I know better than to expect for you to be able to put yourself together quick."

"Hey..."

"I mean it. Take your time. Titan's been out. There's a half pot of coffee in the kitchen. Feel free to use my shower if you want—just lock the door on your way out, yeah?"

Mitzi stared at him, processing all he'd said before she reached for the back of his neck. She then pulled him close, lifting her head enough to steal a kiss. "I think we might keep you."

"Smart as you are pretty." He gave her neck a gentle squeeze and pressed his lips against her forehead, where he mumbled, "I'll call you later."

She nodded, following him with her eyes as he stood. "Go catch bad guys."

"Yes, ma'am," he replied with a wink, popping his sucker back into his mouth.

Atticus said he wanted to leave with the image of her still in his bed, but Mitzi had to admit her view wasn't half bad, either. When he disappeared from sight, and she heard the garage door close behind him, she freed a wistful sigh. She hadn't slept long, but she slept well, and she knew it wasn't because of the mattress or the comfortable bedding under which she still laid. It was the man; the man who exhausted her body with pleasure and then held her through the night; the man who saw to her baby boy and made coffee while she slept; the man who made her belly tingle even when he wasn't in the room.

Mitzi rolled onto her back, hugging his sheets around her as she stared up at the ceiling. She knew she could be impulsive. Some of her greatest success came from acting first and thinking through the details second. She'd learned not to be afraid of failure because it taught her what worked and what didn't—but she'd never been impulsive when it came to men. She was careful and calculated, understanding that love came with sacrifice, and anyone she gave her heart to needed to prove he was worth it. But with Atticus, she didn't feel as though she had a choice.

She was falling in love with him already. She could feel it, and she couldn't stop it.

More importantly, she didn't want to.

She pondered this reality until she heard the jingling of Titan's tags as he entered the room. Propping herself onto her elbows, Mitzi looked down at him as he came to the side of the bed and signaled his desire to join her.

"I'm not sure Atticus has warmed up to the idea of you in his bed, yet," she said, forcing herself to get up. Soon as her feet hit the floor, she scooped her pup into her arms and peppered the top of his head with kisses. "We'll work on him, okay, baby?"

In nothing more than Atticus' t-shirt, Mitzi made her way out of his bedroom, headed straight for his coffee pot. His open shelves made it easy for her to find a mug, and she rummaged her way around until she found some sugar and cream to sweeten her dose of much needed caffeine. With Titan still in the crook of one of her arms, she leaned back against the counter beside the stove, sipped at her beverage, and took in the quiet, picturesque setting of his almost finished kitchen. She admired every detail her eyes could catch—searching for Atticus in each one.

The longer she stood in his space, seeing him through the work of his hands, the further she recessed into her imagination. Then, suddenly, she was dreaming up a collection of menswear. Her gaze grew unfocused as she saw in her mind's eye an ensemble designed for a southern gentleman who liked to work with his hands. She didn't see flannel and work boots, as that wasn't her style; instead, she classed-up a practical look, mentally sorting through a catalogue of fabric choices to give her the feel she was going for. As she sipped at her coffee, her fingers started to itch with her desire to sit down with pencil and paper. There was no question what was on her agenda for the rest of the day.

Her menswear spring collection was going to be inspired by the kind of man she'd only ever found at home. Gianna would love the concept, especially as it coincided with the theme of the new store's opening.

She was yanked from her thoughts by the sound of her ringing phone. She jolted fully upright, trying to remember where she left the device as she made her way out of the kitchen. Following the sound to her purse, which sat on the bench seat at the foot of Atticus' bed, Mitzi lowered Titan to the ground and used her free hand to dig for the phone. When she saw it was Adalynn who had initiated a video call, she grimaced, looked down at herself, whispered a curse and then slid her thumb across the screen before she missed the call entirely.

"Uh, hi, boss. Did I catch you at a bad time? I thought we agreed —"

"No. Yes. You're right. I wanted us to check in with each other this morning. It's totally my fault for losing track of the time. I'm— I'm distracted. I'm sorry."

Adalynn tried to conceal her smile, but her blue eyes sparkled in excitement before she murmured conspiratorially, "I oversaw the packing of your apartment, and I don't recall seeing a men's t-shirt in your sleepwear collection. Are you...*alone* right now?"

Mitzi captured her bottom lip between her teeth as she fought the urge to feel embarrassed. As her assistant, Adalynn had access to more than Mitzi's business life. Much as she tried to keep things professional, their relationship was built on the kind of trust which only manifested after both women exposed their humanity to one another. Mitzi was Adalynn's boss, but that didn't mean they couldn't fill the role of *friend* when it was warranted.

That said, Mitzi had never answered a video call in nothing more than a man's t-shirt and what was left of her makeup after a night in bed. While her inner southern-belle felt exposed in that way which made her feel utterly unpresentable, it was the business owner part of her that felt like she'd shirked on her responsibilities in an uncustomary sort of way.

Freeing her lip, Mitzi sighed, turned, then plopped down onto the bench. "Yes, I'm alone," she finally answered. "I probably shouldn't have picked up, but I didn't want to stand you up and…" She laughed to herself as she played back the comment Atticus made before he left. "And, the truth is, it'll be at least an hour before I'm cleaned up and ready for the day."

"Okay—so, you totally don't have to answer this, but…is this a rekindled thing or a new thing?"

"Uhm, it's new," she stammered before taking a sip of her remaining coffee.

"That's exciting," Adalynn replied, her sentiment mirrored in her gaze. "Right? I mean, I'm allowed to be happy for you. Or, wait, is this a guy worth getting excited over or—"

Mitzi laughed softly, Adalynn's demeanor putting her at ease and reminding her why she and her assistant got on so well. "Yes. Excitement is warranted. But please don't ask me anymore. If we start talking about him, I might not want to stop, and that is *not* why you called. You'll just have to meet him when you come visit."

Adalynn was silent for a beat before she murmured, "You seem happy. *Really* happy. Not that you weren't happy here, but—I'm glad you're there. I miss you, but I can tell your life needed this change. Not that you need me to tell you that."

"No, I'm glad you did. Thank you. Every day I'm here, I'm more certain than ever I'm where I belong; but I left something very important behind, and to know the people taking care of it support me even now, it means everything."

"We're not going anywhere. We're here for you, and we're loyal to Sterling Thread."

"Speaking of," said Mitzi, changing her tone. "I don't want to monopolize your morning, and I've got ideas in my head I'm dying to get on paper—so, let's talk business, shall we?"

"Yes, let's. There are a few things I need to get on your schedule."

"All right. Lay it on me."

chapter fifteen

A FTER A QUICK SHOWER, Mitzi stuck around the house long enough to make the bed and clean her empty coffee mug. She double-checked the front door to make sure it was locked on her way out, then sent Atticus a text as soon as she and Titan were situated in her car.

Me: Thanks for the extra time in bed. And the coffee. And the shower.

Me: Maybe next time...all 3 You.

Smiling to herself, she set her phone aside and made the short trip home. Anxious to get to work, as soon as she was inside she ditched her outfit from the previous night for something more comfortable. Keeping on her strapless bra, she dressed in a pair of nude sweatpants and her matching, slashed-neck, off-the-shoulder sweatshirt. She ignored the state of her unwashed hair as she pulled it into a messy ponytail, grabbed her laptop and her sketchbook, then settled herself at her dining room table. It was a head-down, no-frills kind of workday, and she didn't waste any time before getting started.

She first took care of a few obligatory tasks previously discussed with Adalynn. It had been a long time since she'd prepared to open a store, and she forgot about all the moving parts and finer details that were key to an opening's success. Construction on her shop hadn't even started yet, and the grand opening was tentatively on the schedule for February, but there was plenty to be done in the meantime. When she'd checked off the items on Adalynn's prescribed to-do list, Mitzi set her laptop aside, opened her sketchbook to a blank page, and started drawing the images she'd seen in her head while in Atticus' kitchen.

As it so often did when she was trying to get a design right, time slipped away from her. It was Titan who gently clawed at her legs, reminding her he needed to be fed. She made quick work of filling his bowl and refreshing his water, then grabbed a container of yogurt for herself before she was back at the table, scrutinizing her work. Eventually, Titan splayed himself across her bare feet for a nap. Mitzi kept telling herself she'd get up and take him for a long walk as soon as she got to a decent stopping point; but by the time she was satisfied with two complete looks, comprised of five separate pieces, the sun had long since taken a dive for the horizon.

She sighed as she reached down to run her fingers through his hair, and he immediately rolled onto his back, exposing his belly.

"I'm sorry mama neglected you all day. I promise to take you on a nice, long walk in the morning. Fortunately for us, we've got a backyard now. You want to go outside?"

Titan barked in reply as he rolled over and onto his feet. Already familiar with their new home, he trotted to the back door, his tail wagging in excitement as she followed close behind. Mitzi flipped on the outside light as she unlocked the door. No sooner had Titan stepped foot into the cool evening than there was a knock at her front door. She frowned in its direction, glanced out at Titan—who was preoccupied sniffing around the yard—then decided to leave the door open for him as she went to see about her unexpected guest. When she pressed up on her tiptoes to peer through the peep-hole, her belly tingled, causing a smile to spread across her face.

With one hand still on the doorknob, she propped her other against her hip and waited for him to lift his gaze from his feet. "I thought you said you'd call," she teased instead of hello.

For a second, he merely smirked at her. Then he casually reached into his pants pocket for his phone, tapped the screen with his thumb a couple times, switched the call to speaker, and waited. He didn't have to wait but a second before Mitzi's voicemail message sounded between them. Rolling her lips between her teeth, she stared up at him sheepishly. Suddenly she remembered she came home and got straight to work. Her phone—which hadn't been charged the night before—had obviously died where she left it. In her purse.

Atticus took the call off speaker, but he didn't hang up. His attention still focused on her, he brought the phone to his ear and proceeded to leave a message. "Know this, pretty girl—I call you twice and you don't pick up, I'm comin' over. Considering the nature of some of the open cases on my desk right now, I'd feel a lot better if you'd answer when I called. See you soon. Hope you're hungry."

When he was finished, he hung up and dropped the phone back into his pocket, not once breaking eye contact with her. In an effort to play coy, she asked, "And how are you so sure I wasn't trying to ghost you?"

He laughed, dropped his gaze, and reached up to squeeze the back of his neck. Peering at her from below his lifted brow, he muttered, "Last night wasn't just a great dream, Mitzi. I know you felt it, too. No way a woman with a kiss as sweet as yours has a heart cold enough to ghost a man when he's just gettin' started."

His response took her by surprise and stole her breath for good measure. "Okay," she started to say, reaching for a fistful of his leather jacket. She gave him a tug, but they both took a step toward one another, eliminating the distance between them. "You got me."

"Mmhmm," he hummed as he let go of his neck in order to take hold of the side of hers. "That's what I thought." He grazed his thumb along her jawline, keeping her head titled up as he leaned in for a kiss. Not that she needed prompting. She welcomed his affection, already craving it more than she did the day before. His mouth didn't linger against hers for long. Lifting his head enough to meet her gaze, he said, "Can you be ready in five?"

This time it was her turn to laugh. "Not a chance."

"Ten?" he replied, as if he thought negotiation tactics would really get them out the door faster.

Mitzi pressed both palms against his abdomen as she leaned into him and said, "How about we don't keep track. Tell me where we're going, and I promise no matter how long it takes me, it'll be worth it."

"The Thai place on Elm."

"Okay," she nodded, her mind already in her closet, piecing together an outfit. "Come in. I'll be out in a minute."

It took her ten minutes to decide on the tightest pair of denim jeans she owned, a black blouse speckled in white poke-a-dots—with delicate ruffles around the collar and at her wrists—and a pair of high-heeled, black, suede booties. It took her five minutes to redo her hair, arranging it in a more stylish version of her messy ponytail. It took her fifteen minutes to decorate her eyes in the appropriate amount of shadow, liner, and mascara to befit a dinner date. It took her two minutes to find her tube of red lipstick, plus one more to apply it. By the time she'd accessorized with the perfect gold earrings and coordinating rings, it had been approximately thirty-seven minutes since she disappeared into her room.

Not that she was keeping track.

Mitzi was slipping her arms into her fantastic, pale gray, suede, bomber jacket when she emerged from the hallway to find Atticus sitting at her dining room table. She stopped short when she saw he was flipping through her sketchbook. Part of her didn't mind him looking. He'd seen her naked, and one couldn't get more vulnerable than that. Only, she hated to get anyone's opinion on her work before she'd had a chance to step away from her design and decide for herself if she still liked it.

She opened her mouth, her mind scrambling to find the right words, when he turned and caught sight of her from over his shoulder. She forgot her words all together as his eyes did a slow perusal of her handiwork.

"Mitzi, babe—I want you to know you don't have to do all that for me. Wanted you an hour ago just as much as I want you now. Understood?"

She frowned, not entirely sure how to interpret his comment. On the one hand, it sounded like he was annoyed she'd taken as long as she did to get ready. While part of her *had* gone through the effort for his benefit, that wasn't the *only* reason. Whether it be Shelbyville or Manhattan, she never left home for a night out without a fresh coat of lipstick. However, what he said was kind of sweet. She appreciated knowing he wanted Mitzi the woman, not the trophy. Still, she wasn't entirely sure she *did* understand.

Atticus stood before Mitzi could make heads or tails of his question, and she studied him as he drew closer. He shook his head and offered her a lazy smile as he said, "What I'm tryin' to say is— damn. Didn't need it, but it sure was worth the wait."

Relaxing, she smiled up at him and replied, "Keep talkin' like that and I'll have to touch up my lipstick. That'd be at least another five minutes, and I'm *starving*."

"Dinner first. Let's get out of here."

Mitzi grabbed her purse, knelt to whisper a goodbye to Titan, and then accepted the hand Atticus held out to her. He led her through the front door, waited for her to lock-up, and then escorted her to the passenger side of his Chevelle. It wasn't the first time he'd been such a gentleman, but it warmed her belly just the same. There was something about his kindness even after they'd been intimate that she admired.

Her stomach growled as she buckled herself in and waited for Atticus to fold himself behind the wheel. It was nearly seven, and the only thing she could remember eating all day was a yogurt. Hungry as she was, she didn't regret it. Nothing made her feel content the way she did after a full day of sketching or sewing. It had been weeks since she'd done either with the same vigor and focus she'd experienced that day. Not to mention, had she eaten, she wouldn't be on her way to dinner with the man who had inspired her in the first place.

"How was your day?" she asked him as he eased out of her driveway.

"Frustrating. Case on the top of my pile is gettin' colder by the day. I'm runnin' in circles, hittin' dead ends, and it's not the only case needs my attention."

"I'm sorry. You want to talk about it?"

"Can't really discuss an open investigation, babe."

"I get that," she murmured, shifting in an effort to angle her body in his direction. "I'm not asking for details, but I'm here if you need to unload a little."

He took his eyes off the road in order to look her way. Before he refocused his attention out the windshield, he reached for her hand and laced his fingers between hers. "Appreciate that, Mitz—but I don't want to talk about my day, I want to hear about yours. Saw your sketchbook out. I—"

"No, don't!" she insisted. She lifted his hand until she was holding it in both of hers against her chest. "If you're about to give me your opinion of my ideas—please don't."

"Oh-kay," he mumbled, a frown tugging his eyebrows together.

"Sorry—it's a quirk of mine. It's not that I don't care about what you think, it's just I haven't fully decided what *I* think yet. What you saw was what I was working on today. Tomorrow, after I've had a chance to sleep on it, I'll know whether or not it's as good as I thought it was the moment I finished sketching. If you tell me what you think now, I'll never really know what I thought before my opinion was shaped by yours."

"Fair enough," he chuckled. "Am I allowed to know how your day was?"

She relaxed and smiled at him, dropping their hands into her lap. "Yes. It was quite productive, in all the best ways. And the whole of it was bookended by you—so I'd say it's been pretty great."

Mitzi saw her sentiment mirrored in the small twitch of his lips, and she fell for him a little harder. It was nonsensical, but she didn't fight it.

"Reynolds start work on the store yet?"

"Not yet. He should be ordering materials any day now and hopefully he can get started in a couple weeks. The shop has good bones, so I'm not planning on changing much—just sprucing it up a bit. I'm hoping he's done by the end of the year. Soon as he's finished, I'll have my designers come down and help complete my vision. Then it's up to me to make sure the racks are full of merchandise for the grand opening." As she spoke, her complete to-do list started to populate right before her eyes. Her gaze grew unfocused as she went on to add, "Somewhere in there I'll have to start the hiring process so I have help in the store. Much as I love going in, I try not to work every day. Finding someone as amazing as Adalynn or Gianna is going to be a challenge."

"Something tells me you'll have plenty of applicants anxious to help you out," said Atticus, breaking her trance.

"Maybe."

"Definitely," he insisted. "You're not a nobody around here.

That Sterling Thread sign goes up, and you'll have your pick of employees."

Mitzi bit the inside of her cheek as she stared at Atticus. She felt a pang of nervous excitement in her belly as she considered his awareness of her. Not just her, but her brand. This wasn't the first time he'd mentioned Sterling Thread with an air of familiarity; not to mention, she was certain he wore her fragrance better than any man. It still surprised her.

"Kind of sounds like you've been keepin' tabs on me, Detective Steele."

"Maybe I have."

"Why?" she all but whispered.

He glanced in her direction, and she searched his face for any hint of a clue. Before she could find anything, his eyes were focused on the road again. "Folks in Shelbyville take pride in the people who grew up here only to go and leave their mark on the world. Wouldn't be surprised if Jay hasn't spent more than one entire paycheck on a cart full of your designs. She swears, no one makes sexy look classy like you do.

"You branched out into menswear right before I made Sargent. She bought me one of your jackets to congratulate me. I liked it, so I looked you up. You built somethin', Mitzi—I admire you for that. Anyone around here who doesn't is just jealous."

"Oh," she murmured, feeling flattered.

"You openin' up shop here, bringin' your success back home, it means something to this town. You know it does. You'll find the help you need."

It warmed her heart hearing him talk about what Sterling Thread meant to Shelby. He wasn't the first one to say as much. Nora and the girls talked about the pride they shared with people all over town—women and men alike supporting her by purchasing her merchandise. But hearing how much Atticus believed in her and what she was doing, it meant more. Not because his opinion mattered more or because of his status, but because everything he'd said touched the deepest part of her. He didn't merely believe she was a good designer or a competent businesswoman; he understood where she came from; he understood why the culmination of her success was never going to be found on a runway in Paris. Notoriety would never satisfy her the way it did for some people.

She was always going to be a small town girl with big dreams —dreams not everyone would be able to understand. But she knew Atticus did.

They arrived at the Thai restaurant, the parking lot all the evidence either of them needed to know they wouldn't have to wait to be seated. Whatever dinner rush might have been had gone with the sun. Mitzi smiled to herself as they made their way inside. The food scene in New York might have been incredible, but she wouldn't miss the crowds that filled the best dining rooms at any hour on any weeknight.

Within twenty minutes of being seated, they were served. Conversation between the two of them was as easy as she was growing accustomed. They talked about her early years in the city and how Sterling Thread got its start in a tiny bedroom in Queens. Atticus then colored in the blank spots of his history, bits and pieces of which Mitzi had collected from Nora or Jay in passing over the years. They made each other laugh, they asked each other questions, and before either of them knew it, an hour had come and gone as they sat in a booth that felt more like a private bubble of their own making.

What fascinated Mitzi the most was that even as she was getting to know the man across from her, even though she never really knew him growing up, he wasn't a stranger. Somehow, the familiarity which existed between them made what was developing every moment they were together uncomplicated. She could hardly remember what it was like to be in a romantic relationship that *wasn't* complicated.

The longer she sat across from him, staring into the dark brown eyes trained intently in her direction, the more she longed for him. She remembered what she said the night before—the two of them in bed, her in his t-shirt and tucked underneath his arm. What she wanted now was different than what she wanted a decade ago. Gone was the girl who roamed the halls of Shelby High promising nothing but a good time. Now, she was a woman who wanted to promise someone forever. Crazy as she felt to admit it, she couldn't help but think a future with Atticus Steele tethering her to their small town was exactly what she wanted.

After he settled the bill, Atticus escorted Mitzi to the passenger side of his Chevelle and drove her home. She assumed, upon reaching their destination, he'd come inside with her. This was way, when he didn't follow her over her threshold, she turned and looked back at him in surprise.

"Are you leaving?"

"That's up to you, pretty girl," he started to say as he leaned one of his shoulders against the doorjamb. "I come in, we might be up half the night again."

"Atticus…" She got close and reached for the front of his shirt before she murmured, "Get in here and kiss the rest of this lipstick off of me."

He chuckled and offered her a nod. Pushing himself upright, he replied, "Yes, ma'am."

FOR THE SECOND MORNING in a row, Mitzi woke to the feel of Atticus' fingers buried in her hair—only this time, the sun wasn't high enough to pry its way through the closed blinds, and he hadn't left her in bed alone. As she slowly blinked her eyes open, finding her way to consciousness, she sensed Titan curled up by her feet. With a sigh, she settled her gaze on her lover's face, lit by the dull glow of her bedside lamp.

"We've got to stop meetin' like this," she mumbled with a pathetic frown.

"Won't argue with you on that."

"What time is it?"

"Six-thirty. And, babe, good as you smell—I show up at the station smellin' like you, Abernathy will give me shit about it all day."

Mitzi breathed a groggy giggle as she reached for his face. Curving her palm around his stubble-covered cheek, she said, "Give me a second and I'll walk you out."

"Nope. You, pretty girl, go back to sleep. I'll call you later."

"Okay," she acquiesced, too out of it to put up a fight. She slid her hand from his cheek in order to reach for the back of his neck. No further prompting was needed before his lips were pressed against hers. He pulled away long enough for her to whisper, "Have a good day," and then he was back for more.

Mitzi didn't register the fact that he hadn't said anything in response as he stood to full height. When he reached for an item on her nightstand, she realized he had something more than *goodbye* on his mind. She frowned in confusion when he held up her sketchbook. She knew for certain she'd left it on the dining room table the night before; yet, there it was, in his hand, opened to the mock-up she'd drawn of two streetwear men designs, comprised of her five new pieces.

She looked from her drawings to the man who inspired them, her unasked question in her eyes. He smirked down at her before he said, "Bet all the cash in my wallet these aren't as good as you thought they were the moment you finished sketching them— because they're better than good, Mitzi. I'd have placed an order for this jacket last night if you'd have let me. Now you've slept on it, and I'm tellin' you—these are great."

Speechless, Mitzi didn't say a word as he tossed the sketchbook into the space he'd occupied all night. He then leaned down and kissed her forehead. His lips still grazing her skin, he said, "You're more than a good designer. You're a damn talented one." He kissed her once more, winked down at her, then started for the door.

She watched him leave, knowing there was no way she'd be able to go back to sleep after that goodbye. Still at a loss for words, she didn't move until she heard her front door open and close. Then, rolling onto her back, she reached for her sketchbook and stared at her work. She had to admit, drowsy as she was, one look at her concept and she knew she still liked it after putting space between her and it. But Atticus' opinion made her love it—so much so, she was half tempted to get up, get in her car and take a trip to Nashville to the only fabric store in Tennessee suited to fit her textile needs.

The more awake she became, the more she recognized the impulsivity of her desire. She sighed, hugging her sketches to her chest as she reminded herself she couldn't make final fabric choices until after she'd finished the collection. This made her want to get up and get to sketching; but when she sat up, Titan lifted his head and she knew she couldn't dive into work right away. She had a promise to make good on.

"Mama needs five minutes, then we'll get you leashed up, yeah?"

He responded by crawling in her lap and reaching for a kiss. Mitzi giggled, tilting her chin up so as to avoid his tongue across her mouth, then picked him up so she could get out of bed. Not surprisingly, it took her longer than five minutes to bundle up and make herself look like she hadn't just rolled out of bed, but Titan didn't seem to mind. They strolled around the neighborhood for an hour, as school buses came and went and people began to leave for work. Upon returning to her home, Mitzi fed her pup and then proceeded to get ready for what she hoped would be another productive day.

By nine she was fully dressed with a full mug of coffee in hand. By noon, she'd met with Gianna, her marketing partners, and

Adalynn in one video call after another. When her stomach alerted her to her growing hunger, she opened every cabinet, searched her fridge and her full pantry only to find she didn't have an appetite for anything she had lying around. It wasn't that she couldn't throw together something quick and edible; more like her mind was too crowded with other things to concentrate on such a task.

What Atticus said to her that morning had been festering inside of her all day. Inspired as he'd left her, she hadn't responded. Not to him. Not to herself. Now, she knew subconsciously she'd never be able to focus all that energy until she'd fully processed the extent of her feelings—and there was only one person in the whole world she could talk to about the man who made her feel crazy in the best possible way.

Without giving it a second thought, she grabbed her purse, her phone, and her dog—snagging her keys on her way out of the house. Fifteen minutes later, she pulled open the door of the salon and looked around for Nora. She wasn't at her station, and the other two hair stylists were busy with their own clients. Mitzi was just getting ready to ask one of them if they knew where her friend was when Nora came from the back with a basket full of freshly laundered towels.

"Hey, stranger. Called you yesterday, but I only got your voicemail. What are you doin' here?"

"Yeah. My phone was dead. There's actually a whole long story to go with that—a story I was hoping to tell you over lunch at Rock-N-Joe. Got an hour?"

Nora looked down at the basket in her hands and then smiled at Mitzi. "I think these towels can wait. My next appointment isn't until two. Let me grab my purse."

A minute later, they were walking around the center of The Square, Titan happily leading the way.

"So, what's up? Last I heard, you were goin' to Steele's to watch football Monday night. I thought I'd have an update by now. You been busy?"

"I've been busy, all right. Busy falling—like, Nora, I don't know if I've ever fallen this hard this fast over a guy before. It's making me feel a little crazy. Is that crazy?"

Nora laughed as they looked at one another. Serious as Mitzi was, she didn't bother trying to conceal her own smile.

"I mean it!"

"Okay, well, you were there when I fell for Lawson. It was the hardest fall I've ever had."

"Nora-Jean, we were fifteen. That was literally half our lives ago. We weren't smart enough back then to know better." Even as she said the words, the deepest part of Mitzi knew it was a ridiculous thing to say. It was no throw-away comment when Nora mentioned Lawson.

"We were young and dumb, sure, but we weren't stupid. I knew then just as much as I know now, which is there would never be another Lawson. And you, *you* knew what you wanted. You wouldn't let anyone call himself your boyfriend." Nora stopped a few paces away from the corner of the street and turned to face Mitzi. She popped one of her hips and took hold of her waist as she went on to say, "As a matter of fact, you've *always* known what you wanted. And maybe love has gotten the best of you in the past, but haven't we all experienced that?"

Mitzi shook her head in confusion. "I don't know what you're saying."

"I'm sayin', you guarded your heart against every boy you kissed in high school. Then when you met Drew, even when you started dating Nolan, you took your time allowing yourself to trust them, and not for nothin'."

"Exactly," Mitzi exclaimed, throwing her arm out to emphasize her sentiment. "I've been home, like, a month and Atticus and I have been—whatever we are—for a *second*, and already I can barely stop thinkin' about him. I even started designing an entire collection for my spring line that's inspired by him. I've never done that before. Not even when I was with Nolan, and he was a model! Oh, my god," she murmured, sweeping her fingers across her forehead. She blew out a sigh and continued toward the corner across the street from her new shop. "I really am going crazy."

"But you're feelin' inspired," said Nora as she followed Mitzi from one sidewalk to another. "And you're happy, right?"

Mitzi's feet slowed as her mind filled with memories from the last two nights. It was when she replayed the words he'd spoken between kisses against her forehead that she looked to Nora and admitted, "I spent the night at his place on Monday. Last night, he stayed at mine. I told you the other day he could kiss a girl stupid but...he touches me like no one ever has before. Like *I* inspire *him*. And when he looks at me—it's like he gets it. He gets that I'm still me, even though I've been away a while. I'm a designer of high-end streetwear that sells all over the world, but one of my favorite places in the world is this tiny little corner of it. And every minute I spend with him makes me want to be here more. He's amazing, Nora."

"So, *yes*. You *are* happy."

Mitzi nodded. "Yeah."

"Good. Focus on that. The crazy part? I don't think you can fall in love without goin' a little crazy in the process." As they arrived at their destination, Nora reached for the door, holding it open as she smirked at Mitzi and said, "Things keep goin' how they're goin', I might have to thank Steele for keepin' your ass here forever."

Mitzi scooped Titan in her arms as she crossed the threshold and hid her smile in a kiss she planted in her pup's hair. It felt crazy letting herself think about forever with the Steele who protected her hometown with a badge on his hip; but if there was real truth in what Nora said, maybe going crazy wasn't such a bad thing after all.

chapter sixteen

MITZI TOOK A PULL FROM the bottle of cold beer she'd just uncapped from the fridge. The fizzy pilsner glided over her tongue and raced down her throat, quenching her thirst and sending a zing of excitement toward her belly, still warm from the flame of passion Atticus lit there only a few moments ago. Naked under the button-up she'd swiped from off the floor, her bare feet guided her through the darkness of her home and toward the soft light coming from her bedroom. She stopped when she reached the threshold and propped her shoulder against the doorjamb, admiring the view she hadn't had in three nights.

While they'd spoken on the phone for at least a minute or two every day, Atticus barely had time to sleep in a bed at all, let alone under the sheets with her. With a stakeout on Wednesday, a late arrest on Thursday, and another lead that led to a fruitless raid on Friday—her man had been busy. He'd also been frustrated, with the perp he really wanted still evading him at every turn. Mitzi was half expecting her Saturday night would be spent on the couch with Nora and Evie when Atticus called and promised otherwise.

They'd finally gotten their date at Smithy's, and her Jimmy Choo's did not disappoint. It was safe to say, Atticus liked her in a tight dress and designer stilettos, which was why all of the above were still on the floor—precisely where he'd discarded them. Now, dressed only in the navy boxer briefs she'd helped him out of earlier, Atticus sat on the edge of the bed, his long legs allowing his bare feet to reach the floor with ease. He was a sight to behold—his solid frame of lean muscle accented by his autumn sun-kissed skin, still holding on even as winter grew closer and closer. His hair was a sexy mess, disheveled by the work of her own hands. The only thing about the picture he made she didn't like was his furrowed brow aimed at the phone in his hand.

"Is everything okay?" she murmured, hoping the answer wouldn't have him walking out her front door before the morning light.

"Yeah," he mumbled, his attention still trained on his screen.

Mitzi took another pull of beer. This time, as it made its way toward her belly, there was no zing of excitement; more like a sour taste of nervous anxiety.

"Baby?" she whispered.

His scowl still firmly intact, he shook his head, his thumbs constructing a written reply as he muttered, "Fitz and Ramirez are on patrol tonight. They thought they saw something that might help with my armed robbery case. Not sure it'll pan out; but I'll take what I can get, I guess."

"Do you have to go?"

She held her breath as he finished his text, then held it some more as he set the phone down on her nightstand and turned to look her way. It was the slow, handsome smirk which curled the corner of his mouth that encouraged her to breathe again.

"Damn, you're cute."

It was impossible for her to deny him a reaction in response to him denying her an answer. He was the ruler of perfect timing and one-liners.

"Careful, Atticus Steele—you keep bein' sweet to me, and I'll expect it all the time."

His smirk turned into a grin, causing her belly to flutter.

"Countin' on it. Come 'ere, pretty girl."

She did as she was told and closed the gap between them. When she was in reaching distance, Atticus did just that—taking hold of her waist as he guided her into the space between his legs. When he had her where he wanted her, he reached for the beer she grabbed for them to share and took a long pull. Mitzi smiled, knowing that meant he wasn't going anywhere.

"Put in enough overtime this week," he said after he swallowed. "Tonight's yours—and I'm not done with you yet."

Yeah, she was falling.

She was falling hard.

More than content with his answer, she circled her arms around his waist and leaned in for a kiss. It was a slow, lazy kind of kiss that lingered on until Atticus pulled away and said, "Come with me tomorrow."

"Come with you where?"

"Church. Dinner."

Mitzi jerked her head back a little, caught off guard by his request. "You mean—*Sunday* dinner?"

He chuckled, brought the beer bottle to his lips, then murmured, "Tomorrow is Sunday, Mitz."

Still trying to wrap her mind around what he was asking, she semi-repeated, "You want me to have Sunday dinner with you and your family?"

"Yeah, babe. That's what I'm sayin'."

Suddenly nervous, she slid her hands around to press against his chest. "Aren't those dinners, like, sacred?"

"Sacred? No. Tradition, yeah. So?"

"It's just—I remember the first time Nora was invited over to your parents' house for Sunday dinner. It was a big deal. Even after it became a regular thing for her to be there, it was always a big deal."

Atticus took another swig of beer before he switched the bottle from one hand to another and set it on the nightstand. With his hands free, he wrapped his arms around Mitzi and pulled her closer, looking her right in the eyes. "Babe—this thing between us, it's a big deal."

Mitzi's belly did that thing that made her feel like she'd just dropped from the top of a roller coaster, and her breath caught in her throat for a second. "You think so?" she breathed.

"You don't?" asked Atticus, a slight scowl returning to his brow.

"No, I do." She slid her hands up his chest and wrapped her arms around his shoulders. "I do. We—we've never said it."

"Well, now it's been said. So, you comin'?"

She opened her mouth to respond but then stopped when it dawned on her she was wearing his shirt and nothing else after two *really* great orgasms. It'd been a while since she'd been to church— even longer since she'd been to a Catholic mass. The Bates family was Protestant on the occasional Sunday, but especially on Easter and Christmas. While it certainly wasn't a secret that all the Steeles were Catholic, she was still naked underneath Atticus' shirt.

"Aren't Catholics...*against* birth control? And, by extension, everything we just got finished doing?"

Grinning, Atticus tightened his grip around her and replied, "I'm a practicing Catholic, babe, not a perfect one. Now are you comin' or what?"

Unable to deny the man behind that smile a second longer, she pressed up onto her tiptoes, touched her forehead to his and whispered, "Yeah. I'm comin'."

MITZI WOKE IN ATTICUS' arms the next morning. It was the first time they'd shared a bed and he wasn't already up, dressed, and on his way out the door when she peeled open her eyes. Much as she wanted to stay in bed and wade in and out of sleep with the man at her back, she knew she couldn't. Mass started at eleven and she wasn't going to be the reason Atticus was late.

When she moved to reach for her phone in order to check the time, his arms constricted around her. Clutching her mobile in her hand, she grinned when he buried his face in the back of her hair and mumbled, "Don't think so, pretty girl." His voice was deeper and rougher from sleep, and the sound of it sent a thrill down her spine.

Wanting to give in to his request, she hoped to find she'd woken earlier than she anticipated; but when she awakened her screen and saw it was nearly nine, she closed her eyes and announced, "Baby, I've got to get up. You keep me here much longer and we'll be late."

"And if I see to Titan, how much time does that buy me?"

Mitzi laughed as she rolled over until she was facing Atticus. His eyes were still closed, but as he adjusted his grip around her, there was no denying he was awake.

"Titan's easy. It's me who needs every minute I can get." She leaned in, brushed a soft kiss against his lips, and whispered, "Go back to sleep."

Rather than let her go, he pulled her closer and opened his eyes to half-mast. "Probably a dumb question, but is Titan comin' with us this afternoon?"

Mitzi smiled and whispered, "That an invitation?"

"Right. I need to stop by my place for a change of clothes. I'll just get ready there and come back to get you. I'll take the little guy with me and leave him there. It's closer. We'll swing by and pick him up after church."

"Okay. I'll pack his bag," she murmured happily, running her fingers through his mussed hair. "Now will you go back to sleep?"

"Wake me at ten?" he asked, his eyes already drooping closed.

"I can do that."

She kissed him softly once more and then sat up to get out of bed. This time, he let her go. On her way to the bathroom, she paused and looked back at him. In that moment, she understood exactly why he preferred to see her stretched out underneath the sheets on his way out the door.

During the hour Atticus was asleep, Mitzi managed to shower, moisturize, make a pot of coffee, prep Titan's backpack while he sniffed around the backyard, and blow-dry her hair. Shortly after ten, she stood at the door of her walk-in-closet with her mug still half-full and kissed her two guys goodbye. It felt surreal. While she knew everything didn't have to come with some grand meaning, it was hard denying the reality that she'd never let a man leave with her maltipoo—and yet, she trusted Atticus wholeheartedly.

Mitzi had to force herself to refocus. She downed a large gulp of coffee as she turned to survey her dress collection. She thought long and hard before deciding on one of her own creations. It was a dark teal, long-sleeved, maxi dress made with yards and yards of fine satin. It was designed to drape effortlessly down a woman's body with a skirt that billowed if she twirled. The V-neck cut at the front was formed by the wrap-design of the bodice, and the matching belt—if tied properly—cinched the dress at the waist and allowed for a generous, bow draped at the hip. The sleeves ballooned slightly above the cuffs, adding to the flowy nature of the garment.

With her dress picked out, it was easy for her to accessorize. She decided on a pair of simple, nude, pointed toe, four-inch heels, an assortment of gold necklaces, and small matching hoops for her ears. Forty minutes later, after she'd curled her hair, put on a full-face of makeup, found her way into her dress, and tucked her feet into her shoes, there was a knock at her front door. She was quick to put on a few last-minute rings before hurrying out of her closet. Her dress danced around her legs as she grabbed her phone, found her purse, then took a breath on her way to the door.

When she saw Atticus on her porch, dressed in a pair of gray slacks and a fantastic beige, slim-fit knitted sweater, she remembered exactly for what she'd spent all morning getting ready. Their relationship wasn't a secret. Even though they'd only been dating for a couple of weeks, they'd been seen together enough for rumors to spread. It didn't take much in Shelbyville. But the moment he walked her into that church, the rumors would become truth. This made Mitzi equal parts nervous and excited.

EVERY TIME SHE OPENED the door, he was reminded the prettiest woman in town was his. Every time. He wasn't ready to say it out loud, but he had every intention of making sure she never opened the door for anyone else ever again. She had been worth the wait and then some.

"I like that dress."

"Thank you. I made it myself," she replied, joining him on the porch.

Steele shook his head slightly, a small smile tugging at one side of his mouth. "Why am I not surprised?"

She winked up at him before turning to lock her door, and his smile grew as he shifted his attention down at his boots. Yeah. Mitzi Bates was home grown and pretty as could be. She was also exactly what he'd been waiting for.

It was a ten minute drive to St. William's, and the parking lot was almost full when Atticus pulled in. He spotted Lawson's truck near the back just as his brother started the climb out of the cab. Steele pulled in a couple spots down and tried to pretend he didn't notice Lawson staring his way as he walked around the back of the Chevelle to help Mitzi out of her seat. With her hand tucked inside of his, he started for the church, Lawson falling into step beside them.

"Mitzi," he greeted with a subtle dip of his chin.

"Hi, Lawson."

He shifted his gaze onto his brother, and they locked eyes before he asked, "You tell mom?"

Steele couldn't fight his sly grin as he replied, "What fun would that be?"

The Steeles had been occupying the same pew in the parish for about as long as Steele could remember. Sixth row back. Right side of the aisle. Upon their entrance, the pipe organ was already playing, signaling the start of the service would begin any moment. In spite of the music, the click of Mitzi's heels against the tiled floor marked time to their arrival. Justice—seated on the far side of the pew next to their mother—peeked back at them just as Lawson genuflected and crossed himself before occupying the empty seat next to their father. It was but a glance, yet Steele didn't miss the twinkle which shone in his sister's eyes as she fought a knowing smile.

He missed it when Gale looked their way, his attention focused on Mitzi as he signaled for her to take the spot next to Lawson. He let go of her hand only long enough to genuflect and cross himself. Upon filling the empty space beside Mitzi, he didn't think twice about taking her hand and lacing his fingers between hers. Keaton then leaned forward, caught his son's eye and offered him a playful thumbs up before nodding a friendly hello to Mitzi. She breathed a soft giggle and waved back in response before the organist went silent and the cantor took to the mic.

Over the course of the next hour, Steele held onto Mitzi, guiding her through the motions of the service. It'd been years since he'd brought a newbie to church, but he didn't mind playing teacher. He knew it wouldn't be long before she caught on all on her own.

"The mass is ended. Go in peace," proclaimed Father Milton.

"Thanks be to God," the congregation responded.

As always, the Steeles remained standing in their pew, singing the closing hymn long after the priest's procession. It wasn't until the organ sang the last note that they all returned their hymnals to their rightful place and made their way out of the church.

"Why Mitzi Bates, you sure are a sight for sore eyes. It's been a long time since I've seen you, but you've hardly aged a day. Just a pretty, young thing you are," said Gale as the family descended the front steps.

Mitzi smiled in his parents' direction as they all congregated out of the way. Her grip around his hand tightened, and Steele focused his attention down at her as she replied, "I was going to say the same thing about you, Mrs. Steele."

"Oh, that's just the magic of the salon you're seein'," she teased with a wave of her hand. "I'm grayer than a stormy sky under this chestnut dye."

Steele glanced at his mother, who was just as beautiful and regal as he'd always known her to be. She had the same shoulder-length haircut she'd been wearing for twenty-five years. The only makeup she ever wore was a little bit of mascara, a kiss of blush she said she needed to bring some color to her pale complexion, and her favorite light pink lipstick. At five-nine with a slim build, there wasn't a soul in town that didn't look at Gale and see Justice Steele twenty years down the road—sans tattoos, of course.

"My husband, on the other hand, somehow pulls off a head full of silver hair better than any man I know," she went on to say, patting Keaton on the arm she held onto.

"Not that you're at all biased," he replied with a wink.

Gale winked back and then aimed her smile at Steele. "And you, my dear, look quite handsome on her arm. I'd heard rumors about you two, but—"

"Okay, how about we move this compliment-fest to the house? I'm starving," interrupted Justice. She started to back her way to the parking lot, hiking her thumb over her shoulder, her brow raised in silent insistence. "They're together, obviously. And we all know Mitzi's comin' to dinner, because Steele will never hear the end of it if she doesn't. So, come on."

She didn't wait for anyone to follow her before she gave them her back and headed for her vehicle. Lawson cleared his throat, and Steele looked over just as he shoved both of his hands into his pockets and started after their sister. "I got this. See y'all at the house."

Gale frowned in that way she did when she was disquieted, peering over her shoulder as Keaton said, "Mitzi, you are more than welcome to join us for dinner, but it's only an obligation for one of you."

"We're right behind you, Judge," murmured Steele. "We just have to make a quick stop."

"In that case, I hope you like pot roast."

"Pot roast sounds great," said Mitzi.

"YOU'RE OKAY, BABY," MITZI cooed as Atticus got Titan situated in the backseat. "Mama's not going to hold you in this satin." She reached back and scratched behind his ears as he whined, obviously wanting to ride in her lap. "Lay down, Titan. We'll be there soon."

"How is he with other dogs?" asked Atticus as he closed himself behind the wheel.

Gasping in excitement, Mitzi asked, "Do your parents have a dog?"

"Yeah, babe," he chuckled, backing out of the driveway. "An old German pointer."

"Titan is gonna be so excited. He loves other dogs."

"Good." He threw a smile her way and then she saw it as his

thoughts shifted. Atticus sighed and said, "Listen, I'm sorry about Jay. Hopefully Lawson's got her straightened out by the time we get there."

"Atticus, you don't have to apologize for her. I wasn't offended."

"Maybe not, but it's like Judge said—you are welcome at our table."

"I know." Mitzi reached over to rest her hand on the inside of his thigh. "I also know Jay has nothing against us and she's having her heart tossed around by this Liam guy nobody seems to like. She's my friend, and she's hurting. No apologies are necessary."

Atticus paused a beat, glancing her way before he muttered, "You're all right, pretty girl. Think I'll keep you around."

Their drive was the leisurely kind one could only experience whilst headed toward the country. Keaton and Gale Steele lived twenty minutes from the heart of Shelbyville on what appeared to be at least a couple acres of land. The house Mitzi saw in the distance looked gorgeous even from afar. The closer they got, the more nervous she grew. The Steeles didn't come by strangers very often in their town—all of them embedded in a public service of some kind—which meant Mitzi's nerves were silly. That being said, pulling up to the house next to Atticus didn't feel like it did when she was a teenager, riding up the short driveway of a different address, squeezed into the cab of an old truck with Lawson and Nora.

"When did your parents move out here?"

"They bought the land right after Jay graduated high school. Had the house custom built a couple years later. Four bedrooms, five bathrooms, a garage big enough for all Judge's toys. Mom's been after all of us to hurry up and give her some grandkids so she can watch 'em play from out her kitchen window. We keep tellin' her, nobody told them to upsize their yard just when all of us were out of the house."

Mitzi laughed as she asked, "Do you want kids?"

"As many as I can stand."

Her eyes widened and she tried to keep her voice even when she followed-up with, "And how many might that be?"

Grinning in that handsome way she liked, Mitzi caught on to the fact that she hadn't feigned calm as well as she'd intended. "Three," he replied.

"Oh. Three's good."

"What about you? You want kids?"

"With the right partner, I think I could handle three," she murmured as they came to a stop behind a familiar, grey Chevy truck in the Steeles circle driveway.

Atticus put the Chevelle in park, smirked at Mitzi, then leaned across the distance between them and pressed a gentle kiss against her lips. "Good answer."

"If you two start makin' out in there, I'm totally tellin' mom."

Atticus shifted his gaze out the passenger side window as Mitzi turned in her seat to spot Jay standing a few feet away, her fists poised on either side of her hips.

"She really is a bullet in my ass," mumbled Atticus, making Mitzi laugh.

"Would you mind helping Titan out? I'll grab his leash and make sure he goes to the bathroom before we go inside."

"I'll take him out back, introduce him to Gavel."

Mitzi melted, pressing both hands over her heart as she murmured, "His name is Gavel? That's adorable."

"Judge always has thought himself clever. Come on, before Bullet loses what little patience she seems to have today."

Almost as soon as Atticus reached for his own door handle, Mitzi heard the latch at her door give way. She looked up at Jay, who managed to make an oversized burnt-orange sweater over a short, ruffled, cream, chiffon slip-dress and a pair of knee-high, suede leather boots look effortlessly stylish.

"Can I talk to you for a minute?"

"Yeah, of course," she insisted, gathering her skirt in order to exit the car.

"We'll meet you inside," said Atticus, making his way toward the house with Titan tucked in the crook of his arm.

Mitzi could only manage a nod. For the second time that day, she was transfixed by the sight of her man and her pup. Their bond was easy, in that way two chill guys could always get along, and she kind of loved it.

"Careful, there, Mitz. You might get a little drool on your dress," teased Jay.

Mitzi scrunched her nose, a laugh bubbling out of her as she focused her attention on her friend. "Sorry. I know he's your brother, but the only thing hotter than that man in that sweater is that man in that sweater holdin' my dog."

Smirking, Jay closed the passenger-side door of the Chevelle. "I'll let that slide, mostly because it's me who owes you an apology. Sorry if I was kind of a bitch earlier."

"Oh, don't worry about that."

Jay nodded toward the house. "I haven't seen him this into someone in a while. He seems happy, and you two look really good together."

"Thanks. He's...amazing. He makes me happy, too."

"Glad to hear it. So, we're cool?"

"Of course. Are *you* okay? Things with Liam, are they—?"

"Mitz, there's not enough wine in that house for me to be able to discuss Liam. Raincheck? Girls night soon?"

"I can live with that," Mitzi agreed with a smile and a nod. "Besides, it's about time I had our crew over to my place."

"Cool," Jay sighed as they both started for the house.

"Any advice for getting through my first Sunday dinner?"

"Oh, you'll be fine. Mom and Judge won't bite. We haven't had any plus ones at the table in a while. No doubt, they'll be on their best behavior."

"Does that mean I don't have to worry about your mom dropping hints about grandkids?"

Jay threw her head back and belted a belly laugh that was undeniably contagious. As they climbed the steps leading up to the wrap around porch at the front of the house, she caught her breath and replied, "Not a chance. You're hosed."

chapter seventeen

MITZI TIGHTENED HER LONG, knitted cardigan around her then cupped her steaming mug of coffee in both hands. It was early the next morning as she watched Titan roam about the yard. She took a slow, indulgent sip of her beverage, in no hurry to rush into the new day—too content to replay the previous one. Easy as it would have been to claim her favorite part of Sunday was waking up with Atticus, that wasn't the best part. What was even better was sitting down to dinner with him and his family.

It was obvious their weekly tradition held immeasurable value. There was something about their commitment to one another that was beautiful and rare. One day a week, come hell or highwater, they kept a promise to each other and showed up. Mitzi learned the only times when all five of them weren't together on a Sunday afternoon was when Lawson was deployed as an active duty marine. Even when Atticus and Lawson were playing ball in Knoxville, the Steeles made it work. Dinner wasn't always at

Keaton's table. He, Gale, and Jay made the drive north when it was more convenient; and Atticus drove down from Nashville every week when he was enrolled in the police academy.

Mitzi felt honored having a place-setting just for her. She understood in ways words could not express why Nora had insisted her place at the Steele table was a big deal every single time she sat down with them. For an hour and a half, they ate and talked and laughed with each other. Atticus, Lawson, and Jay also bickered and argued over whose turn it was to do the dishes—as if they were still kids living under their parents' roof. They were a family who loved each other and supported one another. They were a family who did life together, and it showed. They *knew* each other, and Mitzi envied them.

On the drive back into town, Atticus assured her his family was far from perfect. Not every dinner was jovial, and sometimes it felt more like an obligation than some of them wanted to admit. Apparently, a couple years back, Jay and Atticus had gotten into it and were barely on speaking terms for a month. He informed Mitzi, it made for awkward Sunday afternoons; but family dinner required everyone in the family to be there, so they endured the pain until they made up and got over it.

Now, as Mitzi breathed in the cool, November morning air, she thought about her own family. She wondered, had she not run off to New York, if they'd be different now than they were before. More united. More cohesive. Though, no matter how hard she tried, she couldn't imagine a scenario in which she could bite her tongue and ignore the man Trace was. Not to mention, every time he made a pass at her, it was somehow *her* fault. Scarlett's wedding had been the last straw. Regardless of the blame which belonged on her shoulders for the current state of her family's dynamic, she'd been right to stand up for herself.

Nevertheless, part of the reason she came back was because she missed *home.* She missed being a part of the Bates family.

She missed the ease and comfort found amongst the people she'd known her whole life. Spending the afternoon at the Steele residence only reinforced what she knew she was missing. Hard as it was to admit, if she was ever going to get back the good parts she ran away from, she was going to have to make a truly concerted effort.

By the time Titan was finished with his business in the yard, Mitzi made up her mind to turn her hopes into actions that very day. She was mature enough to know, no matter how hard she tried, she, Scarlett, and Dolly would always have their differences which would lead to bickering and disagreements. Still, the unspoken grudges and poorly healed wounds needed fixing, and the only place to start was with Scarlett. As soon as she returned to the warmth of the indoors, Mitzi checked her calendar. Her morning was light, and her afternoon was flexible.

She had enough time to get ready for the day before her weekend sales report call with Gianna. She then checked in with Adalynn to plan the rest of the week. A few minutes before noon, on her way out the door, she hopped on a call with Dax to verbally approve the final draft of his security system proposal. As she was pulling out of her neighborhood, headed for the Whitfield home, she put work out of her mind. Presumptuous as it was to assume her sister had no lunch plans that day, she thought a little spontaneity might make her proposal that much more fun.

When she reached her destination, Mitzi ran her fingers through her hair and checked her lipstick in the rearview mirror before she exited her vehicle and headed for the front door. She could hear the sound of the bell as it reverberated off the walls inside, and she hoped the house wasn't completely empty. She was getting ready to ring a second time when she heard her sister's approaching footsteps.

"Hi," Scarlett greeted, a slight frown pulling at her manicured eyebrows. "What are you doin' here?"

"Are you busy? I thought maybe we could go to lunch."

Obviously taken aback by the suggestion, Scarlett only stared at Mitzi for second. "Did somethin' happen? Do you need somethin'?"

"No," Mitzi breathed through a smile. "Letty, when's the last time you and I did anything just you and me? Can you remember? Because I can't."

Again, Scarlett hesitated, but Mitzi didn't back down. Finally, her sister nodded and said, "I can be ready in ten minutes. I've got a couple errands I need to run this afternoon before the kids are out of school, so I was plannin' on bein' out anyway."

"Okay, great. Name the place, and I'll meet you there?"

"What about Legends? They've got a great cobb salad."

"Yeah, sure. I'll leave now and grab us a table."

"See you there."

Thirty minutes later, the two women were seated across from one another at a booth in the quiet restaurant. After their server took their order and collected their menus, Mitzi pulled in a deep breath, folded her hands atop the table, and focused her gaze on Scarlett. She thought about what it felt like to sit across from Jay the previous afternoon. She remembered the easy way Jay bantered with Lawson, like nothing had changed between them since high school.

"Do you remember when we were younger? When daddy would drop us off at that ice cream parlor in The Square whenever he had to check in at the dealership on a Saturday afternoon?"

"Of course, I do. Charlotte and Brooks love it there."

"God, how did we get here?" Mitzi laughed on a sigh. "We were them, once. Now we're grown women. You've got a family, I've got a business. Back then, being a grown-up seemed so far in the distance."

"Bein' free from responsibility was fun while it lasted, but I prefer my life now. What's better than havin' daddy give us cash for ice cream is doing the same for my kids. Seein' them get excited over somethin' so small—it's a joy only a parent could ever understand. Maybe one day you'll know what that's like."

"I hope so."

"Do you? No offense, but it seems your life is all about Sterling Thread. It's like you said, time can get away from us. I get it that your work is important to you, but you left when you were nineteen. You were in a huge city. You're beautiful and talented and, yet, you were more worried about your talent than your biological clock. You'll be thirty-one soon, and it's like you're still the same stubborn girl you were all those years ago. Determined not to fall in love."

"That's not true. Sure, I've been chasing after my dream relentlessly. But I've let myself fall in love with someone other than fashion design. More than once. Most of us don't find our husbands at fifteen."

"Maybe not," Scarlett acquiesced as she reached for her iced tea. "But you're not gettin' any younger."

"And what about you?" Something in Mitzi's gut told her not to take the bait, but she couldn't help it. She resented the way Scarlett and Dolly looked at her—like they couldn't simply be proud of her for her life choices. "You don't have babies at home anymore. You're a wife and a mother. A great one, even. But what about *you?* What about when you're in that big house all day by yourself? What then? Eventually, Charlotte and Brooks are going to grow up and move out. Then who will you be?"

"Just because you went off and made a name for yourself and I stayed here to start a family doesn't mean my life lacks meaning and purpose. I'll be fine, Mitz. I may not own my own business, but I have a brain, too."

Mitzi leaned back in her chair. She felt like she was fighting a losing battle, and they hadn't even been served their main course.

"I don't want to argue with you. In fact, that's the opposite of what I wanted when I invited you to lunch in the first place. You and I are different. That much is obvious. That doesn't mean we can't get along. We're sisters. It used to be so much easier than this."

Scarlett opened her mouth to respond just as their server arrived with their salad orders. After they each murmured their thanks, silence fell between them as they unrolled their silverware and spread their napkins in their laps. Not sure what to say, Mitzi speared her fork into the bed of lettuce on her plate.

"Sometimes, when Trace has a vacancy in one of his properties, if he's havin' trouble movin' it, I'll stage the space. I've done it a few times. There's a storage facility not too far from his office where all the items I've accumulated over the past couple of years gets stored. It's happened before that the new tenant wants to keep my design, and Trace will up the cost of rent so they can have a fully furnished office space."

"Letty," Mitzi breathed, in awe of what she'd just heard. "I had no idea. That's amazing."

"It's not exactly a career. He doesn't need me to do it very often, but it's somethin' I enjoy."

"I think it's great. Given what you've done with your home, I bet there's not a space you couldn't fill beautifully."

"Thanks."

Scarlett offered her sister a smile before she took a bite of her lunch, and Mitzi started to relax a little. What she'd shared had been an olive branch, and Mitzi knew it was her turn to offer one of her own.

"Atticus—er, Steele and I, we're still seeing each other."

"So I've heard."

"Yeah, that's not surprising," she replied lightheartedly. "Actually, things are getting serious between us."

"Oh? That seems fast."

"I thought so, too, at first," Mitzi agreed as she watched Scarlett take another bite. "I didn't come back with my heart set on finding someone. He took me by surprise. I know you weren't sure of him when I first mentioned my interest, but he's an amazing guy."

Scarlett nodded as she finished chewing, her eyes studying Mitzi all the while.

"I never doubted his kindness. He's got a reputation in this town. A respected one. I'm glad you think he's a good guy. I just— I know his ex. He did a number on her after things ended between them. She moved to Lynchburg to get away from him."

Mitzi pushed her salad around with the tip of her fork as she tried to keep herself from getting defensive. "The way he tells it, they both made mistakes. They weren't right for each other. Simple as that."

"Be careful. It's all I'm sayin'," she said with a shrug. "A man who looks like him with a job like his? Around here, it's so obvious the way women fall at his feet, givin' him a hero's complex. He might be an amazing guy, but he's also a heartbreaker. I don't want you to be one of his victims."

Unable to squelch her exasperation, Mitzi coughed out an incredulous laugh. "You're kidding, right? A few minutes ago, you accused me of not havin' my priorities straight—like I'm going to run out of time to fall in love and start a family of my own. Then when I tell you there's this guy I'm fallin' for, you tell me I should be careful? That I shouldn't put myself out there because he might break my heart?

"You don't even know him anymore. You just assume you do because of the rumors around town. Which is *really* ironic coming from you."

"Excuse me? What's that supposed to mean?"

"How many rumors have you ignored about Trace?"

Scarlett's spine straightened as a scowl creased her forehead. "I don't know what you're talking about."

"Oh, please. Talk about me being a victim—I know I'm not making things up when I see the way Trace looks at other women. I know I'm not because he's looked at *me* the same way. Considering what happened at your wedding—your *wedding*—I honestly can't believe you would allow him to hire that secretary he's got at the office. And just how many secretaries has he had in the last ten years?"

"How *dare* you?" hissed Scarlett.

"You're a smart woman, Letty. I know you've seen it. I know you've let him get away with it."

"You don't know anything," she declared as she dropped her fork. "Trace loves me. He chooses me. Twenty years we've been together. *Twenty.* So don't talk to me about what you know—because you're wrong." She shook her head as she reached for the napkin in her lap and stood to her feet. She dropped the cloth on top of her unfinished salad and reached for her purse as she went on to say, "Whatever your opinion of my husband, he's my choice, and you have no right to judge me for it."

Mitzi watched as Scarlett stormed out of the restaurant with her head held high. As soon as her sister was out of sight, she looked down at her half-eaten lunch, for which she no longer had an appetite. Her heart sank as she replayed the last five minutes. Needless to say, her plan hadn't gone as well as she'd hoped.

Even though she wasn't sure whether or not their server had heard their argument, Mitzi was still embarrassed when he returned to the table. She asked for the check and was quick to pull out her card in order to cover the bill. Once the transaction was complete, she didn't linger but made her way out to her vehicle where she sat with her thoughts behind the wheel.

Part of her was angry with Scarlett. She hated the way her sister needed to be right about everything. It frustrated her how she labeled Atticus as some bad guy in disguise, as if her own husband's flaws didn't exist. Another part of her wasn't angry so much as it was disappointed. The rift which existed between them was easier to work around when she was a thousand miles away. Now only ten miles separated them, but the chasm seemed to stretch on and on, making it impossible to cross and find solid ground.

Too irritated to go home, and certain she wouldn't be productive with her mind in such a state, she started her car and pointed it toward the center of town. It didn't take her long to reach her destination. For the second time that day, she found herself knocking on a door, hoping someone was on the other side.

"Hey," greeted Nora through a grin. Her hair was piled on top of her head in a messy bun, and she had a pencil tucked behind her ear. This was all the proof Mitzi needed to know her friend was spending her day off writing music. "Last I checked, you've still got a key. You could have just come in."

"If you're in the zone, I can go. Your quiet moments are few and far between."

Nora made a face, silently informing Mitzi she was being ridiculous, and then opened the door wider. "Get in here. Somethin's up. What is it?"

"I went to Sunday dinner with the Steeles yesterday," she started to explain as she entered, headed straight for the couch.

"Wow," said Nora. She closed them inside but remained standing at the door, her hand poised on the knob. "That's a big deal. And, not that I was worried, but clearly confirmation Steele reciprocates your feelings whole hog. How was it?"

"Everything you made it out to be and more."

"Yeah. I'll bet."

"Seeing them all together, it made me jealous."

Finally coming unstuck from her spot at the door, Nora made her way onto the cushion next to Mitzi. Bringing her legs up and crossing her ankles, one of her knees propped against the back of the couch, she settled in, silently asking for more.

"They're so close with one another. It's one thing for a family to be like that when everyone still lives under the same roof. It's another thing entirely when their lives go different directions, and yet they make it work."

"And you wish your family was like that," Nora observed.

"Or something like that."

"MB, have you considered they're the exception, not the rule?"

Mitzi sighed and leaned her head back as she let her eyes fall closed. "I wish I would have thought of that before I invited Scarlett to lunch with me."

"Is that where you're comin' from?"

"Yeah. At first, it was fine. I thought we could just spend some time together. But—we got into it, like we always seem to do, and she walked out."

"You knew this part of comin' home was always gonna be hard."

She opened her eyes in search of Nora's and admitted, "Yes. You're right."

"As an only child, I don't feel particularly qualified to give you advice; but my guess is, all you can do is try again."

Mitzi groaned. "You should thank your lucky stars you're an only child."

"You don't mean that. Hard as things might be between you two, you love Scarlett."

She scowled playfully as she demanded, "Stop being right."

Nora laughed before checking the time on her phone. "Speaking of only children, I've got to go grab mine from Aunt Darlene in a half hour—but I'm all ears until then if you want to vent some more."

"Thanks. I'm okay. We don't have to talk about it anymore."

"What about Sunday dinner? Do I get to know how that came about?"

Mitzi smiled as the memory came rushing to the forefront of her mind. She gave Nora the abbreviated version then summarized the morning leading up to the big event. "I've always prided myself on being a good one to take home to the parents. Southern manners and all that. But you should have seen the look on Gale's face when she heard me call Atticus by his name. It was like I'd hung the moon."

"The fact that he lets you call him that says a whole lot about how *he* feels about *you*. I'm sure she loves that for him—which, by extension, means major points for you." Nora's eyes lost focus as she continued, "That woman has a heart of gold. All she's ever wanted for her kids was for them to find the same kind of happiness and love she found in Keaton. I always admired that about her."

Mitzi watched her friend for a moment, a slight pang of regret striking a nerve in her belly. Nora rarely wanted to talk about it, but Mitzi didn't need to hear the words to understand losing Lawson wasn't *just* about losing the man. Even though her friendship with Jay was still intact and the relationship she had with Atticus was on good terms, it all paled in comparison to the whole package. What was worse was that neither of them had moved on. Not really, anyway.

"I'm told it's been a while since a plus one has come to dinner. Atticus brought Faith, until that ended. Jay has never brought anyone. And Lawson…Lawson hasn't brought anyone since you."

Nora shook her head slightly, as if clearing the fog from her mind, and forced a smile. "Jay was never particularly fond of Steele's ex. If I remember correctly, the two of them butted heads over her pretty hard a couple times. In the end, turns out she was right."

"She always liked you," Mitzi goaded.

"Come on, MB. We both know I screwed that up and I can't take it back."

"Maybe not, but it's been five years, and he's still not bringing anyone else to Sunday dinner."

"Mitzi Belle…don't. Please. It's not just me anymore. I've got my own plus one to think about."

"I know, but—"

"Hey, I'm *so* happy for you. I really am. Steele is a good one, and so are you. I don't believe he could have chosen better. I hope there are many more Sunday dinners in your future. You don't have to worry about me. I'm okay. Great, even. And Lawson—Lawson can take care of himself."

Much as she wanted to belabor the point neither of them had moved on for a reason, Mitzi got Nora's message loud and clear. As she bit her tongue, tucking her argument away for safe keeping, she promised herself she wouldn't give up. If anyone deserved a happily-ever-after, it was Nora.

"That just leaves Jay. I still don't know very much about Liam, but I've heard enough to join the club of people who don't like him. Which reminds me—Jay and I talked about having another girls' night soon. My place this time. Think Darlene and Wayde might be up for a sleepover with Evie Friday night?"

"Friday? No plans with *Atticus?*"

"He can have me any other night he wants," she replied with a wink. "Friday's for the girls. You in?"

"Is my name Nora-Jean?"

Mitzi grinned. "Then we're on. I'll let everyone know."

chapter eighteen

MITZI SENT OUT A MASS text to Nora, Jay, Billie, and Reese before Nora left to pick up Evie and Mitzi headed home. By the time she pulled into the garage, she'd gotten confirmation from everyone they were free on Friday and looking forward to a night in at Mitzi's. After getting greeted by an excited Titan, her favorite and most loyal companion, the emotional impact of her foiled lunch with Scarlett had subsided. Disappointed as she still was, she was also calm enough to rationalize her issues with her sister were not going to get solved in one day. She had other business to attend to.

After checking and responding to a round of emails, Mitzi gathered her sketchbook and pencils in hopes of finishing the last of her menswear spring line collection. She had nine pieces she loved, with a pretty good sense of fabric selection, but she wouldn't know for sure until she was done and in the store. With every passing day, the itch to touch and feel the textiles she had in mind grew more intense. This truth was what helped her focus for the rest of the afternoon. It also didn't hurt how every piece she dreamed up, she pictured how it might look on a tall, handsome detective she was claiming as hers.

Her stomach started to growl as the sun started to set, and Mitzi was reminded how she hadn't finished her lunch. With no desire to relive the reason *why*, she shoved aside the memories and focused her attention on making an early dinner, instead. Her head still in a creative fog, trying to reimagine an idea she knew could be better, her meal ended up being far from extravagant. Nevertheless, the baked chicken and steamed vegetables she threw together satisfied her hunger and fueled her mind for a couple more hours of work.

It was nearly eight o'clock when she held her sketchbook out in front of her and tilted her head as she studied the trench coat she'd finally managed to get on paper the way she wanted. Gently gnawing on her bottom lip, she squinted and imagined a similar design but with a few feminine touches for the woman's line. She was getting ready to turn to a fresh page when a knock sounded at her door. Titan, who was curled up with his head rested on Mitzi's thigh, turned to look in its direction as he barked softly.

Before Mitzi got up to see who it was, she reached for her phone, discarded on her coffee table. Aside from a text she hadn't noticed from Nora, there were no other notifications. Another knock sounded as she climbed off the couch, Titan trailing her toward the front entryway. One glance through the peephole confirmed her visitor was exactly who she hoped it would be.

"One of these days, you're gonna drop by and I'm gonna be out with my other boyfriend," Mitzi joked as she opened the door.

Atticus, who stood with his hands buried in the pockets of his slacks, offered her no more than a half-hearted smirk. Mitzi gave him a proper once over, noting his sleeves were rolled up to his elbows, the tie he wore around his neck was loosened, and his collar was undone. His hair looked like it'd seen a lot of his fingers, and his eyes appeared tired.

"I was only teasing," she murmured, joining him on the porch.

"I know, babe. Sorry. Long day."

He leaned down for a kiss, and Mitzi tilted her head back to receive it. As he straightened, she circled her arms around his waist, pressing into him as she asked, "Have you eaten? I made dinner and I've got leftovers. It's nothing fancy, but if you're hungry..."

"I'm starving."

"Okay." She pushed up onto her tiptoes and puckered her lips. Atticus didn't deny her, which brought a smile to her face as she insisted, "Come in. I'll get you a beer and heat you some dinner. You can tell me about your day."

Mitzi let him go, turned to head inside, and made a b-line for the fridge. She had one beer left from a six-pack that had been hanging around since the weekend of her move. As she popped the cap, she made a mental note to start a list of things she'd need to stock-up on for girls' night—booze topping the list.

"So, you're just now leaving work?" she asked, handing Atticus the cold brew.

"Yeah. Thank you." He took a long pull from the bottle then sat in one of the barstools on the opposite side of the counter.

Mitzi pulled out the leftovers, pausing to look at her man when he didn't say more. "Baby, this food's not free. Talk to me."

The same half-hearted smirk tugged at the corner of his mouth, this time joined by a tired, clipped laugh. Atticus shook his head and replied, "The intel Fitz and Ramirez got on Saturday was good. There's chatter. Something's goin' down—but I don't know when or where. I should be back at the station. I shouldn't even be thinkin' about sleep until I can figure this shit out, but the dots just aren't connecting." He sighed, brought his beer to his lips and whispered a curse before he took another pull.

Mitzi's hands moved slowly, her focus divided between her task and Atticus. She'd never seen him this frustrated before.

She remembered the night he caught this particular case and the morning after. He'd been distracted and irritated, but this was different. With every passing day, his patience was beginning to wane.

"You were the one to catch this guy the first time, right? You'll catch him again."

"The question is when. Before he strikes again or after? It just pisses me off how he's outsmartin' me. He's a rat who hides in holes, not a mastermind."

"The first time you caught him, he didn't know what it was like to be behind bars. Now he does. I don't for a second think he's smarter than you, but he's probably smarter than he was."

Atticus grunted his agreement but offered nothing more as Mitzi put his plate in the microwave. While she waited for the timer to sound, she thought about all *Detective Steele* had shared. A week ago, there were no details on the tip of his tongue he was willing to let loose. She wondered just how bad the situation was if now he couldn't keep everything on his mind to himself.

"This...*chatter* you've been hearing? Should I be worried? About you or, I don't know. Billie, maybe? I mean, I know this guy usually sticks to the outskirts of town, but—"

"Hey, no. No. Listen to me," he insisted, extending his arm across the counter, turning his palm face up. Mitzi accepted his invitation and placed her hand in his. "I don't want you to worry. I shouldn't have—"

"Atticus, I want you to be able to talk to me. Your job is tough. Tougher than anyone in town wants it to be. I might not understand the weight you carry, but if we're going to do this—I don't want to be in the dark. I want to support you anyway I can."

"Appreciate you sayin' that, pretty girl, but I'm not the kind of man who's gonna burden you with my shit. I don't want you worryin' all the time."

"And I hear you, but I kind of think dating a detective comes standard with some measure of worry. I'll get used to it. Besides, I'm not the kind of woman who's going to let you shoulder the world all on your own. Those kinds of partnerships never last, and I've got my hopes set on us."

Atticus stared at her for a long moment. Seconds before the microwave sounded, he turned on his seat and tugged on Mitzi's hand. Smiling, she followed his pull until she was standing in the space between his legs. With his opposite hand, cool from the beer he'd been holding, he cradled the back of her neck, keeping her where he wanted her as he brought his mouth to hers.

He kissed her hard and deep, causing her to almost forget all about his dinner, until the microwave beeped a second time. "Baby," she muttered between kisses, not the least bit bothered when he didn't stop. "Your dinner. It'll get cold."

"Let it."

Draping her arms around his neck, she breathed, "Okay."

A HALF AN HOUR LATER, Mitzi occupied the stool next to Atticus. She folded one bare leg over the other, her pants tossed over a chair at her dining room table, along with her shirt, her bra, Atticus' tie, and the undershirt she helped him out of in a wild, unexpected frenzy. She couldn't contain her coy smile as she rested her chin on her shoulder, covered in the button-up which belonged to the man beside her. He was finally eating his twice heated dinner, his chest naked, his belt and his pants still undone. Somehow, he managed to look sexy and not sloppy, and Mitzi found herself wanting more and looking forward to later.

"How is it?" she asked, reaching over to trace her fingertips across his lower back.

Looking her way, he replied, "Hits the spot."

Mitzi's smile grew, loving how she didn't know whether he was talking about her food or her touch. She didn't ask for clarification, satisfied to see the mischievous spark in his eyes. The case weighing him down upon his arrival had been shoved into some far corner of his mind. For the moment, he was all hers, and she had every intention of holding onto him for as long as she could.

"How was your day?" he inquired before taking another bite.

Mitzi's smile began to fade as her most recent memories made way for darker ones.

"Looks like I'm not the only one who needs to unload. What happened?"

She drew in a deep breath and blew out a heavy sigh before she answered, "Scarlett and I went to lunch. We got into it, and neither of us actually finished our order."

"Sorry to hear that."

"Yesterday..." Mitzi hesitated, a frown creasing her brow. "Yesterday, you mentioned there was a time when you and Jay went through a rough patch."

"Yeah. Most days, she's a pain in my ass. Always has been. But for those few weeks? She didn't bug me at all. It sucked."

"What'd you two fight about?"

"Faith."

Giggling softly, she murmured, "Care to elaborate?"

"It was a couple months before she and I broke up. She and Jay never really got along. Jay had some things to say about my relationship I wasn't ready to hear. We fought. But, in the end, she was right."

"Are you sayin' Jay triggered your breakup?"

"No. Faith triggered our breakup. Jay was just lookin' out for me. As her older brother, I didn't think it was her place. As the bullet in my ass, she didn't care what I thought. Why?"

Absentmindedly stroking his back, she confessed, "Sometimes it feels like Scarlett and I have been walkin' on egg shells for years. It's like we can't talk to each other without comparing our lives to one another, like we're in a competition. We're sisters. Maybe women just can't help it—but I don't want to fight with her. I want what your family has. It just seems so easy."

"Babe, you talk about playin' the comparison game with Scarlett, and you're gonna turn around and compare your relationship with her to *my* relationship with *my* sister?"

Mitzi considered what he said, scowled when she realized he had a point, then groaned as she leaned toward him and pressed her forehead to his shoulder.

"For the record, every relationship can't be easy. Sometimes the most important ones are the hardest. If you want things with Scarlett to get better, you've got to work at it."

"I tried," she pouted, lifting her head in order to seek out his gaze.

A lopsided grin curled the corner of his mouth as he replied, "Mitz, sounds like your problems can't be solved over one lunch."

She narrowed her eyes at him, playfully irritated by the way he'd managed to extract the same thought she had earlier from the rational part of her brain. "I don't want you to be right."

Atticus chuckled as he leaned toward her and pressed a kiss against her forehead. "You care, and that's admirable. Give it time."

When he shifted his attention back onto his plate, Mitzi got lost in her thoughts for a moment. She never considered herself to be an impatient person. Everything she'd worked so hard to build required the investment of time. Countless hours and years of dedication. It was obvious the same would hold true for the repairs that needed to be made within her family. Everyone held their own share of blame for all the scars they bore. Mitzi was ready to own up to her part; but she was beginning to wonder if the same could be said for everyone else.

She was pulled from her thoughts at the soft sound of a vibrating phone. Her spine straightened when Atticus took another bite before reaching in his pocket for the ringing device. He didn't look at her, but she knew to brace for what might happen *after* the call when he curved a hand around her bare thigh the same time he swiped his thumb across the screen to answer.

"Lieutenant," he greeted, matter-of-factly. He listened intently for a few seconds and then replied, "Yeah. On my way."

Disappointment settled in Mitzi's belly, and she knew the smile she forced when he finally sought out her gaze wouldn't be bought. Even though she hadn't planned on seeing him that night, now that she had him at her kitchen counter, she wasn't ready to see him go. He disconnected his call and slid the phone back in his pocket, all the while keeping his gaze locked with hers.

He gave her leg a gentle squeeze, his voice low and tender when he said, "Swear to you, I didn't come over here to scratch an itch and fill my stomach. Sorry, pretty girl. Duty calls."

"It's okay," she murmured with a nod.

Atticus studied her closely, his slight scowl an indication he wasn't sure if he believed her.

Appreciative of his concern, her fake smile warmed into an authentic one as she reached for either side of his face. "I mean it. It's okay. You've got a case to close."

"I get this shit off my desk, my load gets lighter, and soon you'll be sick of me droppin' by and spoilin' your plans."

"Lookin' forward to it."

He leaned toward her in response, brushing a kiss against her lips. "Thanks for dinner."

"You're welcome."

Atticus kissed her once more. When he pulled away, she let him go. He scooped the last of his dinner into his mouth before he stood to fasten his pants closed. Smirking her way, he reminded her, "Babe—I'm gonna need that."

She looked down at herself, smiled, then met his eyes. "Right. Give me just a sec."

Mitzi gathered the pieces of her discarded outfit and hurried to her bedroom. Rather than getting fully dressed, she tossed the clothes into the hamper she kept in her closet and grabbed her short, pale pink, satin, kimono robe. She fastened the sides closed with a large bow tied at her right hip, and then folded Atticus' shirt over her arm. She was halfway to the door when she glanced toward her bed, causing her feet to slow to a stop. While it was true Atticus had to deal with work just then, such a reality didn't have to mean they slept alone that night.

Mitzi paused and thought over her idea for only a second before she walked to her dresser and plucked the key out of her trinket tray. Atticus was discarding his plate in the sink when Mitzi returned to the kitchen. He turned to face her as she handed him his shirt, and she watched him shrug it on, all the while palming the token of her affection as she tried to find the right words to say.

"I don't know how long I'll be at work. Might be pretty late, so I'll call you tomorrow."

"Okay. But if it is late—or even if it's not—and you don't want to climb into an empty bed tonight, you don't have to," she assured him, holding open her palm.

He quirked an eyebrow in surprise. "You're givin' me a key to your place?"

Recognizing his question was obviously rhetorical, Mitzi said nothing in reply.

When he was done buttoning up his shirt, he rested his hands on his hips and stated, "That's no small gesture."

"Baby," she began, taking a step toward him as a grin spliced across her face. She watched as his eyebrow dropped, his mouth mirroring hers in a smile. "This thing between us—it's a big deal."

Rather than take hold of the key, he took hold of Mitzi, wrapping an arm around her waist as he pulled her against his chest. "Yeah?"

"You think this *key* says something? Yesterday, I let you leave this house with my dog. If that's not a big deal, I don't know what is."

Atticus chuckled as he leaned in for a kiss. His lips still pressed to hers, he extracted the key from her hand, pocketing it as he straightened.

"Go catch a bad guy," she whispered.

"Yes, ma'am."

THE NEXT MORNING, WHEN Mitzi crawled out of sleep, it wasn't until she reached for her phone that she remembered the last thing she hoped for before she fell asleep. Upon seeing no missed text messages or calls, she turned to examine the other half of the bed and found only Titan, curled up atop her duvet. Before she could feel disappointment, unease took residence in the forefront of her mind. She wasn't concerned by the fact that Atticus hadn't taken her up on her offer to lay his head next to hers at the end of the night—it was *why* he hadn't.

She sat up and pulled her fingers through her hair as she stared down at her phone. Her stomach twisted in a knot as it dawned on her this was the first time she felt truly unsettled about where Atticus was and what he was doing. The deeper the roots of her feelings grew for him, the more his well-being mattered to her. The previous night was not the first or even the second time her man had left her alone in order to chase a criminal. Small as Shelbyville was, Mitzi was beginning to understand, crime was everywhere and Atticus would have more nights at the station than she might like.

Running her teeth over her bottom lip, she contemplated whether or not to text him. Real and honest as their relationship was, she didn't want to be *that* girlfriend, checking in on him unnecessarily. Neither did she want him to believe she wasn't thinking and *worrying* about him while he was knee deep in a case. Suddenly, and irritatingly, her decision to text or not to text felt like a game she didn't want to play.

Before she could make up her mind, Titan made his way into her lap. When he tilted his head back, brushing his wet nose against the underside of her chin, Mitzi tossed aside her phone and snuggled her pup in her arms.

"I think you're on to something, Titan," she cooed, kissing the top of his head. "Actions speak louder than words, don't they?" He licked her arm, as if in reply, and her decision had been made. "Let's get you outside. Mama's got to get ready."

Rather than joining Titan in the chilly, morning air with a cup of coffee, she kept an eye on him from the back door's window while rearranging her schedule for the day. With her intended destination putting her near The Square, she decided it was good a time as any to check in at the shop to see what kind of progress had been made in the last week. She assumed not much, as the required materials might still be in transit, but with any luck, she'd catch Palmer on-site. Even though it was a few months out, Mitzi was looking forward to having someplace to go to work other than her living room couch or dining room table. Fortunately, she was almost ready to put her sewing room to good use.

With her calendar up-to-date, she let Titan inside and then hurried back to her room to get ready. The weather inspired her outfit choice of the day. Before hopping in the shower, she laid out a pair of distressed, black jeans, a plain, white tank top, and her red and black, triple breasted plaid blazer. In an effort to keep her look ultra-casual chic, she opted for white sneakers to complete the outfit.

After she'd washed and moisturized from head to toe, she styled her hair in a short, low ponytail and put on a full face of makeup. Her lipstick of choice was a dark, matte red. She cuffed the sleeves of her blazer and accessorized with an assortment of jewelry which classed up her ensemble. A few rings, a couple bracelets, a dangling necklace, and a couple stud-earrings later, she was overdue for a cup of coffee.

But first—donuts.

With Titan in tow, she set out for her first destination. After she walked out of the small, local donut shop she got an even *better* idea. An additional stop and fifteen minutes later, she was parked in front of Rock-N-Joe, hoping she'd missed the early morning rush.

"Titan, you be good and stay right there, okay?" she insisted, looking him right in the eyes. "You can have a treat when I get back, but you have to stay right there, okay baby? The donuts aren't for you, sweet boy."

She stared at him a second longer, intent on sending a clear message, and then she hurried inside. It was a few minutes after nine, and Mitzi smiled to herself in relief when she found only a couple people ahead of her in line with Billie manning the cash register. There was hardly any wait at all before it was her turn to place an order.

"Hey, how you doin'?" she greeted, her tone more cautious than chipper.

"I'm fine..." said Mitzi hesitantly. "How are *you* doing?"

Billie narrowed her eyes studiously before she murmured, "You haven't heard."

"Haven't heard *what?*"

"Have you been by your shop this mornin'?"

Mitzi's stomach dropped and a rising sense of anxiety made her heart rate pick up speed. "Billie, just tell me what happened."

She drew in a deep breath and blew it out in a huff, reaching up to pull her hair away from her face as she continued to stare at Mitzi. It was quiet obvious she didn't want to be the bearer of bad news. The longer it took her to speak, the more nervous Mitzi became.

"Faye's shop got hit last night. News hasn't broken about who did it or why, but everyone in The Square is shaken up this mornin'."

"Wait, what? When did this happen?" she asked, even though she intrinsically knew the answer. Before Billie could confirm her suspicions, she was already questioning why Atticus hadn't told her.

"I think it was between eight and nine. Rumor has it, the perp wasn't expectin' anyone to be there. What message he was tryin' to send or what he thought he'd find in Faye's till is beyond me. Obviously, she's one of the busiest shops in The Square—but her cakes aren't cheap, and people don't pay with cash like they used to."

"Oh, my god, is Faye okay?"

Suddenly, Mitzi didn't feel like stopping by her store anymore. Flashbacks from her own break-in tried to cloud her mind with fear, but she willed herself to stay in the present.

"Faye's fine. It was Taylor who was workin' late in the kitchen," she replied, speaking of Faye's niece. Holding her hands up in a reassuring manner, she was quick to add, "Taylor is also fine. She was the one to call the cops. As soon as the guy realized she was there, he bailed."

"I don't understand..."

"Welcome to the club." Her gaze shifted for a second, and the smile that curled her lips spoke of the line which was apparently forming behind Mitzi. Her gray eyes sought out Mitzi's hazel ones. "I know that news isn't what you came in here for. Can I ease your worry with a cup o'Joe?"

"Um—yeah. Actually, do you know Steele and Abernathy's order?"

Laughing softly, Billie started tapping at the screen in front of her. "Is my name Willamenah Holt? What else can I get for you?"

"Medium Americano Girl with a pump of vanilla."

"You got it."

Mitzi pulled out her card to pay, all the while wondering if the break-in at Faye's shop was connected to the armed robber Atticus was after. The fact that he'd left her place around the time of the incident, compounded with her waking up alone, it made her feel unsettled in a way she knew she wouldn't be able to shake until she got some answers. What made it all worse was her own selfishness. She couldn't help but wonder why he hadn't told her what happened. Frosted by Faye was right next door to her store. Regardless of whether or not her shop was occupied, she didn't like the thought of Atticus keeping this news from her.

"Hey—all of this is gonna end soon. Long before your shop is open. I really believe that."

Mitzi shook her head, her mind turning over thoughts faster than she could process them. "Billie, what if you're next? Or the salon where Nora works? I'm not worried about me. It just—I know what it's like to be in Taylor's shoes. Or the guy who was held at knife point on the edge of town. It's scary."

"Yeah. I know. We just have to trust our boys in blue. I do, and you should, too."

Mitzi sighed, knowing her friend was right, yet still nervous all the same.

"We'll have your order right out. If you hear anything good from the guys, call me?"

"Absolutely, I will."

Mitzi stepped aside so Billie could help the customers who were waiting to be served. It was another five minutes before Mitzi's order was complete, but she hardly noticed the time. Gathering the drink tray in her hands, she returned to her Fusion and carefully situated herself behind the wheel. She barely noticed how Titan was sitting obediently, almost exactly as she'd left him, and she forgot about the treat she promised him before she'd left him alone with donuts in the backseat. She was too preoccupied.

When she pulled into the parking lot at the station, she identified Atticus' Chevelle in an instant. She knew it wasn't the car he drove while he was on duty, but she hoped he was there, just the same. It took a little finagling, but she was headed inside with her purse over her shoulder, Titan's leash around her wrist, and three coffees balanced atop a box of a dozen donuts without delay. In spite of the treats, gone were her intentions of a lighthearted first surprise girlfriend visit.

"Mornin'. Can I help you?" asked the uniformed officer behind the raised front desk.

"I hope so. Is Detective Steele here?"

"Yes, ma'am."

Mitzi smiled, relieved by the amusement she felt at his polite if not oblivious response. Raising her eyebrows in question, she went on to clarify, "Is it okay if I go back to see him?"

The young officer hesitated a moment, his gaze assessing her closely. "Things are a bit hectic at the moment, but somethin' tells me it'll be my ass if he finds out I turned a woman with a face like yours away on account of us bein' a little busy. Let me walk you on back."

"Thank you," she murmured as he made his way out to escort her.

She'd never been inside the police station before. While she wasn't a perfect angel growing up, she wasn't a rebel rouser, either. The building's interior design was outdated and looked as old as it was. Nevertheless, there was a buzz of activity in the place as the officer lead her toward the back of the precinct, broadcasting how little the staff cared about the decades old paint on the walls

Atticus was sitting on the edge of a desk, his arms folded across his chest, a deep scowl creasing his brow, and his attention captivated by Reed. In similar fashion, Detective Abernathy had his arms crossed over his broad chest, but he was on his feet, shifting his weight from one leg to the other as he spoke. Both men looked wrinkled, frustrated, and tired. Atticus had more scruff on his face than Mitzi had ever seen on him. Attractive as it was, she didn't relish the sight, knowing there was only one reason he hadn't shaved—because he hadn't been home.

"Sarge? You've got a visitor," announced Mitzi's escort.

Atticus looked at the officer, his scowl still intact, until he shifted his gaze onto Mitzi. Reed looked at her from over his shoulder as Atticus stood and inquired, "Mitzi, what are you doin' here?"

His tone was curious and gentle, but he still had an intense look in his eye that shook her confidence a little. It was like first thing that morning all over again, when she couldn't decide whether to text or not to text; whether to live with her assumptions or seek answers. Only, now she was standing in the middle of the police station with coffee and donuts.

"Are those...*donuts?*" asked Reed before Mitzi could find her words.

Unlike Atticus, Reed's tone sounded offended. His quirked eyebrow only made Mitzi wonder if she'd misjudged Detective Abernathy. She thought he came complete with a sense of humor.

"Baker's dozen of assorted deliciousness from I Love Donuts. I also brought you some of Billie's coffee."

All at once, Reed's face lit up with a huge, lopsided grin. "You're a saint. Also—the stereotype is totally true, and I'm famished," he stated as he turned to free her hands.

"The Americano is mine," she murmured as he took the items to his desk. Not that she was overly concerned about her coffee in that moment. As Reed flipped open the lid to the box of donuts, Mitzi's attention shifted back onto Atticus, who hadn't moved an inch.

"Sweet of you to bring us breakfast, pretty girl, but you didn't need to go out of your way."

His words reminded her exactly how far out of her way she'd already gone, and she reached inside of her purse for the bag of Dum Dums she'd purchased from the grocery store before stopping at Rock-N-Joe.

"I actually—I woke up and you weren't there. I thought maybe it meant you had a really long night. I wanted to surprise you. But then I got a little surprise of my own." Holding out the bag, she asked, "Did you know it was Faye's shop that got broken into before you left my place last night? Why didn't you tell me? I thought I told you I didn't want to be left in the dark, Atticus. My shop—"

Grabbing the bag of suckers with one hand, he took hold of hers with the other and insisted, "Come with me."

The next thing she knew, they were closed in an interrogation room. Atticus tossed his candy onto the steel table then rested his hands on his hips—one atop the gun Mitzi noticed for the first time, the other next to the shield he wore clipped to his belt—before fixing his eyes on her. It would have been a lie for Mitzi to say she felt at ease, but she tried to mask her discomfort as she stared right back into his dark brown eyes.

"Call came in last night, I was told the chatter we'd heard had turned into action, and I reported to the station. When I left, intel was still comin' in. By the time I got the specifics, a clerk at a gas station in Bell Buckle had been robbed at knife point. What happened at Faye's was a decoy. Collared the little shit at midnight. I spent the last four hours in this room with the perp, tryin' to get him to talk. That's all I can tell you. Been busy, babe. Want nothin' more than a shower and a bed right now—what I don't need is you gettin' funny ideas about what I'm not tellin' you and why."

"Oh," she whispered.

It's all she could think to say. Having obviously put her foot in her mouth, she sealed her lips closed and stared up at him sheepishly. He'd never been so short with her before, but she didn't blame him for his tone. He was doing his job, a job the whole town trusted him to do, and she was making it personal.

A long moment of silence passed between them as they stared at one another—then Titan sat to give himself a scratch, rattling his tags and jarring Mitzi to speak.

"I'm sorry. I'm not—I'm not that woman who shows up at her boyfriend's work and demands to know why he didn't come home the night before. I was really only dropping by to say hi, but then

I talked to Billie and…Atticus, business robberies freak me out. I know my shop's not open yet, but the thought of something happening to my friends who work in The Square…" Mitzi closed her eyes, shook her head, and sighed. She wanted to apologize, but it was turning into a justification.

"Hey." Atticus spoke softly, and Mitzi opened her eyes at the feel of his hand on her cheek. "You've got to know what happens to you matters to me. If ever I think you're in danger, I won't keep you in the dark. As for the rest of this town, I'm doin' my best to get this guy." He pulled his hand away from her face and raked his fingers through his hair. "My best is all I've got."

"Hey," she mimicked, taking a step toward him. She rested a hand against his chest and murmured, "I believe I recall you tellin' me you were a damn fine detective. I don't know anyone in Shelby who would disagree. Least of all me. You're going to get him. I know you are." She glanced out of the blind-covered windows of the interrogation room before she met his eyes and asked, "Am I allowed to kiss you in here?"

A small smirk curled the corner of his mouth ever so slightly as he breathed a quiet chuckle. Without saying a word in reply, he leaned down and pressed his lips to hers in a chaste but satisfying kiss.

"Call me when you're on your way home?" she asked as he straightened. "I can come to you tonight if you want company."

"Yeah, pretty girl. I'll call you later."

"Okay. I'm just gonna grab my coffee and get out of your hair."

"Mitz?" he asked as she turned for the door.

She stopped and hummed, "Hmm?"

"You really are a sight for sore eyes."

Mitzi didn't know it until it hit her—but his compliment soothed the dull ache she felt upon waking, before she made up her mind to come to the station. Even in the midst of a difficult morning, even after she'd falsely accused him of keeping her in the dark, he still had a way of making her feel wanted. It touched her in a way she couldn't match with words, and so she simply smiled sweetly in reply.

chapter nineteen

MITZI WOKE WITH A START. She hadn't meant to fall asleep; at least, not before she'd heard from Atticus. The soft, early light of dawn alerted her she hadn't just dozed off, she'd crashed and slept through the night. In spite of her visit to the station the previous morning, she couldn't help but to feel troubled by the whole situation. For most of the day, she managed to put it in the back of her mind so as to focus on finishing her sketches. Much as she wanted to check-in at the shop, she thought it would be better not to see what damage might have been done at Faye's place. It would only bring back memories from the not-so-distant past, and she had enough to worry about without inciting her anxiety.

It was on the evening news where she was informed the man who broke into Frosted by Faye was the cousin of Kevin Casey, the felon who was now wanted for *two* armed robberies in Bedford County. Upon hearing the news, the nerves Mitzi had tried to ignore most of the day became unavoidable. She clutched her phone for the rest of the night, hoping to hear from Atticus.

At nine p.m., it took everything in her not to send him a text in order to check-in with him. He assured her he would call her later. He was a man of his word. Moreover, he was busy working on a very important case. She trusted him. She trusted the relationship they were building. She had also assured him she could handle being the girlfriend of a detective, even if that meant the burden wasn't always light.

By eleven p.m., she found herself on the phone with Nora. She needed someone to help calm her down. With every minute, Atticus was getting closer and closer to forty-eight hours with no sleep. She didn't need to be a police officer to know lack of rest led to lack of clarity and focus. It was her best friend who reminded her Atticus wasn't alone. His partner had his back, and Mitzi needed to learn to trust him, too.

She had no idea when she fell asleep, but as she was startled awake, her first instinct was to reach for her phone in search of a message from Atticus. Except, before she moved an inch, she felt her man at her back, one of his arms draped heavily over her waist.

He used his key.

Mitzi's eyes drifted close again as she exhaled in blissful relief. Any tension in her body awakened just a second prior was chased away by the presence of her detective, safe and sound and in her bed. Blindly, she ran one of her hands along his forearm, in search of his hand. She felt her way over his wrist and then laced her fingers between his. Her touch triggered a response, and he curled his fingers around hers as he brought both of their arms across her chest before he pulled her closer. Her belly tingled in excitement when she felt his lips press into the space between her neck and her shoulder.

Atticus freed a deep exhale but said not a word, making Mitzi wonder if he was awake or still sleeping. After a full minute of silence, she smiled to herself, certain she was falling in love with a man who responded to her touch and pulled her close even while he was unconscious. Aware of just how little rest he'd gotten in the past couple of days, the last thing she wanted to do was wake him. Having gone to bed without him three nights in a row, she didn't relish the thought of leaving her bed now that he was in it—but neither could she stay underneath the sheets all morning.

Wanting Atticus to get as much sleep as he could, she decided to snuggle with him for a few minutes and then gently extract herself from his hold. It wasn't until she pulled her hand away from his that he started to stir.

"Where you goin'?" he mumbled, his gravely voice deep and sexy.

"Hi, baby," she whispered as she tried to catch a glimpse of him from over her shoulder. "I'm getting up. You go back to sleep."

Tightening his hold around her, he insisted, "Stay."

Mitzi bit her lip, fighting her smile before she rolled onto her opposite side, putting her face to face with Atticus. His eyes were still closed, but even without looking into them, she saw the evidence of his exhaustion. He now wore three days of stubble, and the dark circles above his cheeks alerted her to the reality that he must not have been asleep for long.

Gently resting one of her hands against his scruffy cheek, she grazed her thumb back and forth across the sensitive skin beneath his eye. "I've got to get some work done before I drive up to Nashville."

He frowned sleepily. "Nashville?"

"Mmhmm. I'm picking out fabrics today." He grumbled in reply, and she breathed a quiet giggle. "Go back to sleep, baby."

As she continued to stroke his face, he said nothing. Mitzi watched silently as he fell back into a deep sleep, then she brushed a featherlike kiss against his lips before carefully climbing out of bed.

On her way to the bathroom, she caught Titan's eyes as he lifted his head and looked at her. Mitzi smiled at him as she rounded the foot of the bed, wondering if he was going to jump down to follow her or stay curled up where he'd settled, at Atticus' feet. As if he'd seriously contemplated his options, Titan huffed a sigh and rested his head on his paws, clearly content precisely where he was. She didn't blame him one bit.

Wanting to be the least bit disruptive, Mitzi took a quick shower, skipping her hair wash. When she emerged from the steamy bathroom fresh and wrapped in a towel, she paused on her way to her closet, taken by the view—both her favorite boys sleeping in her bed. She also noticed the toiletry bag Atticus had abandoned on the nightstand, and his clothes piled in a heap on the floor. There was no telling how worn out he must have been. To think that, at whatever time he was able to leave work behind, rather than going home and falling into bed, he packed a few essentials and found his way back to her—it warmed her insides and made her belly tingle.

Yeah, she was definitely falling in love.

As she gazed upon him a while longer, an idea came to mind. Hoping not to miss her window of opportunity, she hurried into her closet and swapped her towel for a robe. Then, as quickly and quietly as possible, she went to her work room and rummaged through her things for a measuring tape. Every time she cut a new pattern for a piece in her collection, she worked with the same set of measurements—her own, for her women's clothing, and Nolan's for the men's line. He was her very first male model. Once she had the fit right, it was easy for her to adjust for various sizes to be sold from the rack. But this time, she didn't want to use Nolan's measurements. This time, she had someone else in mind.

Both her guys slept through her task as she took a few rough measurements, scribbling them down for safe keeping. When she was finished, Mitzi started a pot of coffee and, quite proud of herself, she went about completing her hair and makeup. Keeping it neutral, she was finished with her face in no time; and her hair was just oily enough to do exactly what she wanted without a fuss. She styled it half up, with a messy top-knot, and half down. Doctored coffee in hand, she spent a couple minutes in her closet before she decided on a long-sleeve, navy floral t-shirt dress, which draped low around her knees. By the time she was dressed, it was nearly nine, making her just in time for her call with Gianna.

It wasn't until she settled at her dining room table with her laptop that she thought about grabbing earbuds. She grimaced when Gianna's call came through, and she was quick to answer as she glanced toward the hallway. She'd left her bedroom door cracked, in case Titan wanted to grace her with his presence.

"Hey, you," greeted Gianna.

"Hi, good morning," Mitzi murmured in return.

Immediately noticing something was off, Gianna frowned curiously and asked, "Why are you talking so softly?"

Mitzi couldn't help but giggle, noting how the woman had softened her tone, too.

"Sorry," she replied, speaking a little louder. "Atticus is sleeping in the next room. He's had a really long couple of days, and I don't want to wake him."

Gianna's frown turned into an intrigued yet pleased expression. "You know, I've heard that name quite a few times, now. A picture would be nice. Or, better yet, an introduction."

Mitzi grinned, knowing her friend didn't know the half of it. She still hadn't told her how Atticus was the inspiration for her spring line—or what she planned on calling it.

"I don't have any pictures of him, yet. I'll work on it. As for an introduction, that can always be arranged. I don't think he's going anywhere."

"I like the sound of that." She paused a moment. "You know, I miss you. But, I've got to say, you seem really happy and inspired lately. Whatever's in the water down there, it's done you more good than I thought it would."

"It's home. It always was and always will be."

"I know what you mean."

With a contented sigh, Gianna changed the subject, diving into business. The two met for an hour and a half. Almost as soon as they said their goodbyes, Titan came into the room. He pawed at Mitzi's legs, signaling his desire to be let outside, and she was happy to oblige. While he handled his business, she refreshed his water bowl and poured him some breakfast. When she let him back in, he headed straight for both.

Mitzi was returning to the table when she spotted Atticus at the mouth of the hallway. The day before, he'd called her a sight for sore eyes. She was convinced he had no idea what he did to her looking the way he did. His hair was mussed from sleep, his eyes a little puffy. He wore no shirt, and the top button of his jeans was left undone. He was far more than a sight for sore eyes.

"Hi," she breathed.

"Mornin', pretty girl," he mumbled, still sounding half sleep.

"Did you get enough rest?"

"Hell of a lot more than I've gotten all week."

Mitzi smiled sympathetically. "Want some coffee? I can heat some up for you."

"Coffee'd be great."

With a nod, she went to the kitchen, took down a clean mug, and filled it close to the brim with the leftover coffee which had gone cool in her pot. Just as she popped the mug into the microwave, she felt Atticus at her back. Happiness flooded her entire body at the feel of his arms circling her waist. He pressed a kiss into her hair before he breathed in deep, as if still waking up; and he held her tighter as he let it all out in a slow exhale.

With her hands free, she folded her arms over his, taking hold of his elbows, a signal she wanted him to stay close. In their shared moment of contented silence, she realized how much she'd been missing him before she woke up in his arms. Even though they'd seen each other every day going on five days, the absence of him from the moment she left the station until he'd sleepily asked her to stay with him in bed—it made her anxious. Not about their relationship, but about what it meant to tie to her heart to a man who wore a gun to work.

The reality of his job wasn't lost on her. From their first date until that very moment, she'd seen how committed he was to his job. His commitment was as noble as it was admirable—but the case he was working was getting more intense. He was getting buried in it, and she needed to be held by him in order to remember he was a damn fine detective and she didn't need to fret so much.

"Babe?" he mumbled into her hair.

"Hmm?"

"Coffee's done and you're still holdin' on to me. What's on your mind?"

Her eyes immediately shifted up at the timer on the microwave and told her he was right. She hadn't heard the beep, too consumed by her thoughts.

"Mitz," he prompted once more.

"Last week, you were busy. Late nights. Stake outs."

"Babe—"

She uncrossed her arms and spun around in his hold to face him as she pleaded, "Let me finish. What I'm saying is, every night I didn't see you because you were at work, you'd call me. This time was different. This time, you knew I knew where you were—because you left here to go back to the station; and when my day ended, yours kept going. But yesterday, after I came to see you, we agreed you'd call."

"Mitzi, by the time I was headed home for a shower, it was after one—"

"I don't care that you didn't call because you didn't want to wake me up. You made up for that by usin' your key. I'm just saying, I'm gonna worry. I'll worry less when you call. And if you don't call— I'm going to hang on a little longer when you're home."

He studied her for a few seconds before he leaned his head down to touch his forehead to hers. "Careful, pretty girl. You keep it up, and I just might fall for you."

Sliding her hands up his bare arms, she pressed up onto her tiptoes, wrapped her arms around his neck and whispered, "Countin' on it."

She barely got the words out before his lips were sealed with hers. He kissed her slow and sweet, until his coffee needed another reheat. After he finally got his mug out of the microwave, Mitzi made her way to the dining room table as he went to fetch some cream out of her fridge.

"What's this about a drive up to Nashville today?"

"There's a huge fabric store up there. I need to do some shopping so I can start makin' my sketches a reality."

"How long will you be in the store?"

"I don't know. Maybe an hour or two. Depends on how fast I can find what I want or if I change my mind about something. Why?"

"I'll drive."

This made Mitzi turn around in her chair. When she did, she saw Atticus casually leaned against the counter, taking a slow sip of caffeine.

"You will?"

"We'll go to lunch up there first. Then, yeah, I'll get you to the store. I've got to be back by five. Workin' tonight. Might not have a chance to take you out again until Friday."

"I've got plans Friday. I'm hosting girl's night."

"Even more reason for me to take my pretty girl to lunch today."

Speaking through a grin she replied, "Careful, Atticus Steele. You keep it up, and I might fall for you."

He chuckled into his mug and mumbled, "Coutin' on it."

IT WAS THE END of a long week, and Mitzi could think of no better way to step into the weekend than with a night full of good food, great wine, and more laughter than she could stand. She hadn't exchanged a single word with Scarlett since she stormed out on their impromptu lunch date; Kevin Casey was still out there hiding; and Atticus was burning it at both ends—but for a few hours, Mitzi almost forgot she had anything to worry about.

Jay, who volunteered to be everyone's designated driver that night, was sprawled out across Mitzi's couch, laughing hysterically as Mitzi, Nora-Jean, Billie, and Reese tried to remember an old cheer routine choreographed to the billboard hit Nora and Mitzi's senior year. "I Gotta Feeling" by the Black Eyed Peas was blasting from Mitzi's Google Home as they talked over each other, shouting instructions in their intoxicated state. They were being loud and obnoxious, Mitzi's face hurt from smiling so much, and it felt good.

Titan, enlivened by all the excitement, was barking as he watched the women clap their hands, rattle imaginary pom-poms, and bounce around between fits of laughter. It was when Titan stopped barking at them and raced for the door that they realized they had company. Mitzi didn't bother to turn down the music as she followed after her pup, her friends moving to look toward the entryway, all of them peering from over the back of the couch. Mitzi scooped Titan into her arms before she twisted her locks free. At the sight of two uniformed police officers on her front porch, her breath caught in her throat.

"Oh, shit," laughed Jay.

"Fitz? Ramirez, what are you doin' here?" Reese asked. Mitzi looked over her shoulder when someone cut the music, and she could suddenly hear her friend approaching.

Their names sounded familiar, but when the handsome, Hispanic officer smirked knowingly at Reese, Mitzi was sure she'd never seen him or his partner before. She was halfway in love with a man who had beautiful brown eyes—but Ramirez had his own set too gorgeous to forget.

With his hands resting atop his utility belt, it was Officer Fitzgerald who replied, "We got a noise complaint."

"You can't be serious. We weren't bein' *that* loud." Reese furrowed her brow as she looked to Mitzi and murmured, "Were we?"

"Which one of her neighbors called it in?" inquired Billie as she, Nora and Jay completed the squad at the door. "It's imperative I know. Anyone who spoils girls night does *not* get whipped cream on their latte."

Ramirez exchanged a look with Fitzgerald, and Mitzi squinted at the officer with the blue eyes. She couldn't tell if it was the wine, the lighting or the truth—but she could have sworn he was trying not to smile. He cleared his throat and raised his eyebrows at Billie as he asked, "You have any idea what time it is? It's late. Folks are tryin' to get to bed."

When Ramirez covered a cough with his fist, turning his face away from the women, Mitzi shifted her attention onto him.

"This is a prank. It's gotta be," insisted Billie, taking the words right out of Mitzi's mouth. "Who put you up to it? Jed? Crew? I know it wasn't Bishop. He's still gettin' free coffee from me after he got shot at my neighbor's house a couple weeks ago."

"Please," grumbled Ramirez with an eyeroll. "He got nicked."

"Don't be jealous, Diego. You still get the boys in blue discount."

"Hold on a second," said Mitzi, speaking for the first time. She shook her head, trying to ward off the effects of the alcohol in her system, but to no avail. Forging ahead anyway, she frowned and continued, "We're not criminals. There's an *actual* criminal hidin' somewhere in this town. Shouldn't you be more concerned about him?"

Whatever amusement she'd seen in Fitzgerald's bright blue eyes waned as he replied, "We're just on patrol tonight, ma'am. Call came in and we answered. Rest assured, between the Shelby PD and State

Patrol, we're on the hunt for Casey."

Hugging Titan closer, Mitzi's frown deepened, her intoxicated thoughts latching onto one word. "Did you just call me...*ma'am?*"

This made Nora laugh. Her giggle was so contagious, soon they were all laughing, Fitzgerald and Ramirez watching with expressions which broadcasted their entertainment.

"Look, we know y'all were just havin' a good time. We're not here to give you any grief. We'll let you off with just a warnin' if you break it up and head on home."

"Fitz, that's ridiculous," argued Reese, folding her arms across her chest. "We're not a bunch of rowdy teenagers throwin' a rager, keepin' up half the neighborhood. I wear a shield just as well as you. Not to mention, you're talkin' to Steele's sister and his woman."

Again, Fitzgerald and Ramirez exchanged a look wrought with meaning Mitzi couldn't interpret. Ramirez then said, "McKnight, difference between you and us right now could be tested with a breathalyzer."

Reese gasped just as Fitzgerald raised his hands placatingly. "Just break it up, would you? Any of y'all need a ride home?"

"Son of a judge," muttered Jay. She choked out a dry laugh and added, "He's gonna pay for this."

Mitzi turned to ask what her friend meant, but before she could open her mouth to speak, Jay was headed back to the living room.

"My Jeep's certainly more comfortable than the back of an RMP. If you're rollin' with me, come on."

"What?" Mitzi turned her back on the officers as she exchanged confused glances with Nora, Reese, and Billie. "You're actually leavin'?"

"Mitz, hon, you're drunk. It won't be five minutes after we walk out that door and this'll all suddenly start to make sense."

"It will?" asked Nora.

"Yeah. Trust me. We're ready to go." With her purse slung over her shoulder, she waved at the confused women in encouragement.

"Come on. I'll explain in the car," she added with an eyeroll.

Mitzi, still confused, scowled at Jay then looked over her shoulder to find the two men who'd spoiled their night still standing on her porch. When she felt a hand on her shoulder, she looked up to find Jay smiling down at her.

"Thanks for tonight. It was a blast. Sorry for leavin' you with the mess. Tell Steele he's on dish duty."

She scratched the top of Titan's head and then made her exit, walking straight between the officers with a shake of her head. Soon, Mitzi was being showered with farewell hugs from the rest of her gang as they all filed out, one by one. When she stood inside her home alone, both officers dipped their chins as they wished her a good night, and she watched them go, still unsure how her night had come to such an abrupt end.

Her disappointment was heighted in her intoxicated state, and her mouth fell into a pout as she shut and locked her front door, placing Titan at her feet. Making her way back into her living room, she looked around at the evidence of her guests and sighed. Admittedly, it was getting pretty late, and she had a little league game to go to the next day—but she still felt wide awake.

She was gathering the last of the empty wine glasses, placing them carefully in the sink, when a knock came at her door. Before she headed that way, she glanced around her living space, wondering if one of her girls had left something behind. Spotting nothing, she pulled her fingers through her hair as she went to answer. As soon as she peeked through the peep hole, suddenly everything Jay said upon her exit made sense. She should have known. Maybe she would have been able to piece it together if not for the cabernet sauvignon in her system.

Mitzi freed her locks and swung open the door. It irked her how the sight of him standing casually on her porch, chewing on a Dum Dum made her want to smile. She tried to fight it as she squinted her eyes at him and pressed her fists against her hips.

"You called the cops on us?"

Atticus grinned, and the mischievous look in his eyes was irritatingly sexy.

"Thought they'd never leave."

"You called *the cops* on us?" she repeated.

He shrugged. "It's been a tough week. Figured they could have a little fun. Callin' on a house full of beautiful woman on a slow night makes the shift not so long."

Kind as his gesture sounded, and happy as she was to see him, she wasn't yet ready to let him off the hook. This time, she leaned toward him and enunciated every word as she repeated, "*You called the cops on us?*"

For a second, he merely stared at her. Then, in one swift motion, he pulled the white stick out of his mouth, shoved it into the back pocket of his jeans, and stepped into the house, forcing her to retreat. As soon as he'd cleared the door, he kicked it closed then leaned down and reached for her. With one arm around her waist, he grabbed for her thigh with his other hand, lifting her from her feet and guiding one of her legs around his hip as he spun her around and pressed her back against the door. Her body acting instinctively, she wrapped herself around him, holding on to his shoulders as her breath caught in her throat.

His gaze fixed intently on her face, his voice rumbly and low, he spoke. "Knew you were occupied tonight. Knew you'd be home. Knew you'd be drinkin' with your girls. Planned on droppin' by when they left and lovin' on my pretty little thing until you passed out. So I got in the Chevelle quarter to midnight. Drove by, spotted Jay's Wrangler, and turned around. Stayed home long enough to have a beer. Drank it slow. Thought about you. Twelve thirty, drove by again—that damn Wrangler was still parked in your driveway, so I drove around the neighborhood, wonderin' how drunk you'd be when I got here; wonderin' how hot I could get you. Then I imagined you wild and loose, inhibitions gone, taken me for a ride

—and I was headed back your way, wantin' you alone.

"Called in a favor, babe. Couldn't wait any longer. Haven't touched you in days. Your man missed you. So, yeah—I'm the reason Fitz and Ramirez showed up at your door. You mad?"

By the time Atticus was finished with his explanation, Mitzi was practically panting, her mind filled with her own fantasies, all of which spurred a tingling sensation between her legs. She hugged him closer, her whole body aching for him as she tried to string together a coherent response.

"You're not playin' fair," she breathed, running her nose down the side of his.

"You mad?" he repeated, his lips grazing hers.

Rather than use her words, Mitzi moaned as she sealed her mouth around his. He responded immediately, holding her tighter as he kissed her back deep and hard. In that moment, his lips had never felt more right, his tongue had never tasted so good, and she couldn't get close enough. As he leaned into her, pressing her flush against the door, she took hold of his face and hummed in pleasure. When she felt the evidence of his arousal, heat washed over her like a tidal wave, and she thought she might burn from the inside out if she didn't get out of her clothes.

Mitzi tore her mouth away from his, short of breath as she kissed her way along his jaw until her lips were at his ear. "Take me to bed, baby," she whispered. "I want to go for a ride."

Atticus didn't need to be told twice.

chapter twenty

MITZI'S ALARM CLOCK WENT OFF at nine-thirty the next morning. She groaned pathetically at the sound. Her head ached and her eyes felt glued shut, making it nearly impossible for her to move. Fortunately, she wasn't in bed alone. She sighed in relief as she felt Atticus reach over her in order to silence her wakeup call. As the room grew quiet, Atticus wrapped himself around Mitzi, pressing a sweet kiss against her bare shoulder. While her alarm made her want to pull the sheets over her head and hide, her man's affection made her want to snuggle in his arms all day.

She knew neither option was a possibility, but this didn't stop her from tucking herself more snugly into Atticus' chest. He kissed her again, this time against her forehead, before he mumbled, "Alarm?"

"Brooks. Football," she managed.

"Hmmm."

Their exhausted exchange made her giggle, and she forced her eyes open as she tilted up her chin. The light which poured into the room reminded her of her headache, and her amusement morphed into a whine. Hearing it made Atticus open his eyes. As the two stared at each other, memories of their early morning activities flooded Mitzi's mind.

They were all over each other for hours. There was no doubt in her mind, it was the hottest sex of her life, and she loved every second of it. There was something about Atticus that was different from any other man she'd ever loved. She trusted him with her body more than anyone who had ever touched her. This unlocked an uninhibited passion which didn't need the aid of alcohol—the effects of which had worn off long before Mitzi found sleep.

The pounding in her head was a result of the sugar in the wine, her lack of hydration after a full, active night, and not nearly enough rest. She needed caffeine—*stat.*

"What are you doin' today?"

His hand beneath the sheets, Atticus traced his fingertips down the length of her spine and across the small of her back as he replied, "You tell me, pretty girl."

"Brooks. Football," said Mitzi, speaking through a lazy grin.

"You got it."

When his hand traveled down and over her backside, her nipples pebbled. She stared into his eyes, his gaze unwaveringly settled on her, and she saw flashes of their fervent intimacy there. Following his lead, she slid her hand over his hip and felt her way across his back. "I had fun last night," she whispered.

He smirked. "Me, too."

"You still owe me for callin' your buddies, though."

His smirk stretched into a smile. "Worth it."

Giggling, Mitzi leaned into him a little more, and his grip around her backside tightened.

"I need coffee. The good kind. Will you make that happen?"

"I can do that. We can stop by Billie's on our way to the field."

"Actually, I promised Evie she could come. She stayed with Nora's aunt and uncle last night, so I've got to go pick her up from there. If I go get her and you go get coffee and we meet at the game, we can stay in bed a few minutes longer."

"I like that plan."

"Good. Me, too."

They stayed in bed for another twenty minutes, touching each other tenderly. When Mitzi finally forced herself up, she pressed a parting kiss against Atticus' mouth and headed for the shower. Much as she wanted to take her time, she knew she didn't have that luxury, so she hurried through her usual routine. No sooner had she stepped out of the shower than Atticus popped his head into the room to let her know he was on his way out.

"What time is the game?"

"Eleven."

Atticus raised his eyebrows as a crooked smile pulled at the side of his mouth. "You're kiddin' me, right?"

"No. Why?"

He laughed as he looked her over from head to toe. "I've learned one thing for sure—Mitzi Bates needs more time than you've got to get ready." Still chuckling to himself, he pressed a kiss against her damp temple. "I'll see you there."

She watched him leave, spurred on by his implied challenge. She then looked at her reflection in the mirror and sighed. He had a point, and she wouldn't pretend otherwise. Whatever she could manage in the next twenty minutes wouldn't be her best, and it certainly wouldn't be enough to avoid the unsolicited opinion of her mother. Nevertheless, with the hope of a strong, hot coffee at the finish line, Mitzi got to work.

Rather than blow-dry her hair, she pulled it back into a small, messy bun and added a pale pink knotted headband for good measure. She then spent fifteen minutes putting on her makeup, all the while accepting the fact that miracles didn't happen in fifteen minutes. While she didn't look as bright-eyed and fresh as a new spring morning, she'd covered her bases. When she was satisfied with her efforts, she hurried to her closet and pieced together an outfit as quickly as possible. A pair of high-waisted jeans, a pink, gray, and cream color-blocked, lantern-sleeved sweater, and a matching set of gray slip-on sneakers later—and she was as put together as she was going to get.

"Titan?" she called, hurrying from her closet. "Titan, come to mama. We got to go, baby."

Her maltipoo came trotting into the bedroom only to follow her out and toward the kitchen, where she bagged a couple treats to take with them. It took her longer than she preferred to find his leash, and she sighed exasperatedly as she tossed both things into her purse.

"We're so totally going to be late," she mumbled under her breath, gathering Titan with her keys and her bag.

Thirty minutes later, she was fifteen minutes behind schedule. Even though the park's lot was full of vehicles, it wasn't hard for Mitzi to spot her guy waiting for her. He was leaned against the driver's side door of his Chevelle—somehow both showered, shaved and effortlessly handsome. She didn't need to see behind his sunglasses to know as she, Evie, and Titan made their way toward him, he was watching them with a smug glint in his eye.

"Don't even say it," she insisted when she was in hearing distance.

"Wasn't gonna," he replied with a cocky grin. He took a sip of coffee as they finished their approach, then turned to grab the carrier from off the top of his car. He held it out for her, and Mitzi immediately reached for the largest option available and downed a healthy swing. Atticus only chuckled before he squatted down in front of Evie, offering her the remaining beverage. "Hey, Evie. Got you a hot chocolate."

"I love hot chocolate!" she gasped.

"What do you say, Evie Belle?"

"Thank you, Dedective Steele."

"You're welcome."

As he stood to full height, Evie looked up at Mitzi and asked, "What do *you* say, Auntie Belle?"

This made Atticus bark with laughter, which spurred Evie's tinkling giggle, both of which brought an unstoppable smile to Mitzi's face.

"*Thank you*, Detective Steele."

"You're welcome, pretty girl. Now, what do you say we go watch some football?"

"Yes. And we have to hurry. We've already missed the first quarter and part of the second."

Atticus looked down at Evie, obviously assessing just how fast her little legs could carry her. It took him only a second to make up his mind, and then she was propped against his chest, both hands clinging to her hot chocolate as she sang "*Whee!*" while they walked briskly toward the appropriate field. Mitzi spotted Trace first, standing near the sideline with his arms folded across his chest. She'd noticed this was his stance only when the Cyclones were playing defense, which meant Brooks was not on the field.

Charlotte was standing with her father, but Scarlett and Dolly were in their usual positions—settled into their collapsible chairs. Somehow, in the hustle of her morning, Mitzi forgot about the last conversation she'd had with her sister; or, more accurately, the fact that they hadn't spoken since. Of course it had crossed her mind how their paths would meet. Uncomfortable as she imagined it would be, skipping out on Brooks' final game of the season wasn't an option. She'd missed enough in her niece and nephew's lives, and she wouldn't miss any more so long as she could help it.

Yet, the days leading up to the game had been distracting in their own right. Aside from Atticus and his caseload, and worrying about who might be the next business to be targeted around town,

Mitzi had allowed herself to zone out for a day and a half—focusing only on her spring line. She'd been sewing up a storm with the haul of fabric she'd purchased in Nashville in the middle of the week. It brought her the kind of peace she'd only ever been able to find sitting at her machine, the sound of the bobbing needle drowning out her aimless thoughts.

Now, she was wholly aware of how far away she was from her modest home studio and the creative space she kept for herself in her mind. She hadn't prepared for this moment. She hadn't decided the appropriate course of action. In truth, what happened between sisters the previous Monday wasn't born in a single moment; it was the result of a much deeper issue which had been a sore spot in their relationship for years—none of which would be solved at a little league football game. As the distance between them grew less and less, Mitzi wondered if there was enough coffee in her cup to help her keep their unresolved issues tucked away.

When Mitzi began to slow her pace, Atticus moved to put Evie back down on her feet.

"No, no, wait!" she gasped, looking at the ground and then at Atticus. "Can I stay up here?"

Righting himself, he smirked at the little girl, and Mitzi's heart melted. She'd seen his crooked smile more than a few times, but there was something different about it now—aimed at Evie. It was sweeter. It was precious. It made her knees feel a little weak.

"Make you deal. You can stay up here until my coffee's gone."

Evie bit her bottom lip in contemplation. "How much do you have left?"

"'bout half."

She paused once more. "Okay. But just don't drink so fast."

"Promise," he assured her, speaking through a grin.

Mitzi was so wrapped up in their exchange, she was caught off guard when Scarlett drawled, "Nice of you to show up. You've only missed most of the first half."

She didn't bother looking Mitzi's way as she spoke. Dolly, on the other hand, tilted her head back to glance up at the new arrivals. "Atticus Steele, as I live and breathe. Didn't know you'd be here this mornin'. It's good to see you, honey," she greeted warmly. "You, too, Evie." She then settled her gaze on Mitzi, sighed and said, "You look tired, dear."

Mitzi forced a smile as she tried to remind herself she knew that was coming. Miracles didn't happen in fifteen minutes, and two sips of her lukewarm Americano weren't enough to chase away her exhaustion or the dull ache she still felt at her temples.

"Good to see you too, mom. I'm sorry I'm late. I'll apologize to Brooks after the game. Did we miss anything?"

"Let's be honest, you've missed a lot—not the least of which was his first touchdown of the game."

"Come now, Scarlett. Now's not the time or the place," chided Dolly softly.

Mitzi bit her tongue and shook her head as she looked out onto the field. She'd only been in their presence for a minute, and she knew just how screwed she was. It wasn't a surprise that Dolly knew her girls were in the middle of a fight—neither should it have been that her mother had picked a side. Just like always, it was her against them, regardless of how valid her side of the argument was.

"Aunt Mitzi!" called Charlotte.

Mitzi followed the direction of her niece's voice in time to see her break away from her daddy's side as she hurried over. The affection she received as Charlotte walked straight into her arms was like healing balm to an open wound.

"Hi, beautiful."

"Mom said you weren't comin'."

She couldn't help but to cut her eyes at her sister before she insisted, "Wouldn't have missed it."

"Can I hold Titan's leash?"

"Sure. Keep him close, okay?"

Charlotte nodded, taking the leash from Mitzi, and then looked up over her aunt's head. "Hey, Evie."

Evie wiggled in excitement and then looked at Atticus as she requested, "Okay, I can get down now."

"You got it."

As soon as Evie was on her feet, she was practically attached to Charlotte's hip, and the two of them let Titan sniff his way through the grass, headed toward the endzone. Mitzi watched them for a moment, hopeful her niece would always stay so sweet.

"Hey," muttered Atticus, grazing the back of one of his fingers down Mitzi's cheek.

She turned and lifted her chin to meet his gaze and saw his silent question reflected in his brown eyes. It didn't take a detective to read the room. It was as frigid as an ice bath. Before she could assure him she was fine, a whistle sounded on the field and Trace interrupted their private exchange.

"Steele? Haven't seen you in a minute. What are you doin' here?" he asked good naturedly, closing the distance between them.

Trace extended his hand and Atticus responded in kind, greeting his old friend with a shake. "Thought that much would be obvious." He tossed a wink at Mitzi to drive home his point.

"Right, right." Trace folded his arms across his chest as he aimed a knowing smile at his sister-in-law. "Might of heard a rumor about you two."

Just like always, his smile made Mitzi uncomfortable, the distrust she felt toward the man so deeply rooted she couldn't see around it. She brought her coffee to her lips and took a slow sip as she directed her attention out at the field, where the Cyclones defense was lining up for the fourth down.

"Surprised they don't have you tied up at the station, after the news cycle we've had this week."

The whistle sounded again, and Mitzi hoped with every fiber of her being this would make Trace return to his spot on the edge of the sideline. It was one thing for him to be an asshole to her or her sister. She was used to that sort of behavior. It was another thing entirely for him to puff out his chest in an effort to assert some sort of superiority over Atticus. If she wasn't in muddy waters already, Mitzi would have fired a comeback of her own—but she inhaled slowly and held her breath for a moment instead. The pounding in her head seemed to grow louder when the game started up again, but Trace didn't budge.

"Oh, come now, Trace. Steele's not the only man on our police force, and everyone needs a break now and again," pipped in Dolly.

Again, Mitzi raised her coffee to her lips, wishing she could journey to the opposite side of the field in search of Sterling. If nothing else, she knew he was far more interested in the game than Atticus' schedule.

"We've got guys workin' 'round the clock. We're gonna catch this guy—I can promise you that." As he spoke, Atticus reached for Mitzi's hand. When he laced his fingers between hers and squeezed, her nerves began to settle.

"Trace, sweetie, Brooks is takin' the field again. Let's stay out of their business and watch the game."

Pointed as Scarlett's comment was, Mitzi couldn't have said it better.

It was in the middle of the third quarter when she couldn't stand the bitter silence from her sister any longer. With her hand still engulfed in Atticus' grip, she asked the girls if they wanted to walk Titan around to the opposite side of the field in order to find Sterling. All parties were in favor, and they set out on a leisurely trek to the other sideline.

"You want to talk about it?" asked Atticus along the way, giving her fingers a gentle squeeze.

"Not now, thanks."

He didn't press, for which Mitzi was grateful, and the rest of the game was enjoyed with far less tension in Sterling's company. In the end, the Cyclones took the win, and seeing Brooks' excitement was worth all the trouble she'd endured that morning. As the crowd of families cheered, the boys stormed the field in victory. It reminded Mitzi of what it felt like after a win under the Friday night lights. Thinking about the countless games she attended in her cheerleading uniform then brought back flashbacks of the night before, and the girls' night shenanigans which culminated in even sweeter memories with some of her dearest and oldest friends.

"Aunt Mitzi, are you gonna come to lunch with us?" asked Charlotte, relinquishing Titan's leash.

"We can't today. After I give Brooks a squeeze, we've got to go."

"Okay," she replied, her casual shrug meant to mask her disappointment. "Pops, you're comin', right?"

"Yeah, sweetheart," answered Sterling, smoothing his hand over her hair affectionately. "Go on back to your mama. I'm right behind you."

After a quick round of farewells, Charlotte obeyed. As soon as she was out of earshot, Sterling looked at his daughter and asked, "How long is this fight with your sister gonna last this time?"

"Daddy—"

"I don't want to hear it, Mitz. Y'all are grown and I'm not gettin' in the middle of whatever you've got goin' on. But I'll tell you one thing." He paused and raised his brow for added effect. "Thanksgiving's right around the corner and I don't want nothin' but peace at my table, understood?"

"Yes, daddy."

He nodded in approval of her response and then looked to Atticus with an outstretched hand. "Good to see you, Steele," he said as they shook. "So long as you're holdin' on to my baby girl like you are now, you're welcome at my supper table, too."

"'Ppreciate the invite, Mr. Bates."

"Auntie Belle, are we gonna take me to mommy now?" Evie

inquired as Sterling took his leave.

"I thought we might stop and get some lunch first. Maybe some ice cream." Mitzi waggled her eyebrows at the mention of the sweet treat. "How does that sound?"

"I want ice cream!"

"Thought you might like that idea. We've got to go congratulate Brooks, and then we can go."

Evie then turned to Atticus, smiled up at him shyly and asked sweetly, "Can I have a ride?"

In an act that proved he found Evelyn Belle just as undeniable as Mitzi did, he squatted down on his haunches, reached over his shoulder, and tapped his back. "Climb on."

With Evie on Atticus' back, and Titan leading the way, his tail wagging furiously as they headed toward the excitement, Mitzi found Brooks in order to praise his team's effort and say goodbye. Not in the mood for another exchange with Scarlett, Mitzi didn't bother to find the rest of her family before she pointed her little entourage toward the parking lot.

"Mitzi, babe, if I'm gonna make an appearance at Sterling's table, I think you need to read me in on the details of this cold war between you and Scarlett."

Jerking her head in surprise, she stared up at him and replied, "You'd come to Thanksgiving dinner with my family? No way Gale doesn't make a great spread for the holiday."

"I know better than to doubt the reputation of Dolly Bates. Besides, I'm a grown man. I can eat two dinners. Don't change the subject."

"I…" She cut herself off before she could argue that hadn't been her intent. Even if it was true, she didn't particularly relish the idea of unpacking the fight her dad had insisted she resolve. "The thing is, my problem's not with Scarlett. Not when you really boil it down. I just wish she wasn't so blind when it came to her husband. He's not as good to her as she deserves, and she ignores it."

"Wait, are we talkin' 'bout the same Trace and Scarlett we just left? I know we aren't as tight as we once were, but—Scarlett's been it for Trace since we were kids."

Mitzi scrunched her face in confusion. "Maybe you don't see it because you're a guy, but he has got a serious wandering eye. Not to mention, he can be a shameless flirt. I would know. I'm one of his victims. But God forbid anyone acknowledge that's *not* how a husband should treat his wife."

"Has he ever stepped out on her?"

"Not that I know of, no. But that's not the point." Mitzi huffed out a sigh as she came to a stop and looked up at him. "If I ever heard someone say they saw you make a pass at someone, or heard you say somethin' flirty or inappropriate to any woman who wasn't me? We'd be over. When you're committed to someone, there are boundaries you don't cross. Scarlett turns a blind eye and a deaf ear about any such rumor. She has for *decades*."

"Okay," muttered Atticus carefully. He stared into Mitzi's eyes for a long moment, and she watched as he thought about his next words. Finally, he said, "I'm not gonna say you're wrong, pretty girl. Maybe Trace has got a bit of a rubber neck—but he's also still got a ring on his finger after all this time. From where I'm sittin', and I'll grant you it's not very close, they're the high school sweethearts who actually made it."

Narrowing her eyes at him suspiciously, she tried to tamp down the irritation which was beginning to cloud her mind. "I'm sorry, are you takin' my sister's side right now?"

"Babe, I'm not takin' any sides. I'm just telling you what I think."

"You want to know what I think? I think you sound like everyone else. I'm not wrong about him, and it's infuriating that *nobody* will admit it but me."

"Mitz—"

"Evie Belle, climb down, babe. I changed my mind about lunch. I think we should skip it and go get ice cream. Just you and me."

This time, it was Atticus who scrunched his brown in confusion as he helped Evie off his back. "Mitzi, come on."

"No, Atticus. You were in *my* bed last night which means you're supposed to be on *my* side. And I'm way too tired to try to convince you of something you should already understand. I will talk to you later. We're gonna go."

Taking Evie's hand, Mitzi walked away, all the while trying to remember the last time she and Atticus parted without a kiss. Upset as she was, she couldn't recall.

Forty-five minutes later, after they each devoured a heaping scoop of ice cream from the parlor in The Square, Mitzi used the key she'd yet to give back to Nora to grant them entrance into the apartment. Evie burst through the door the first chance she got, spotting her mother right away. She sat tucked into the corner of the couch, a blanket over her lap, and her journal propped on her knee.

"Mommy!" Evie yelled as she skirted the coffee table and collided into the woman.

"Hi, baby. I missed you," Nora giggled. She wrapped her arms around her little one before planting a kiss on top of her head.

"I owe you an apology." Mitzi grimaced as she closed the door and leaned against it, watching their exchange. "I was upset and I kind of took it out on Evie."

"What?" asked Nora, glancing over her shoulder.

"We had *ice cream!*" announced Evie, still riding her sugar high.

Speaking through a barely contained laugh, Mitzi explained, "We kind of skipped lunch and went straight for dessert. That was, of course, after Atticus gave her a hot chocolate at the game. She is *totally* amped up at the moment, and it's my fault. So, I'm sorry."

Nora chuckled and took hold of either side of Evie's face. "You had fun, didn't you?"

"Yes."

"Good. Kiss." Evie did as she was told, planting a sticky kiss against her mother's lips. "Go wash your hands and wipe your mouth, mini-me. I'm gonna make us some lunch, okay?"

"Okay," Evie chirped before skipping down the hall, Titan trotting along after her.

"Thanks for hangin' out with her this morning," said Nora as she unfolded herself from the couch.

"Oh," Mitzi sighed with a wave. "You know you don't have to thank me for that."

"No, I do. It was really nice to take this morning slow. Last night was great, but I definitely felt the consequences of it when I woke up. You, on the other hand, don't look too worse for wear," she teased on her way to the kitchen. "And if Jay was right, your night didn't end when we left."

A flashback from the wee hours of the morning sparked a tingling in her belly which was immediately followed by a pang of something akin to regret. "Yeah. I had a late night."

"Okay, not that I'm lookin' for details, but that doesn't sound like a good time."

"No, it's not that," she admitted, dragging her feet as she followed her friend to the kitchen. She dropped her purse on the counter's ledge, then propped her hip against the dishwasher. "Last night was—hot. Really, really hot."

"*But?* You said you were upset. What happened?" prompted Nora as she rummaged through the fridge, pulling out the necessities for sandwiches.

"He had a front row seat to the aftermath of my latest blow-up with Letty. When we were leaving the game, he asked for details, I gave them to him, and he sided with Scarlett."

"What'd he say?"

Mitzi gave her the full play-by-play of their spat. By the time she was done, Nora-Jean was calling Evie to the table, where a quartered sandwich and half a sliced apple awaited her.

"MB, don't hate me for sayin' this but...he *does* have a point."

"But I'm not wrong," she argued.

Nora handed her a sandwich. "No. You're not." Mitzi took it, but opened her mouth to speak rather than take a bite. Before she could utter a word, Nora shook her head, pointed at the sandwich and demanded, "Eat that and listen to me for a second. You know *I* know Trace is the same man he was the night he made Scarlett a Whitfield. I see what you see, no doubt about it. You are not wrong in your character assessment of him. But—much as you don't like him—Scarlett loves him."

Speaking with her mouth half-full, Mitzi shielded Nora from the turkey and cheese she was in the middle of consuming and countered, "That much is obvious. But just because she loves him doesn't mean she should let him disrespect her the way he does. That's *not* love."

"Okay, but, think about it. It's like Steele said. They're the high school sweethearts who made it. Whatever the dynamic of their relationship, there's something there that keeps them together. I know better than most—sometimes love isn't enough, which means they've got an extra something that works for them."

"What—avoidance? Obliviousness? Denial? And even if that is their secret, it doesn't change anything. She's allowed to have an opinion about how I live my life and the men I date, she's allowed to judge me but it's not okay for me to dish it back?"

"No, of course not. Look, your relationship is complicated. When you were in New York, the distance made it easier to manage. Now that you're back home, you've got to deal with all your sh—" She hesitated, glanced at her daughter, and then amended, "crap. Crap that's been unresolved for way too long. You knew—"

"I know, I *know*. I knew this part would suck. I signed up for this when I decided to stay."

When Nora-Jean finished putting her own sandwich together, she picked it up and started for the table, nudging Mitzi's shoulder with her own as she passed. Pausing to look her friend in the eye, she murmured, "You've got to find a way to get past this—to get past your opinion of Trace. He's not goin' anywhere. More importantly, you shouldn't let him rob you of the relationship you want with your sister. You know if there was a dumb guy between you and me, we wouldn't let him tear us apart."

"Yeah, well, you're too smart to hitch your wagon to a dumb guy. Besides, I haven't given up hope that Trace and Scarlett won't end up the only high school sweethearts who make it."

Nora rolled her eyes, shook her head, and continued to the table. "If I knew havin' you home meant I was gonna hear you beat that old drum over and over again, I might not have encouraged you to stay," she said playfully.

"Someone has to keep hope alive." Mitzi smiled slyly, pulling out her own chair to take a seat.

"*Yeah, well,*" Nora repeated mockingly, "We're not talkin' about me. Anyway, kind of sounds like you might need to talk things out with *your* Steele."

Glancing down at her sandwich, Mitzi's smile faded. She knew Nora-Jean was right, but it didn't make her ready to admit it. Truth of the matter was, if it wasn't for Nora, she might of thought herself crazy. For years, it felt as though everyone had labeled Mitzi the irrational one, which was a subtle way of deeming her the bad guy of the bunch. Trace and Scarlett's wedding might have been eleven and a half years ago, but the way her mother and Scarlett swept the incident under the rug, the way her daddy pretended he didn't know, and Trace's complete lack of remorse made it difficult for time to form a cloth over her eyes.

She didn't like Trace. In all the time she'd known him, he never gave her a reason to change her mind about him. He might have been a decent father, a faithful husband, and a successful businessman—but that didn't make him *good*. Mitzi was sure of it. She wasn't fooled by his handsome features, his big smile, or his pretty blue eyes. It was those very same eyes which made her uncomfortable in the first place. While she couldn't blame Atticus for not having ever noticed, it stung hearing him defend the man. Right or wrong or somewhere in between, she wasn't ready to accept Atticus' opinion on the matter.

"This afternoon, I think what I need is lunch with my best friend and her mini-me and then a long date with my couch, my dog, and reruns of *Project Runway*."

Nora studied her a moment and then nodded her understanding. "I'll allow it. Somethin' tells me *Atticus* will still be around when you're ready."

chapter twenty-one

M ITZI WOKE UP WITH THE SUN the following morning, curled up under a blanket on the couch, Titan snuggled close to her chest. She furrowed her brow, the grogginess which accompanied her first waking moments after a hard slumber making it difficult for her to remember when she'd found sleep and why she wasn't in her bed. Pulling in a deep breath, she took in her surroundings.

There were take-out boxes from her dinner on the coffee table. Her phone was close by, likely dead having not been plugged in at the end of the previous day. Glancing over at her television, she remembered the hours she spent binging her favorite fashion duo —Heidi Klum and Tim Gunn. She must have fallen asleep partway through season eight. She'd seen it at least a dozen times. Mondo and his bold print choices usually had a way of lifting her spirits.

Even though she felt sufficiently recovered and well rested after much-needed sleep, the more awake she became, the less at peace she felt. She needed to talk to Scarlett. She needed to talk to Atticus. Yet, she didn't feel clear headed or objective enough to start either conversation.

Titan began to stir. Noticing she was awake, he kissed her chin, which made her smile. "You want to go for a walk, baby? Hmm? I think I could use one." At her suggestion, he got up on all fours, stretched, and gave himself a shake. When he was finished, he looked right at her, as if to proclaim he was ready when she was. "Okay. Give me ten minutes."

After she discarded the evidence of her dinner, she went to plug in her phone before stopping in the bathroom to splash water on her face. Having slept in the leggings and t-shirt she'd lounged in for the evening, Mitzi did little more than throw on a roomy, fleece pullover before tucking her feet into a pair of warm, fuzzy ankle boots. Fairly certain she wouldn't run into any of her neighbors before eight a.m. on a quiet, November, Sunday morning, she didn't think twice about her appearance as she fastened Titan's leash and headed for the door.

They walked for nearly forty-five minutes. The fresh air did Mitzi good, and the distance they traveled was just enough to wear out her pup. As soon as they returned to the house, she freshened his water bowl, poured him some breakfast, and hopped in the shower. Knowing Atticus had church, she promised herself she would call him after he had dinner with his family. Having made up her mind he deserved more than a text, she didn't even bother to look at her phone after she blow dried her hair and got dressed. With time to kill, she put on a pot of coffee and then headed into her workroom.

A couple days earlier, she'd cut the pattern for the leather jacket Atticus had commented on after the first time he'd ever seen one of her sketches. Now seemed as good a time as any to stop playing around with paper and start working with the leather she'd purchased in Nashville. Three hours, two cups of coffee, and a tin full of straight-pins later, the pieces of her jacket were draped over the shoulders of her mannequin. She was so focused on what she was doing, she didn't hear it when the front door opened and closed. Neither did she notice when Titan jumped down from her sewing chair and trotted into the next room. It wasn't until she heard the sound of his approaching boots that she turned and watched as Atticus filled her open doorway.

Her heart skipped a beat at the sight of him.

It wasn't the way he looked in navy dress slacks, a crisp, white button-up, and his worn, black-leather jacket. Though, that certainly didn't hurt. It wasn't the way he casually invited himself inside, or how he cradled Titan in the crook of his arm, like they were buddies. Well, not entirely. It was the look in his eyes. In his beautiful brown gaze, she saw he'd waited long enough, and he had no intention of waiting any longer. She saw what she hadn't admitted to herself until that moment.

She'd missed him terribly, their time apart and the silence between them different than it had ever been before.

"I'm sorry," she breathed. Those two words seemed to fall short, so she sighed and added, "Turns out, I have a short fuse when it comes to my family and our issues. I shouldn't have walked away from you like that."

"We're gonna disagree sometimes, Mitzi. We'll probably fight, too. But I respect you and that head on your shoulders. You're not just a pretty face—and I'm not just some washed up jock."

"I know," she whispered, taking a step toward him. She felt a knot as it began to take shape in the back of her throat, catching her off guard. She gasped quietly, in an effort to control her bourgeoning emotions and said, "I didn't mean to make you feel that way. I just—for so long, it's always felt like everyone has taken her side over mine. When I left, it was partly because of Trace, and no one came after me. Not once did my parents even suggest so much as a visit. And every time I came back, everyone wanted to pretend Trace was perfect, but I see right through it. Sometimes it seems like I'm the only one who does. I don't like him, and I don't like it when everybody takes his side, makin' me the black sheep in my own family."

Atticus furrowed his brow in thought as he leaned down to place Titan back on his feet. When he straightened, he slid his hands into the pockets of his slacks, nodded and replied, "Okay. I'll admit, there's a lot to unpack in all that."

"But you still think I'm wrong?"

"Babe, I swear to you, I'm not lookin' at this situation through the lens of right or wrong. The way I see it, there's only so much you can control here. Seems pretty obvious to me, Trace isn't goin' anywhere. I'm not sayin' you have to like it. Hell, you don't even have to like *him*—but you have to live with him. Like it or not, he's part of your family. And I won't sugar coat it, pretty girl; in my experience, you want to keep your seat at Sterling's table, you're gonna have to forgive and move on. You're the one who decided to come back."

Mitzi sighed, sealing her eyes closed tight as she buried her fingers in her hair. He was right. Furthermore, he was only repeating what she'd told herself weeks ago. Nora-Jean had called her brave for coming back and facing the problems her family had been avoiding for years. Only, at present, she wasn't feeling so brave. A small part of her wanted to tuck tail and run, cowardly as it was.

"God, it would be easier to go back to Brooklyn."

"Hey," called Atticus softly. Mitzi opened her eyes and dropped her hands to her sides at the feel of his fingers at her chin, tilting up her head. When he had her full attention, he shook his head once and declared, "I'd follow you as far as the county line, Mitz—but you go further than that, and I'll be forced to drag you back, kickin' and screamin'."

A half-hearted smile curled the corner of her mouth before she leaned forward, pressing her forehead against his sternum. "I'm not goin' anywhere, Atticus."

He smoothed a hand over her hair and then kissed the top of her head. "We good?"

Mitzi paused long enough for a breath, then steadied herself as she pulled away from him in order to look into his eyes. "You tell me."

Before he spoke, Atticus reached into his pocket and pulled out a key. Holding it up for her to see, he said, "For the next time you feel like sayin' sorry."

Her belly clenched in nervous excitement as she looked from him to the key and back again. "You mean I can only use that when I screw up?"

"Take the key, babe," he said, speaking through a smirk. "Use it whenever you'd like. Next time you need a little space, feel free to come on over when you've had all the space you need."

"Atticus Montgomery?" she asked, plucking the key from his grasp.

"Right here, Mitzi Belle."

Smiling up at him, she murmured, "Please kiss me."

"Yes, ma'am."

And so he did, long and slow; deep and wet, until Mitzi was weak at the knees.

With both his hands buried in her hair, cradling the back of her neck, he severed their lips and propped his forehead against hers. "We don't stop, I'll want to start takin' your clothes off, and we don't have time for that. How long will it take you to get ready?"

It took her a second to come out of the haze of their kiss in order to string her words together. "Ready for what?" she managed.

"Sunday dinner, pretty girl. I don't show up with you and Titan ridin' shotgun, I'll never hear the end of it. Already got an earful for comin' to church without you."

"You did?"

"Wouldn't lie about such a thing."

This made her smile. Much like the embrace from her niece the previous morning, the Steeles' desire to have Mitzi at their table was an invitation which soothed her heart. While her man's family could never replace her own, it felt nice to be wanted so unabashedly. Knowing the road ahead of her with the Bates and Whitfields was still paved with roadblocks and potholes, she was relieved to have been offered the gift of a reprieve.

"Give me thirty minutes?"

"Kick off was twenty minutes ago. If you hurry, we'll be at the house before halftime. We can tune in on the radio along the way."

"It's that late already?" she gasped, pushing her way out of his hold and hurrying for the hallway. "Fifteen minutes. Twenty, max." She halted at the door, then spun back around and insisted, "Before the sun goes down, I need to fit you into that jacket. I'd do it now, but I need at least twenty minutes for a fitting."

Atticus turned to look over at the mannequin and then met Mitzi's gaze with a raised eyebrow and a sly smile. "Hell, yeah."

Grinning, Mitzi chuckled, winked, and then raced for her closet, feeling happier than she thought she could be that day.

IT WAS MONDAY MORNING, a week since the horrible lunch date with her sister, and Mitzi found herself standing on Scarlett's front porch, willing herself to lift her hand and ring the bell. Fearing she'd get the cold shoulder if she merely called or texted, Mitzi had decided to show up unannounced. Her intentions were good, and all she could do was hope that was enough.

After a couple long minutes, she shook her head at herself, pressed the doorbell, and then held her breath. When she heard her sister's approaching footsteps, she let out a slow exhale. It took Scarlett longer than was necessary to unlock the door, which made

Mitzi's heart heavy—but she didn't move, silently declaring she wasn't going anywhere.

When the door finally swung open, Scarlett didn't say a word. For a moment, intentions be damned, Mitzi wanted to turn around and walk away. In the silence, her sister was claiming she was the victim; she was in the right; she was owed the apology. It took everything Mitzi had in her to tamp down her stubborn pride and force herself to confront the situation head on.

"Can we talk? Please?"

Scarlett continued to say nothing but turned and headed into the house, leaving the door open in the coldest invitation imaginable. Mitzi stifled a sigh as she closed them both inside, following her sister toward her living room. Scarlett took a seat on her immaculate, beige couch, folding one leg over the other as she clasped her hands together atop her knee. Mitzi opted to stand.

"Okay. It's obvious you want an apology, so here it is," she began to say, setting her purse on the coffee table. "I'm sorry for tellin' you the truth. I'm sorry for havin' an opinion you don't like. I'm not entirely sure how we get past this, but I hope we can."

"Wow. That was *some* apology."

"Don't you *want* to be friends again? To be a family? Maybe it's not important to you. Maybe you don't care anymore. If that's the case, I'll leave right now."

"I can't believe you're pointin' the finger at me," argued Scarlett, sitting forward with a scowl tugging at her perfectly manicured eyebrows. "My God, you're so selfish sometimes. You've had it in for Trace *forever*. He's my *husband*, Mitzi. If you can't accept that, after all these years, that's *your* problem, not mine. We've been a family all this time. It's *you* who left."

"Fine. Okay. You're right. I left. And, yeah, I don't like Trace—but I *love* you. This isn't me bein' selfish. It's me tryin' to look out for you."

"I don't need you lookin' out for me. I don't know how many

ways to say it, but I choose him—flaws and all. He's the father of my children and the love of my life. Contrary to what you might think, you don't know everything. You haven't been around for the majority of my marriage. You don't see the way he loves me. Or maybe you don't want to. Again, that's on *you*. I wish you would stop actin' like you're better than me—like you're better than all of us. You're not."

Scarlett's outburst took the breath out of Mitzi's lungs. She gaped at her sister before easing herself down onto the opposite end of the couch. Speaking barely above a whisper, she replied, "I don't think I'm better than you."

"Don't you? All those years ago, you left without so much as a goodbye, like you didn't need us. Then all your dreams came true. And maybe you didn't give daddy any grandbabies, but you named your brand after him, as if to remind us all that he's always had a soft spot for you. It didn't matter if you broke his heart when you left, and it didn't matter how far away you were, you weren't gonna be forgotten. Then you come back here and act like you never left; like nothin's changed when, in fact, everything has changed."

"That's what you think?" asked Mitzi, her eyes brimming with tears. "That's what you think of *me?*"

"Yes. I do."

Mitzi swallowed hard as she lifted her gaze toward the ceiling, in a futile attempt to keep from crying. The truth hurt. For a moment, she thought she understood how hard a blow it must have been for Scarlett every time she reminded her of Trace's worst habits. She was sorrier than she'd ever been for opening old wounds better left stitched closed.

"I was tired of waitin'; tired of fallin' short while everyone around me was movin' on with their lives," she murmured, her voice strained as she tried to talk around the knot in her throat. "I didn't leave because I didn't need you. I left when it felt like no one needed me. It wasn't until you called me and told me you were pregnant with Charlotte that it even felt like I might have been missed."

Mitzi sniffled and shook her head, still looking anywhere but into her sister's hazel eyes.

"I named my brand after daddy because everything I learned about runnin' a successful business, I learned from him. No one works harder than Sterling Bates. I saw it growin' up—but I got a front row seat when I was workin' for him at the dealership. I knew I'd never make it in the fashion industry if I didn't follow his example. And I was right.

"Whatever success I've found, it's because of all of you. I had a mom who raised me with a certain standard of beauty, and an older sister who lived up to that standard while raisin' a family of her own. I've never strived to be better than any of you or this town. Shelbyville's my home, and I've only got one family. I just wanted to make everyone proud. Myself included."

Her tears slowed to a trickle as she finished speaking, and she forced herself to look at Scarlett before she stood to her feet. Swiping her fingertips across her cheeks, she drew in a deep breath, blew out a sigh, and then reached for her purse.

"I didn't know. I didn't know you felt that way. I'm sorry."

She didn't make it two steps before Scarlett grumbled, "Damnit, Mitzi."

Mitzi stopped, glanced over her shoulder, and watched as Scarlett held out her hand.

"Don't go."

With that, Mitzi's tears came rushing back. She returned to the couch, dropping her purse on the floor as Scarlett pulled her into a hug. It had been a long time since they'd held each other. Too long. And it felt good—necessary.

"You're pain in the neck, you know. Always have been," Scarlett sniffled. She pulled away, and they both wiped at their cheeks as she continued. "Look, I don't want to fight. I want to be glad you're back

—for Charlotte and Brooks' sake, for mom and daddy..."

"And you?"

Scarlett blew out a heavy sigh, sweeping a bit of hair behind her ears as she dropped her gaze. "You're not the only one in this town who feels the way you do about Trace, but he's not the man people assume he is. They just don't know him. There's a part of him only I get to see. He showed it to me when I was fifteen years old, and I've loved him ever since.

"What hurts me isn't your opinion of Trace. He's a grown man. He can defend himself. What hurts is your opinion of *me*—like I'm just some stupid woman trapped in a relationship." She paused long enough to look Mitzi in the eye. "I might not have a fancy career, and I'm not the reason we can pay for this big house, but I'm proud of the life I've made for myself, and I'm proud of the family Trace and I have made together."

"Oh, my god, of course you are," insisted Mitzi, taking hold of one of Scarlett's hands. "You should be."

"Even so, you were wrong about us not needin' you." Scarlett's voice was soft and strained as she fought to hold back her tears. "Bein' Scarlett Whitfield isn't as easy as it was bein' Scarlett Bates. We've always been well off with daddy—but it's different with Trace. The circles we run in because of the number of zeros in our bank account...well, let's just say I don't have very many friends who would stick around if one day we lost it all.

"And I know how that sounds. It's not the worst problem a woman can have. But the older my babies get, the harder it is for me to ignore it. I can't tell you how many times I wished you were here, just so I'd have someone other than mom to talk to."

Much as Mitzi wanted to argue she was in New York and not dead, she was beginning to understand the hurt went both ways. Their situation wasn't as simple as *right* or *wrong*. All they had were the mistakes made in their pasts and the opportunity to fix what was broken in the present in order to preserve their future. There was no room for blame. Just as Atticus had told her the day before—they needed to forgive each other and move on.

"Well, I'm here now. Catch me up?"

Scarlett coughed out a laugh, and the sound brought a smile to Mitzi's face. She didn't realize how much she missed being responsible for that laugh.

Her sister squeezed her hand before letting go and tracing her fingers over the skin beneath her eyes. "You want some coffee?"

"Yeah. I'd love some," Mitzi murmured, warmed by the invitation to stay a while. "And Letty?"

They stood together, and Scarlett waited silently for Mitzi to speak.

Adjusting her bag over her shoulder, she found the words for the honest and sincere apology her sister was owed—the apology they both needed in order to begin again. "I really am sorry about how my opinion of Trace made you feel. From now on, I'll keep it to myself."

Scarlett merely nodded, but that was enough. Nothing more needed to be said. They were moving on.

chapter twenty-two

"**W**AIT FOR MAMA HERE, TITAN. I'll be right back, okay?" Mitzi kissed the top of his head and ran her hand along his spine before she left him in the front seat to gather her first load. She might have gone a little overboard at the craft shop, but she wasn't sorry. She wasn't sorry at all.

With her arms laced with the handles of five bags stuffed full of decorations, she made her way toward the house. Using the key Atticus had given her a couple weeks prior, she granted herself entrance and headed straight for the corner in his living room, where she'd already decided his new Christmas tree would go. She'd done all the hard work of finding the perfect assortment of ornaments and tree dressings. Now all she had to do was convince him to buy the tree.

They'd been arguing about it since the day before Thanksgiving.

Smiling to herself, Mitzi turned to head back to her car to fetch her pup and the groceries she picked up for dinner. Her day had been packed. Then again, that was becoming the trend as they got further and further into December. It wasn't merely the usual hustle and bustle of Christmas taking over. With Palmer and his team nearly done with renovations at her shop, she was preparing to put her own finishing touches in the place. From art pieces to hang on the wall, to unique shelving to display her Sterling Mist collection, she was working with her team to make her new spot everything she wanted it to be.

She'd also been sewing in every spare moment she could find. Her living room had become an extension of her spare bedroom studio space, housing the racks with her completed pieces. Her men's collection was finished with just a couple designs from her women's collection that needed tweaking. She was cutting it close, but just after the holidays, she planned on making a trip back to New York to spend a couple days with her seamstresses. They'd have a month to get enough sewn for the soft launch of her new line in her new shop and her Brooklyn storefront. After her grand opening in February, she planned on launching the spring line broadly.

Much as she poured her heart into her latest designs, *home* and *love* stitched into every item, she could hardly wait to share them with the world.

Once she and Titan were in the house, Mitzi immediately went about unpacking her grocery haul and starting on dinner. She was still learning Atticus' storage system, which was a bit awry amidst his ongoing remodel work, but she managed. As he liked to tease, she was to blame for his kitchen's currently unfinished state, as she was occupying all of his free time. In turn, Mitzi insisted he'd have more time if he wasn't working such long hours, which always brought them to the inevitable impasse. Truth of the matter was, it had been a few weeks since Casey had struck, and it made Atticus nervous. Apparently, chatter among the seedier crowd had gotten pretty quiet. The quieter they grew, the more focused Atticus became.

Mitzi understood he was merely doing the job he loved—but neither did she apologize for wanting to be with him when he was around; even if that meant climbing into his bed at night and waiting for him to get home so he could join her.

Though, that night was going to be different. That night, he promised he'd be home by seven. He didn't know it yet, but they were going to have a romantic shrimp risotto dinner while they watched the Steelers play the Vikings in the Thursday night football match-up. After nearly an hour in the kitchen, and right on cue, she heard Atticus enter the house. As the click of his boots against the hard floor got closer, she abandoned the pot on the stove, their food nearly ready, and headed for the bottle of wine she'd left by the sink. She was inserting the corkscrew when she felt her man at her back.

"Hi, baby," she cooed as he took hold of her waist and gave her an affectionate squeeze.

Rather than use his words to say hello, he used his chin to sweep away the hair covering the side of her neck and then kissed her there. His lips still grazing her skin, he asked, "You want to tell me what's in those bags in the middle of my livin' room?"

She grinned as she continued to twist the corkscrew. "They're actually *not* in the middle of the room. They're in the corner— where your Christmas tree is gonna go."

He breathed a laugh, kissed her neck once more, then lifted his hands from her sides in order to reach for the bottle of wine. As he took over the task of uncorking their beverage for the evening, he tried once more to make his case. "Babe, you want a tree so badly, why don't you get one at your place?"

"Because, if you hadn't noticed, I've been spending my nights here. My place is cluttered with my work, and you've got the perfect spot for a beautiful, luscious tree."

He grunted in disagreement as he reached over her head for a couple glasses. Before he could pour either of them a serving, she turned so they were facing one another and smiled up at him as she took hold of the lapels of his sports coat. "You're failing to imagine the full magic of a tree decked out in ornaments and warm, golden lights."

Atticus smirked. "Am I?"

Pressing up on her tiptoes, she leaned into him and whispered, "Want to know what's more romantic than having sex by candle light?"

Mitzi watched in delight as his smirk morphed into a grin. "You playin' me or promisin' me?"

"Oh, I would never kid about sex by tree light."

"Mmmhmm," he hummed as he descended for a kiss. "What's for dinner, pretty girl? Smells good."

Snaking her arms around his shoulders, she held onto him a moment and kissed the underside of his jaw. It was her silent way of saying just because he changed the subject didn't mean she was giving up.

"Shrimp risotto. Are you hungry?"

"Yeah. We watchin' the game?"

"Yes. You pour the wine, I'll fill our plates?"

He nodded and they separated in order to fulfill their respective tasks. Atticus finished first, carrying their glasses into the living room and powering on the television. When Mitzi made her way into the next room a couple minutes later, he was coming from the hallway—his jacket off and his boots gone. He was working his sleeves up his forearms as they settled in on the couch, just in time for kickoff.

"Hey," Atticus mumbled, stealing her attention before she took her first bite.

"Hmm?"

For a second, he said nothing as his eyes danced around her face. Then he leaned over and pressed a kiss against her temple, pulling away as he said, "Thanks for dinner, pretty girl."

"You're welcome."

Mitzi didn't have to ask him if he liked it. He devoured his first serving and helped himself to another. During the second quarter of the game, he topped off their wine, and at halftime he took care of their dishes while she took Titan out back for a break of his own. At the top of the third quarter, all three of them were on the couch —Mitzi snuggled close under Atticus' arm; Titan curled up behind her legs, his head resting atop her bent knees. As the third quarter ended and the fourth began, both of Mitzi's guys were asleep.

It was as ordinary a night as they came, and there was nowhere else she wanted to be.

FOUR MINUTES AFTER MIDNIGHT, Steele's ringing cell phone yanked him from his sleep. As he jerked awake, he tightened his hold around Mitzi, still stretched out along his side and tucked under his arm, her cheek pressed against his bare chest. He pulled in a deep breath and fumbled with his free hand for the device, hoping to silence it before it woke his woman.

Steele frowned when he saw it was the station calling, but he didn't hesitate before tapping the screen and bringing the phone to his ear. "'ello?" he grumbled.

"Detective Steele, sorry to wake you, but we've got a situation at the station."

"What kind of situation?"

"There's a woman here, claims to be Kevin Casey's girl. She's in pretty bad shape, Sarge. Tried to get her to talk, but she said she won't speak to anyone but the lead detective on Casey's case."

"Shit. Okay," he replied, now fully awake. "I'm on my way. Do me a favor—wake Abernathy, too."

"Yes, sir."

Steele ended the call without another word and then carefully tried to ease Mitzi off of him and onto a pillow.

"Baby? Where you goin'?" she murmured sleepily.

"Got called in. Go back to sleep."

Rather than lay down, she propped herself up and peered at him through the darkness, softened only by the pale light of the moon.

"What happened?"

"Babe, go back to sleep," whispered Steele, leaning down to press a kiss in her hair. "I'll be back as soon as I can."

"'Kay," she sighed, resting her head once more. "Be careful."

"Always am."

Five minutes later, after throwing on jeans and a t-shirt and extracting his gun from the safe in his closet, he grabbed his leather jacket, shoved his feet into his boots and was out the door. The streets were quiet, and he was at the station in under ten minutes —his thoughts spinning as fast as the wheels of his Chevelle. If it really was Casey's girl waiting for him, it was going to be one hell of a break.

"Where is she?" Steele asked the officer manning the front desk the second he burst through the main entry.

"We put her in interrogation room A, detective."

"Abernathy?"

"Not here, yet, sir."

Steele nodded but said nothing else as his stride took him into the bowels of the station, toward his desk. He stopped at the break area to pour himself a cup of what he was sure would be a mediocre serving of coffee, but he was in need of a jolt. The day before had been long in and of itself. Barely twenty minutes into the new day, and he knew he didn't have the luxury of any excuse for a lack of focus, which meant he could use all the help he could get.

As he sipped slowly at the black liquid, he continued to his desk, glancing toward the window and through the blinds of interrogation room A. He couldn't see much, but what he did see he didn't like. Then again, it wasn't altogether surprising, either.

"What have we got?" called Reed as he hurried in Steele's direction.

It didn't escape Steele's attention that Reed was still dressed in the clothes he'd been wearing during their last shift; neither did he look like he'd been called out of bed. Curious as he was about his partner's whereabouts, they had more important matters to discuss.

Steele jerked his chin toward the woman. "Jittery as hell. Beat up, too. If I had to guess her poison of choice, I'd put her on meth. Don't know what brought her here, but I sure am lookin' forward to findin' out."

"Let's do this."

Reed led the way, and the woman jumped as they entered the room. She looked to be about thirty-six or thirty-seven; but knowing Casey was only twenty-nine himself, Steele guessed it was the drugs that put an extra ten years on her. She was skinny as a rail, her blonde hair a dull yellow, the long strands wispy and thin. At one time, she might have been pretty—but the woman who called herself Casey's was a mess. She looked between the two of them before her gaze settled on Steele.

"You. You're the one who caught him the first time. Your face—it was all over the news."

He set his coffee down on the far corner of the table, folded his arms across his chest and replied, "I'm Detective Steele. This is my partner, Detective Abernathy. You wanted the men after Kevin Casey—here we are."

She shrank back in her seat and sealed her mouth shut, scratching at her forearm anxiously. Steele read her like she was an open book. As if the reality of where she was and the consequences of her actions had finally caught up to her drug-muddled brain, she was having second thoughts. Steele pulled the chair out from underneath the table and sat across from her.

"What's your name?"

"Bette. Bette Sutton."

"He give you that bloody lip, Bette? Hmm?" No longer brave enough to look him in the eye, she shifted her attention down at her lap. Steele pressed on. "What about that black eye? He do that to you? My guess—probably wasn't the first time."

"He ain't a monster," she grumbled, frowning at him. "He's never—he just freaked out, okay? He was high, and he freaked, and I—got scared. I didn't have nowhere else to go."

"Where is he now, Bette? We'll go get him," said Reed. "You willing to press charges?"

She shook her head, but as her entire body began to rock back and forth, it was obvious she wasn't turning Reed down. She was agitated. She was anxious. She was keeping something from them.

"What aren't you tellin' us?" asked Steele.

"I told him to stop. I told him—after his cousin got picked up? I *told* him, it was only a matter of time. I told him!" she repeated, her voice growing louder as she rocked herself harder. "I told him. If he got caught again, I wasn't gonna wait for his ass. I told him."

His voice still calm and low, Steele inquired, "Is he planning another job, Bette? Is that why he freaked out? You told him to stop, he got mad, and he took it out on you?"

With tears streaming down her face, she sealed her eyes closed tight and nodded her confirmation.

"When?" asked Reed.

"Tonight."

Steele cursed under his breath as he stood to his feet. The scraping of the chair's legs against the floor caught Bette's attention, and she looked up with wide eyes.

"Where?"

"I don't know," she cried.

"Now's not the time to hold out on us, Bette," Reed insisted.

"I'm not."

Steele narrowed his eyes, not quite sure he believed her.

"You know he's up to something, right?" Reed pressed. "Did he talk to you about it? Did you overhear a conversation between him and someone else?"

When she remained silent, Steele jumped in, switching tactics.

"You came to us, remember? We can't help you if you don't tell us everything you know, right now. A name, an address, you've got to give us *something*—otherwise, we're done here. You're on your own, you understand?"

She hesitated a second too long, and Reed lost his patience. He swore, smacking his hand against the wall as he started to take his leave. He took one step over the threshold before Bette murmured, "Madison."

Reed paused, glancing back at her from over his shoulder.

"Madison? What does that mean?" Steele asked.

"I don't know." She shrugged and shook her head from side to side. "He just kept sayin' he was gonna fuck Madison all night long —and then he was gonna take me away if I shut my mouth."

"Steele, Abernathy!"

Both men looked in the direction of the man hollering their names and saw their Lieutenant waving them over. Unlike Reed a few minutes ago, Carlson looked like he'd just rolled out of bed and started barking orders—the first of which was for Steele and Reed to join him in his office. Both men hurried from the room.

Before they could come to a stop, Carlson announced, "Dispatch just got their second call reporting an armed robbery in the last twenty minutes."

"What?" spat Reed.

"Second? Why the hell didn't anyone tell us about the first? Where?"

Carlson waved off the first question and answered the second. "He hit the Speedway on Madison. Radio car got to the scene and—"

"Fuck—*Madison*," Reed muttered, jogging toward his desk. He swiped his set of keys from the top drawer, and Steele began to back his way out of the room.

"He's not done," he told his Lieutenant. Then he and Reed were both jogging for the door. "Get a unit to every convenience store on Madison now," Steele yelled over his shoulder.

"On it."

Reed had the SUV started by the time Steele hauled himself into the passenger side. The tires screeched against the pavement as Reed gunned it out of the station's parking lot, lights flashing and siren singing.

"How do we play this?"

"If he hit the Speedway first, he was in the center of town. He's workin' his way out. A call came in for his second stop, which means he's onto his third."

"Or maybe he's already on to number four. How many gas stations are there on Madison, anyway?"

Steele, having already pulled up a map on his phone replied, "Four. Circle K would be his last stop. Go there."

"Copy that."

What would usually take them seven minutes took them three, the SUV flying through the quiet streets under the weight of Reed's lead foot. The strobe lights of a radio car could be seen at the first gas station they passed, and the sirens of other approaching units could be heard coming from multiple directions—but they were the first to pull into the lot of Circle K. There was an old, faded, Buick sedan parked right out front. No witnesses had ever been able to positively ID Casey's vehicle, but the unmarked car was impossible to miss that night.

Reed stopped the vehicle at a diagonal, parking behind the Buick and blocking any possible escape route. Without a word spoken between them, both men jumped out of the cab and started for the convenience store. Steele took two steps before he saw him. Kevin Casey was making a run for it—except, when he stepped foot outside, he noticed the detectives.

He stopped in his tracks and cursed. In a split second, Steele knew he was on one. He was being reckless and stupid. *More reckless and stupid than usual.* He'd gone weeks without getting caught, but that night was different. After their chat with Bette, Steele wasn't surprised by the wild look in Casey's eye, but he was curious.

"It's over," he called out, lifting his hand to rest on the gun at his hip. "Put the knife—"

Steele didn't have a chance to finish his sentence before Casey took off, headed for the field to the right of the gas station. Without thinking twice about it, Steele initiated his pursuit on foot, Reed trailing behind him, sirens of an approaching radio car sounding in the distance.

"Police!" shouted Steele. "Freeze!"

With at least six inches in height to his advantage, and an athletic build suited for the job at hand, Casey barely made it into the overgrown grass before Steele tackled him to the ground. Yet, what the perp lacked in speed, he made up for in strength —fueled by stubbornness, adrenaline, and whatever drug flooded his system. He bucked his head back, clipping Steele's jaw, and throwing off his balance. Before he could establish a good grip on Casey, pinning him firmly to the ground, he managed to maneuver his way onto his side.

"Drop your weapon," Steele demanded as he tried to pin down the man's arms.

Unsurprisingly, Casey did not comply. With a grunt, he threw his left elbow back and swung it up, catching Steele in the side. *Hard.* The force of the blow was as unexpected as it was jarring, and he lost his hold on Casey as he fell backward.

Having been relieved of the full weight of Steele on top of him, Casey whirled around and in one, swift motion, he hurled himself at the detective and plunged his knife directly into Steele's side. Whatever fight he had in him was temporary suspended. The burn of the blade piercing his insides caused him to freeze. He fell onto his back, and Casey went with him, staring down at him with wide, crazed eyes.

Only, it wasn't Casey whom Steele saw as he gasped for air. It wasn't Casey he felt as he grabbed onto the man's jacket. He wasn't at a gas station, in a field, fighting off a felon—he was in his kitchen with a pretty girl in his arms. For a split second, Mitzi was all he saw. Her big, hazel eyes. Her bright, playful smile. He smelled her perfume. He heard her giggle. He felt her lips brush the underside of his jaw in her cute, flirty effort to convince him to buy a Christmas tree.

Should have gotten the damn tree, he thought.

Then the pain at his side brought him back to the here and now.

The burning sensation he'd felt initially was nothing compared to the fire which seemed to spread from the inside out, causing him to clench his teeth and groan. It wasn't until he heard Reed yelling that he blinked, and the haze of confusion dissipated completely.

Casey had removed the knife, and Steele's heart was beating overtime as blood spilled from his wound. When Casey stood, Steele gasped for air, his adrenaline taking over as he reached for his gun. A shot was fired before he could lift his arm and aim at the man who was now running toward the tree line. It took a moment for Steele to gather the strength to grip his weapon and steady his aim. Two more rounds were fired from Reed's gun, but Steele had Casey in his sight.

He fired three times. The last shot hit its mark. At the same time Kevin Casey went down, Steele's head fell back, his eyes drooped closed, and the pain he'd felt subsided into something far worse. He felt nothing but cold.

THE FIRST TIME HER phone rang, she heard it as if it was in her dream. The second time it rang, the sound woke her— but the interruption in the dead of night was discombobulating.

For a moment, she couldn't remember where she was. When she looked beside her and saw the place Atticus should have been, she panicked, not remembering that he'd gone. Then, as if her ringtone was her tether to the here and now, she recalled his departure. He'd been called into work—but now it was *her* who was beckoned from her sleep by a call.

Finally reaching for the device, she squinted at the screen and saw Jay's name before she answered, "Hello?"

"Mitzi, you have to get up. It's Steele."

She shot up in bed, her hair falling around her face as she gasped, suddenly wide awake. "What? What happened? Where is he?" The words fell out of her mouth almost faster than she could speak them, keeping pace with the increased speed of her heartbeat.

"He was stabbed, I guess. I don't know. Reed called Judge, Judge called Lawson, he called me—we're on our way to Vanderbilt. I don't know—I don't know the details."

"But is he okay?" asked Mitzi, already out of bed and frantically searching for her pants in the dark.

"He wasn't wearin' his vest," was Jay's only reply.

This halted Mitzi in her tracks, as if the news was a blow to the chest, knocking the wind from her lungs.

"What?" she whispered.

"I don't know anything else. I'm in my Jeep now."

"Okay, okay," said Mitzi. She shook her head, in an attempt to shake away the fog of worry which had begun to make her thoughts hazy. It didn't help, but she forced her body to keep moving anyway. "I'm coming. I'm—I'm leavin' now."

"Drive safe."

"You, too."

chapter twenty-three

S HE HADN'T BRUSHED HER TEETH or washed her face. The only attention her hair got was from her hands, having run her fingers through it frantically. Dressed in a pair of jeans, the t-shirt she'd been sleeping in, and the well-worn UT sweatshirt she'd snatched from Atticus' closet, she practically ran through the parking lot and toward the emergency room entrance of Vanderbilt Hospital. Without even so much as a lick of lipstick on, she would have felt practically naked; but given where she was and why, she was lucky to have a bra on, which was all she had the capacity to manage at nearly two in the morning.

The bright florescent lights inside the hospital were abrasive. It took Mitzi's eyes a moment to adjust, and another few seconds for her to catch her breath and focus her mind, which felt on the verge of sensory overload.

"Mitzi, sweetie, we're over here."

She jerked in the direction of Gale's voice, and her stomach dropped when she saw the crowd which had assembled for the one and only Atticus Steele. Gale was sitting beside Keaton, clinging to his hand as if he was her lifeline. On her opposite side was Jay, whose long legs were curled up against her chest, her head resting on her mother's shoulder. Lawson was standing in the corner, his arms folded tightly across his chest, his back leaned up against the wall. But it wasn't the sight of the Steele family which made her stomach hurt with angst—it was all the cops.

Reed was pacing the room, like it would kill him to stand still. His shirt had blood on it, and she knew without a doubt it wasn't his. Lieutenant Carlson occupied the chair to Keaton's left, looking tired and wrinkled. Officers Fitzgerald and Ramirez, still in uniform, stood side by side, both looking her way with expressions she couldn't interpret. Bishop and Jed were there, too. Somehow she knew, they, like her, had been in bed but had come as soon as they heard.

"Hey." Mitzi gasped in surprise when she felt Reese take her hand. Looking over at her friend, also in uniform, her reflexes were triggered, and she instinctively held on tight. "We came as soon as we could get away."

"What do we know?" asked the tall, handsome blond Mitzi knew was Reese's partner. For the life of her, she couldn't remember his name, but she was grateful he'd asked the question she couldn't find the voice to ask herself.

"Nothin' yet," the lieutenant replied.

Mitzi wondered if no news was good news, but she couldn't convince herself that was true. She hated not knowing what was going on or how it had transpired. The uncertainty of it all made her want to cry, but her tears wouldn't come—as if the stress of the situation was an internal dam preventing her from releasing anything that would relieve her mounting anxiety.

"Tell me the sonofabitch who did this is behind bars," Billie demanded as she entered the waiting room. One glance, and Mitzi recognized the woman had chosen to cling to her anger in order to keep herself together.

"He's dead," muttered Reed matter-of-factly. "Steele saw to it. Fuckin' hero even when he's bleedin' out."

Mitzi's breath caught, incapable of processing the good information with the bad.

"Well..." Billie stated, her tone a little weaker than it had been a second ago. "Okay, then. I can live with that."

Jay extended her arm, reaching for her best friend, and Billie didn't hesitate.

"Mitz? Mitz, maybe you should sit," Reese kindly suggested.

It was when Reese sandwiched Mitzi's hand in both of her own that Mitzi realized the intensity of her grip. When she looked into Reese's light brown eyes, she knew she was never going to get through the night or survive the wait without her own best friend. Even with a room full of support, love, and family, it wasn't enough —not when the man of her dreams was *bleeding out*.

"Will you—will you call Nora?" she whispered.

Reese nodded and insisted, "Sit for me and I will."

Mitzi obeyed, Reese made the call, and twenty minutes later, Nora was rushing through the door—Evie still in her long-john, floral pjs, hair wild, half sleep, and wrapped around her mother. The pressure inside of her chest was mounting, her need to cry undeniable, but Mitzi's tears still wouldn't come even as Nora took the seat next to her and immediately began rubbing her back comfortingly.

"Hi. Any news, yet?"

Mitzi shook her head and furrowed her brow, both thankful her friend had come and regretful she'd asked her to. "I'm sorry for gettin' you both out of bed."

"Are you kidding?" Nora scoffed. "My Evie-B loves that man. So do you. I'd be pissed at you if I found out about this a second later than I did."

A knot crawled its way into Mitzi's throat at Nora's statement. Suddenly, the fact that she *did* love Atticus, but she hadn't yet told him, was all she could think about.

As if she'd read Mitzi's mind, Nora looked her straight in the eye and said, "He's gonna be okay."

"Then why haven't we heard anything?"

"The doctors are makin' sure I'm right," she answered confidently.

It was another long twenty minutes before a doctor finally came into the waiting room, looking for the family of Atticus Steele. Keaton, Gale, and Jay all joined Lawson on their feet in response, but they weren't the only ones anxious for an update; neither were they the only ones who stood.

The doctor took note of his, and a small smile pulled at the corner of his mouth as he made his way over to Atticus' parents. Mitzi got closer, desperate to know if she was allowed to draw hope from that small expression. Noticing her out of the corner of his eye, Keaton waved her over, wrapping an arm around her shoulders when she was in reach, silently declaring she belonged with them.

"Detective Steele suffered a stab wound in the right side of his abdomen. The good news is, the blade got caught on the zipper of his jacket pocket. The bad news is, his attacker was still able to penetrate the abdominal wall, and the tip of the knife did pierce his liver. As far as I can tell, the liver wasn't damaged enough to warrant surgery. We'll be monitoring him closely for the next couple days to make sure surgery is not required.

"Steele did lose a significant amount of blood. We started a blood transfusion, which will take a few hours to complete, and he'll need plenty of rest, but he should be fine."

"Oh, thank you Lord," Gale breathed.

"Can we see him?" asked Jay.

The doctor looked at Jay, then at Gale before his gaze settled on Mitzi. The tiny smile she'd seen earlier came back, this time in his tired eyes. "Yes. He can have two visitors at a time in fifteen minute intervals—but first, he's asking for Mitzi. Something tells me that's you."

Her heart skipped a beat as she looked at the rest of his family and then back at the doctor. "Yeah, I'm Mitzi."

"I'll take you to his room."

Every muscle in her body told her to go, but it didn't feel right leaving Gale behind. Atticus might have been the love of Mitzi's life, but he was Gale's first born child, no matter how old he got. As she stepped out from underneath Keaton's arm, she held out her hand in invitation. Gale's eyes, wet with tears, lit up as she accepted Mitzi's offer.

"I knew you were a keeper," she sniffled.

For the first time in an hour, Mitzi smiled.

Even with favorable news from the doctor, the journey to Atticus' room felt long. When they finally made it to the door, a nurse was on her way out. With a smile, she assured them he was only resting his eyes, but he was still awake and anxious for visitors. Gale, letting go of Mitzi's hand, encouraged her over the threshold with a gentle push. As soon as they were both inside, Atticus opened his eyes.

He was pale and he looked exhausted, but he remained as gorgeous as he'd always been. For the first time since she answered Jay's call, Mitzi breathed a full, deep breath. As her lungs expanded with air, the pressure in her chest was released—like the dam within had suddenly malfunctioned. Seeing Atticus in a hospital bed was a reality check. She'd never seen him so vulnerable; but the truth was, regardless of his rank, his bravery, or his strength, beneath his shield, Atticus was still just a man.

But he was *Mitzi's* man.

On her next exhale, all the tears she couldn't cry before came rushing out of her. Whatever safeguards had been erected in her mind in the waiting room, they vanished. She sobbed so hard, her entire body trembled. He was right there—alive and breathing —but the possibility that he might not have been had the circumstances been different, it devastated her. Her affection for him was overwhelming and startling, as if she'd fully realized it all at once and in that very room.

"Come 'ere, pretty girl. Come 'ere," demanded Atticus.

She tried to get a hold of herself as she closed the distance between them, but it was no use. With the IV hooked up to his right arm, Atticus extended his left one, wrapping his fingers around the nape of her neck and drawing her into his shoulder upon her approach.

"I'm okay, babe," he mumbled, kissing the side of her head. "Listen to me—I'm gonna be fine."

She closed her eyes, leaned into him, and held onto his forearm with both hands. It took her a minute to calm down enough to catch her breath, his smooth, deep voice soothing her all the while. As her tears subsided, she lifted her head from his shoulder, reached for either side of his face, and kissed his mouth. Once. Twice. Three times. When she pulled away, his eyes stared intently into hers as he moved to dry her tears. Something about his touch set her off again. Except, rather than bottomless relief, she felt irate.

Jerking out of his reach, she planted her fists on her hips and cried, "What were you thinking? Do you have any idea what it's like gettin' a call at two in the morning hearin' your boyfriend's been *stabbed* and he wasn't wearin' his vest? You said you'd be careful! That's not careful! Nobody asked you to be a hero, least of all me. You can't scare me like that ever again—do you understand me?"

She paused long enough to rake her fingers through her hair. Before he could get in a word, she continued, "I get that you're never gonna be the guy ridin' a desk—but I swear to God, if you *ever* go after an armed criminal without your freakin' vest on *ever* again, you won't see me naked for a *long* time. A *long time*, Atticus!"

Smirking, Atticus raised his eyebrows, glanced behind Mitzi, and then met her gaze once more. "You done?"

"No," she huffed. Her eyes welled with fresh tears as she murmured, "I love you. And I'm not just sayin' that because you're lyin' in a hospital bed right now. I loved you yesterday, and the day before, and the day before that..." She hiccupped on another sob she was trying to hold back.

His smirk morphed into a lazy grin as he crooked a finger, signaling he wanted her closer. Giving into his silent request, she put herself back in reaching distance. He buried his fingers in her hair and pulled her close enough to kiss. His lips grazing hers, he whispered, "Soon as I get out of here, I'm gettin' you a Christmas tree." She gasped, utterly elated, and he kissed her, holding on longer than he should with his mother watching. Then, not bothering to pull away, he mumbled, "I love you too, baby. I promise not to be so reckless next time."

"Okay," she whimpered before he kissed her one last time.

When their lips parted, Atticus kept her close, but he spoke not a word. For a long moment, Mitzi watched him stare at her, like it was important for him to take in every detail of her face.

"Baby?" she breathed, her eyebrows knit together in concern. "You okay?"

"Shit like this goes down, they say your life flashes before your eyes." He paused a second and swept a bit of her hair behind her ear. Grazing the back of his knuckles down her cheek, he murmured, "All I saw was you."

"Careful, Atticus Steele," she warned, mimicking his gesture with her own fingers against his stubble covered cheek. "I just stopped cryin'."

His smirk returned and it made her want to kiss him—so she

did.

"Do me a favor?" he asked when she pulled away.

"Anything."

"Sit with me a while."

"I'd love to. You have no idea how much. But the doctor said only two of us at a time for fifteen minute intervals. You've got a whole room of people who want to see you."

"Babe?" he muttered with a frown. "I was stabbed. Think that means I get to call the shots. You stay. Now, pull up a chair."

Mitzi didn't need to be told twice. She straightened, wiping away the remnants of her tears as she searched the room for a chair. Spotting two against the wall on the opposite side of the bed, she pulled one up right along side of him, wrapping her fingers around his as she sat. Gale, who stood silently at the door throughout the duration of their exchange, wore a small, confident smile as she finally stepped further into the room.

"She might be small, but she knows how to roar. I had half a mind to give you an earful myself, but I believe your sweetheart will follow through on her threat, and I can't top that."

Gale winked at Mitzi who couldn't help but to blush in response. It was then Mitzi realized she'd boldly proclaimed Atticus had access to her naked—in front of his *mother*. Wise and mature as she was, Gale ignored Mitzi's rosy cheeks and focused her attention onto her son.

Combing her fingers through his hair she said, "Son, let's not meet here again soon, okay?"

"Deal."

Gale only stayed a few minutes before she left the room to fetch Keaton. He walked in, hand in hand with Jay, who said hardly anything. But when Jay laid her head on Atticus' chest, just over his heart, it was clear no words could say more. They stayed for ten minutes, each of them promising they would be back later in the day, and then left to tag-in Lawson.

Atticus' nurse, who came by during a quiet moment, was finishing up when Lawson, Reed, and Lieutenant Carlson filled the doorway. She quirked an eyebrow and shook her head, waving a finger for good measure, as she tried to block them from the room.

"I'm sorry, gentleman—two at a time. We're already makin' an exception, here. His body has been through enough for one night. He needs to rest, not entertain. One of you has to go and wait your turn."

"I'm his brother," stated Lawson.

The nurse nodded, then looked to Reed who announced, "I'm his partner."

"I'm his Lieutenant."

"And I'm his nurse," she said with a shrug.

"I outrank everyone here, and I need to have a word with my detective."

Not to be outdone, she folded her arms across her chest, popped her hip, and replied, "You don't outrank me, sir. Not in this hospital."

"Kendall, it's okay. Let them in," Atticus insisted weakly.

Mitzi squeezed his hand. It wasn't lost on her how all the attention was sucking up what little energy he had left.

This time, the nurse directed her attitude at her patient. "Detective Steele, how's your head?"

"Pounding. But if you split them up, whatever conversation we're about to have will happen twice. Please, let them in."

Kendall sighed, shifted her attention toward the men still waiting at the door, and instructed, "Five minutes. Brother can stay —but the cops get five minutes and then you'll have to come back tomorrow, get me?"

Mitzi liked her.

"I'll be back in five minutes," she assured them, taking her leave.

Reed opened his mouth to comment, but Atticus spoke before he could, clearly only interested in answers. "Casey?"

"You got him in the lung," reported his partner. "Didn't make it to the hospital."

His grip tightened around Mitzi's fingers, but he said nothing in reply.

"You broke protocol," said Carlson. Even Mitzi could recognize the reprimand in his tone.

"You were there," Atticus argued. "The call came in, and we responded. As soon as we got on the scene, he made a run for it."

"I heard the story. You still broke protocol."

"I was *not* going to let him get away. I made a judgment call. Given the circumstances, I don't regret it."

"Different circumstances, different outcome."

"I did my job."

Carlson said nothing for a few seconds, and everyone watched as the two men stared each other down. Finally, Carlson said, "I've got a team at his place now, tyin' up loose ends. Case will be closed by mornin'."

"And Bette?"

"Lucky break," muttered Reed. "Lot of that goin' around tonight. You al'right?"

"Fine. Glad it's over."

"Had a word with the doc. You're benched for the next six weeks."

"Shit," he grumbled, rubbing at his eyes with his free hand.

"That's not the end of it," continued Carlson. "Want you to go easy for a bit. Take some time. Step foot in the station before the new year, and I'll send you packin'."

"What?" asked Atticus, scowling up at the lieutenant.

"You heard me. When's the last time you used any of your vacation time? Probably can't even remember. You're out until after the new year. That's an order."

Lawson chuckled under his breath, and all eyes fell on him. He glanced at his brother and then settled his gaze on Mitzi. "Good luck keepin' him down."

She smiled because she knew he had a point. Still, she replied confidently, "I'll manage."

After what Mitzi was certain was five minutes on the dot, Kendall came back to shoo *the cops* out of the room. Reed insisted he'd be back, Carlson reiterated his command for Atticus to stand down a while, and then it was just Lawson.

"Three tours in Afghanistan, and somehow, right here at home, you're the one givin' mom and Judge a scare."

"Hardly more than a flesh wound. Everyone will forget it happened in a couple weeks."

Mitzi scoffed and pinched at his leg. "Did Kendall up your morphine? Because you're talkin' crazy."

Atticus breathed a quiet chuckle as his eyes fell closed. Clearly exhausted, he didn't bother opening them as he said, "I'll be just fine."

Lawson gave his brother's shoulder a squeeze then, looking over at Mitzi, said, "Either of you need anything, just call."

"Actually, there is something I could use your help with."

"What?"

"I'm gonna try and stay as long as they'll let me. I left Titan at Atticus' place. Do you think you could stop by with Nora so she can take him home?"

"Uh...yeah. Okay."

"Thank you. There's a bag around here someplace with Atticus' things," she started to say, looking around for said bag.

"Don't worry about it. I've got a key." He ran his fingers through his hair and then glanced down at his brother. "I've got work all day tomorrow. I'll try to swing by after."

"You should go get some sleep."

"Yeah."

As he was turning to take his leave, Nora and Evie arrived at the door. Just like she had been when they came rushing into the hospital, Evie was still wrapped around her mother. Nora hesitated before stepping into the room, smoothing a hand down her daughter's back as she murmured, "Can we come in? Once Evie understood why we were here, she insisted we couldn't leave without seein' him."

"Of course," said Mitzi, standing to her feet. Edging closer to Atticus, she ran her fingers through his hair, wondering if he might stir for one last visitor. "Baby?" she whispered, only wishing to wake him if he wasn't too far gone.

"Hmm?" he hummed.

"Evie's here."

Atticus pried open his eyes, looking at Mitzi before shifting his gaze in search of his little friend. When he found her, a small, tired smile played at the corner of his mouth.

"Hi."

Evie didn't respond at first. Clinging to Nora's neck, she studied Atticus, concern tugging at her brow. It took her a moment to process what she was seeing. Finally, she murmured, "Mommy said you got a big owey and the doctor had to fix you."

"Yeah. But I'm gonna be okay."

Still frowning suspiciously she asked, "Does it hurt?"

"A little," he lied with a reassuring smile.

"But you're gonna get better?"

"I am."

"Promise?"

"I promise."

"Okay."

Noticing she still looked a little unsure, Mitzi attempted to distract her from what she guessed was the same sense of helplessness she harbored. "Evie Belle, do you think you could do something for me?"

Evie merely nodded in reply.

"I need someone to keep an eye on Titan for the next day or two.

Especially at night. He doesn't like to sleep alone. Will you snuggle him for me while I stay here with Atticus?"

"Mmhmm. Where is he?"

"We've got to pick him up," answered Nora, kissing Evie's cheek. "We'll go right now, okay?"

Evie nodded again, and her lack of words said it all. She was tired. They all were. It had been a long night.

"Tell everyone to head home and get some sleep," Atticus instructed Lawson.

"Will do."

By the time Lawson, Nora, and Evie were out of the room, Atticus was half sleep again. Mitzi, who had every intention of settling in for the night, resumed her spot in the chair beside the bed.

"Mitz?"Atticus mumbled, his eyes still closed as slumber continued to beckon.

"Yeah?" she asked, reaching for his hand.

"Titan's not the only one doesn't like sleepin' alone."

Speaking through a quiet giggle, she replied, "I'm right here. Not goin' anywhere."

"Bed's big enough for two, pretty girl."

"Atticus—"

Peeling open his eyes just a sliver, he reminded her, "Knife went in my right side. Left side's good as new."

Shaking her head, she fought a smile and argued, "I doubt Kendall would approve."

"I was stabbed. Think that means I get to call the shots."

Her smile broke through, morphing into a grin as she stood from her chair and made her way to the other side of the bed. "I'm startin' to think I'm going to hear that a lot."

"Long as it works."

"Mmmhmm," she hummed, lowering the bed rail.

She glanced toward the door, hoping Kendall wasn't around.

Mitzi liked the woman when she was throwing her sass at other people, but she didn't want to be on the receiving end of it. Satisfied the coast was clear, she then carefully climbed in beside Atticus, snuggling against his good side. With his arm draped around her, he freed a heavy sigh, and drifted off to sleep without another word.

Mitzi thought for sure it would take her a while to find sleep herself. The last couple of hours had been a whirlwind. This was the first silent moment she had to truly process all of it. Though, emotional as the night had been, her man was going to be okay. That measure of truth offered her peace; and the warmth of his body along with the steady rhythm of his heartbeat, sounding from the monitor, was better than a lullaby. Mitzi was out before she knew it.

chapter twenty-five

Three weeks later...

MITZI DIDN'T NEED ANOTHER REASON to love Atticus any more—but the longer he gazed at her, tracing his fingertips along her hairline, the harder she fell. He was still inside of her, still fitted between her legs after the most tender lovemaking she'd ever known. They were swaddled in a light blanket, stretched out on his couch, the only illumination in the room coming from the soft, warm glow of the Christmas tree.

"I love you," said Atticus, his voice barely above a whisper.

Mitzi's entire body reacted to the declaration. Her legs tightened around his hips, her belly tingled, her heart swelled, and as she stared up into her favorite pair of dark brown eyes, she tickled the hair at the nape of his neck. It wasn't the first time he'd said it, and she knew it wouldn't be the last. What she did know was she was absolutely certain she'd never tire of hearing it.

"I love you, too," she murmured.

Right then, connected with her man, she understood what it meant to be crazy in love. She no longer questioned why Scarlett only had eyes for Trace, or why Nora had hitched her heart to Lawson when they were just kids. What she refused to let herself experience in high school, she now felt in full force. She was fitted with her own blinders. There never was and there never would be anyone she loved more than Atticus Steele.

As if he had exclusive access to her thoughts, a sexy, crooked smile tugged at the corner of his mouth. The sight made her giggle. Atticus silenced her with a kiss which only reminded her of what they'd just done. It made her want to do it again. With no place else they needed to be, she was confident she could get her way.

After Atticus was stabbed, the subsequent weeks leading up to Christmas had been a bit of a whirlwind. Between keeping the man down so he could properly heal, putting the final touches on her spring line, working with her interior designers sourcing furniture for her store, frequent check-ins with Palmer as his team started to wrap up construction, *and* Christmas prep—it was a wonder Mitzi had any energy left to spare. But that was the magic of Christmas. It was reinvigorating.

It came as absolutely no surprise when the Steeles welcomed her with warm, open arms into their traditions. Having Atticus by her side with her own family had been a gift in and of itself. When she came back to Shelbyville, she knew life would be different. In some ways more challenging, as she dealt with the unresolved issues with her family; in other ways more fulfilling, as she reconnected with her roots and the only place which had ever truly felt like home. What she didn't anticipate was how much better her life would be.

Sometimes she missed New York, but she'd brought the best part of her time in the city home with her. Bringing Sterling Thread into The Square was like the culmination of the dream she carried in her heart for most of her life. And the people who helped keep her dream alive, they weren't going anywhere, and they were only a plane ride away.

"Come to New York with me," breathed Mitzi between kisses.

"Okay," Atticus murmured, his lips still grazing hers.

"Tomorrow."

This made him lift his head in order to properly see her.

"Tomorrow?"

She nodded. "You aren't due back at work for another week. I could introduce you to Adalynn and Gianna. They're dyin' to meet you. We could stay for New Year's Eve; I could show you all my favorite places. Besides, if I don't get you out of here, you'll start buildin' something. The doctor said—"

"Babe, I remember what he said," he interrupted on a chuckle.

"So, tomorrow?"

He hesitated, shaking his head at her, his smile still found in his eyes. "My spontaneous woman."

"Is that a yes?" she asked, speaking through a grin.

"Yeah, pretty girl. It's a yes."

MITZI GOT HER WISH and Atticus made love to her again before they got up and made travel arrangements for the following day. Their flight left late in the afternoon. By the time they were ready to go and headed to the airport, they hardly had a chance to tell anyone they were leaving. A few hurried texts were sent after they'd made it through security, and then it was just Mitzi and her guys.

Even though Manhattan and Brooklyn were nearly as familiar to her as Shelbyville, it still felt as though she and Atticus were going on an adventure. It had been years since Mitzi had the chance to play tour guide to a loved one from home. She tried not to think about the fact that no one from her immediate family had ever given her such an opportunity. Picking at those wounds did her no good. Besides, they were in a good place now. It might have taken her coming home to get there, but such a compromise had yielded more happiness than she could ever have imagined.

It was half past eight when they checked into their hotel. Mitzi made quick work of getting Titan settled with a fresh bowl of water and some food before kissing him goodbye, promising to be back later. As she and Atticus rode the elevator back down to the hotel lobby, she tightened her wool coat around her, tugging the belt at her waist to keep it closed. She then looked at her man, and the smile he painted on her lips was undeniable.

He stood casually with one of his hands tucked into the front pocket of his faded jeans, his simple, gray, long-sleeve, thermal t-shirt hugging his chest the way she liked. He was sexy without even trying—which was all the reason why he made her spring collection's men's leather jacket look *so good*. She'd gifted him his own exclusive release edition for Christmas, after his favorite jacket was ruined the night he was stabbed. Though, hot as he was in her design, it was freezing in the city, especially after dark.

"Are you sure you're gonna to be okay walkin' a few blocks? We could grab a taxi."

"Babe—not my first time someplace cold. I'll be fine."

"Okay. But tomorrow I'm buyin' you a scarf," she insisted, reaching for his free hand.

He winked at her, giving her fingers a squeeze in response.

"There's this Japanese restaurant I want to take you to, but I'm sure the place is packed right now. We'll make a reservation while we're in town. Tonight, I thought I'd take you to this all night diner I like. *Total* greasy spoon of a spot."

"It's your world, pretty girl. I'm just along for the ride."

Grinning, she leaned into him and declared, "I'm so happy to be here with you."

This earned her a kiss in reply, just as the elevator doors opened with a chime.

Both of them more than a little hungry, they didn't waste any time walking to the restaurant of Mitzi's choosing. They dined for an hour and then ventured back out into the cold. Instead of returning to their hotel, they wandered toward Brooklyn Bridge Park. Mitzi didn't realize how much she missed the incredible view of the New York City skyline in the dark of night. It had never been more romantic than it was that night as she stared at it while tucked underneath Atticus' arm.

"It's spectacular," he said, causing her to look up at him. "It really is. But I prefer the sky full of stars back home."

Her gaze still trained up at him, she watched as he admired the city lights, her belly tingling at his words. She didn't need another reason to love him, but he'd just given her one. Her man was a detective in a small town. He lived for Sunday dinners with his family, watching football with a beer and the boys at Gypsy's, and protecting the citizens of Shelbyville from the bad guys. He was the kind of man who could look at the Big City and appreciate its beauty without getting entranced or enticed into the hustle which came with its own price of admission.

She'd known and loved men who let their ambitions drive them rather than the other way around—but Atticus was different. He was stronger. He was more grounded. He was noble, and she admired him so much.

They stood together on the pier, until the cold wafting from the water got to them both, and then headed back to the hotel. It didn't take them long to ready themselves for bed, but sleep wasn't on either of their minds as they slipped between the sheets. They succeeded in exhausting each other before slumber beckoned, then slept until the sun was pouring through the uncovered window. Though, it was Titan who insisted they needed to wake.

"I'll take him out," Atticus said, pressing a kiss against Mitzi's bare shoulder.

"You don't have to. I can get up."

"Come 'ere, boy," he insisted, ignoring her suggestion. Titan climbed over Mitzi as Atticus sat up, clearly interested in showing favoritism to whomever was ready to go first.

"Wait, he needs his vest. Will you grab it from his bag? I'll put it on really quick."

Atticus fetched it, donning his own clothes as Mitzi bundled her pup for his walk. Admittedly, they were out the door faster than Mitzi would have been. She got up and hopped in the shower, in an attempt to get a head start in her few minutes alone. While she wasn't in a rush, she was excited to surprise Gianna and Adalynn with her visit to the boutique that morning. She was also looking forward to being in her store again. It had been a couple months since the attack which sent her running scared. The last time she was at the boutique, she remembered the overwhelming feeling of anxiety which seemed to rob the place of the magical feeling she'd ascribed to her pride and joy.

She wasn't scared anymore. Certainly not with Atticus at her side. She was ready to return to her little slice of Brooklyn. Moreover, just like all of her favorite places in New York, she was looking forward to sharing it with the man who owned her heart. She wanted him to have all of her, including the piece of herself she'd left behind.

Atticus was gone for forty-five minutes. While that gave Mitzi plenty of time to bathe, moisturize, and blow-dry her hair, she was close to sending out a search party when she finally heard the latch on the door give way.

"Baby, did you get lost?" she asked, emerging from the bathroom wrapped in her robe.

"No. I got coffee."

She spotted him just as he was letting Titan off his leash. When he stood to full height, he held out the cardboard carrier, offering her the cup marked *Americano*.

"Atticus Montgomery, you are my favorite human."

He laughed under his breath as she took her coffee, then kissed her when she puckered her lips in a silent request. An hour later, both of them caffeinated, showered, and ready for the day, they exited the hotel, Titan excited for another walk in his hometown.

The boutique didn't open until eleven, and Mitzi was certain they'd arrive about twenty minutes before then on foot. Knowing her crew, she surmised they were already at the shop, dutifully preparing for the day ahead. She didn't know what she'd done to deserve them, but she was so incredibly grateful for their loyalty.

The closer they got, the more giddy Mitzi grew. It felt good, and she didn't try to down play her excitement. She even walked a little faster as they took the last turn onto the block of their destination. She was about to point out the sign above her store's door when she noticed Gianna. She was standing out front on the sidewalk clearly arguing with someone. It took Mitzi a moment to recognize him; but when she did, she felt her stomach drop.

"Oh, my god," she breathed, picking up her pace.

"Mitz?" asked Atticus, matching her quick steps with ease.

She didn't answer him, her attention glued to the arguing pair. It was Gianna's raised voice she was able to hear first.

"You can't keep coming here. She's gone, and I won't tell you where she is. Get that through your head."

"It's important, Gi. Please—you have to help me. I *need* to see her."

"You need to move on. You need to get out of here. My answer is *never* going to change. I won't help you."

"You don't understand."

This time, as he spoke, he grabbed hold of her biceps and got in her face.

"Hey! Get away from her," cried Mitzi. She let go of Atticus' hand in order to shove at Nolan, taking both him and Gianna by surprise.

"Oh, my god. What are you doing here?" Gianna gasped, her tone a mix of dismay and delight.

Before she could form a single word, Nolan interrupted. "Baby, god, where've you been?"

He took a step toward her, but then Atticus was there, standing at her side, his arm outstretched in an unmistakable sign that Nolan was not welcome anywhere near her.

"How 'bout you watch who you're callin' baby?" he muttered with a scowl.

Nolan looked from Atticus to Mitzi, confusion tugging at his brow as he inquired, "Who the hell is he?"

Mitzi was speechless. She hadn't expected to walk in on— whatever was going on. She hadn't seen Nolan in months. Even before she moved back to Tennessee. He was skinny. Too skinny. He had bags under his eyes, like he hadn't slept in a week. Looking into his dull, brown irises, she thought she saw a glimmer of the beautiful man she'd once known, but there was desperation where she once saw passion. There was something so hollow about him. It broke her heart a little.

"Nolan, what are you doin' here? I told you—I told you not to come around. Puttin' your hands on Gianna like that? What the hell?"

"I've been looking for you. Where've you been?"

He tried once more to close the distance between them, but Atticus stiff-armed him a second time. "You need to back off."

"What the—" He cut himself off, frowning at Atticus before returning his attention to Mitzi. "Who the hell is this guy, huh?"

"I'm not *this* guy. I'm *the* guy," stated Atticus matter-of-factly.

"What's that supposed to mean?"

Until that moment, Mitzi wasn't sure whether or not Nolan was high. But a man who looked like him, weak and scrawny in the shadow of a man who looked like Atticus, he would *have* to be high to argue with such an opponent.

"*The* guy—as in *the* guy who knows how she takes her coffee. *The* guy she paints her lips for. *The* guy keepin' her warm at night. And *the* guy who will kick your ass if you lay so much as a finger on her. Now, I believe both of these women have made it pretty clear you're not welcome here. You need to leave."

Nolan huffed out a sigh, then looked to Mitzi. "Baby, please."

"I will call the cops," threatened Atticus. "And while I'm at it, I'll help these two file a restraining order."

"Mitzi," he cried, still not deterred.

"Get out of here, Nolan. Just go. You've caused enough trouble."

"Baby, that wasn't me!"

For the third time, he tried to advance on Mitzi, but Atticus had had enough. He stepped in front of her, blocking her entirely as he asked, "How much do you have on you? Hmm? I call the cops right now for harassment, what might they find in your pockets? Somethin' tells me, that look in your eyes, you're not walkin' around empty handed."

"Man, fuck you." He sounded sure of himself, but even as he spoke, he started to back away.

Atticus took a step toward him and reached for his phone. "You don't get gone, and I'll pin you down myself until the cops show up."

Nolan muttered a curse under his breath, turned on his heel, and ran. Atticus then turned to address Gianna. "He comes back again, don't even speak to him. Just call the cops."

She nodded. "I've been trying to keep the police out of it but you're right. I don't know what else will keep him away."

"You've been trying to keep the police out of it?" Mitzi asked, now holding Titan in her arms. "Gianna, how long has he been comin' around?"

"A month. Two, maybe."

"Two *months?* I've been gone for less than three. He's been comin' around almost the whole time I've been gone, and you didn't tell me?"

"Mitzi, he's a pest, nothing more. Look at me, I'm fine. Adalynn's

fine. And the store? It's great. I saw no point in worrying you. Now
—can I hug you? I still can't believe you're standing right next to
me."

Gianna didn't wait for Mitzi to respond before she had her
arms around the woman, gently squishing Titan in their embrace.
Then, in an obvious attempt to avoid the issue at hand, Gianna
wrapped an arm around Mitzi's shoulders and ushered her inside
the store, declaring she had to see Adalynn. As soon as they were
over the threshold, the smell of Sterling Mist for him and for her
filled her nose—the scents complimenting each other in that way
she cherished. Mitzi couldn't help but smile to herself. Much as she
missed the familiarity of her store's smell, she'd come to love her
scent more than anything on one man in particular.

Being in her store for the first time in months was something
she didn't want to take for granted. She had every intention of
discussing the issue of Nolan further; but for the moment he was
gone, and the conversation could wait. As Gianna went into the
back to get Adalynn, Mitzi unleashed Titan and freed him from his
vest, letting him loose in the store that really was his home away
from home. She then stood with a sigh, looked around, and stopped
when her gaze met her man's brown-eyed stare.

"Well, this is it. What do you think?"

A smirk curling the side of his mouth, he replied, "I think I'm a
lucky guy."

"Oh, you're not just a lucky guy," she said teasingly, closing the
distance between them. "You're *the* lucky guy."

His smirk stretched into a grin as he wrapped one of his arms
around her waist, pulling her into his chest. "You makin' fun of
me?"

"Not at all. You were a little possessive out there. It was kind of
hot."

"Yeah?"

"Mmhmm," she assured him with a nod. "The real question is,

did you scare my ex away for good?"

"If he's got any brain cells left, I'd say yeah," said Gianna.

"Hey, boss! This is such a surprise. Why didn't you tell us you were coming?"

"Then it wouldn't be a surprise," she laughed, pulling away from Atticus in order to greet her assistant properly. "But, really, it was a spur of the moment kind of trip. I wanted to show Atticus the city. There's nothin' like New York at Christmas. Anyway, we got in last night and this is our first stop this morning."

"So we finally get to meet Atticus."

"Yeah," murmured Mitzi, smiling up at her guy. "Atticus, Gianna and Adalynn."

"It's nice to meet you," he said, shaking each of their hands. "Folks at home call me Steele. You can, too."

Adalynn's eyebrows shot up. "Steele? As in...the *Steele Collection?*"

Atticus frowned. "What?"

"Oh, my god—this is one of yours, isn't it?" said Gianna, taking a step toward Atticus. "I noticed it almost as soon as I noticed him, but seeing it up close? Babe, this is perfect."

Mitzi stifled a giggle as Gianna began to slowly circle her man, using both her hands and her eyes to examine the leather jacket he wore. Atticus quirked an eyebrow at Mitzi in confusion.

"My spring line. It was inspired by this guy I sort of fell in love with. I'm callin' it the Steele Collection. I haven't told anyone back home, yet."

She watched as he processed this news, the confusion on his face giving way to something akin to stoic awe. For what felt like a full a minute, he didn't say anything, his silence causing all three women to stare at him in wait.

Finally, he muttered, "Pretty girl?"

"Yeah, baby?"

"I'm gonna kiss you now."

This earned him not just one but three smiles as Mitzi murmured, "Okay."

epilogue

One month later...

MITZI SAT IN ONE OF THE ROSE HUED, tufted armchairs situated at the front of the store, one leg folded over the other as she tried to pretend she wasn't tired of talking. The blogger she was speaking to sat in the matching chair opposite her. The phone recording their interview was sitting on the small side table between them, the bouquet of flowers beside it a charming reminder she'd done it. She'd brought Sterling Thread to Shelbyville. The boutique was beautiful. It was everything she dreamed it would be and then some. In just a few days, the whole town would know it, and she could hardly wait to share it with them.

"One last question," said the blogger.

Mitzi forced a smile and nodded. This was her sixth interview in an hour. She understood the point of the press party and private grand opening was for her to talk with journalists and bloggers about the new store, the Steele Collection, and the future of Sterling Thread. It was exclusive, intimate, and purposeful—but she wanted to do more than speak with the press and the Instagram influencers her marketing team had sourced and invited to the party. Her closest friends and family were also in attendance, and she'd barely gotten a chance to speak with them since the evening began.

"Thank you so much for your time," said the writer, gathering her phone.

"Thank you for comin'," replied Mitzi, standing to her feet with her guest. "I hope you enjoy the rest of the party."

As if right on cue, Gianna walked over with a gift bag and Adalynn with a glass of champagne. The bag was given to the blogger, but the champagne was meant for Mitzi. She took a long, slow sip, swallowed, and then freed a heavy sigh.

"Please tell me that was the last one. I feel like I've been stuck in this corner all night, and it's *my* party."

"You've got a few photo ops we need to make sure you get, but then you should be free to mingle for a while," Adalynn promised. "I'll let you finish that glass before I force you in front of a camera. How's that?"

"Thank you," breathed Mitzi before bringing the glass to her lips again.

"Scarlett sure does know how to throw an event," said Gianna, her eyes dancing around the store. "I can't get over how amazing it looks."

"Right?" Adalynn gushed. "I was *this close* to packing my bags and moving down here, afraid of trusting anyone with your brand outside of us—but she gets it. It's obvious."

Mitzi smiled at Adalynn, her heart warmed by the sentiment behind her comment. She then looked around and saw what her team saw. The room was full of Mitzi's ideas. The furniture, the fixtures, the clothes, the accessories. Palmer Reynolds helped her build the shell she needed in the shop; her interior designers helped flesh out the full concept, and Mitzi's designs gave the place purpose—but it was Scarlett who thought of all the little finishing touches. The fresh flowers, the gorgeous balloons, the champagne and cake bites.

When she approached her sister with the idea of hiring her as the store's general manager, she knew she could trust Scarlett to bring that southern charm Mitzi believed was synonymous with *home*; but looking around, she was almost ashamed at how she underestimated the woman. Of course, Scarlett could be trusted with Mitzi's brand. They were sisters, after all. More than that, they were Dolly's girls, which meant they'd been born with style.

"I'm in good company down here. Besides, I need you in New York. But you are always more than welcome to come visit as often as you'd like."

"Given some of the guys I see wandering around tonight, don't be surprised if we visit often," teased Gianna.

Mitzi laughed, took another sip of champagne, and found herself searching the crowd for the one hot guy she'd claimed as her own. When she spotted him across the room—in his dark jeans, blue button-up, stellar gray sports coat and the cowboy boots he loved—she let herself bask in his beauty for a moment. He was standing in a group, listening as Bishop told some story with a drink in one hand and his wife, Lexy, holding on to his other. Jed, Reed, and Jay were there too, all of them captivated and seemingly entertained.

Tired as she was of interviews, Mitzi couldn't deny how incredibly happy and proud she felt to be exactly where she was doing exactly what she was doing. When she first launched Sterling Thread and made her first sale, she wasn't sure anything would be able to top that feeling of accomplishment. Then she opened her boutique in Brooklyn, and *that* became the pentacle of success. But that night, in her new store, she was sure she'd never felt so content.

This was the height of her career. Not because another building had her brand's name printed on the door. Not because writers in the fashion industry came from New York, Atlanta, and as far south as Miami to get the first scoop on her new flagship location. Not even because she knew this was only the beginning of a fresh start in a new year. What mattered more than any of that were the people who showed up to support her.

The man who stood across the room with a Dum Dum tucked into his cheek was at the top of her list of people to thank after the night was over. The last several weeks, Mitzi had been a bit of a crazy woman trying to get everything done. Turned out, Atticus had the patience of a saint, and she loved him for it. In fact, she loved him for so many reasons, she stopped keeping count. As soon as she was finished with the obligatory parts of her evening, she had every intention of spending the rest of the night with him by her side.

As if he could feel her lingering gaze, Atticus looked away from Bishop and glanced at Mitzi. He winked, she grinned, and then he rolled his sucker from one side of his mouth to the other. Mitzi wondered what flavor he had. She'd have to kiss him later to find out.

No sooner had Mitzi polished off the last of her champagne than Adalynn was whisking her around the shop for her next round of press coverage. It was Nora and Billie who rescued her a half hour later, insisting she'd spent way too much of the night working and not enough time enjoying the fruits of her labor. Nonetheless, before she knew it, guests were starting to say goodnight.

"It's still early," Jed pointed out, throwing his arm around Billie's shoulders. "A few of us are movin' this party over to Gypsy's. You're comin'," he demanded, raising his eyebrows at Mitzi.

"As long as there are chili fries involved, I'm in."

"Done," Bishop promised.

"We'll catch up." As he spoke, Atticus ran a hand down Mitzi's back and then hooked his arm around her waist. She leaned into him, silently expressing how much she craved his affection. She hadn't shared nearly as much time with him that night as she intended.

All their friends left with plans of reuniting in a few minutes, and suddenly the store was quiet, save the music still playing overhead.

"The caterers just finished cleanin' up. I'll be back sometime tomorrow after I get the kids off to school to take down the balloons. Do you need anything else from me tonight?" asked Scarlett.

Mitzi noticed her parents and Trace standing out on the sidewalk, obviously chatting while they waited for her sister to call it quits. Stepping away from Atticus, Mitzi wrapped her arms around Scarlett and murmured, "Go home. Get out of those heels. You deserve it. Thank you so much for everything."

"We wouldn't be here without you. If I haven't said it already, congratulations. I'm proud of you."

"Okay, now you just need to get out of here before you make me cry," Mitzi teased, pushing away her sister.

"Al'right. I'll see you tomorrow. Bye, Steele."

"Goodnight," he replied with a dip of his chin.

As Scarlett took her leave, the music cut off, and then it was Gianna and Adalynn making their way from the back, each of them with their purses over their arms.

"Boss, you didn't have to stay. We could have locked up for you."

"It's okay. I've got it."

"Hope y'all are joinin' us at Gypsy's," said Atticus.

"Best waterin' hole you'll find in Shelbyville," added Mitzi.

Adalynn laughed and replied, "You just called it a watering hole. If that's not small town, I don't know what is. We're in. See you in a few?"

"Right behind you."

As the two women headed toward the door, Mitzi started for the back to gather her own things. She didn't get two steps before Atticus had her by the hand.

"Not so fast, pretty girl," he muttered, tugging her toward him.

Mitzi went without protest, smiling up at him as she circled her arms around his waist.

"Sorry I was so busy tonight. The turnout was insane."

"Don't apologize. You were doin' your thing. Looked good doin' it, too."

"Thanks, baby."

Mitzi pressed up onto her tiptoes and reached for a kiss. Atticus leaned down and gave her what she wanted, lingering long enough for her to taste the remnants of his sour apple Dum Dum. It was when he pulled away that she noticed something was up. It was like he didn't want to leave.

"Atticus? Everything okay?"

"Judge always taught me to follow my gut. He told me it was God's way of pointin' us in the right direction when we're too hard headed to make sense of it in our mind. All my life, I've been followin' his advice. Knew one day, when I met the woman I was meant to be with, I'd just know. Can't make sense of it, pretty girl —but my gut told me you were it the first time you walked by this empty store. Now, here we are."

Mitzi held him tighter as the memory of that chance meeting raced through her mind. It made her belly tingle remembering the look in his eyes when he glanced back at her from over his shoulder.

"Watchin' you tonight—I don't think I've ever been so proud of anyone. And it's not just about tonight. All this..." he paused long enough to take in their surroundings and then continued, "it's incredible. But the way you're sharin' it with your sister? With this town? Babe—only one thing could make me more proud."

The next thing she knew, Atticus was down on one knee. Mitzi jaw fell open, genuinely surprised at what was happening. She could hardly pull in a breath as she stared at him in shock.

"Wait, what?" she breathed, clapping both her hands over her chest.

"I know we've only been doin' this for a few months, but I think forever with you wouldn't be long enough. And nothin' could make me more proud than callin' you my wife. Mitzi Belle Bates, will you marry me?"

As he asked the question, he snapped open the box Mitzi hardly realized he was holding, and revealed a gorgeous, oval diamond ring. When she tried to say something in reply, the only sound that came out of her was a startled sob. Realizing her best bet was to act rather than speak, she nodded as she reached for his face and bent down to press her mouth to his. She felt his smile as he returned her kiss, and it made her giggle even as tears ran down her face.

Atticus squeezed the back of her neck with his free hand, kissing her hard once more before he mumbled, "Let me put the ring on, pretty girl."

"'Kay," she sniffled as she straightened.

He took her hand and fit the ring in place before he got to his feet. Mitzi held her hand in front of her face, still a little shocked, and then looked up at her man.

"Atticus Steele, I love you." She reached up and wrapped her arms around his shoulders, pulling him close as she whispered, "I love you so, so much. I always will."

He smirked as he folded her in his arms and touched his forehead to hers.

"Countin' on it."

Murfreesboro, TN

IT'D BEEN MONTHS SINCE his last kill. He wasn't sure if he could remember the warmth of her blood. The smell of her fear. The passion in her scream. It'd taken him too long to find another—but he'd had to be careful. He'd had to be patient. He'd had to blend in on his hunt for the perfect woman.

In Nashville, it was easy. He could be nobody. He could be as invisible as the next stranger, completely unmemorable. But he couldn't stay there. Not anymore. Not if he was going to get his message across. He had to work his way toward home.

Murfreesboro wasn't home for him, but it was where she laid her head. He'd been watching her. Studying her. Learning her. It had been weeks. He couldn't wait any longer. He had to have her. He had to taste her. He was itching for a kill—and tonight was the night.

Shelbyville, TN
Thirty-four hours later...

REED PULLED IN A deep breath and scrunched his brow as his ringing phone yanked him from his sleep. It was Saturday, if he was remembering correctly, and he had no plans of getting up with the sun. He squinted open one eye and sighed when he saw who was trying to reach him. Looked like whatever plans he had that morning were about to be made for him.

"Abernathy," he grumbled in hello.

"You see the news?" asked Steele.

"Late night. Haven't seen anything but the back of my eyelids."

"There was another murder. Closer, this time. Same M.O."

"Shit. Lieutenant callin' us in?"

"No. Just wanted to put it on your radar."

"Copy that, partner."

"Murfreesboro. Franklin was bad enough. Murfreesboro is way too close for comfort."

Reed opened his eyes and frowned. He felt the woman at his back, the warmth of her body seeping into his, and he knew Steele was right. She wasn't this killer's type, but that didn't silence the part of him wanting to rise up and protect her at all costs. He looked down at his waist and the ink-covered arm holding onto him.

"Yeah," he finally said.

"Right, well—I've got to go. I'll hit you up later."

"Yeah."

They both hung up without another word, and Reed tossed his phone back onto his nightstand.

"Everything okay?" whispered Justice, her lips grazing his bare shoulder.

The truth was, everything wasn't okay. Not so long as he was lying to his partner. But Justice kept saying she wasn't ready. He promised they would go at the pace she chose, and he cared about her too much to push.

"Reed?"

"Yeah, princess. Everything's fine."

Reed and Justice's story will be next in the Beneath the Shield series. But first, in a Vollucci Security/Beneath the Shield crossover novel, Lawson Steele and Nora-Jean Bates get a second chance at romance. Keep reading to check out a sneak peek from my next novel—Steeled.

He tossed his keys onto the kitchen counter, cluttered with junk mail and old receipts he'd been meaning to throw away for weeks. Guided only by the faint light of a streetlamp reaching its way through his apartment's living room window, Lawson headed straight for the fridge. It was mostly empty. Traveling back and forth between Nashville and Shelbyville meant a lot of miles on his truck and not enough time for a grocery run. He knew he needed to do better, but that night he didn't have the energy to worry about it. He reached around his stash of Gatorade and grabbed himself a beer. It had been that kind of day.

He enjoyed his work. He'd only been with Vollucci Security for a few months, but it was turning out to be a decent fit. His boss, Cruiz Moretti, had proved to be more friend than foe; and the owner, Leo Vollucci, was a respectable guy. In a way, the men who made up their crew were like family—the women in their lives making it so —and he somehow managed to be lucky enough to be adopted into the fold.

It was the concept of family that had him sitting in the dark of his sparsely furnished apartment, nursing his ice-cold beer.

For eight years, he was part of a brotherhood only his fellow soldiers could ever comprehend. Even if he wasn't wearing the uniform anymore, he still belonged to the corps. It would always be a part of him. It gave him purpose for so long—the kind of purpose that truly meant something. When he got out, he understood he'd never find anything like he had with the men in his unit—but, by the grace of God, he managed to find a brotherhood of a different kind. And he was grateful.

After he retired from the Marines, Lawson never thought he'd find himself in the company of celebrities the likes of Ashley Hicks or Sage McCoy. Both artists were global sensations on their way to becoming musical legends of their time. But Vollucci Security was founded on the good reputation Leo had earned after nearly a decade at Ashley's side. It was no surprise when Hicks called Vollucci for a couple extra bodies that week. Though, what Lawson experienced the last couple of days was different than he'd expected.

The two singer songwriters were in Nashville working on a collaboration piece. Both men had brought their families. There were six kids between the two of them. The paparazzi and their fans loved to see them; McCoy and Hicks loved to keep their children's faces off the internet. Along with their personal security, Lawson was hired to be one more body and one more set of eyes to help combat the frenzy that came as a result of two beloved Grammy award winning artists in town with their clans.

There hadn't been any real threats, given the amount of time the group was in the studio. The kids seemed to be used to the environment, and Corie and Millie entertained them and enjoyed each other's company like women do. It was the way Ashley and Sage interacted with their kids between takes which stuck with Lawson even now, after a long day.

There was a time in his life when he'd wanted that—a wife and kids of his own. A home. A real one, like the one he grew up in, not the bleak apartment which was little more than a roof over his head right now. In some ways, that felt like a lifetime ago.

In all of his thirty-two years on the planet, there had only ever been one woman he'd wanted enough to marry. Much as he loved her, he'd managed to screw up his chances. It had been six years since he'd watched the love of his life walk away. Even so, on days like this one, it was hard for him not to think of Nora-Jean Barton; hard for him not to dream of her and all they could have been. Much as he knew he should move on, the best he'd ever been able to do was shove her into the darkest corner of his mind in hopes of muting his longing.

Worked a lot better when there were a few state lines between them. Hell, worked better still when there was an ocean separating them. But Shelbyville was home. It's where his family was. It's where he always knew he'd settle. He was a small-town kind of guy. The pace of life suited him well, especially after the war he'd seen. When the opportunity to move back presented itself, he couldn't pass it up—even if it put him in close proximity to her.

Masochistic as it was, he took another pull from his beer, swallowed, closed his eyes, and let his mind conjure her face. She'd always be the prettiest girl in all of Tennessee.

Steeled: A Vollucci Security/Beneath the Shield Crossover Novel

Available Now!

ALSO BY R.C. MARTIN

Vollucci Security Series
Severed
Wired
Steeled

Savior Series Duet
Guarded
Tethered

Tennessee Grace Series
Background Noise
Backwoods Belle
Rock-N-Roll Christmas

Foolish at Heart Series
Fool for Him
Fool for Her
Fools in Love

Mountains & Men Series
Encore Worthy
Worthy of the Harmony
Worthy of the Dissonance
Worthy of the Melody

Made for Love Series
The Promises We Keep
Reckless Surrender
The O'Conners
So Much More
Chasing After Me

Standalones
The Lies of Bryn van Doren
Heartless
The Bridgewater Case
Stealing Home

ABOUT THE AUTHOR

There's a place where your mind can escape,
your body can find rest, and your heart can soar –
and R.C. Martin wants to take you there.

In a voice all her own, she strives to capture the magic of
a kiss, the passion in a lovers' embrace, and even sometimes
the breathtaking ache of a broken heart. A true believer
in the power of love and the grace found in redemption,
you can trust this hopeless romantic to take you on an
emotional ride that leaves you forever changed.

www.rcmartinbooks.com